The Conquest of the Air

The Conquest of the Air
Forty Days of Aerial Navigation

by
Alphonse Brown

translated, annotated and introduced by
Brian Stableford

A Black Coat Press Book

ISBN 978-1-61227-143-9. First Printing. February 2013. Published by Black Coat Press, an imprint of Hollywood Comics.com, LLC, P.O. Box 17270, Encino, CA 91416. All rights reserved. Except for review purposes, no part of this book may be reproduced or transmitted in any form or by any means, electronic or mechanical, including photocopying, recording, or by any information storage and retrieval system, without permission in writing from the publisher. The stories and characters depicted in this novel are entirely fictional. Printed in the United States of America.

Introduction

La Conquête de l'air: 40 jours de navigation aérienne by Alphonse Brown was originally published in Paris by Glady Frères in 1875.

The preliminary page devoted to listing other works by the same author lists one title as "*sous presse*"—*La Retraite des quarante-cinq*—and four "*en preparation*": *Avant le deluge, Le Fleuve mystérieux, Aventures extraordinaires du capitaine Bob Kincardy* and *L'Ère nouvelle*. In the event, only one of these titles appears to have been published, *Aventure du capitaine Bob Kincardy* being the subtitle attached to Brown's second published book, *Voyage à dos de baleine* [A Voyage on a Whale's Back] (1876); there is no way of knowing whether the others were completed or not, although the first-named must surely have existed in a finished state, and would presumably have appeared had the publisher survived.

Perhaps the other titles on the list only reflected the author's initial ambitions, but in so doing they suggested that he wanted to be a much further-ranging writer than he eventually became. In the event, the great majority of Brown's other published works stuck closely to the groove first hollowed out by *La Conquête de l'air*, in working on the borderland of the popularization of science, celebrating the contribution that new technologies would inevitably make to the exploration of the globe that was making such rapid progress in the mid-nineteenth century and attracting so much interest and enthusiasm as a component of social progress.

Within the history of the French popular fiction, *La Conquête de l'air* is significant in two ways: narrowly, in terms of its specific theme, that of the potential development of aviation; and more broadly, in terms of its literary method and underlying attitude—to wit, its contribution to the development of the subgenre of Vernian fiction and its subtle but vital modification of that genre. The former significance is more obvious, being necessarily in the foreground of the text, but the latter is arguably more important providing a back-cloth.

As Brown's text proudly points out, the French had led the way in the development of aeronautics, thanks to the Montgolfier brothers and all those who sought to follow their example. It was in France, in consequence, that the problem of aviation—directed flight no longer at the mercy of the wind—was felt most acutely and its solution sought most assiduously. Corollary to that attention was the fact that it was in France, too, that the problem of aviation came in for its most wide-spread and intense literary consideration, thus making a cru-cial contribution to the development of the kind of fiction that became known in France as *roman scientifique* [scientific fic-tion] and eventually became known internationally as "science fiction."

Consideration of the problem of aviation in the mid-19th century was initially focused on the simple problem of how to add a power source and a steering mechanism to a balloon, so that it could be driven in a desired direction instead of drifting in the wind. There was, however, a second way of approach-ing the issue, which deflected the focus away from the possi-ble development of more ingenious lighter-than-air craft to-ward the invention of new species of heavier-than-air flying machines. In Paris, the most significant publicity for the latter approach was provided by the foundation in 1863 of a *Societé d'encouragement de la navigation aérienne au moyen du plus lourd que l'air* [Society for the Encouragement of Aerial Nav-igation by Heavier-than-Air Means] by the flamboyant "Félix Nadar," whose actual forename was Gaspard, and who was usually known simply as "Nadar."

Nadar had initially made a name for himself as a carica-turist for the newspapers, but had developed a passion for bal-looning and a passion for photography—two interests whose combination made him the most significant pioneer of aerial photography. Nadar's fascination with ballooning had already assisted his friend Jules Verne to make his crucial literary breakthrough with the publication of *Cinq semaines en ballon* (1862; tr. as *Five Weeks in a Balloon*) and it was only natural that Verne should become the secretary of the society, although the two men appear to have quarreled bitterly thereafter and Verne's association with it was brief. As things turned out, Nadar's active promotion was also soon compromised when he commenced experiments with his own balloon, the aptly-named *Le Géant*, which crashed on its second flight in October 1863 and left Nadar crippled. That did not prevent him, however, from combining his efforts with those of other members of the society to found the periodical *L'Aéronaute* in 1867, or from instituting a *Compagnie d'Aérostatiers* during the Franco-Prussian War of 1870-71.

Of all these publicizing efforts, the last was undoubtedly the most striking; although the efforts made by the Compagnie's balloonists to assist in alleviating the siege of Paris had only limited success, they did provide useful data about enemy positions and carried a great many dispatches. One of them, the *Armand-Barbès*—named after one of the revolutionaries of 1848 who had gone into exile after the *coup-d'état* that founded the Second Empire—carried the Minister of the Interior, Léon Gambetta, to the besieged city to Tours in order that he might organize resistance to the invading Prussians. Like Barbès before him, Gambetta was a far-left Republican, and one of the other two balloons forming Nadar's fleet (which eventually expended to sixty-six) was named the *Louis-Blanc* after another similarly-exiled hero of the 1848 Revolution. No possible doubt was left that the aeronauts were defending the Paris of the Commune, not Napoléon III's corrupt and collapsing empire. Significantly, the third member of the initial trio was the *George-Sand*, named after one of the key figures of the French Romantic Movement, who had written a striking fantasy about a symbolic balloon voyage in *Laura, voyage dans le cristal* (1865). Had Nadar not quarreled with Verne, he might well have made a different

7

choice; *Laura* was directly and admittedly inspired by Verne's early works.

As a resident of Bordeaux who remained firmly anchored to that city,[1] "Alphonse Brown" (whose actual forename was André) did not have the opportunity to join Nadar's society for the encouragement of aviation, or to enlist in the Compagnie d'Aérostatiers, and he would certainly have had reservations about the political slant of the latter enterprise, but he undoubtedly took an interest in the events in question, and it seems probable that the reason that Nadar only receives a single and very brief direct mention in the text of *La Conquête de l'air* (in a list that includes other members of his society) is that Brown was aware of Nadar's quarrel with Verne, and inevitably took the latter's side, even though he had probably never met Verne, and only knew him through his works. Those works had obviously made a deep impact on Brown, whose own text is a virtual homage to Verne, acknowledging his inspiration explicitly as well as in the sincere flattery of imitation.

La Conquête de l'air was by no means the first literary work to address the question of aviation, but it was a landmark nevertheless in its determination to tackle the question earnestly and to provide propaganda for its importance. There is a sense in which the most surprising thing about that objective is that it still remained to be tackled, because Jules Verne had let it well alone, perhaps because his quarrel with Nadar had soured any prospect of writing a novel that would have been construed as—and would, indeed, have been—publicity for Nadar's society. Brown's description of a hypothetical heavier-than-air flying machine was by far the most detailed so far produced, and it set a standard that several subsequent writers attempted heroically, and undoubtedly consciously, to follow.

---

[1] A few further details of Brown's life and career are provided in the introduction to the Black Coat Press edition of his novel *City of Glass* (ISBN 9781612270234, 2011; originally *Une Ville de Verre*, 1890-91).

It is not surprising that the hypothetical flying machines of the future had played a central role in the fictional element of Félix Bodin's pioneering prospectus for *Le Roman de l'avenir* (1834)[2], nor that one such machine should have played the crucial symbolic role in S. Henry Berthoud's pioneering dramatization of the psychology and sociology of scientific endeavor in "Voyage au ciel" (1841; tr. as "A Heavenward Voyage"), nor that their extravagant development should have taken pride of place in the triumphant culminating episode in Victor Hugo's magisterial account of human history, *La Légende des siècles*, "Plein air" [Open Sky] (1859). Nor is it surprising that absurd and dangerous aviation technologies are singled out for satirical abuse in such deliberately anti-progressive fantasies as Charles Nodier's two-part "Perfectibilité" (1833)[3] and Émile Souvestre's *Le Monde tel qu'il sera* (1846; tr. as *The World as it Shall Be*). The notion was inevitably central to French speculative fiction even before the advent of Jules Verne.

Alphonse Brown must have been familiar with most, if not all, of the works cited above, and had probably also read Alfred Driou's *Aventures d'un aéronaute parisien dans les mondes inconnus* (1856),[4] which features a rapid world tour similar in some respects to, though far less scrupulously planned than, the one he describes. He was, therefore, writing in the knowledge that there was a rich existing tradition of such works, but he singled out Verne as his primary and overriding influence because he was so impressed with the manner in which Verne integrated technical and didactic material into stories that had action, color, verve and reader-appeal of a

---

[2] tr. as *The Novel of the Future*, Black Coat Press, ISBN 978-1-934543-44-3.

[3] tr. as "Perfectibility" in *The Germans on Venus*, Black Coat Press, ISBN 978-1-934543-56-6

[4] tr. as *The Adventures of a Parisian Aeronaut in Unknown Worlds*, Black Coat Press, ISBN 978-1-61227-067-8.

kind that none of the previous writers had attempted, let alone achieved.

The fictitious aircraft described by Félix Bodin bear far more resemblance to Brown's than any others featured in previous attempts, but it is unlikely that Brown took much direct inspiration from that source, the resemblance in question resulting logically from a similar line of argument as to how heavier-than-air flight might be made practicable. We now know that Brown's argument in that respect is flawed, but it certainly seemed plausible at the time that, given that birds are heavier than air but can nevertheless fly, technology might well find the secret of such flight by imitating birds. Brown is given credit by some historians for an early use of the term "aéroplane" in *La Conquête de l'air* (the term had actually been coined by Joseph Pline in 1855) but as readers of this translation will observe, he does not intend that word to mean what it subsequently came to mean. In common with all his contemporaries, Brown had no inkling of the principle of physics by virtue of which a fixed wing can generate lift, and therefore has not the slightest idea that flight might one day be possible using rigid and immobile wings. He takes it for granted that if humans are to emulate birds, their technological wings will have to flap.

We also know now that Brown's solution to the problem of powering his hypothetical machine is similarly impractical—but again, it was by no means implausible at the time. He was right to conclude that the best motors then available— steam engines—were unlikely ever to be adaptable to aviation, because they were simply too heavy in proportion to their power output, and his effort to get around that problem shows commendable ingenuity for its time. Even writers of a slightly later era, who were aware—as Brown was not—of the principle of the internal combustion engine, often had difficulty in seeing that as a better solution. If one compares Brown's flying machine with later similarly-detailed descriptions of hypothetical heavier-than-air machines, such as those featured in

Les Aventures extraordinaires d'un savant russe (1888-96)[5] by Henry de Graffigny and Georges le Faure and *Fleur de Bagne* (1901)[6] by Goron and Émile Gautier, it is not obvious that Brown's suffers by comparison, even though the later writers had much better models from which they might have taken inspiration.

The design of the aircraft featured in *La Conquête de l'air* is, however, a secondary matter, even though the novel goes to such great pains to offer details of its construction and functioning. The real issue at stake is what it can do, and what it will mean for the future of human society. It is, of course, implausible that anyone inventing such a machine would try to go around the world in it without any preliminary trials at all, but that is not relevant to the point of the story, where the journey in question, in spite of the wealth of detail carefully added to it, is purely symbolic. The trip around the world is made in forty days, that being exactly half the duration given such tremendous emblematic significance by Verne's best-seller *Le Tour du monde en quatre-vingts jours* (1872 as a *feuilleton* in *Le Temps*; 1873 in book form; tr. as *Around the World in Eighty Days*).

What Verne did in the novel that was to become and re-main his most famous was to dramatize the manner in which the world had been "shrunk" by new modes of transport—primarily railways, steamships and the Suez canal, although balloons inevitably play their part. In that respect it was thoroughly realistic—so much so that people not only began to try to match or beat the imaginary record in question, but, in the case of George Francis Train, to claim that they already had, and had therefore inspired the novel; Thomas Cook added round-the-world trips to the itineraries offered by his organiza-

---

[5] tr. as *The Extraordinary Adventures of a Russian Scientist* (2 volumes), Black Coat Press, ISBN 978-1-934543-81-8 and 978-1-934543-82-5.

[6] tr. as *Spawn of the Penitentiary*, Black Coat Press, ISBN 978-1-61227137-8.

tion in the same year as the novel's *feuilleton* appearance. Brown's halving of the magic figure was a calculatedly-striking statement of the extent to which the advent of aviation might "shrink" the world by a further dramatic increment, and thus make a crucial contribution to the formulation of a community of nations and peoples: a single vast multicultural array, in which differences of race religion and culture would no longer, and could no longer, lead to thoroughgoing social isolation.

We now know that Brown's ethnography is as mistaken as his technology; his descriptions of other cultures and their brief interactions with his heroic voyagers embody prejudices of his time based in missionary propaganda and the superficial impressions of pioneering explorers, and we can now appreciate the distortions and inadequacies of those sources. The underlying argument is, however, perfectly sound, and we also know that Brown was absolutely correct in his anticipation that aviation would bring different peoples together in a very dramatic way, fundamentally altering their attitudes to one another and their interactions with one another. It is notable, too, that in this respect there is a distinct difference between Brown's endeavor and those of Jules Verne, reflecting a fundamental difference of attitude.

As Michel Butor has pointed out in one of his essays on Verne (whose English translation can be found in *Inventory*, 1969), Verne's tales of exploration are often more about getting away than getting to a destination; his various vehicles are as much ends as means, and there is a sense in which his "utopian ideal" is to be cast away, like the protagonists of his longest work, *L'Île mystérieuse* (1874; tr. as *The Mysterious Island*), on an implausibly comfortable and well-supplied "desert island," far from stressful contact with the mass of human beings. That novel was a sequel to Verne's second most famous book, *Vingt mille lieues sous les mers* (1870; tr. as *Twenty Thousand Leagues Under the Sea*), whose misanthropic anti-hero lives aboard a magical submarine that is, in essence, a world of its own, entirely self-sufficient, and whose only intercourse with world society consists of sinking the occasional ship belonging to a nation that the significantly-named Captain Nemo does not like.

When Verne finally did get around to writing his own romance of aviation, *Robur le conquérant* (1886; tr. as *The Clipper of the Clouds*), he modeled it on *Vingt mille lieues sous les mers*, and although that decision might have something to do with not wishing to be seen to be imitating his own imitators, *Robur le conquérant* goes to a perhaps-undesirable extreme in distancing itself attitudinally from *La Conquête de l'air*, stressing opposition and separation rather than collaboration and communication. Verne does appear to have thought of himself as a champion of progress, but his works do not always give that impression—when his early anti-utopia *Paris au XXe siècle* (written 1863, published 1994) was belatedly rediscovered, it demonstrated the full extent of his anxious reservations—and many of the writers he tempted to follow in his footsteps were much more wholehearted in that championship than he was. Alphonse Brown is perhaps the cardinal example, who did at least as much as anyone else, in his first two published novels and the feuilletons he subsequently contributed to the *Journal des Voyages* and *La Science Illustrée*, to give the subgenre of Vernian fiction a more robust stance in promoting the philosophy of progress in its original sense—which is to say, the conviction that scientific progress is inevitably and inextricable bound up with social progress toward liberty, equality and fraternity.

Alphonse Brown was not nearly as elegant or compelling a writer as Jules Verne, and he never had any change of emulating Verne's commercial and critical success. Although he improved with practice, the first endeavor shows him at his most awkward, with no real grasp of characterization and a dire addiction to tedious lists; in many ways he could serve as a model of all the bad habits that modern science fiction writers are routinely counseled to avoid at all costs. Those faults do not, however, distract from the significance of what he was attempting to do, nor the fact that it was worth doing. Although he was consciously following in the footsteps of others, in terms of his method, Brown was nevertheless a genuine pioneer in terms of his direction and thrust, and he deserves full credit for his efforts.

Initially, I attempted to make this translation from the copy of the Glady Frères edition made available on line via archive.org, scanned at the New York Public Library. That scanning job was, however, horribly botched, resulting in the total loss of four pages and the blurring or interruption of many others. There was a single copy of an abridged reprint edition available for sale via amazon.fr, which I was able to purchase and use to restore the continuity of the text, but because of its abridgment, some of the replacement passages probably do not contain all of the text contained in the original. It is a shame that the apparent availability of the existing on-line copy will presumably act as a disincentive to anyone else who might want to scan the text properly and conscientiously in order to create a reliable electronic version of the text.

The principal problem offered by the translation was that of place names, many of which have become obsolete since 1875, sometimes making it difficult to identify the inevitable few that were misrendered by the typesetter (usually because of a failure to interpret the author's handwriting correctly). To a large extent, I have stuck to Brown's versions of place names, but I have altered his orthography in numerous places where modern spelling would be more easily recognizable to contemporary readers. This means that the conventions followed in the present text are not entirely consistent, but the same is true of the original. I have corrected all the mistakes that I could identify, but a handful of instances remained where I could not determine the intended reference and had no alternative but to reproduce place-names as printed that do not seem ever to have been in use.

In order to economize on footnotes I have added Christian names to some citations where only surnames are provided in the text, in order to make the references clearer.

Brian Stableford

THE CONQUEST OF THE AIR

Chapter I

On the first of September 187* at eight o'clock in the evening, several people were assembled in the conversation room of the Grand Hotel in Arcachon. A sudden reduction in the temperature and the fine but concentrated rain that was falling outside explained that unusual gathering. It was necessary to kill time, as people say in vulgar terms, and the bathers were killing it by chatting. Sometimes, however, there was a lull in the conversation, and everyone listened silently to the splashing of waves on the sandy beach or the roar of the wind shaking the branches of the pine trees.[7]

Several groups had formed; everyone, according to his character, his humor or the caprice of the moment, was able to vary his chat. In one corner they were talking literature, in another, the discussion was entirely political; here, women were discussing fashion; there, serious financiers were pompously raising the 3% to the level of a social principle. The most animate group, however, was the one whose members were talking about distant explorations and the voyagers who had undertaken them.

"Yes," exclaimed Sir Walter Donderry, an Englishman as plump as a Rabelaisian monk and as red-faced as a poppy,

---

[7] This location is significant; Arcachon was a newly-constructed town in 1875, commissioned by Napoléon III in 1857 specifically to accommodate and facilitate a new fashion for "bathing stations"—seaside resorts to which the rentiers of Paris frequently retreated in the hot month of August, by means of recently-constructed railways, and where they routinely mingled with foreign tourists. It is about 55 kilometers from Brown's home town of Bordeaux.

17

"yes—and I don't say this, Messieurs, to wound your national susceptibility, my compatriots alone have the perseverance and boldness that overcomes the obstacles and braves the dangers into which voyagers penetrating into unknown regions often run."

The United Kingdom is the foremost nation in the world!" added Harry Catlen, a former manufacturer from Birmingham, endowed by his fortune with the title of Esquire, sententiously.[8]

"The English sometimes push conceit and vanity to the point of stupidity," a Russian whispered in the ear of a Frenchman whom hazard had set beside him.

"It's a malady of which we have rid ourselves, but which we have transmitted to the British islanders," the Frenchman replied, in a low voice.

"Monsieur Kisseloff," Sir Walter Donderry put in, "I didn't hear the words you addressed to Monsieur Dambielle, your neighbor, but I'll wager a thousand pounds sterling that they weren't in praise of the English."

"You're right, Sir Walter, and..."

"Oh, of course! I understand your reflections. National arrogance is almost as detestable as individual arrogance. The comment thrown into our conversation by the honorable Mr. Catlen, Esquire, is calculated to aggravate the nerves of the man least equipped with patriotic fiber—even a simple subject of the Prince of Monaco or a meager citizen of the Republic of Andorra."

"However," said Harry Catlen, "the United Kingdom is..."

"Is the foremost nation in the world. Agreed, my dear Harry—but think, and don't repeat it so often. We must extend our amiability to foreigners if you want us to have any right to theirs."

---

[8] "Esquire" is not a title limited in English usage to the rich, but Brown seems to be unfamiliar with its actual usage.

"Well said, in the opinion of Will Tooke!" said an American from Kansas who had not yet opened his mouth.

"You're appreciation flatters me, Mr. Tooke," added Sir Walter Donderry, "for it is stupid prejudices that makes nations rivals."

"Personally," said Dambielle, "I approve of praising one's fatherland, even emphatically. You might find that ridiculous or humorous, Messieurs, but my conviction is unshakable."

"Every good Englishman," said Catlen, "ought to proclaim that the United Kingdom is..."

"The foremost nation in the world," added Dambielle, with vivacity. "Well, I can say as much of France, Monsieur Catlen."

"No, because the United Kingdom is..."

"Please, gentlemen," Sir Walter interjected, "don't remain on that terrain any longer, for the best arguments are never appreciated in such cases, and sometimes degenerate into regrettable quarrels. The man who is indifferent to his fatherland is unworthy and despicable, but what can you do to grant that superiority justly, which each people claims solely for itself?"

"Why, then," asked Kisseloff, "did you assert just now that the English alone have boldness and perseverance enough to venture into unexplored regions?

"Forgive me, Monsieur de Kisseloff; I did not intend to be exclusive. I know that all civilized nations furnish intelligent and courageous pioneers, but in England, the passion for long voyages and the research of the unknown preoccupies all minds; it's a fever, a frenzy! Among us, explorers are more numerous than anywhere else; I would make you a detailed list, but count and compare, and you'll be convinced that it's without the slightest vanity that we claim the first rank.

"Moreover, gentlemen, the scientists, journalists and conscientious and impartial writers of other nations render us justice. At this moment, I am reading with the keenest pleasure the works of Jules Verne, a French author whose merit is appreciated all over the world, and I notice that his heroes are almost always English. I'm not talking about the *voyages extraordinaires*, in which erudite fantasy and originality play the major role, but purely scientific and literary works in which the most difficult adventures are related. There is Captain Hatteras, an Englishman, who becomes the first to reach the cold Arctic regions; there is Dr. Ferguson, Kennedy and Joe, three Englishmen who, in *Five Weeks in a Balloon*, launch themselves into the air and cross the whole of Africa; there's Jasper Hobson, another Englishman, who is the hero of the dramatic plot of *The Fur Country*; and there is Phileas Fogg, still an Englishman, who goes *Around the World in Eighty Days*."

"I'll stop you there, Sir Walter," said Dambielle. "I beg you to note that Phileas Fogg is not alone—that his servant, Passepartout, a Frenchman, accompanies him and plays an important role in the course of the work."

"And I affirm," added Will Tooke, "that the Americans have got closer to the North Pole than the English."

"I know all that as well as you do, gentlemen," said Sir Walter Donderry. "For Arctic explorers, America can victoriously oppose to us Kane, Hayes and Captain Hall, who have all surpassed the eightieth degree of latitude. I also know that Passepartout, in *Around the World in Eighty Days*, relieves the monotony of a journey at full steam, if I might express it thus, but that certainly doesn't prevent the French author about whom we're talking from rendering justice to our nation in preferentially choosing the actors in his dramas from among the English."

"The English," said Dambielle, "are greatly encouraged by the scientific societies of their country and have more money to spend than we do. If money is the sinew of war, it's also that of the endeavors of peace and progress. In France, it's the scantiness of our resources that often stops us; without that, we'd be as good as he English."

"Better!" put in a man of about thirty leaning nonchalantly on the mantelpiece, and who had seemed until then to be listening to the conversation distractedly.

Everyone turned round. Each of them, by means of his expression, seemed to be demanding an explanation.

"Is it necessary to extol Phileas Fogg," continued the man who had interrupted, "because he went around the world in eighty days? Gentlemen, I'll wager that I can do it myself in forty days."

"Are you mad, Valdy?" asked Dambielle, moving closer to the man who had spoken so boldly.

Sir Walter Donderry was gripped by a fit of laughter that lifted up his abdomen in violent jerky somersaults. "Oh, Monsieur Valdy," he said, still laughing, "I wouldn't want to neglect, in your regard...the respect that...well brought-up people...owe to one another...but, truly, your proposition is so funny...oh, it's obvious that we're in Arcachon, and that Arcachon is Gascon territory..."

"Gascon territory, a former possession of the United Kingdom," Harry Catlen, Esquire, put in, peering curiously at Valdy. He too was surprised and bewildered.

"Messieurs," Valdy repeated, "I'm willing to bet. My proposal is quite serious."

"Have you the legs of an antelope?" asked Sir Walter Donderry. "Have you the powerful fins of a shark, or the wings of a bird?"

"Who knows?" Valdy replied, simply.

"But the most up-to-date and best-known means of transport don't permit us to suppose a speed..."

"Messieurs, the bet is still on offer."

"Well then, let's bet!" cried Harry Catlen, Esquire.

"Not yet," said Dambielle, "I'd like to believe that Monsieur Valdy will think about it and take back his rather boastful proposition."

"Well, so be it!" Valdy said. "Twenty-four hours is sufficient to reflect. Tomorrow, I'll renew my offer."

"Do you intend to make this voyage of circumnavigation alone, Monsieur?" asked Will Tooke.

"No, certainly not—but I intend to choose those who will accompany me."

"Your confidence is persuasive. With your permission, I'll be one of your companions."

"With pleasure, Monsieur Tooke, for you seem bold and resolute to me."

"Thank you." The American shook the Frenchman's hand.

They continued chatting for a little while longer. Gradually, the drawing room emptied, and no one remained but Valdy and Dambielle. The latter employed all sorts of arguments to persuade his friend to retract, but Valdy was unshakable. The two young men separated slightly annoyed with one another.

The rain had stopped. Dambielle went out on to the terrace briefly and smoked—or, rather, chewed—a cigar. He was about to go back in to go to bed when he was accosted by Kisseloff.

"Forgive me, Monsieur Dambielle," the Russian said to him, "but would you do me the honor of chatting with me briefly?"

"As much as you please, Monsieur Kisseloff—although I suppose you want to talk to me about Valdy and the ridiculous wager that he wants to make with Sir Walter Donderry."

"It is, indeed, Monsieur Valdy about whom I want to talk, if you'll permit. You're his friend, I believe."

"Since childhood."

"Then you know him very well. Do you think that he is a man to carry his projects through?"

"If he affirms that he can travel around the world in forty days, he's capable of doing it in thirty-nine. By what means? I don't know—but take it from me that he'll attempt the impossible in this reckless adventure, even if it costs him his life."

"That reassures me, Monsieur Dambielle. For a moment, I thought that Monsieur Valdy was nothing but a vulgar charlatan."

"No, no—Valdy is sometimes eccentric, but he's serious and knowledgeable. Moreover, his eccentricities are no longer surprising when one knows the mental tortures that he's endured. Take note—suffering has marked his forehead with an indelible trace. The fixity of his gaze, the pallor of his face and the sad smile that sometimes parts his lips inspire a profound pity."

"And yet Monsieur Vardy is young, and despair has not yet entered his soul."

"I hope you're not mistaken, Monsieur—but I fear that a suicide might be hidden behind this crazy enterprise that he's meditating. He's like a soldier weary of life, who, not wanting to put an end to his days himself, throws himself into the thick of the action during a battle."

Would it be indiscreet to ask you the cause of your friend's affliction? Perhaps I can help you to calm him down."

"Thank you for your good and generous words, Monsieur Kisseloff; I'll tell you everything about my friend without beating around the bush. Marcel Valdy and I were born in X , a small town situated a few leagues from Bordeaux, and went to school together. That explains, briefly, the friendship that unites us.

"A few years ago, Valdy wanted to marry Berthe Férandier, the daughter of a high-ranking judge who had recently retired. One cannot spend thirty to forty years in the latter profession without one's character acquiring the spitefulness of a harpy. One day, Père Férandier slammed the door in Valdy's face and told him not to come near his daughter again. Marcel loved Berthe, and she seemed delighted with her future husband. Nothing, in fact, seemed to presage a rupture; the fortune, honorability and proportionate age were very similar in the two fiancés.

"Soon, we had an explanation of the revolting actions of the former judge. As sly as a fox, and as crafty as a Norman, he had caught in his net one of his former colleagues, the Marquis de Béconnais, an insignificant magistrate but a worthy man, considerably enriched some time before by unexpected inheritances. He was the son-in-law dreamed off by Monsieur Férandier—and his daughter would be a Marquise! Berthe allowed herself to become intoxicated by her suitor's large fortune—or was she yielding to the pleasure that certain women experience when they adorn themselves with trinkets and satisfy their vanity? I don't know, but she became the Marquise de Béconnais.

"It was a terrible blow for Marcel Valdy; he couldn't understand why a beautiful young woman, endowed with all the graces, would consent to marry a decrepit old man. I won't describe the fits of rage he had, during which he trembled like a madman. That state of continual agitation was succeeded by a malady of languor; for a time, we thought he was going to die. When fever gripped him, and delirium tortured him, he never ceased crying out for Berthe, his darling Berthe, his beloved Berthe.

"Finally, Monsieur, youth triumphed over dolor, and Valdy recovered rather suddenly. Since then, he has conserved a kind of misanthropic sadness, a surly tone that has sometimes distressed me; but Marcel was not one of those effeminate, romantic individuals who live in a perpetual affectation. His education was careful and extensive; so, in order to combat painful memories, he surrounded himself with books and instruments of physics and chemistry, set up a laboratory and worked with a feverish ardor.

"In order to distract himself, and perhaps to instruct himself, he traveled, and was away for here long years before returning to X***. We he came back, he was accompanied by two mariners named Cardounet and Pickerreek. He accommodated them for a long time and always treated them with the most perfect amity. Cardounet and Pickerreek were rough and rather coarse individuals, but they enjoyed life and were cheerful rogues. Whenever the two matelots left, Valdy urged them to return promptly, and they reappeared after each voyage, to rest from the fatigues of their long and perilous crossings.

"In company with the mariners, Valdy underwent a change that surprised us; a frank cheerfulness replaced his black sadness, and he became the most outgoing person one could meet. About two months ago, Pickerreek and Cardounet left my friend again, and he became more eccentric, odder and sadder than ever. I persuaded him to come and distract himself in Arcachon, and—should I confess it to you?—I'm here partly for his sake. I try to amuse him, hoping that time will make him forget Mademoiselle Férandier and…but the bet he wants to make with Sir Walter Donderry had just set all my plans back.

"That, Monsieur, is all I can tell you about Valdy."

"Thank you, Monsieur Dambielle," said Kisseloff.

The two young men walked for a few minutes without saying a word. Suddenly, the Russian stopped, and emerged from his reflections. "Monsieur Dambielle," he said, "those whom the Lord puts to the proof are always the elect. Look at all the great men who honor the nations; they only produced their masterpieces, or made their astonishing discoveries, after having undergone ordeals in which weaker natures would have succumbed. Monsieur Valdy is not a vulgar individual. Suffering has weighed upon him, but he reacted with hard labor. He will show the woman who disdained him that talent is worth more than a title or a fortune. Who knows whether the fruit of his sleepless nights might not be manifest in an invention that will astonish all of humankind?"

"Your enthusiasm is admirable, Monsieur Kisseloff, but I fear that it might be a tacit approval of Valdy's projects."

"That's true. The strangeness and unexpectedness of the proposal made a deep impression on me, and now, instead of trying to dissuade him, I shall be the first to encourage him."

"But you'll be spreading oil on the fire."

"No matter! Tomorrow, I shall ask Monsieur Valdy to accept me as a traveling companion. If he consents, he can count on a devotion proof against anything, and a gratitude that will only end with my life."

"He might drag you into a perilous adventure..."

"Where would the merit of triumph be if there were not dangers to brave and obstacles to overcome? I shall accompany Monsieur Valdy and...but I shall impose one condition on him."

"What?"

"That there are no Englishmen among us."

"Has Harry Catlen, Esquire, filled you with disgust for his compatriots?"

"The English have all pretentions. It's necessary to show them what can be done without them, and better than them."

"If you fail, they'll laugh at you...and they'll win your money, for I assume that you're going to bet, along with Valdy."

"My fortune is at your friend's disposal."

"You're as crazy as he is, Monsieur Kisseloff, but your heart is good. Permit me to shake your hand."

"With pleasure."

The two young men walked for a while longer, chatting about insignificant things, and then went back in to go to bed. Before they parted, however, they heard Harry Catlen exclaiming: "In the entire United Kingdom there's no one as mad as Mr. Valdy. Tomorrow, I'll bet...and I'll win."

"Perhaps," said the Russian.

I dare not affirmed that Kisseloff's sleep was untroubled and dreamless. As soon as dawn broke, he knocked discreetly on the door of Valdy's room.

"Come in!" called the latter.

Valdy received his early visitor in very simple garb. Several maps were extended in front of him and, for want of compasses, he was measuring certain distances with a graduated meter rule. It was evident that he had sacrificed part of the night to geographical studies.

"I beg your pardon for disturbing you," said Kisseloff, "but I've been waiting impatiently for daylight for two hours. The proposal you made yesterday has preoccupied me, and..."

"And you doubt too, don't you?"

"On the contrary; I have the greatest confidence in you. At any rate, I'll explain myself without bating around the bush. I'm Count Ivan Kisseloff, an officer on the staff on the Russian Ministry of War. I have an annual income of 25,000 roubles, and I'm putting my entire fortune, and my person, at your disposal."

Odd and—let us say the word—eccentric as Valdy was, he could not master his astonishment or prevent himself from looking at his interlocutor in amazement.

"Well, Monsieur," said the Russian. "Do you accept?"

"Monsieur Kisseloff," Valdy replied, "the spontaneity of your generous offer moves me, but I ought not to, and cannot, draw you to your doom. Am I certain of success?"

"Yes, for you have faith in your work."

"That's true—I have faith in it, but also resignation. When I depart, I might never be seen again."

"You didn't present all those objections to Will Tooke."

"Will Tooke is older than you are; then again, he's an American from the Far West—which is to say, one of those powerful individualists that only the New World can furnish; one of those men who confront danger for the pleasure of confronting it and put all their abnegation into the pursuit of the smallest and greatest endeavors."

"I know that people nurse prejudices against Russians. For you Occidentals, we are still, to some extent, the ancient Scythians."

"No, Monsieur Kisseloff; in Russia, as everywhere, there are people for whom progress is not a vain word. You alone would serve to prove that, but I fear that you might be the dupe of your imagination. You have been seduced by the unexpectedness and boldness of my projects. Soon, lassitude and disgust might replace the effervescence of your spirit. Moreover, you're an officer, bound by certain duties whose demands you cannot avoid with impunity."

"Oh, Monsieur, that last consideration does not prevent your accepting me as a traveling companion! In Russia, we love adventures that are out of the ordinary; the Minister to whom I'm attached knows that science requires volunteers, and sometime victims. He'll be eager to grant me the leave I need. Come on, Monsieur Valdy—don't refuse my request."

"Well, all right. You have the fine aspirations, the ardor and the courage of youth, which realize great things. You'll be a useful auxiliary."

Kisseloff thanked Valdy warmly and left him without referring to the condition he had mentioned the previous evening.

"Bah!" he said. "Monsieur Valdy is betting against the English; he won't take any of them." That judicious reflection soothed him and rendered him the happiest of mortals.

As one can imagine, all the conversations held in Arcachon on the second of September 187* revolved around Valdy. The latter, it must be admitted, encountered little approval. The English colony, in particular, jeered at the temerity of the Frenchman and promised to subject him to a humiliation that he would remember.

Sir Walter Donderry was thoughtful, however; he was seen walking with Dambielle and heard talking to him animatedly. Sir Walter was certainly a Englishman in the full meaning of the term, but if he possessed the qualities of his compatriots, he did not have the ridiculousness that characterizes them. Having traveled a great deal, and seen a great deal and leaned a great deal in consequence, he was exempt from certain weaknesses and a certain arrogance. He was an eminent man, owing the consideration he enjoyed to his broad education, his high intelligence and the benefits that he distributed discreetly around him. His generosity was extreme and he strove to put into practice the Scriptural dictum: *He passeth over the earth like a beneficent dew.*

He was, therefore, saddened that his provocations had driven Valdy to make the wager. His protruding belly seemed diminished by a third and his joyful and benevolent face, ordinarily crimson, took on violet tints—a sure sign, in him, of violent emotion and great irritation. He resolved to try anything to prevent Valdy from attempting his enterprise.

Finally, the impatiently-awaited evening arrived. The vicinity of the Grand Hotel, the vestibule and the conversation room were overflowing with people. It was generally believed that something extraordinary was about to happen. Commentaries followed their course; the most bizarre, baroque and guttural exclamations escaped the crowd for foreigners still holidaying in Arcachon.

Eight o'clock sounded. Valdy, accompanied by Dambielle, Ivan Kisseloff and Will Tooke, came into the conversation room. A near-religious silence immediately fell.

"Messieurs," said Valdy, "I have wagered that I will go around the world in forty days, but I omitted to submit the condition essential to my departure. I request a year in order to make preparations."

Sir Walter Donderry breathed more easily. He thought that the Frenchman was retreating, and he was delighted. Harry Catlen, Esquire, grimaced and sniggered.

"I have the habit of keeping my promises," Valdy went on, severely. "You are perfectly at liberty not to wager, Monsieur Catlen, but I affirm to you that on September the first next year, I shall set out."

"Setting out is nothing; coming back is the difficult thing," said Harry Catlen.

"I shall come back if it pleases God," Valdy added. "Now, Messieurs, I have another objection to present to you. I count on going around the world by traveling westwards; you are not unaware that, in that direction, the days are lengthened by four minutes per degree, which is twenty-four hours in $360°$; I shall therefore lose the day that I would gain if I were to steer eastwards; I shall return on the eleventh of October and not the tenth. It is forty days that I request for my expedition, and it is forty days that you must grant me. My fortune amounts, in round figures to nearly a hundred thousand francs; I wager a hundred thousand francs."

"I also wager a hundred thousand francs with Monsieur Valdy," said Ivan Kisseloff.

"And me the same," added Will Tooke.

A general rumor succeeded the silence so scrupulously observed until then. The members of the audience consulted one another. The Englishmen, and even blonde Englishwomen, initially amazed by the audacity and self-confidence of the Frenchman, were offering to wager sums larger than those proposed. Dambielle recorded the stakes. Harry Catlen, Esquire, would wager a hundred thousand francs, Sir Walter Donderry fifty thousand. The remaining hundred and fifty thousand francs would be divided among several individuals of various nationalities.

In order to avoid any misunderstanding, it was agreed that Marcel Valdy would be in Arcachon in a year's time, that he would leave on the first of September and return after having traveled around the world in forty days. For the return, a rendezvous was arranged at the Café de Bordeaux in Bordeaux on the evening of the eleventh of October. The proofs of the exact accomplishment of the rapid excursion would be furnished by letters and newspaper articles.

"Monsieur Marcel Valdy," said Sir Walter Donderry, "I've wagered two thousand pounds against you, but I hope I shall lose them."

"You have a noble character, Sir Walter, and I understand your apprehensions. Be assured that I am not engaging lightly in an adventure in which I have nothing to gain but money if I succeed, and ruination if I fail. I am devoting myself to a scientific task, which might perhaps be destined to change all our social relations. Salomon de Caux was locked up as a madman,[9] Galileo was persecuted, Denis Papin pau-

---

[9] The engineer Salomon de Caus, or Caux, published *Les Raisons des forces mouvantes* [The Principles of Motive Force] in

30

perized, Robert Fulton mocked by his compatriots and mistrusted by the governments of Europe—and yet those valiant minds endowed humankind with the most unexpected and marvelous discoveries. Shall I despair before the struggle? Shall I withdraw because no one has confidence in me? No, no—that shall not be."

"You're right, Monsieur Marcel; sternly-tempered natures triumph over everything. May it please God that you succeed, even if I have to sacrifice another two thousand pounds."

Valdy was interrogated from all directions; he was begged to reveal the means he intended to employ in order to carry out his voyage, but he made no reply. Toward the end of the evening he met up with Kisseloff and Will Tooke, and spoke to them briefly.

"Messieurs," he said, "I thank you for the confidence of which you have given evidence, and I count, with your aid, on confounding the mockers and the skeptics. At this moment, I can't give you any explanation. Can you arrive at the Hôtel de Bayonne in Bordeaux on the first of February next year? I shall be entirely at your disposal, and we can draw up our plans.

"I'm traveling for some time in Syria and Egypt," said Will Tooke, "but on the first of February, I'll be in Bordeaux."

"When he's informed of the goal of my voyage," Ivan Kisseloff added, "the Minister of War will grant me permission. Count on me."

The Russian and the American shook Valdy's hand cordially, and left.

1615 containing a description of a steam-driven pump, which caused François Arago to name him as the true inventor of the team engine. Like Denis Papin, who has a much more justified claim to that invention, he was a Huguenot, and religious prejudice played some part in determining that he did much of his work outside France, in England and Germany.

Chapter II

Five months after the episodes we have just related, on the morning of the first of February 187*, Will Tooke arrived in Bordeaux and went to the Hôtel de Bayonne. He asked a bell-boy whether two travelers by the names of Kisseloff and Valdy were in residence. The reply was negative.

"Oh well," he said. "As I'm expecting these gentlemen today, and they won't miss our rendezvous, I'll reserve the two rooms adjacent to mine. It'll be easier for us to confer together."

"As you wish, Monsieur."

At eleven o'clock, Will Tooke went down to the restaurant and was served one of those substantial lunches that a true Yankee orders, and which the staff at the Hôtel de Bayonne are able to prepare. Afterwards, he went to the Place de la Comédie, marching phlegmatically, and mingled with the strollers who always clutter the broad pavement in front of the Café de Bordeaux, a sort of small-scale Tortoni where foreigners, businessmen, financiers and so on gather at certain times.

Suddenly, the American heard himself hailed. The voice came from a cab.

"Will Tooke!"

"Kisseloff!"

The usual compliments were exchanged and hands were shaken vigorously.

"And Marcel Valdy?" asked the Russian.

"Not yet arrived," Will Tooke replied.

"As long as nothing unfortunate had happened to him," said Kisseloff.

"Bah! I've booked a room for you and anther for him. By virtue of a kind of intuition with which I'm familiar, I knew that you'd arrive."

The Russian and the American went to the hotel. Will Tooke noticed that Kisseloff had brought a domestic, but a rather ugly domestic such as one rarely sees.

"What do you intend to do with that ape?" he asked.

"'That ape' will be introduced to Monsieur Valdy, and I hope that he'll be very useful to us, if he's permitted to accompany us."

Without raising any further objection, the American saluted Dernghuiz—that was the name of Kisseloff's servant—and assured him that he was delighted to make his acquaintance. Dernghuiz only made a monosyllabic reply, for good reason—he spoke a dialect that only his master understood.

Dernghuiz was one of the most successful specimens of the hybrid family that inhabits the plateaux and deserts of central Asia, which seems to be formed of a mixture of the Indo-Germanic and Mongolian races. A seemingly-frail body supported a rather large head; his nose was rather flat; his lips, of medium thickness, were surrounded by a sparse and fleecy beard. His small, keen eyes denoted a boldness proof against anything and a free-ranging intelligence.

That servant of a new and scarcely civilized kind was, however, utterly devoted to his master and obedient to his slightest sign or gesture. Between themselves they had establish a sort of "mute language," which economized on words and sometimes avoided them. The Tatar might have been compared to the faithful Grimaud popularized by the talent of Alexandre Dumas in *Les Mousquetaires de la Reine*, who only opened his mouth at rare intervals to utter a few sparse monosyllables.

Gratitude bound Dernghuiz to Kisseloff; the latter had saved his life during an expedition directed against a few turbulent tribes on the Pamir plateau. Instead of treating him as a rebel, Kisseloff had busied himself securing his loyalty by care and good treatment.

Will Tooke and Kisseloff waited in vain for Valdy for most of the day. They dined copiously, however, and in order to cheer themselves up a little they decided to spend the evening at the theater. They were getting up from the table when a carriage arrived with a frightful racket, and stopped in front of the Hôtel de Bayonne.

"It's him!" said the American.

The Russian hurried out to the coaching entrance, but stepped back abruptly. In the carriage in question he did not make out Valdy's voice. A forceful curse and mocking exclamation were pronounced because the gates were not opened quickly enough. Marcel was better brought-up than the new arrivals. Finally, the latter got down, cursing and grumbling at the coachman, who had not come to lower the foot-plate.

"Hey, out there, cab-parrot, is it to be paid twice that you move about so much?"

"Put on your gloves to talk to Mossieu, Pickerreek—he's an ambassador with a number."

Pickerreek! That name was a revelation. Ivan Kisseloff remembered the conversation he had had with Dambielle on the evening of the previous first of September. Pickerreek and Cardounet! Those names advertised Valdy's presence to him.

In fact, one of the mariners called out: "Open your eyes at the cathead, Monsieur Marcel; this vagabond coachman wants to kill the poor people; he hasn't lowered the footplate."

"Of course!" said the American. "I knew that Valdy would come. My presentiments are never mistaken."

Marcel Valdy excused himself for arriving so late, and offered the pretext that his good friends Pickerreek and Cardounet had delayed him."

"Your room is booked," said Will Tooke.

"Let's go," Valdy replied.

The six men installed themselves in the room and Valdy unrolled a map of the world with a stereographical projection, into which he stuck several pins.

"You're still intent on attempting the adventure with me?" he asked.

"Yes," replied Tooke and Kisseloff, firmly.

"I shall submit my plans for your appreciation immediately. We have forty days to travel around the world; that's an average of two hundred and fifty leagues a day to cover, as you can see. That's trivial, for it's not uncommon for a locomotive to reach a speed of a hundred kilometers an hour, which is twenty-five ordinary leagues—but a locomotive can only travel overland; then again, it's often slowed down by inclines, and winding bends that it can't take rapidly without bringing about a catastrophe, a derailment or an explosion. With my system, nothing will stop us. Mountains, rivers, deserts, lakes and stretches of sea are covered without obstacles, without requiring the slightest detour. Messieurs, it's a voyage of aerial circumnavigation that we're going to undertake."

"In a balloon!" Pickerreek interjected. "I know about that. When the Prussians besieged Paris, I went up in a wicker basket and passed over their lines."

"It's not in a balloon that we'll be traveling," Valdy added. "I won't give you the technical details of the apparatus I've invented, but I guarantee its success. For us, distance will no longer exist. If it pleases us, we can travel five hundred leagues in a day."

As one can imagine, the astonishment of the audience increased.

"Messieurs," Valdy continued, "the air only offers insignificant resistance; the currents it contains will work to our advantage; then our normal speed will double. You have often heard mention of various ascents in which sixty, eighty or even a hundred kilometers are crossed in an hour by balloons; well, that speed is nothing compared to those attained by migrating birds. Quail, which seem so poorly equipped for flight, cross the Mediterranean in eight hours; swallows reach us from Senegal in two or three days; a falcon belonging to Henri III, which escaped in the forest of Fontainebleau, was recaptured the following day on the island of Malta. You've all heard talk of the rapidity of passenger pigeons, and I'll cite you a few facts supported by observation. A few years ago, in 1854, six swallows were captured in Paris and transported to Vienna in Austria, where they were set free at eight o'clock in the morning. Two of them returned to Paris at one o'clock in

35

the afternoon, the third at two-twenty, another at four o'clock, and two were lost en route. About three hundred leagues had been traveled in five hours.

"Some raptors one beat their wings once per second, but nevertheless advance with a vertiginous rapidity. We have the proof of it in a story in the *Nouvelle Gazette de Zurich* of 26 August 1863, reported by Doctor Hoefer in his work *Les Saisons*.[10] 'A group of tourists,' he says there, 'left Coire to make an ascent of the Stützerhon, which is 2,576 meters high. From the summit of the mountain they perceived an enormous eagle, which, having taken off from Calanda beyond the Rhine, headed for the Stützerhon in order to go, after a slight detour, to settle on the side of the Rothorn. The duration of the flight was five minutes; the interval between the point of departure and the point of arrival has been estimated at two and a half leagues. The eagle must therefore have traveled a distance of 3,000 Swiss feet in three seconds, which corresponds to a speed of 35.6 meters per second.'

"The eagle in question must have been traveling at nearly a hundred and thirty kilometers an hour. Some sea-birds draw away from coasts to distances that the fastest ships can only reach after several days of navigation, and yet return to their roosts every night.[11]

"With steam, humans have partly suppressed distance, but its power is only dominant over the earth and the oceans. The air has not yet been conquered. The balloon has not yet fulfilled any of the promise predicted by the scientific minds of the end of the eighteenth century. I share the opinion of Monsieur Babinet[12]: the notion of the direction of balloons is absurd, for that kind of apparatus, inflated with gases lighter than air, whose ascensional force increases by reason of its

---

[10] Ferdinand Hoefer, *Les Saisons: études de la nature* (1867).

[11] The author adds a footnote remarking that frigate-birds are often encountered more than four hundred leagues out to sea.

[12] The physicist Jacques Babinet (1794-1872), a prominent popularizer of science.

volume and the difference of densities, presents a surface as extensive that the slightest breeze, the smallest zephyr, will always triumph over the blades, paddle-wheels and helices with which they are equipped. 'How can balloons like the *Flesselles*, for instance, which measures a hundred and twenty feet in diameter,' Monsieur Babinet said to the Association Polytechnique, be made to resist and maneuver against the currents? It would require a force of four hundred horsepower per meter to mount a near-equal contest between the wind and the sail of a ship. Suppose, which is impossible, that a balloon could carry with it a force of four hundred horsepower; that great effort would be utterly useless, for we immediately appreciate that, under that pressure, your balloon would crash in its fragile envelope. Imagine all the horses in a regiment attached by a rope to the nacelle of a balloon, and the only result would be to shatter your balloon into fragments.'

"The problem of aerial navigation cannot be resolved by balloons, and I have looked elsewhere. During the unfortunate war that my fatherland fought against Prussia, a host of inventors surged forth, proposing the most ridiculous motors and the most eccentric means to facilitate locomotion in the atmosphere. Personally, I carried out and fulfilled my duties as a volunteer; when evening came, or even during the night-watch, I thought and reflected profoundly. I recognized that all the projects with which the newspapers were filled could not stand up to serious examination, and that humans would only rise up and steer in the air after having found a motor combining great power with extreme lightness.

"Several people have proposed steam; among them, I call special attention to Messieurs Giffard and Crocé-Spinelli. Giffard, during his celebrated experiment of 22 September 1852, rose into the air with a light and cleverly-constructed steam engine, but the machine rested in the nacelle.[13] If the

---

[13] Henri Giffard made the first powered and controlled balloon flight on 24 September 1852, from Paris to Trappes, 27 kilo-

motive force had propelled the balloon rapidly, the loss of Monsieur Giffard would have been inevitable, in consequence of the explanations given by Monsieur Babinet. His attempt was bold but imprudent. Croce-Spinelli restricted himself to describing light motors applicable to aerial navigation, and thought that a twenty horsepower machine would fulfill all the conditions required by the demands of atmospheric locomotion.[14] The weight would be reasonable, but water and fuel would undoubtedly take up a lot of space and would add their weight to that of the machine. You see, therefore, Messieurs, that it is impossible, for the moment, to put into practice the theories I have just mentioned."

"Perhaps it's electricity that you'll employ," Ivan Kisseloff put in.

"No," Vardy replied. "Electric motors are costly and heavy, and their force is insignificant. Thus far, with a weight of eight hundred to a thousand kilograms, it has not been possible to obtain more than four or five horsepower. For the moment, know that I shall make use of an agent whose force is incalculable. Messieurs, our motor will be liquefied carbonic acid gas. If you have any knowledge of chemistry you will understand that I can dispense with a boiler and combustible fuel, and that we can give our motor the lightness sought in vain until now."

"Aren't you afraid of explosions?" asked Kisseloff.

---

meters away, but could not return because the contrary wind was too strong.

[14] The author adds a footnote explaining that these lines were written "before the dolorous *Zénith* disaster." The aeronaut Joseph Croce-Spinelli had set an altitude record aboard the *Étoile polaire* in 1874 and set a record for the duration of a balloon flight aboard the *Zénith* in March 1875, but an attempt to break the altitude record in the latter balloon in April 1875 lead to his death by asphyxiation, along with Théodore Sivel, although their travelling companion, Gaston Tissandier, survived and went on to attempt further exploits.

"When the apparatus that will transport us through the air has been constructed," Valdy said, "you can study the precautions I have planned to prevent explosions."

"We have confidence in you, Monsieur Vardy," said Will Tooke, "and if, unfortunately, it's necessary to blow up in mid-air, we'll, we'll blow up."

Pickerreek and Cardounet emitted groans that were scarcely approving. Dernghuiz, as a true philosopher, had crouched down in a corner and was sleeping tranquilly.

"Messieurs," Vardy continued, "we are going to draw up our itinerary. We shall depart from Arcachon on the first of September; we shall traverse France, and England and head for Greenland, calling in at the Faroe islands and Iceland."

"We won't be warm," Cardounet put in.

"It's not by virtue of mental caprice hat I've chosen that direction. You must understand that my apparatus, during that first experiment, will have certain imperfections that I will only discover definitively after a certain lapse of time. I don't want to expose you to a descent into the sea. As a safety measure that you will appreciate, I need to distance myself from land as little as possible. Originally, I had resolved to go along the coasts of Spain, Portugal and Africa and set out toward America from Senegal, but the expanse of sea that separates the old continent from the new world is too great, and doesn't offer sufficient landing-places to attempt the adventure. By steering northwards and stopping at the Faroes and Iceland, we'll reach the boreal lands without running any great risks.

"We'll cross Greenland, the Davis Strait, Baffin Island, the Foxe Basin, Southampton Island and eventually arrive in American territory at Repulse Bay or Chesterfield Inlet. From there, we'll go along the coast of the Dominion of Canada and land at Fort Churchill. We'll be able to cross the entirety of North America without exposing ourselves to great distress by virtue of cold and snowstorms, so we'll descend as far as the fortieth parallel, taking Denver, the capital of Colorado, as an objective. We'll follow the Nelson River, pass over Lake

Winnipeg and arrive in Denver having traversed the immense plains that separate the hills of Missouri from Kansas.

"Then we'll cross the Rocky Mountains, the land of the Mormons, the territory of Oregon, and venture into the cold regions of British Columbia and the Alaskan peninsula. From that peninsula we'll reach Asia by following the Aleutian Islands. From Kamchatka we'll head into southern Siberia and travel the entirety of Asia, passing over the lands of the Khalka Mongols, the Gobi Desert, the Koukou-Noor, Tibet, Nepal and Hindustan to end up in the confines of the Gujarat peninsula. Our task will then become easier, for, in order to return to Europe, we need only follow the coasts of Baluchistan as far as the Strait of Hormuz, those of Arabia as far as the Strait of Bab-el-Mandeb, those of Abyssinia, Egypt and the regency of Tripoli, and we'll arrive in Algeria, then Spain, and finally France.

"You'll observe that I've almost never left land, and, save for rare exceptions, we'll be constantly in countries where the people are not hostile to us. Above all, I'm avoiding major centers of population and big cities, for our excursion would then be slowed down by the curiosity we'll excite. Now, Messieurs, it's necessary that each of us makes arrangements to deposit, in the various countries we'll traverse, good provisions of ethyl alcohol and hydrochloric or sulfuric acid, agents indispensable for the manufacture of the carbonic acid that we shall need. Personally, I'll take charge of establishing depots of those materials in the Faroe Islands, Iceland, Greenland, Egypt, Arabia and Algeria.

"I'll establish my depots in the whole of America and the Aleutian Isles," said Will Tooke.

"Siberia, China, Hindustan and Baluchistan will be my concern," added Ivan Kisseloff.

"Above all," Valdy continued, "don't neglect my final recommendation, because success depends on your care and precision. It's of no particular importance that the various depots of bicarbonate of soda and hydrochloric acid are in one place rather than another. Navigating in the air, a detour of twenty, thirty or forty leagues is a bagatelle. The essential thing is that we always find sufficient fuel for my apparatus and that you identify in an absolutely precise fashion the places where we can, if might put it thus, take on provisions. The rest is up to me, and I hope that Providence will aid us."

Will Tooke uttered an entirely American hurrah.

"Monsieur Valdy," said Ivan Kisseloff, "we're crossing the entirety of Asia?"

"Yes."

"Don't you think that a man who has lived the life of the nomadic peoples and knows their language might be very useful to us?"

"I agree."

"I have that man at your disposal; he's one of my servants, Dernghuiz, who is sleeping over there in that corner."

"He can join us. I'll enlarge my apparatus slightly; there'll be room for all of us."

"Dernghuiz!" called Kisseloff.

The Tatar woke up and ran—or, rather, bounded—toward his master.

"You see these men," the Russian said to him, in his own language. "They're my friends; they'll become yours. In time, we'll be departing for a distant exploration, in which we won't be spared fatigue ad danger; promise to be as devoted to them as you are to me. When you're tired, they'll relieve you; when you're in peril, they'll help you. Like you, they're good and courageous."

Dernghuiz folded his arms across his chest, looked attentively at Valdy, Will Tooke, Pickerreek and Cardounet, and then, passing before them, he bowed his head.

"Master," he said, "I am the friend and slave of your friends."

"But if Dernghuiz goes with us," Cardounet put in, "how will he carry out the orders given to him? He doesn't understand us."

"Yes," Ivan Kisseloff replied, smiling. "Dernghuiz understands sign language. Try."

Cardounet decided to commence the trial immediately. By means of an animated pantomime, he asked for a drink. The Tatar disappeared, and soon came back carrying a carafe full of water and a glass. Cardounet made a scornful grimace, not addressed to Dernghuiz but to the carafe. Pickerreek joined in with his companion, and never, in any puppet theater, has Pierrot been seen to execute in a more expressive fashion the gestures of a man uncorking a bottle, pouring a drink from it, looking lovingly at the vermilion liquid, raising it carefully to his lips and savoring it with the delectation that is the sole prerogative of highly-qualified gourmets or drunkards.

Dernghuiz smiled and disappeared. He came back a few moments later carrying several bottles of a Saint-Émilion recommended by its age and vintage.

"Good!" said Cardounet, "we'll make something of our new comrade."

The bottles were uncorked and everyone drank to the success of the future voyage. The toasts were frequently renewed, so, when the time came to separate, Pickerreek's and Cardounet's eyes were sparkling like carbuncles.

When Valdy had taken his leave of his friends, a waiter knocked softly on the door and came in with a mysterious expression.

"Are you Monsieur Valdy?" he asked.

"Yes."

"A woman who has been waiting for a short while desires to speak to you."

"A woman!"

"Yes, Monsieur: a woman, accompanied by a maidservant, who reserved a room while Monsieur was drinking with the friends who met in his room."

"Tell her that I can't see her now."

"Monsieur, the lady insisted strongly on seeing you as soon as possible. She says that her visit cannot be put off."

"Send her up, then."

The waiter did not need to have the last instruction repeated. One may deduce that his insistence was rewarded by a
large tip. A few minutes later he reappeared, accompanied by
a woman dressed in mourning, whose face was hidden by a
thick veil.

Valdy recognized the visitor immediately.

"Berthe!" he exclaimed. Then he revised the appellation:
"Madame la Marquise de Béconnais."

"Call me Berthe," said the young woman, extending her
hand to him. "For me, you have never ceased to be Marcel."

"Oh, Madame," Valdy replied, sadly, "the wound you in-
flicted on my heart has not healed yet."

"Forgive me, my friend; I was obliged to yield to the inflexible will of my father. He thought that the glamour of a
title and a large fortune would make me happy. Alas, he was
mistaken—but I can't blame him, and I don't want to talk
about a past that is dolorous for you and for me. I've come to
tell you that I'm free, completely fee, and that I can dispose of
my hand."

"You're a widow, then?"

"Yes. Monsieur de Béconnais died about a year ago, in
Italy, to which I had accompanied him. He appointed me the
heir of everything he possessed. Today, I'm rich enough for
you and for me. Some time after my marriage, Monsieur de
Béconnais recognized all the torments by which I was afflicted, and yet he didn't complain; he had a delicate mind and a
good heart. In exchange for the deference he showed me, the
distractions he tried to procure for me and the generosity he
showed toward me, I surrounded him with care and showed
him all the gratitude of which I was capable.

During his final illness I stayed with him, watched over
him and helped him with a devotion exempt from calculation
and self-interest. Before dying, he called me to him. 'Berthe,'
he said to me, 'I thank you; you have tried to brighten my dying, but your cares were futile; my days were counted. My
fortune belongs to you; I leave it to you without imposing any

egotistical conditions. Be happy with the man you loved; I've been assured that he is worthy of you.'"

As she finished speaking, the young woman sat down and put her hand to her eyes. Large tears were trickling down her cheeks.

Marcel understood that the widow's grief was sincere, and he respected it. But a battle began in his head in which passion and reason clashed. His adored Berthe was there, having come to offer herself without restrictions, more beautiful and more gracious than ever. However, was she not the primary cause of the suffering he had endured, the grim misanthropy that had taken possession of him, the more or less bizarre projects that he had formed and which he was about to risk his life to accomplish?

Eventually, he broke the silence and said to Madame de Béconnais: "It's too late, Berthe."

"You don't love me any longer, Marcel?"

"Berthe, don't be mistaken with regard to the meaning of my words. You're as dear to me as before, and your benevolent visit is making my heart overflow with joy, but I can't be your husband. Believing that I had lost you, I have conceived the most reckless enterprises; I'm bound by engagements that I cannot break without being accused of idle boasting and cowardice. If you have any concern for my honor, don't persist."

"Has your friend Monsieur Dambielle deceived me, then? Yesterday, when I saw him and told him what I intended to do, he said to me: 'Go, Madame, see Marcel as soon as possible; dissuade him from carrying out his projects. You alone will have sufficient influence to stop him.' I don't know what you're meditating, Marcel, but he seemed to sense that you were in danger; I ran to you to ask you, to beg you, not to throw yourself head-first into the most hazardous adventures."

"Don't worry, Berthe; since I thought you were lost forever I have grown pale over books; I have tried the most audacious experiments; and I sense that I shall succeed…now more than ever, for if I acquire a little glory, it will reflect upon you."

Then Marcel told Madame de Béconnais about his life of strife and hard work. His convictions, his hopes and his self-confidence rendered him eloquent and gave his words the warm insinuation that always captures the imagination, so the young widow was soon seduced by what was extraordinary and great in Valdy's conceptions. Her approval, tacit at first, became expansive, and she encouraged that which she had initially criticized.

That sudden conversion perhaps related to mysteries of the heart that no one can explain. A beloved individual is always seen with all perfections, always surrounded by a resplendent aureole. At any rate, Madame de Béconnais squeezed Marcel's hand and said to him: "There's nothing to prevent our getting married. I too am bold. I'll go with you and share your fatigues."

"What? You!"

"Do you refuse?"

"Oh Berthe, how worthy you are of being loved!"

Madame de Béconnais withdrew, and Valdy, after having gone to bed, had none but pleasant dreams. Thus, the following morning he was more cheerful than he had ever been known to be before.

Will Tooke and Ivan Kisseloff did not pay any great attention to that change of mood, but Pickerreek and Cardounet said to one another: "How joyful he is, Mossieu Marcel! The Saint-Émilion is still producing its effect. It's necessary to confess that it was exceedingly good!"

"Thunder! Don't talk to me about it. If the sea resembled that, I'd like to be a shark forever!"

Chapter III

After the last episodes we have just related, the reader will understand that the widowed Madame de Béconnais soon became Madame Marcel Valdy. The pleasures of the honeymoon did not prevent Marcel from ripening his projects, however. He was too deeply committed to recoil. Moreover, he was no longer seeking to satisfy the vanity of his self-esteem, but to realize one of those scientific endeavors, one of those unexpected discoveries, that sometimes change the face of the world. He set to work immediately.

To shelter himself from unwelcome curiosity, he set up a work-yard on the edge of Parentis Pool, near Parentis-in-Born, a village almost lost in the Landes a few leagues from Arcachon. The Bordeaux-Bayonne railway, passing a short distance from Parentis, was convenient for bringing the materials indispensable to the construction of the apparatus. Valdy fenced the construction site in with pine-trunks, and only admitted the workmen necessary carry out the work. Needless to say, Pickerreek and Cardounet carried out the most active surveillance, and pitilessly chased away idlers attracted by curiosity. In addition, they played important roles, one as foreman and the other as butler, and carried them out to everyone's satisfaction.

Pickerreek, whom everyone called "Pick" for shot, was from Dunkerque, a town in which, as he put it, everyone is "born a cabin-boy," lives as a mariner and dies as an old sea-dog if the sea, sufficiently clement not to swallow you up in its abysses, eventually throws you back among the landlubbers because your muscles are ankylosed, rheumatism has paralyzed all your limbs and the sperm whales wouldn't deign to swallow your old carcass.

Pickerreek, we may say, was one of the most accomplished of those northern mariners who, beneath an apparent phlegm, combine the solid qualities that a man of the sea ought to possess. His patience and impassivity were almost proverbial. Squalls, high winds, tempests and dead calms—nothing surprised him. Whether it was necessary to replace the carpenter or furl the sails when the wind was bending the masts, he was ready for anything, and committed himself philosophically and dexterously to the various tasks he was given.

Although his mind was good, his physique was scarcely graceful. Beneath a skin tanned by the sun a turbercular nose protruded, strewn with a handful of warts and a few bristling hairs, lit up as if it were coated with red lead. "Oh, what a nose! All the world is astonished by it!" Cardounet sang. It was a ruby the color of fire, reflecting sparks from its golden mount. We think, however, the Dunkerque gin had something to do with that emphatic tint.

Although deprived of the graces that characterize the head of the Apollo of the Belvedere, Pickerreek's face was martial; a thick beard, slightly disheveled, trimmed into a collar, framed it agreeably and partially concealed a permanent inflammation of the right cheek. Sometimes, Pickerreek pursed his lips and a reddish ejaculation escaped therefrom. The inflammation was explained: Pickerreek chewed tobacco! What do you expect? No man is perfect, especially one of those matelots reeking of tobacco and tar, one of those unpolished matelots whose callused hand we fops would not deign to shake, but who confronts death proudly every day.

Cardounet was the opposite—or, to put it in maritime terms, the living antipodes—of Pickerreek. Two inches shorter, he was also thinner and wirier. His vivacity and impressionable nature declared clearly enough that he had been born on the banks of the Garonne. A talkative braggart and storyteller, like most southern mariners, he always had words on his lips to make one laugh, or a joyful song. Several incidents in his life would not have been unworthy of the funniest chapters of a comic novel. He had started out as a cabin-boy, then, weary of sailing, had joined a troop of actors touring southwestern France—but his dramatic triumphs could not take away his highly-developed appetite for voyages, which he claimed to undertake for pleasure an instruction. However, malicious tongues asserted that in his artistic career he had collected more apple-cores and whistles than laurels and money. At any rate, Cardounet had taken passage on another ship, bound for Senegal, and since then, save for rare exceptions, he had remained, as he put it, faithful to Thetis—for it is necessary to say that Cardounet, in his capacity as a smooth talker, enameled his picturesque conversation with citations borrowed from the dramatic repertoire that he had studied.

Pickerreek and Cardounet had met up on a ship in the southern seas. How did two such disparate men come to be bound by an unalterable amity? Explain it as you will, it was a fact. Pleasures, difficulties and dangers all became common to them and one never took ship without the other. Valdy had run into them on a steamer serving South America, and, in the mental irritation in which he found himself as a result of Berthe Férandier's marriage to Monsieur de Béconnais, was seduced and charmed to encounter the friendship and rectitude of those seemingly coarse natures. Sympathy is contagious; Pickerreek and Cardounet divined the immense dolor that was overwhelming the stranger, and had done their best to soothe it. Gratefully, Valdy became the friend of the two mariners. We have seen that he was always glad to welcome them to his home and treat them like spoiled children. A long time ago he had selected them as his first traveling companions.

Valdy had conscientiously studied the complex problem of aerial navigation. More than once, we must confess, doubt had taken possession of his mind. Doubt, we say to our shame, is an integral part of the French temperament. In any scientific, artistic, industrial or commercial endeavor, we do not much care for innovations, and debate long and hard before putting them into practice. In the meantime, foreigners take the discoveries and replace the arguments with trials, often crowned with complete success.

Action is almost always better than theory. The English found applications for steam and the Americans for electricity while our Academies were making or listening to speeches.

Valdy, torn between the partisans of dirigible balloons and those of heavier-than-air flight, fortunately understood that quarrels, no matter how learned they might be, envenom individuals without producing the slightest progress, and considered that the pettiest experiment would prove more than the reviews emanating from the various societies that have the pretention of directing science. It was then that he resolved to put his astonishing conceptions to the test.

The conquest of the air! What a dream and what glory! Since the most remote times, humans have sought to dominate the atmosphere and render it the docile agent of their omnipotence; thus, no discovery was more loudly hailed with such enthusiastic acclamation as that of aerostats. Diderot had dared to say, so great was his confidence in progress, that people would go to the moon one day, but his hyperbolic expression was surpassed by the confident words of the old Maréchal de Villeroi, who had witnessed the first ascent in a hydrogen balloon.

"*They* will find the means of no longer dying," he said, "but it will be when I am dead!"

Aerostats, however, have existed for almost a century, and have not kept any of the promises that Benjamin Franklin himself, so sagacious and judicious an intelligence, seemed to anticipate when he said, in speaking about the Montgolfier: "It's a new-born child!" Today, the child is almost a centenarian, and it has not advanced.

From the very beginning, people believed in the possibility of steering balloons: Gaspard Monge, Jérôme Lalande, Meunier de La Place, Guyton de Morveau and Marcellin Bertholet, to name only the most remarkable scientists of the era, affirmed that the problem would be easily resolved. Their affirmation lived as long as roses are said to live: "the space of a morning." The work of Meunier[15] is particularly noteworthy,

---

[15] Meunier de La Place published one of the first scientific papers on aerostats, "Mémoire sur l'équilibre des machines aérostatiques" (*Journal de physique*, juillet 1784)

but Meunier never sought to steer. By means of an ascensional force that he produced at will he sought the atmospheric currents that would carry him. From there to true direction, it is a long way.

Unfortunately, the aeronauts who came after Meunier imitated his methods meekly, without daring—or perhaps without being able—to depart from the rules he had traced. We can cite the principle attempts of the partisans of dirigible aerostats—attempts that never yielded a successful result: Scott and Martinville in 1788; Calais, in the Jardin Marbeuf, in 1801; Jacob Deghen in Paris in 1812; Pauly in London in 1816; Edmond Genet in New York—a projected attempt only—in 1825; Dupuis-Delcourt and Regnier in 1829; Le Comte de Lennox in 1834; Eubriot in Paris in 1839; Dupuis-Delcourt and Van Hecke in Brussels in 1847; Petin in Paris, New York and Mexico in 1850; and Delamarne in Paris in 1864.[16]

If we do not mention the experiments of Blanchard, it is because we think that they are sufficiently well-known; however, we cannot pass in silence over that of Alban, the director of the Javel factory, which appeared, momentarily to be completely decisive. Alban, with his associate Valet and a carpenter named Truchon, departed from Paris in August 1785 with a balloon, the Comte d'Artois. The nacelle was equipped with a powerful pair of wings, imitating those of a windmill, whole exceedingly mobile central pivot tilted both vertically and horizontally. It was, properly speaking, one of the first applications of the helix. In calm weather, Alban could almost steer, and his ascensions of the thirteenth, seventeenth and eighteenth of September seemed conclusive—but on the nineteenth, a moderate wind having got up, he was obliged to have himself taken in tow to return to the point at which he had

---

[16] These details and others related to the same subject were probably taken from Louis Figuier's history of ballooning, included in *Les Grandes inventions anciennes et modernes* (1861) and reproduced in *Les Merveilles de la science* (1867).

departed (from Saint-Cloud to Javel). The experiments that followed were even less successful.

Giffard's fine experiment of 25 September 1852, which he has repeated since, denotes an uncommon boldness, but, as we have demonstrated by invoking Babinet's arguments, it could not succeed. At the most, it prevented the gyration of the balloon, Giffard's balloon being ovoid in shape. We are firmly convinced that it is not necessary to raise a steam engine into the air to obtain that result. Recently, Monsieur Dupuy de Lôme has recommended a system of compressed air, which has produced nothing. All the art and science of aeronauts has been stalled by a confusion identified a long time ago by Dupuis-Delcourt: "It is necessary, above all," that author wrote, "to steer the balloon and not the nacelle, as everyone has complacently attempted to do."

After the seekers of air-currents came the partisans of heavier-than-air flight, most notable among them Messieurs Nadar, Joseph Pline, Gustave Ponton d'Amécourt, Gabrielle de la Landelle, etc.—but these gentlemen have been too preoccupied with organs of propulsion rather than motors. The entire problem resides in the production, as Valdy said, of a movement combining great energy with extreme lightness.

He thought about finding that motive force in the properties of liquefied carbonic acid gas, and we shall soon explain the manner in which he intended to make use of it. Incontrovertibly, the arguments of the partisans of aviation have contributed more to the problem of aeronautics than the experiments carried out by means of balloons. Even so, Valdy did not entirely reject the ascensional force of the classic aerostat, but as he would have had difficulty in some countries in procuring the necessary hydrogen gas, he wanted to utilize it at the departure and operate thereafter in its absence.

All those who have occupied themselves with aerial navigation have imagined apparatus having the most bizarre and unconventional forms. However, humans have always had a perfect form before their eyes, the form *par excellence*, which only needs to be imitated to have some chance of success.

"And now," says Arthur Mangin,[17] "if anyone asks me how I imagine one might succeed in navigating in the air, I show them a bird and I say: imitate that; construct a vessel whose specific density has the same relationship with air as that bird. Give it an analogous form, and above all, strive to find a motor capable of replacing the muscular force of the animal and producing a movement of sufficient energy and rapidity without harming the lightness of the apparatus."

Several scientists have opposed aviation taking inspiration directly from birds, and among them we notice in particular two valiant spirits, two eminent popularizers of science: Wilfrid de Fonvielle[18] and Louis Figuier.

"Many well-educated people," the former writes, "confuse aerial navigation with the more or less bizarre inventions of empiricists who seek a means of steering in the air by imitating birds; but human genius, which has had no need to copy fish in order to tame the oceans, will not have to plagiarize nature to achieve the conquest of the air."

If only people had always plagiarized nature. How much fumbling avoided! How much fruitful work! How much suffering spared! Nature, however unconscious it appears to us, nevertheless holds the key to all secrets that humans have sought for long centuries.

It is true that maritime navigation does not imitate fish, but fish swim beneath the surface of the water, while ship sails with only its keel immersed; everything that is above the flotation line is in the air. Whatever Wilfrid de Fonvielle says, it has been necessary to imitate nature, which offered a perfect model of naval construction when it put before our eyes the

---

[17] In *La Navigation aérienne* (1869). Mangin was a prolific popularizer of science who wrote books on numerous topics.
[18] Wilfrid de Fonvielle (1824-1914) had an unusually long and prolific career as a scientific journalist, which included a stint as editor of the aeronautical journal *L'Aérophile*, founded in 1893; the highlight of his career as a balloonist came when he escaped from Paris in one during the Prussian siege.

modest palmiped. Penguins making use of their vestigial limbs as paired fins are triremes, galley moving by means of the force of oars; elegant and graceful swans, rapidly cleaving the waves assisted by the wind caught in their partly-opened wings, are fine sailing-ships, immense clippers presenting all their sail to the atmospheric current and matching steamers for speeds. Every time that a human being, a new Glaucus, has wanted to explore the abyssal depths, he had been obliged to imitate fish. Submarine boats cannot have any other form. That of Monsieur Villeroy, which thus far realizes the best nautical conditions, is a veritable metallic fish.

Now, this is what Louis Figuier says:

"The enthusiastic defenders of Monsieur Ponton d'Amécourt's aeronef posit in principle that it is necessary, to combat the air, to be heavier than air, and they cite birds as examples. The argument does not appear to us to be decisive. Undoubtedly, a bird at rest is heavier than air, but who has weighed a swallow while it is flying in the sky? Birds' lungs are extended through the greater part of the abdomen; their bones are riddled with air-filed channels; their entire body encloses an infinity of tiny cavities, membranous pockets with valves. All these cavities dilate and fill with warm air during flight. In addition, their feathers function as miniature montgolfiers, to such an extent that the specific weight of the bird changes considerably due to that insufflation of arm light air through their entire body. Finally, the large surface area of their wings, horizontally deployed, presents a relatively considerable resistance, if one compares it to the weight of the muscles that represent the motor apparatus. It is thus permissible to suggest, in spite of the contrary affirmation of the new school, in conformity with the opinion of the physicians and physiologists of the last century, that a bird in movement is almost as light as air."

Louis Figuier only develops this argument theoretically. However, all serious ornithologists—Charles Bonaparte, Bresson, Vieillot, Lesson, Wilson, Audubon, Temminck, Toussenel, etc—recount facts that absolutely give the lie to

Figuier's they. They tell us that the sanguinary raptors fall upon their prey, grip it in their powerful claws and transport it to their nests, neighbors to the clouds. Audubon, that marvelous observer, who spent part of his life in the depths of dark forests, has seen the fierce bearded vulture and the bold sea-eagle raise in the air, to great heights, the inanimate bodies of wild turkeys, swans or lambs weighting up to forty pounds. It cannot be denied that the flight is more difficult and heavier, but in sum, the bird, carrying a burden, is no longer in its normal state, and we are firmly convinced that it is then heavier, and much heavier, then air.[19]

Some naturalists think that a bird weighs about fix or six times as much as the volume of air that it displaces. We almost share that opinion; but the error of the majority of inventors in aviation stems from a very simple cause. They almost always attempt to give the propulsive mechanisms they envisage a vertical ascensional force. By virtue of Archimedes' principle, a balloon possesses that force to the highest degree, but a bird is completely deprived of it. We do not count the slight effort it makes in leaving the ground to take flight, for that is a thrust, a jump. On the other hand, it possesses the force of horizontal projection, of *gliding*, which permits it to attack the air obliquely—which Alphonse Pénaud, after serious research and savant calculations, regards as the key to aerial navigation.[20]

---

[19] The author inserts a footnote to say that in chapter VII several examples of children being carried off by eagles are cited. Fortunately, his argument is not dependent on such dubious anecdotes.

[20] Brown presumably knew about Pénaud's 1871 model airplane the Planophore, powered by a twisted rubber band, which demonstrated the viability of fixed-wing flight, but was undoubtedly more interested in the ornithopters with which he began experimenting in 1872. Brown could not know in 1875 that Pénaud would commit suicide in 1880, at the age of thirty,

Marcel Valdy had understood all the advantages of an apparatus similar to a bird, and in its construction he employed the lightest materials, principally cork, silk, rubber and aluminum. His marriage had enriched him, and he was no longer alarmed by the expenses he had to meet. The lack of capital often impedes the best projects, and every inventor is happy when he has no need to have recourse to partners and shareholders who, in exchange for their money, believe that they have the right to comment on and direct everything.

What, in the constructed apparatus, would replace the muscular force with which a bird is equipped? We have already said that electric motors only produce an insignificant force, and steam engines are excessively heavy; furthermore, their weight is increased by the quantity of water and fuel that serves to activate them. Valdy then thought about employing liquefied carbonic acid gas.

Everyone knows that carbonic acid gas is exhaled in animal respiration, and that it is absorbed by plants, without which the atmosphere would be vitiated. Everyone knows, too, that there are carbonated springs; the famous Grotto del Cane, near Naples, is the most frequently-cited example. The gas is abundantly distributed in nature; we shall make a summary study of its properties in order to understand the role that Vardy had reserved for it.

Chalk, marble and calcareous rocks are compounds of carbonic acid and lime. They give off carbonic acid when they are subjected to the action of a reagent such as sulfuric or hydrochloric acid. The gas is colorless and invisible, with an acrid odor, inappropriate to respiration and combustion, heavier than air, and can be decanted like a liquid. (It weighs 1.984 grams per liter, while an equal volume of air weighs 1.29 grams.) At atmospheric pressure, water dissolves its own volume of carbonic cid, and its solubility increases in proportion to pressure. Foamy beverages—beer, lemonade, champagne,

---

after failing to find financial support for his plans to build full-sized aircraft.

Seltz, Vichy and Spa waters, etc., have an effervescence relative to the quantity of carbonic acid that they contain in solution.

Michael Faraday has liquefied carbonic acid, Charles Thilorier has succeeded in solidifying it. In either state, it is a powerful refrigerant, and if one presses the solid between the fingers it disorganizes the skin and flesh like incandescent material. Placed in a vacuum and mixed with ether its evaporation is retarded and the temperature descends to minus 110 degrees, the temperature at which mercury congeals in a matter of minutes, and liquefies or solidifies the majority of the gas. At present only six gases can be cited that have resisted this powerful means of refrigeration, to wit, oxygen, nitrogen, hydrogen, carbon monoxide, nitrogen dioxide and protocarburet of hydrogen.[21] In the liquid state, the tension of carbonic acid is enormous; above that fifteen degrees it reaches five atmospheres. To obtain a similar result with water would require a temperature of more than 265°.

Steam engines never have a force as great as that which carbonic acid can furnish, especially if it is rapidly generated. Then again, one is not embarrassed by water and combustible fuel, which are exceedingly cumbersome; their volume and weight will be, according to our current scientific knowledge, an invincible obstacle to the raid realization of the best projects.

Bicarbonate of soda contains twice as much carbonic acid as sodium carbonate, which can be readily obtained in immense quantities by the Leblanc method. When one desires to produce a certain quantity, one ordinarily uses the former salt. To liquefy the carbonic acid, one employs two cast iron containers connected by a metallic tube. One is called the generator, the other the receptacle. The generator contains bicarbonate of soda, water and a tubular copper vessel filed with sulfuric or hydrochloric acid. So long as the vessel remains

---

[21] "Protocarburet of hydrogen" was an early term for the gas now known as methane.

vertical, there is no mixture or emission; as soon as the generator is sealed by a metallic screw-cap, it is gradually tilted by rotating the pivot that supports it; the sulfuric acid mixes with the bicarbonate of soda and water, and the reaction commences immediately. The carbonic acid is instantly emitted, but as its volume is between a hundred and a hundred and fifty times greater than the interior of the generator it is compressed and liquefied. The chemical operation raises the generator to a temperature superior to that of the receptacle, so, by means of the tube connecting he two cylinder, the liquefied carbonic acid flows into the cold receptacle and remains in that receptacle, pure of any mixture. The connection opened by the metallic tube is closed, the generator is uncovered and one begins again. One thus obtains, according to the capacity of the receptacle, as many liters of liquefied carbonic acid as one desires.

This experiment presents serious dangers and must be carried out prudently, for liquefied carbonic acid exceeds a pressure of five atmospheres and receptacles can explode and project their shards over some distance, like a bomb. Several chemists have been killed or injured in this way.

The generator and receptacle are usually two cast iron cylinders reinforced by hoops and bars of wrought iron, so they are very heavy. In order to make them lighter while conserving the same solidity, Valdy, following the example of the eminent chemist François-Louis Donny, constructed them in aluminum bronze, over which he superimposed felted material surrounded by steel bands. In order to prevent explosions, he placed these dangerous instruments in a metal basin filled with water and surrounded by damp cloth.

The receptacle! There, then, is the heater, but a heater without a large hot surface, without supplementary tubing, without boilers, without a fire—in sum, reduced to the simplest expression, and disposing an immense force. For the transmission of the movement, it was only necessary to imitate the steam engine, and that was what Valdy did.

The carbonic acid cannot be taken from the receptacle in the liquid state; as soon as it is brought into contact with the air it tends to resume its original state, launches forth as a jet of gas, absorbing heat from the ambient surroundings, and produces a considerable drop in temperature. That sudden expansion gives it a formidable elastic force, and nothing is easier than to conduct it into a cylinder furnished with a piston, slide-valve or distributor, ultimately maneuvering in the same fashion as the pistons of a steam engine.

We have said that Valdy gave his aerial ship the form of a bird. In fact, it was a gigantic ovoid balloon forty meters long, solidly constructed in sheets of cork-oak and larch, linked together by an aluminum framework. The varnish employed for aerostats covered the envelope inside and out in such a way as to render it impermeable. The employment of cork-oak and larch is explicable in terms of their characteristic properties, which are, for the former: lightness, due to its cellular structure and the elasticity of its cell-walls, and impermeability, resulting from the disconnection of each cell from the others; and for the latter: its resistance to the action of the air and humidity, and lightness, since its specific weight in only 0.628. The top of the balloon would only be slightly bulbous, for that upper part had to make room for the voyagers, the various items of motor apparatus, two powerful vacuum pumps, and the instruments necessary for scientific observations and the security of the crew. It is needless to add that a cage of wicker and rope surrounded that upper part, in order to offer efficacious protection against falls, and that six grooved metal rods supported the mass of the balloon. It could thus be taken up or down at will.

Two immense wings pivoted in the vertical sense around a metallic armature disposed on top of that kind of empty-sided hull that we have described. It was in the construction and disposition of these wings that Valdy's ingenuity had been exercised to the highest degree. Each one was forty meters long and presented to the air a surface of eight hundred square meters—a total of sixteen hundred square meters for the apparatus, not including the mass of the balloon. It is unnecessary to be astonished by these figures. We are convinced that aviation will be unable to pas from theory to practice if one employs apparatus with a smaller surface. Archytas and a few mechanics have certainly constructed artificial birds and insects that rise up into the air,[22] but the specific lightness of their automata serves them almost as well as the ingenious springs that give them movement—movement without continuity, as in all toys.

Moreover, aeronauts themselves have understood for a long time that in order to navigate in the air it is necessary to employ veritable vessels of colossal dimension. To be convinced of that, one only has to consult Dupuis-Delcourt's curious report *Sur l'application de l'art aerostatique aux transports par air*, presented to the Ministry of the Interior on 16 May 1845, the works of Eugène Farcot, Gabriel de La Landelle etc. And after all, what is a length, or rather a wingspan, of a hundred meters for an apparatus designed to attempt a decisive test of aviation? Have we not seen gigantic aerostats? The *Flesselles* was forty meters in diameter, the *Géant* as much, with a volume of six thousand cubic meters each!

In order not to prolong this digression, we shall not describe here the marvelous structure of the organs of movement in birds. It is sufficient to know that the wing, moved by the pectoral muscles, goes up and down. On the upstroke it encounters a great deal of resistance on the part of the air, so it describes a rotational movement and presents itself edge-on. The scientific studies of the Societé Française de Navigation Aérienne[23] had inspired and guided Valdy in the construction

---

[22] The allegation that Plato's friend Archytas constructed a self-propelled bird-like flying machine was made five centuries after his death by Aulus Gellius. It might be true, but Brown's "certainly" is a trifle strong.

[23] This society was founded in 1872 and took over publication of the journal *L'Aéronaute*, founded in 1866 by members of Nadar's society for the promotion of heavier-than-air flight.

of the two immense propellers. He rejected, however, the employment of alternative organs of movement, like the steam engines providing circular movement that have been anticipated by some constructors.[24]

The axle moved by the piston had four flywheels; two of these flywheels were equipped with crank-shafts themselves surrounded by hooked rings that served to retain multistranded metal wires. These wires, supported by iron rods several meters long, passed over pulleys divided into several branches and were attached to the wings at certain points, in such a way as to provide extra support and avoid any kind of vacillation. The rotation of the flywheel pulled the wire, whose extremity, securely fixed to the ring, described the same circle as the crank-shaft. That circular movement, as is evident, extended or diminished—according to the diameter of the crank-shaft—the length of the wire held between the wing and the pulley, producing an alternating elevation and lowering.

The lowering of a wing is, incontrovertibly, the essential condition of flight; a bird strikes the air more rapidly and with more force in the descendant movement than the ascendant one. Valdy therefore placed a counterweight under the balloon. The center of gravity was thus better determined and the lowering of the wing effectuated more rapidly. The rotational movement of the wing, which serves for the horizontal movement of a bird, was produced by an extension of the piston, which, in going back and forth, pulled two straps attached to the extremities of the wings.

We shall not say anything about the mathematical studies that Valdy had been obliged to undertake in order methodically to design the various accessories of his apparatus, for that

---

[24] The author inserts a footnote; "Principally Monsieur Rikkers' vertical machine." The machine in question was described in an 1872 issue of *L'Aéronaute*, but its designer remains obscure. Some of the other members of the society included in a subsequent list have similarly been lost to view.

subject would be arid and would lead us to considerations that would be more appropriate in a scientific work than a book without pretentions primarily designed for the popularization of aerial navigation, a neglected science that has fallen into almost complete discredit.

And yet, what admiration will be reaped by the man who subjects the atmosphere to his domination and succeeds in defying its storms and tempests! What a triumph for the man who renders himself the master of the skies!

Unfortunately, we must agree that, save for rare exceptions, aerostatic ascensions are in the domain of frivolity and amusement, and that the partisans of aviation have run up against the ridicule that is such a powerful weapon in France. However, it is France that created aerostatics, was the first to share the kingdom of the Empyrean with the clouds and the winged children of the air, and ought to be the first to strive, with neither pause nor relaxation, for the realization of a fecund discovery.

Listen to an Englishman, James Glaisher: "It is France, I do not hesitate to say aloud, that has the prerogative of setting the example, for balloons will remain suspect so long as France is not occupied with them. Why should one expect other nations to have confidence in aerostats if the country to whom their invention is owed hastens to desert them? Who would dare to defend the art of aeronautics if the French, who have been called into the skies by a long tradition, are the first to recognize its vanity?"

After the bold aeronaut, after the scientist, listen to the poet Alphonse Toussenel:[25]

"If humans, from Icarus to Montgolfier, Desrosiers and Nadar, have continually striven to take possession of the domain of the birds, which forms an integral part of their globe,

---

[25] In *Le Monde des oiseaux, ornithologie pasionnelle* (1853-55), the second part of *L'Esprit des Bêtes*, a supposed analysis of the natural symbolism of animals by a Fourierist utopian writer.

it is because God has lodged the idea of that conquest somewhere in a secret recess of their brains, in order that it might
serve as a compass and a spur to their scientific efforts. Aerial
locomotion is, in fact, not only a condition of the realization of
the true fraternity of peoples but a supreme goal of science. It
is the highest and omnimodal form of locomotion that summa-
rizes all others. The light aerostat of immense proportions is
the chariot of fire that passes over the waters, the ship that
runs over the surface of continents, which laughs at the fury of
the elements and rises above the tempest, which scorns all
obstacles but respects the work of God everywhere, dispensing
with filling in valleys and piercing mountains at the whim of
the homicidal locomotive. Now, human genius, docile to the
indications of instinct, has already planted its flag in the region
of the clouds; it has climbed higher than the eagle and the
condor, and the hour is not far distant when it will reign as
sovereign mater over the fields of the Empyrean."

Let us accept hat augury; let us hope that indifference
and general apathy will be replaced by toil and laborious research. One of God's elect will solve the sphinx's riddle. So,
we salute, if it is permissible to express it thus, the dawn of
atmospheric navigation, in following the curious and patient
studies of the French society that has made devotion, talent
and abnegation the order of the day, and whose members—
Messieurs Janssen, Crocé-Spinelli, Motars, Hureau de Villeneuve, Frion, Saco, Hauvel, Penaud, Caron, Sivel, Paul Bert,
Berthelot, Cornu, Farcot, Wilfrid de Fonvielle, de La Landelle,
Marey, Ponton d'Amécourt, de Quatrefages, Renoir, Tessié du
Motay, Wurtz, etc., etc.—have sufficiently distinguished
themselves.

In the construction of the wings Valdy employed the
lightest and most malleable materials, principally silk and
aluminum; their inferior part was concave and its flexibility
was neutralized by attachments disposed at intervals like the
steel ribs of an umbrella. To steer that mass, or rather, that
large surface—that aeroplane, in a word—it required a rudder.
Still copying nature, which does what it does well, Valdy re-

placed the rectifying feathers of a bird with a fabric chassis placed at the rear of his apparatus. He added an additional vertical frame, a true rudder that operated changes of direction while the former served to accelerate the ascent or descent.

By the twentieth of August, the aerial apparatus was finished. Pickerreek and Cardounet wanted to baptize it and give it one of those bombastic names so frequently used for warships, but Valdy simply called it the *Céleste*. Only indispensable instruments were embarked: compasses, barometers, thermometers, hygrometers, sextants, etc., etc, and it was agreed, in order not to overload the apparatus, that the travelers would not take any baggage except for some thick blankets and that they would buy their changes of underwear en route. As for provisions, they would be the least cumbersome and provided for two or three days at the most.

The workmen employed by Valdy never knew what the machine they were constructing was designed to do. As they were perfectly-treated and well-paid they did not ask any questions about the work they were instructed to do.

At Arcachon, Valdy's various preparations were unknown. If the foreigners and travelers heard mention, by chance, of a workshop almost lost in the depths of the heath, near Parentis-en-Born, they thought that it was a matter of an automatic sawmill for processing pine.

They had nothing to do, therefore, but wait patiently for September the first.

Chapter IV

Finally, the much-anticipated day drew near. On the thirty-first of August the guests at the Grand Hotel in Arcachon were conversing animatedly about Marcel Valdy's impending voyage, as to whether or not he would set out. All conversations revolved around that affirmation and denial.

Harry Catlen, Esquire, jeered as heartily as only an Englishman can jeer; his doubts had been converted into convictions and he issued loud assurances that he was preparing to take possession of the four thousand pounds sterling that he had wagered.

Sir Walter Donderry was anxious. The question of money was of scant relevance to him, and he would certainly have sacrificed the fifty-thousand francs at stake if Valdy had decided not to attempt the perilous enterprise. His conscience was subject to unaccustomed twinges. He was perfectly well aware that in human hands, science realizes gigantic and bold projects that seem to belong to the realm of the supernatural, but he dreaded a catastrophe that seemed to him to be inevitable.

"Since you claim that you can to rise up into and steer in the sky," he said to Valdy, "there's no need, in order to convince us, to fly around the world. Conduct your experiment here; go from Arcachon to Paris. If you accomplish that trajectory, we'll declare ourselves satisfied. I'll undertake to rally all those who have wagered against you to that idea."

"Monsieur Catlen would mock us unduly," Kisseloff interjected.

"And it's because of Mr. Catlen's stupid appreciations that you're going to hurl yourself against insurmountable obstacles?"

"No," said Valdy, "it's for science."

"You're mad. Your madness has something sublime and irreflective about it, which even tugs at me, but I think, sagely, that one ought not to immolate oneself for science at the first strike. Damn it, my friends, no one chose the middle of the ocean for the first attempts at steam navigation; to begin with, they tried out pyroscaphs on the Elbe, the Saône, the Seine and the Clyde. In case of failure, help was at hand, and the inventors had the recourse of saving themselves by swimming. I think Fulton acted prudently in not confronting the wrath of the sea and making his first journey on the Hudson. Who goes slowly goes far, says an Italian proverb; put that aphorism into action and I dare to affirm that you'll succeed, and that your glory will be no less dazzling and no less merited."

"We've bet on one thing," said Will Tooke. "That's to go around the world in forty days. We don't have the right to change our conditions."

"I like it when people express themselves thus; it proves an uncommon virility and boldness, but there's a woman among you—a woman we all esteem, since we have met her— and reasons of humanity forbid you..."

"Oh, have no fear for me," Berthe Valdy interjected. "French women have hearts full of intrepidity and devotion."

"I know that, Madame," Sir Walter added, smiling. "Mr. Catlen grinds his teeth every time someone mentions Joan of Arc."

"And damn it," said Cardounet, "the sight of the fair sex is an encouragement for the French soldier and mariner. We'd never weaken or falter before Madame Marcel."

"By the rigging of the Flying Dutchman, what's the point of so much discussion?" Pickerreek continued. "We're all set to go; we have to go—so let's go, and the sooner the better!"

Sir Walter Donderry did not raise any more objections. The energy and courage of his contradictors amazed him. He almost regretted not being able to accompany the bold voyagers. In his long peregrinations he had braved so many perils and escaped so many dangers that he wondered seriously why the idea of embarking with Valdy had not occurred to him sooner.

At any rate, he added mentally, to console himself, *if this first attempt doesn't succeed, I can try in my turn...*

It will be remembered that Marcel Valdy had imposed an obligation on Kisseloff and Will Tooke to have sulfuric or hydrochloric acid, bicarbonate of soda and ethyl alcohol deposited along the route to be followed, in order continually to renew the elements of motive force. He had taken personal change of establishing depots in the neighboring countries of Europe. We shall list the names of the various places to which the materials had been sent, omitting the names of the depositories, the details and the observations that each had broadly communicated in order to avoid errors and confusions.

Valdy's depots were in the British Scilly Isles, the Isle of Man, the Hebrides, the Orkneys and Shetlands; the Faroe Islands; Reykjavik in Iceland; Hasik and Aden in Arabia; Zoulla in Abyssinia; Souakim and Marakah in Nubia; Aswan, Medinet-al-Fayoum and the Oasis of Siouah in Egypt; Benghazi and Tripoli in the Regency of Tripoli; and El Aghouar and Nemoura in Algeria.

Kisseloff's were in Petropavlovsk in Kamchatka; Okhostk, Oudskoï, Blagoveshchensk, Nertchinsk and Kiatcha in the lands of Amor and Siberia; Ourga, Karakorum and Sou-Tcheou in China; Lhasa in Tibet; Katmandu in Nepal; Oude, Adjemir and Karachi in Hindustan; Gwadar in Baluchistan; and Bandar-Abbas in Persia.

Will Tooke's were in Godhaven on Disko Island and Christiansaab in Greenland; Salisbury Island in Baffin Territory; Fort Churchill, Fort York, Fort Severn and Fort Garry in the Dominion of Canada; Fort Abercrombie and Fort Saint-Pierre in Dakota; Fort Laramie in Wyoming; Denver, Colorado; Ogden, Utah; Unionville, Nevada; Salem, Oregon; Olympia, Washington; Fort Chilcotin and Fort Simpson in British Columbia; New Archangel, Fort St. Nicholas and Fort Alexandre in the Territory of Alaska; and Ounalaska, Tanaga and Attou Islands in the Aleutians.

Valdy organized the various items of information given to him for subsequent consultation without hesitation. He spent the rest of the day buying indispensable tools and weapons in company with Pickerreek and Cardounet.

When the sun had disappeared over the horizon, the conversation room of the Grand Hotel gradually filled with sedentary and foreign bathers. Not one of those who had placed wagers the previous year missed the rendezvous. The stipulations of the bet were renewed and definitively settled. Harry Catlen formulated his doubts and contradictions impertinently. Kisseloff replied hotly; Sir Walter Donderry put an end to the argument with his benevolent intervention and diplomatic tact.

"Messieurs," said Valdy, "faithful to the promise I made, I shall depart tomorrow, the first of September. If I am not in Bordeaux on the eleventh of October next, having gone around the world, you will have won the three hundred thousand francs that Messieurs Kisseloff, Will Tooke and myself have bet against you."

Then, taking Sir Walter Donderry aside, he added: "Sir Walter, you are a true gentleman. The honesty of your character and the nobility of your heart has inspired an esteem in me that one never feels for vulgar individuals. I beg you, on behalf of all my companions, to be the witness of my first efforts! Tonight, at about one o'clock in the morning, we shall leave for Parentis; at daybreak, we shall launch ourselves into the aerial sphere."

"I'm grateful for the deference that you testify toward me," said Sir Walter, "and I accept your proposition with pleasure."

Gradually, the drawing rooms of the Grand Hotel emptied, and everyone retired to savor the repose of sleep.

At about half-past midnight, a large family "brake," a vehicle with ten or twelve seats, drawn by four Landais horses, stopped in the courtyard of the Grand Hotel. The service staff woke up the travelers who were to leave for Parentis. After a few moments, Sir Walter Donderry, Dambielle and the entire crew of the *Céleste* took their places.

The forty kilometers separating Arcachon from Parentis-en-Born were traversed in less than four hours, and dawn was beginning to turn the sky gray behind the clouds when the brake arrived at the construction yard.

On perceiving the *Céleste* crouched on the ground like an immense bat, Sir Walter and Dambielle could not suppress their astonishment. They walked around the aeronef twice while asking Valdy a host of questions. The latter gave them the requested information amicably, but as he feared that unwelcome visitors might arrive he proceeded immediately with the preparations for setting sail. The balloon had been filled with hydrogen the day before, and three receptacles enclosed a good quantity of liquefied carbonic acid. The generators were ready to function if more were needed. Madame Valdy, Will Tooke, Ivan Kisseloff, Pickerreek, Cardounet and Dernghuiz climbed up on top of the balloon by means of a rope-ladder. Having assigned everyone a place and immediate duties, Valdy went to the rear and took hold of the tiller.

Sis Walter Donderry made his adieux in emotional terms and wished the *Céleste* a fortunate voyage. Dambielle furtively wiped away a tear that had moistened his eyes. But Valdy showed so much confidence and courage, and his companions seemed desirous of supporting him with so much devotion and energy, that the sadness and apprehension of the final moments dissipated like a dewdrop in the breath of a zephyr, and hope entered every heart.

"Pay attention!" cried Valdy. "Release the mooring-ropes, open the tap on the receptacle, keep watch on the piston-rod and the straps. Forward ho!"

The flywheels rotated, the transmission was engaged and the immense wings rose up. A click was heard, a grinding, and a formidable noise produced by the armatures and the action of the air violently expelled, but the *Céleste* only experienced a few oscillations.

And that was all!

Valdy felt all his blood flowing back toward his heart; cold sweat beaded his brow; a thousand bizarre and contradictory thoughts went through his head and a sharp doubt gripped his mind. After so much patient research, laborious studies and dogged labor, to arrive at failure and disappointment! That was certainly enough to crush the most resolute man. However, he mastered his emotion, remembering that a check is sometimes occasioned by secondary causes and that a similar misadventure had overtaken Fulton when he launched the first steamboat. He descended to the ground, inspected the *Céleste* minutely, making sure that no fissure had allowed hydrogen to escape and that all the accessories of the apparatus were in good order.

"Perhaps your aeronef is overloaded," said Sir Walter Donderry.

"I think it doesn't have enough." Valdy replied.

Dambielle thought that his friend had gone mad and that disappointment had unhinged him. Could one rationally allege, in fact, that an object seemingly anchored to the ground needed to be heavier in order to rise into the air? Never had a paradox been so obvious and casual. Valdy caused the wings to maneuver again and observed attentively. Finally, a sigh of relief and a cry of joy escaped his breast.

"Messieurs," he said, "in the construction of the *Céleste* I have made the error of excessive dimensions. My alary system is too extensive. In order to depart we shall have to elevate the aeronef by a few meters.

It was true.

When a bird flies it presses against the air and thus finds a resistant point of support. It is easy to understand that if the column of air agitated b the wings is too restricted, the elasticity becomes almost null and the thrust insignificant. It is for those various reasons that ducks skim the surface of the water before taking flight and martins fallen accidentally to earth cannot take off unless they find an unevenness in the ground. In giving large dimensions to the surface of his wings, Valdy thought that he would have a greater ascensional force, but that arrangement deprived him of a fraction of the air intended to generate it.

In his treatise on aerial locomotion[26] Étienne-Jules Marey formally condemns overly extensive surfaces, based on the calculations of Monsieur de Lucy.[27] "In fact," he says, "if we suppose two objects of the same form—two cubes, for example—one of which is twice as large as the other in diameter, each of the faces of the larger cube will be four times as large as that of the smaller, and the weight of the larger cube will be eight times as great as that of the smaller. Thus, for all geometrically similar solids, the linear dimensions having a certain proportion, the surfaces will increase as the squares and the volumes as the cube of that proportion. Two birds similar in form but one of which has twice the wingspan of the other, will have surface area of the wings in a ratio of one to four and weights in a ratio of one to eight.

"Dr. Hureau de Villeneuve, based on these considerations, has sought to determine the surface area of the wings that would be necessary for a bat with the weight of a human being to fly; he found that each wing would need to be three meters long."

All things considered, it was preferable for the *Céleste*'s wings to be greater in extent than that relative to its weight, for it would facilitate gliding flight and save on motive force.

Valdy set these reflections aside and went back to take his place at the rudder. Thanks to the six grooved metal rods supporting the mass of the balloon, it was easy to give it four more meters of elevation. Valdy repeated his commands, and cried in a thunderous voice: "Forward ho!"

Immediately, the wings flapped and the *Céleste* shook. At first it skimmed he ground and advanced slowly in the direction of Parentis Pool, but once Valdy had given the tiller a

---

[26] *La Machine animale. Locomotion terrestre et aérienne* (1873-4)

[27] There are various secondary references to de Lucy's "Poids et mesures des animaux volants" (1865) but the original is elusive, and it might be that Marey had privileged access to it.

vertical twitch the immense machine inclined slightly backwards and took on a more rapid propulsion.

It was a grandiose, magical, sublime spectacle that no one could describe.

Dambielle was astounded. Sir Walter Donderry allowed all the exclamations of surprise and admiration to escape from his lips. Momentarily, his astonishment was translated into the most inconceivable gestures; serious and English as he was, he took off his hat and threw it in the air. That strange last farewell was understood; the voyagers replied to it with a formidable hurrah, and Cardounet, who liked decorum in all things, unfurled in the wind a large flag in the French colors.

The *Céleste* rose up, further and further, and advanced into the sky. At first, it executed a few irregular movements, because no one was familiar with aerial maneuvering, but gradually, under the intelligent direction of Valdy, who never ceased to exercise the most active surveillance, it progressed—or, rather, flew—more easily. With various tools in hand, according to circumstances, Pickerreek scrupulously inspected all the accessory mechanisms, readjusted anything that seemed defective, and brought about useful improvements.

The members of the *Céleste*'s crew were all amazed by the result obtained, but Dernghuiz' surprise was translated into a sort of terror that his master found it difficult to calm. He attributed the ascent to something supernatural, and it would not have taken much for him to prostrate himself before Valdy, to invoke and worship him as a god.

"What's our altitude?" Marcel Valdy asked.

Ivan Kisseloff looked at the barometer and replied: "The mercury column is at 67 centimeters; we're at a height of a thousand meters."

At that moment the rays of the rising sun struck the *Céleste*, which suddenly seemed to be surrounded by a crimson aureole, while the earth, plunged in the semi-darkness of the morning twilight, gradually emerged from the gray shadows covering it. The sky, striped with cirrus clouds with gilded contours, became gradually bluer, reflecting its azure over the inferior layers of the atmosphere. In the distance, the vast sea was visible, gently raising its waves, iridescent in the first gleams of daylight, swaying the sails of small fishing-boats and replying to the cries of sea-birds with a sad and lazy song.

That awakening of nature, which everyone except poets and lovers contemplates with indifference, took on unknown and grandiose proportions at a height of a thousand meters. The voyagers were delighted. Pickerreek and Cardounet confessed that they had never seen a spectacle as admirable. Will Tooke, in spite of his habitual impassivity, found excited expressions to translate the impressions he felt. Madame Valdy gazed at the infinite horizon and repeated several times over, emotionally: "Look, see how beautiful the works of God are!"

Parentis Pool and the narrow strip of land separating it from the ocean were crossed in a matter of minutes. Then Valdy set a course northwards and resolved to follow the French coast in order not to risk falling into the sea in case of an accident.

Soon they perceived Arcachon and the clumps of pine trees in the midst of which the bathing station is coquettishly situated. The bay was reduced to the proportions of a pool; the Grand Hotel resembled an eight of spades fallen from a deck of cards and forgotten on the floor.

"If Harry Catlen can see us," said Cardounet, "he must have a mouth as wide as a hatchway and a face as long as a mizzen-mast!"

The reflection made Ivan Kisseloff smile.

Chapter V

The *Céleste*, favored by a southerly breeze, made rapid progress. The silence of the high regions was only troubled by the whistle of the wings striking the air violently and the dull purr of the flywheels. The barometer indicated a height of two thousand meters. Madame Valdy complained that she was experiencing oppression and dazzlement—in brief, the malaise one experiences during ascents and is known as altitude sickness. Valdy decided to fly at an altitude between a thousand and twelve hundred meters and set the tiller in order to descend. The aeronef obeyed the maneuver and drew nearer to the ground.

It is easy to measure exactly the height one is at. It is well-known that the weight of air on a mercury bowl elevates the metal in a tube; that is the principle of the barometer; in consequence, the heavier the air is, the higher the mercury column rises. At sea level it is 77 centimeters; at a thousand meters, 67 centimeters; at two thousand meters, 60 centimeters; at three thousand meters, 53 centimeters; at four thousand meters, 47 centimeters; at five thousand meters, 36 centimeters; etc. In order for the *Céleste* to maintain the designated height, it was necessary for the mercury to vacillate between 65 and 67 centimeters.

Soon, a white line became perceptible standing out from the distant mists; it was the Cordouan lighthouse, reduced to tiny proportions. It produced an optical effect that astonished the voyagers. The entire terrestrial and aquatic surface they could see seemed to be depressed and take on a concave form; the projecting points were effaced, and no relief was any longer perceptible; that phenomenon, often observed by aeronauts, is attributable to refraction.

The beginning of that first experiment in aerial navigation promised a greater success than they had hoped. The *Céleste* was behaving well. While the wind was behind her, it

.

only flapped its wings every two seconds, thirty per minute, and the impulsion it received maintained it perfectly, permitting it to advance at a speed of nearly a hundred kilometers an hour.

"Everything's going well," said Cardounet. "Suppose we eat! What do you think, Pick?"

"Umm!" replied Pickerreek, as a sign of approval.

"The diabolical cold up here has hollowed out my stomach, and I could eat all the beans in the hold of a three-master."

"And I could drink a good cupful too," added Pickerreek.

"That's understood, of course!"

Cardounet addressed himself to Valdy. "Captain, with your permission, may we ingurgitate a little nourishment?"

"Yes," Valdy replied, "but don't abandon your posts."

"Have no fear."

A cold fowl was carved by Madame Valdy and everyone had, as the vulgar phrase has it, "a snack." Simple and inexpensive as that breakfast was, it was swallowed cheerfully and with a hearty appetite. Dernghuiz drank water; Pickerreek and Cardounet seemed scandalized.

"Don't go spoiling Dernghuiz for me," said Kisseloff, laughing, "by turning him into a drunkard."

"Oh, Monsieur le Comte, how can you have such a low opinion of us? When Dernghuiz leaves us, he'll know how to clink glasses. A man isn't a man if he doesn't empty a bottle with his friends when the opportunity arises."

Kisseloff was about to challenge that singular appreciation when the *Céleste* experienced a shock that caused him to reel and turn round. The direction had suddenly changed and the aeronef was advancing toward the sea.

An easterly wind had got up and was beginning to blow violently. Undoubtedly, the *Céleste* could struggle against a moderate wind, but it was necessary not to think of flying directly into an atmospheric current of a certain force. Even birds never fly into the wind when it is too impetuous. In order not to exhaust themselves in futile effort, they fly through the air sheltered by the sinuosities of the terrain. The swift and the swallow, the best sailors of the air, always proceed thus.

The sandy coats of the Vendée were ahead of them; from the *Céleste* the Île de Yeu was visible, to which they were getting ever closer, and which Valdy designated as a landing-place if the wind remained contrary. He could not explain the sudden turbulence of the aerial layers, however, and instructed Will Tooke to throw out several pieces of paper and follow their evolutions with a naval telescope. The American obeyed immediately and recognized, after brief observation, that the pieces of paper described a large arc and then took a northerly direction.

"All's well," said Valdy. "Our journey won't be interrupted. We've encountered some turbulence that is drawing us off course. Let's take action to avoid it."

The *Céleste* descended, circled a few times, and finally encountered the current favorable to its course at about eight hundred meters above the ground. Valdy immediately set a northward course again, and continued to follow the coast. When they arrived over the mouth of the Vilaine, however, he had to veer north-westwards in order to reach the western extremity of France, and from there to fly toward the Scilly Isles.

It was nearly five o'clock in the evening when the voyagers perceived the cliffs of Cap Saint-Mathieu. Below Ploudalmezeau, a little Atlantic port on the Pointe de Corsen opposite the Roches de Porsal, Valdy spotted a bare and deserted heath; he pointed it out to his companions as the first point of descent.

Before setting forth over the sea, it was prudent to take every precaution and to make sure that no damage had been sustained. The *Céleste* made a gliding spiral descent. Thanks to that maneuver, imitative of a bird, there was no sensible impact.

On seeing that mass descending to earth, several Breton shepherds who were grazing their flocks on the heath felt an extraordinary terror and ran away, shouting and waving their arms. They raised the alarm in a few miserable villages that could be made out in the distance, and church bells could soon be heard ringing at full tilt. It was a call to arms, a summons always heeded in that ancient Armorica, a land of heroes, but also, in numerous places, a land of ignorance and superstition.

Valdy was under no illusions about the plangent ringing that he heard. He knew that a thoughtless crowd begins by striking out instead of reasoning, and that the aeronef would inevitably be destroyed and broken into a thousand pieces, so he ordered that the preparations for a new ascent should be made as rapidly as possible.

The balloon's hull was carefully inspected; the generators received copious provisions of hydrochloric acid and bicarbonate of soda; a sufficient quantity of liquefied carbonic acid filled the receptacles. After half an hour, Valdy gave the signal to depart.

He was just in time. Groups of men and women could be seen converging from various points of the horizon, talking angrily, proffering threats, armed with sticks, pitchforks, scythes and a few rifles. Toward the east, behind a small hill strewn with spare heather, hymns could be heard.

A procession—a veritable procession, with the curé, the verger and the beadle at the head, and banners and holy images deployed, appeared on the crest of the hill. It did not have a very peaceful appearance; the verger was brandishing his halberd and a few of the faithful were showing their fists. A frightened shepherd had recounted that the Devil had come to place his claw on Breton soil! One can imagine the emotion produced by that news in a village that only had rare communications with the external world. Half by inclination and half under duress, before the exasperation caused by this singular news, the curé had been obliged to put on his surplice and stole and march solemnly toward the monarch of Hell, in order to chase him away by means of ablutions of holy water and ceremonies of exorcism.

But the *Céleste* was rising upwards! A dull murmur escaped from every throat. The voyagers laughed at the disappointment and surprise of the crowd. Madame Valdy, however, took pity on the terror and ignorance of the poor Breton peasants, and to reassure them, she threw the following note into the air.

Aboard the Céleste.
First attempt at aerial navigation.
Monsieur le Curé, don't forget us in your prayers; perhaps we shall die for science!

The sheet of paper floated for a few moments and fell to earth. The boldest young men approached, but dared not touch it. Finally, an old soldier picked it up and took it to the curé. The latter read it and understood. He calmed the agitation of the multitude by speaking to them about aerostats, giving them a few technical explanations and gently mocking the shepherds for their terror, assuring them that the fall and ascent of the *Céleste* had nothing supernatural about it.

Gradually, the groups dispersed and the heath was deserted again. Only a few old women committed to devotion and saintly benevolence affirmed that it was the Devil, and nothing but the Devil, who had appeared on the Breton cliffs to announce to the hardened fisher-folk that the hour of desolation was nigh!

The *Céleste* disappeared into the first mists of the evening.

Now it was a matter of a crossing, with all its uncertainties and perils. In case of accident, there was not a single point of relief—not an islet or a rock on which they could descend. Nothing but the sea and its profound abyss! Aboard the aeronef, therefore, everyone competed in the ardor of their labor. Pickerreek, Cardounet and Dernghuiz liquefied carbonic acid; Will Tooke and Ivan Kisseloff supervised the wings, the flywheels and the straps; Madame Valdy oiled the apparatus operating the transmission; Marcel Valdy still held the tiller and consulted the compass.

The *Céleste* advanced at a vertiginous speed; the piston was producing two or three strokes per second. After an hour of that frantic progress, Valdy affirmed that they had covered more than half of the part of the Channel separating France and England. Another hour, and they would land in the Scilly Isles.

The Scillies form a little archipelago of a hundred and fifty-five islets, punctuated by reefs always battered by the waves, deprived of trees and partly arid. Only a few of them are inhabited, the others serving as pasturage. The archipelago is situated about fifty kilometers from Land's End, the most westerly point of Cornwall and all of England.

Valdy consulted the itinerary. The depot of bicarbonate of soda and hydrochloric acid was on St. Martin's Island, in the home of the lighthouse-keeper. Having darted a rapid glance at the map in order to ascertain the exact location of the island be maneuvered in order to make it out—for dusk was replacing daylight—and landed on a small rocky plateau.

On perceiving the aeronef, the lighthouse-keeper experienced all the effects of extreme fright, but when he saw human beings like himself, made of flesh and bone, sliding down the sides of the balloon he was reassured. He approached the newcomers and greeted them cordially. His wife, his two children and a few islanders joined him in offering their services. Will Tooke responded to the worthy folk's advances with a few gracious words and enquired about the deposit confided to them.

"I know what you mean," said the lighthouse-keeper. "Some time ago, a coaster from Falmouth brought me some packets and cylinders that I had to give to a Frenchman answering to the name of Marcel Valdy. Is Marcel Valdy among you?"

"That's me," Valdy replied.

"I'm at your disposal, Sir."

Since eating breakfast at an altitude between a thousand and twelve hundred meters, the crew had had no meal. Cardounet avowed that he was famished. Adequate provisions were brought down from the larder to the rock and Madame Valdy, rolling up the sleeves of her dress, prepared to replace the absent cook—but Pickerreek, Cardounet, Will Tooke, Kisseloff and the islanders were opposed to her playing the role of a vulgar servant.

The islanders ran to their homes, paltry cabins, and came back, some of them bearing fresh or salted fish and others thin poultry and a few items of feathered game. By means of two large stones, an oven was briskly improvised; appetizing soles were grilled on the top while the snipe and two shoveler ducks were roasted on primitive spits methodically rotated by the patient Pickerreek When everything was done to a turn, Valdy sat the lighthouse-keeper down next to him and invited everyone to share the modest feast. The invitation was accepted, and soon, nothing could be heard but he sound of jaws chewing the foodstuffs.

"What a fest!" said Cardounet.

And, indeed, everyone did honor to the repast. The sky was clear, the atmosphere tranquil, and the sea, scarcely agitated, mirrored the stars. The poor inhabitants of St. Martin's Island only knew wine by reputation, so to speak, vines not growing anywhere in the Scillies, so, when they drank a few mouthfuls of the vermilion liquid, their tongues were delirious. The worthy people asked for a host of explanations; they could not understand how an apparatus as large as the *Céleste* could rise up into the air and fly like a bird. Will Tooke accepted the responsibility of the conversation and replied amicably to all the questions addressed to him.

"In sum," Cardounet asked, "how far have we traveled?"

"A trivial distance," Valdy replied. "About eight hundred kilometers."

"And you call that trivial?"

"Yes. By flying for fifteen or sixteen hours a day we could easily cover two thousand kilometers, but it's necessary to allow for detours and accidents, and I think we'll rarely manage more than fifteen hundred kilometers."

"That's already a considerable speed," Ivan Kisseloff put in.

"Yes, for a trial of aerial navigation, but when larger and lighter machines are constructed, more manageable than the *Céleste*, on which crews can work in shifts, it will be possible to travel immense distances. Don't be surprised by my figures; aerostats have often exceeded the average speed we attained today—only to mention those that were launched during the Prussian siege of Paris, I'll cite the *Louis-Blanc*, which traveled at 64.5 kilometers per hour; the *Garibaldi*, at 92.5 kph; the *Égalité*, at 87.42, the *Ville-d'Orléans* at 93.33; the *Volta*, at 69.09; the *Steenakers*, at 119.33; and finally, the *République Universelle*, at 132."

"That's fast going," said Pickerreek.

"That speed is nothing compared to those attained by certain birds. The falcon and the swift fly eighty leagues in an hour. Eighty leagues an hour, you hear! Imagine momentarily that those birds had no need of rest or nourishment; by flying straight ahead they would cover 1,920 leagues—which is 7,680 kilometers—every twenty-four hours. They'd need a little less than five days to fly around the world, passing over both poles."

"Do you believe that humans can ever compete with the birds?"

"Why not? Our power, though limited, is a manifestation of that of God, and no one knows what prodigies it might realize. I don't intend to affirm that a circuit of the globe will be executed in five days, for contrary winds, unexpected tempests and inevitable catastrophes would deflect or halt the flight of aeronefs, but I do claim that our speed today is distinctly second-rate and that it can easily be doubled, if not tripled. Humans have vanquished the fastest terrestrial runners; they compete with sharks and cetaceans as fast swimmers; the day will come when they will challenge the birds in the fields of the Empyrean, and perhaps defeat them."

"Let's hope so, for the confusion of Harry Catlen," said Ivan Kisseloff.

"You don't seem to like the English much," Madame Valdy put in.

"I detest them."

"The welcome offered by the good folk of the Scillies ought, however, to attenuate the effect of your prejudices."

"Oh, Madame, the inhabitants of the Scilly Isles aren't English. They belong to the Celtic family, and are more nearly your compatriots."

"If they belong to the same family as us, the relationship must be very distant."

"Don't believe, Madame, that conquest has destroyed their nationality. Beneath a seemingly coarse and rugged nature, they conceal honest, simple and virtuous sentiments, while the English—the true English—are swollen by conceit and pride, like a strutting turkey."

"You're unjust Mr. Kisseloff, and..."

"Madame," Pickerreek, "don't speak English any longer to the Count. It annoys him..." Mentally, he added: *And we'll find out why, damn it!*

The time for sleep had arrived. The lighthouse-keeper offered Madame Valdy his best room; the men, having set up a sail in the form of a tent on the deck of the *Céleste*, stretched out their blankets, lay down side by side, like soldiers in camp, and went to sleep.

Early the next day, the bicarbonate of soda, hydrochloric acid and ethyl alcohol were carried aboard the aeronef. The voyagers and the worthy islander of St. Martin exchanged warm handshakes and separated as the best of friends.

Valdy hesitated briefly over the route to take. Should he follow the English coast? That would be more prudent, but its profound indentations would lengthen the journey considerably. The previous day, however, they had cross the Channel at its widest point successfully, and it would be useful to become accustomed to danger. The latter consideration removed all uncertainty.

The *Céleste* rose up to an altitude between a thousand and twelve hundred meters and set a direct course for St. David's Head in Pembrokeshire. Two hours later, they flew over Milford Haven, St. Brides Bay, the town of St. Davids and followed the St. George's Channel, which connects the Atlantic with the Irish Sea. The vast bays, or rather gulfs, of Cardigan and Caernarvon were rapidly crossed; they distinguished the Isle of Anglesey, separated from the principality of Wales by the Menai Strait, spanned by the famous Britannia tubular bridge, one of the marvels of modern industry. No incident marred that journey of about 350 kilometers. The weather was fine and the wind blew steadily from the south. The crews of numerous ships crossing the Irish Sea watched attentively for a long time as the aeronef continued on its course.

While they were crossing the arm of the sea separating Anglesey from the Isle of Man an accident occurred that gave the voyagers confidence in the skillful dispositions made in the construction of the *Céleste*, and reassured them regarding the danger of a fall. Either because the pressure was excessive or it had been strongly shaken, one of the tubes taking carbonic aid from the receptacle to the piston was breached. Immediately, the wings stood up almost vertically, and the fall commenced. Brave and energetic as our voyagers were, they experienced a fearful panic. Fortunately, Pickerreek, Will Tooke and Valdy immediately recovered their habitual composure.

"Cardounet! Ivan!" shouted Valdy. "Pull the straps that produce the descendant movement of the wings. Will, replace the broken tube by a rubber one. Pickerreek, put a full receptacle in place of the empty one. Do it quickly, but without hurrying."

The fall continued slowly, for the *Céleste*, obedient to its momentum, was descending obliquely. When, thanks to the efforts of Cardounet and Ivan Kisseloff, aided by Dernghuiz and Madame Valdy, the wings has assumed a horizontal position, the fall slowed down further. Valdy calculated that the aeronef would cover a distance of approximately two leagues before falling into the sea, but Pickerreek and Will Tooke did not waste any time. In a few minutes, everything was back in order. The transmission of the movement operated as before, and the *Céleste*, rising up to more than fifteen hundred meters, advanced toward the Isle of Man, passed over its entire length and came down to land on a buttress of Mount Snaefell near the little port of Ramsey.

The Isle of Man, with a surface area of about 110 square kilometers, has been transformed by its valiant inhabitants. It was once arid, bare and desolate; now it is cultivated and fertile. The hydrochloric acid and bicarbonate of soda depot was in the house of a fisherman in Ramsey. Pickerreek and Cardounet went to look for it and to buy a few fresh provisions. Whether because the *Céleste* had not been seen, or because the islanders were busy with their quotidian labors, very few of them came to examine it.

The voyagers, delighted to escape a curiosity that was sometimes inconvenient, ate lunch with a hearty appetite and departed again. The aeronef rose up, but Valdy noticed that it was not as readily obedient to the rudder, and that it was undulating—or, to put it better, imitating the characteristic flight of birds with long tails, principally the magpie and the wagtail. The wind was variable and the weathervane sometimes indicated sudden clams.

"I recognize that," said Pickerreek. "There's a squall somewhere."

"That's possible," said Valdy, "but I attribute the change to the geological configuration of the country toward which we're heading. Scotland is covered with mountains, and the aerial currents, running into those masses and abruptly interrupted, rise, deviate, struggle and turn back, producing turbulence. In order to avoid the mountainous masses, we'll leave out the Hebrides and head toward the Orkneys, following the eastern counties of Scotland. That way we'll shorten our route by about two hundred kilometers and navigate more easily."

The *Céleste*'s prow turned eastwards, heading over the Solway Firth, a short distance from the counties of Kircudbright and Dumfries, and finally reached land. Then they distinctly heard the whistle of a locomotive, and perceived two trains executing their maneuvers near an almost imperceptible village and railway station.

"Messieurs," said Valdy, laughing, "we're flying over a town celebrated throughout the entire world. That's Gretna Green."

"What's that?" asked Pickerreek.

"Gretna Green!" replied Cardounet, who was not sorry to be able to show off his knowledge. "I can explain that. Suppose that you want to embark on the sea of marriage; you go to the father of a young woman and you say to him, 'I'll charter your daughter!' But you're ruddy and stale, you've caught more sunburn while sailing or hauling the reefs than you have gold in your pockets, and you're as broke as an infantryman who hasn't a sou. The father replies: 'It's not you who'll be the helmsman of our existence; I want a well-to-do shipwright.' Damn it! What a humiliation for a true matelot, who's seen all colors and all dyes. But the girl, who's smitten with you, says: 'One can marry in spite of the contrary winds; pull in all your halyards, charge the masts with sail and let's go!' You leave together, you make fifteen knots and you arrive in Getna Green. There, you find a worthy blacksmith, explain your predicament to him, have a drink with him, sign his register, and there you are—married in perpetuity, with the Devil himself unable to get you out of it, just as if the Maire and the curé had certified it!"

This picturesque explanation amused the voyagers; scarcely was it terminated than they made out the Cheviot Hills—the chain of hills separating England from Scotland—in the distance. Their highest summits reach a thousand meters in height.

The *Céleste* rose up to three thousand meters. Either because the climatic conditions were more favorable or because Madame Valdy was getting used to a thinner atmosphere, she did not feel ill. As rapid as an arrow, the aeronef traversed the counties of Dumfries, Selkirk, Berwick and Haddington, and the Firth of Forth, reaching the North Sea. She came back over land again and followed the fifth meridian west of Paris in an almost straight line, heading for North Ronaldsay, one of the Orkneys, designated on the itinerary as a port of call for rest and replenishment. It was four o'clock in the afternoon when they passed over Banff, the principal town of the county of the same name, a small port situated on the Moray Firth. Two hours later, the *Céleste* landed in a meadow in North Ronaldsay.

The Orkneys, separated from the northern tip of Scotland by the Pentland Firth, form an archipelago if sixty-seven islands, about half of which are inhabited. We are leaving out the skerries, numerous desolate rocky islets sometimes covered by the high tides, on which seaweed is collected that serves for the manufacture of soda and to which myriads of sea-birds come to rest at dusk. The islands are exposed to violent storms; the force of the wind is such that trees cannot grow there unless they are sheltered behind walls or rocky hollows.

As she landed, the *Céleste* ran along the ground for some while; Pickerreek was forced to moor it solidly to avoid the shocks induced by the gusts of wind. As in the Scillies, the crew entered into communication with people of simple and honest mores. The islanders of North Ronaldsay, almost all fishermen or sheep-farmers, hastened around the voyagers and offered their services. In spite of "a breeze that wasn't quilted," to use Cardounet's expression, the meal was eaten in the open air, seasoned by the finest condiments that anyone could desire: appetite and good humor.

The bicarbonate of soda and hydrochloric acid deposited in the home of an old mariner was transferred aboard, and everyone made provision to spend the night as comfortable as possible. Toward eight o'clock, however, the sky was covered by clouds and a fine cold rain began to fall. The voyagers accepted the hospitality offered by the islanders. Cardounet, Pickerreek and Dernghuiz, however, did not abandon the *Céleste*.

"We've seen many others," said the first, philosophically.

"And stood up to them," added the second, sententiously.

Dernghuiz made it understood that it was a matter of indifference to him whether he slept in a house or under the tent. He stayed with the two mariners.

Chapter VI

The next morning, the third of September, the sun did not put in an appearance. Gray and black clouds ran slowly through the sky, agglomerating and swirling. At ground level the weather was quite calm, and a feeble swell was lifting the waves of the sea.

"What do you think of the weather, Pickerreek?" asked Valdy, anxiously.

"Captain," the replied, using the title by which Valdy was now habitually addressed, "when we left the Isle of Man I told you that a squall was bursting somewhere; the squall has certainly burst, and we'll feel its repercussions, unless it prefers to pay us a call."

"Then it's prudent not to leave yet?"

"Oh, that's not what I mean, for I've noticed that when it leaves port, a ship is almost always heading into the wind, but goes just the same—but we won't make such rapid progress tacking as by taking a straight course."

"You're stating the obvious, Pick," said Cardounet.

"That's possible, but what's said is said, and in the captain's place, I know what I'd do."

"What would you do?"

"I'd set a course over land and not stray far from the coast."

"That's good advice, but it's impossible to follow today. We have to time to lose, and we need to be in Iceland tonight, having called in at Shetland and the Faroes. It's a long journey."

"Well, Captain, I think it's prudent not to touch down in Shetland and head straight for the Faroes. How many leagues is it from North Ronaldsay to the Faroes?"

"Between sixty and seventy.

"Storms rarely begin in the morning; we have every chance of landing in the Faroes before being inconvenienced by the squall."

"Let's get under way, then."

The preparations for departure were carried out immediately. Ivan Kisseloff noticed that Dernghuiz was displaying in an unfamiliar urgency and that, emerging from his habitual mutism, he was speaking and singing in his own language. A rapid glance cast at the basket of bottles gave him to understand that Pickerreek and Cardounet, in order to combat the cold and commence the servant's education, had downed two bottles of an excellent Médoc.

Yielding to the demands of his two comrades, Dernghuiz had drunk the fine wine—while pulling a face, but, in the end, he had drunk it—and the wine had made him merry. Pickerreek, delighted with his pupil's willingness, had taken condescension so far as to offer him a monstrous plug of tobacco, but the Tatar had refused politely.

The chronometers marked seven o'clock in the morning when the *Céleste*, abandoning North Ronaldsay, rose into the sky. To begin with it encountered adverse currents, but at an altitude of about fifteen hundred meters it found an aerial layer that was almost completely calm, and was able to advance at a speed of a hundred kilometers an hour. The temperature dropped, however, and the voyagers, tested by the abrupt change, covered themselves with blankets and furs.

It was with a keen sentiment of pleasure that that the crew, after a rather difficult navigation, made out the Faroes, recognizable by Mounts Skalingefield, 680 meters high, and Slattaretind, 900 meters high, the first situated on Stroemoe Island and the second on Oesteroe, the largest two in the group. The *Céleste* landed on Stroemoe, near Thorshawn, the capital of the Faroes. Can one give the title of capital to a township consisting of a hundred wooden houses? Thorshawn, however, the residence of the civil and military authorities that Denmark sends to administer its colony, passes for a big city when one compares it to Westmanshawn and Kongshawn, which claim the title of city but only have fifty houses.

The unexpected arrival of the *Céleste* produced a veritable revolution in Thorshawn. The bailiff and the seneschal[28] put on their ceremonial robes and came out, followed by a part of the population, and cordially bid the voyagers welcome. None of the travelers understood Danish; fortunately, the functionaries had a smattering of English, and the conversation was conducted in that language.

When the islanders had satisfied their curiosity completely, the reception became even more courteous and more amicable. The bailiff gallantly offered his arm to Madame Valdy, led our aerial explorers to his dwelling and ordered a copiously-served table to be set up. The bicarbonate of soda and hydrochloric acid, deposited in the abode of a member of the noble corporation of grocers—doubtless the only one on the island—were transferred from his humble shop to the aeronef.

While the meal was prepared, the voyagers toured Thorshawn and were quite astonished to encounter, in that miserable corner of land, everything constituting the elements of an advanced civilization: a church, several schools, a hospital, a library of more than three thousand volumes, a branch of an international bank, etc.

"Truly," said Madame Valdy, addressing the bailiff, "everything you've shown us here is a marvel! I expected to find beneath your gray skies the monotony of the countries of the far north, but I'm filled with admiration."

"Madame," the bailiff replied, "the Faroes seem very sad for those who, like you, arrive without transition from sunny lands, from your beautiful and radiant France, but they are pleasing when one has visited them, when one knows the loyal, helpful and honest character of the people who inhabit them."

---

[28] The author insets a footnote to explain that the bailiff is in command of the armed force, and the seneschal in charge of the police.

"The cold must be terrible here?"

"No, Madame. Thorshawn is almost exactly on the sixty-second parallel, but the temperature rarely falls below 32° Fahrenheit—zero Centigrade—and the snow only covers our countryside for about a fortnight."

"Undoubtedly that's because of some branch of the Gulf Stream, which skirts your archipelago," said Will Tooke.

"Yes," the bailiff relied, "but on the other hand, if we're spared intense cold, it's very damp, and mists often envelop us everywhere. Of the seven days constituting the Christian week, scarcely two are bright. In spite of that slight inconvenience, everyone is happy here, and if you asked one of our eider-hunters to abandon his homeland and his difficult métier in exchange for a more hospitable land and a more lucrative position, he'd refuse."

"Every bird thinks his nest beautiful," interjected Cardounet, who sometimes gleaned in the fields of Sancho Panza.

"Especially if the bird is able to embellish it," the seneschal replied. "Our islanders have tried everything to charm their cloudy abode. When they're weary of working, they gather together to read or play chess. No one here is ignorant."

"I beg your pardon, Monsieur Seneschal," said Ivan Kisseloff, "but I'm astonished to learn that the noble game of chess, somewhat neglected in Europe, has found a refuge here."

"It's true. Go into any cabin, into the most wretched house in Thorshawn, and you'll find a chessboard hanging on the wall. Do better: challenge one of our men—the one who seems to you to have the least aptitude—and if even you can beat him, you'll be convinced that he's highly skilled."

"Well, I'd like to see that."

"Try."

Two stools and a chessboard were brought. Ivan Kisseloff chose for an adversary an individual of gauche and unintelligent appearance. The game commenced immediately, ad a circle of numerous spectators formed around the two players. In spite of his skill and concentration, the Russian understood that he had found a master. In less than five minutes he was checkmated, to the great joy of the islanders, who laughed at his discomfiture.

"Are you convinced?" asked the bailiff.

"I've been beaten hands down, Monsieur Bailiff, and I ask your permission to invite my adversary to lunch, to prove to him that I don't bear a grudge."

"Your wishes are commands, and hospitality is the order of the day in the Faroes. Let's go to table then—our modest lunch is ready."

The "modest lunch" was notable for the abundance and variety of food. It was one of those copious meals that are served in northern countries, before which Pantagruel and Gargantua would have been easily and admiringly delighted. Four or five species of feathered game, Bremen hams, roast mutton, fresh and salted fish, poultry, pâtés and conserves of every sort—such was the menu drawn up by the bailiff's wife, who supported her husband in receiving his guests graciously. And all of it was washed down by pints of a beer that was a trifle harsh for throats accustomed to savoring the wines of France, although that slight inconvenience was lessened by Pickerreek and Cardounet, who left the table and returned laden with a few bottles brought from the aeronef. The joy then became more expansive, and numerous toasts were drunk. They drank to France, to Denmark, to the success of the first aerial voyage, and to the health and friendship of all those the hazard had brought together in such a strange fashion.

The hour of departure was approaching, however. In order to arrive in Iceland that same evening, it was necessary not to prolong the halt. The distance still to be traveled was six hundred kilometers.

While the voyagers were preparing the *Céleste*, the bailiff, the seneschal and a few old fishermen looked at the cloudy horizon and shook their heads anxiously.

"I don't know," the bailiff said to Valdy, "what happens high in the air when a tempest is blowing at ground level, but it would take a lot to make me embark now, even on a three-master."

"Have no fear, Monsieur Bailiff," Valdy replied. "A hurricane can ravage the sea without agitating the upper layers of the atmosphere.

"Then God bless your efforts and your enterprise!"

Final farewells and sympathetic good wishes were addressed to the voyagers, and the *Céleste* rose up, to the enthusiastic cheers of the brave Faroe islanders. The atmosphere was still agitated, and in order to encounter the favorable current that it had fortunately found on leaving North Ronaldsay, the aeronef circled for a while, passing over Westmans Gulf.

Westmans Gulf is a harbor of sinister appearance formed by thirty gigantic rocks whose bare summits extend to four hundred meters in height. Their assembly has something bizarre and fantastic about it. One might think that the rocks were the petrified heroes of Valhalla, the sanguinary paradise of the Scandinavians, waiting, in a supreme expiation, for the grim Odin to call them back to the company of the gracious Valkyries. In that place, the sea, always somber and agitated, growls, moans and howls with all the tones of distress and hopeless complaint. When furious winds collide with those enormous masses of granite, the noise redoubles and augments the horror of the spectacle. However, many thousands of aquatic birds haunt those frightful rocks; every species establishes its separate dwelling there.

It was these birds that attracted the attention of the voyagers; they were rallying to the land from all directions; their instinct warned them that a tempest would soon be unleashed. Only the petrels were racing over the sea, skimming the crests of the waves and agitating their long wings joyfully. Pickerreek and Cardounet were not unaware that the petrel is the bird of storms, the bird that mariners, in their energetic and imaginative language, call the Scarecrow and Satanic, and which justifies those names by the feverish delight that takes possession of it when a storm is brooding.

Having executed several circuits, the *Céleste* encountered a relatively calm layer of air, and Valdy steered in the direction of Iceland without recourse to tacking, convinced that aerial locomotion had nothing to fear from the tempests that are the scourge of maritime navigation. Meanwhile, the sky became increasingly veiled and the rare ships they perceived were furling all their sails and tying the jib of the staysail to the mizzen.

"We know that maneuver," said Pickerreek, observing the sea with a telescope. "It's a bad sign when the storm-jib's rugged. For a while, it's definitely preferable to fly than sail."

Down below, the wind was blowing alternately from the west and the west-south-west, and its violence was increasing by the minute. The voyagers were anxious. They understood that they could not outrun the tempest, that they would only land in Iceland after great difficulties and a long delay; and that in a region completely devoid of land—for there is not the slightest islet between the Faroes and Iceland—they might encounter some danger impossible to avoid.

The *Céleste* climbed to more than three thousand meters and her wings beat swiftly; her speed reached nearly a hundred and fifty kilometers an hour, and she advanced with that vertiginous rapidity for a hour and a half.

Suddenly, she went into a mass of thick mist and plunged deeply into it. The voyagers could no longer make out anything around them; the aeronef, advancing silently, seemed to be isolated in a formless and nameless chaos. The hole that she made in the mass of vapors undoubtedly produced some meteorological phenomenon, and provoked an unexpected perturbation, for a frightful ululation was heard, similar to the sound of thunder, and the wind, ripping violently through the fog, dispersed it and converted it into clouds that rose up while rotating. Immediately, a diluvian rain, driven almost horizontally by the violence of gusts, began to fall.

The *Céleste* spun around several times and was carried in an eastward direction. Valdy understood that it was impossible to struggle against the storm. He tried to climb, but the torment was raging at every altitude. Then he envisaged the situation in which he and his companions found themselves, and was gripped by fear.

There was no possibility of landing in Iceland or of returning to the Faroes. The wind, still blowing from the west, was taking the *Céleste* away from those islands, and the nearest land was the Scandinavian peninsula. They could not determine the *Céleste*'s exact position, but Pickerreek and Valdy thought that they were somewhere near the sixty-fourth parallel and the thirteenth degree of west longitude. The land toward which they were being driven was on the tenth degree of east longitude, which was twenty-three degrees of difference. And in front of it was the infinite sea, the glacial Arctic ocean, so sad, so somber, and without the slightest port of call.

Only one chance of salvation remained; that was to find a ship and let themselves fall in close proximity to it—but in that abandoned region, only frequented by a few sparse whaling vessels, would they encounter a vessel that could pick up the aerial shipwreck victims? Then again, how would the rescue be organized if the desired vessel were spotted? The fury of the wind was increasing incessantly, enormous waves were undulating the surface of the sea, crashing into one another, folding up, breaking and projecting their foam to considerable heights.

"Well then, it's all over for us!" Valdy murmured.

And yet—O mystery of the human heart!—in that extreme peril, Valdy rejoiced I seeing that the *Céleste*, his creation, the fruit of his intelligence, was comporting itself well in the bosom of the agitated regions. The aeronef became, so to speak, an integral part of the tempest and advanced with all the rapidity of the wind, without experiencing any shocks or oscillations. Sparse wing-beats raised it to the selected altitude.

"We've never traveled so quickly," said Cardounet. We're certainly going more than two hundred kilometers an hour."

"So much the better!" cried Valdy, enthusiastically. "I knew that we'd attain unprecedented speeds. The future is ours."

The courageous inventor was talking about the future, at the moment when he found himself in the most critical situation! His companions, in spite of their energy, were beginning to despair.

Will Tooke was peering into the distance, but the curtain of rain prevented him from seeing more than a hundred meters ahead.

Ivan Kisseloff gritted his teeth convulsively and said: "To die! To die! And it's Mr. Catlen who predicted that I would die miserably and that our enterprise would be abortive."

That race in the wind continued for several hours; to complete the misfortune, night fell: a black night without the slightest glimmer or reflection of that obscure clarity, as Corneille puts it, that the stars shed and permits guidance in the dark—and in every direction, there was the sea, the infinite, and the unknown.

Then Valdy was afraid, not for himself but for those he had drawn along, assuring them of success: for his dear Berthe, who, in exchange for his love and devotion, was about to be subjected to all the terrors of a horrible death. His head spun, and he came to think that his temerity demanded an exemplary punishment. Had not Prometheus been chained to the Caucasus?

He called to his companions, squeezed their hands effusively, and begged their pardon.

"It's me who is killing you," he said, several times over.

Distressingly, his despair was infectious; his valiant comrades, bewildered and terrified, maintained a bleak silence. Like the savage who lies down in his canoe when he can no longer fight against the force of the rapids, they were waiting for death without making any attempt to avoid it.

Fortunately, Madame Valdy reacted against the sinister impressions that were overwhelming her. An unspecifiable fugitive hope filled her heart; she understood that it was necessary to shake off and reject the frightful torpor that had taken possession of the crew and that, by fighting, it was possible to save themselves.

"Why are we trembling when we need to do something?" she cried. "If we have to die, let's not do it without having exhausted our strength ad our resources. God never abandons those who toil and hope!"

"Oh, Madame," said Ivan Kisseloff, "you alone among us are strong and heroic."

"Bless you, Madame," added Will Tooke. "You're reviving my failing courage!"

"A thousand million cannonades!" cried Pickerreek. "So it's the women who are the men and the men the women now. If it's necessary for us to swallow the gaffe, it won't be without a fight!"

Valdy remembered that among the instruments placed abroad the *Céleste* there was a Bunsen pile. He moistened a few couples, produced the current, and electric light soon illuminated a limited space. By means of a reflector turning on a pivot, they searched in all directions, but perceived nothing except black clouds confused with the waters. However, that light, projecting its brought white glare into the distance, comforted the voyagers' souls, if one might put it thus. They were no longer traveling in thick darkness, and the isolation seemed less dismal and painful.

Suddenly, Dernghuiz uttered a strident cry.

"What is it?" demanded Ivan Kisseloff.

"There! There! A light!" replied the Tatar, pointing eastwards.

Everyone looked in the direction indicated, but no one could distinguish anything.

Was it the beacon of a ship tossed by the tempest? Was it the tremulous light of one of those resinous torches of which the Norwegians make use? Or had Dernghuiz been the victim of a hallucination?

"Are you certain that you saw a light?" Kisseloff asked.

"Yes, Master," the Tatar replied, without hesitation. "It shone in my eyes, as fleeting as lightning, and disappeared in the darkness."

"Silence! Listen!" shouted Pickerreek, thunderously.

At that command, pronounced with authority, everyone fell silent. For a few seconds they heard nothing but the rhythmic beating of the wings and the whistling of the wind, which was still howling with the same rage.

"Ah! A thousand portholes!" said Pickerreek. "we're saved! Listen, Captain, Monsieur Marcel…listen!"

"Well, what?" demanded the voyagers.

"The scale of the tempest's changing. Just now, it was screeching in falsetto like a publican refusing credit; now it's as hoarse as a quartermaster who's drunk more *schnick* than tea!"[29]

"What does that prove?"

"It proves that we've quit the sea and we're over land!"

Joy—one of those immense joys that cause the heart to overflow with hope and optimism—chased away all dread. The aeronef descended; the light was projected downwards; Valdy scanned the terrain as best he could, selected a bare spot, and the *Céleste* landed, although somewhat at hazard, without any impact or shock.

Castaways landing on a hospitable shore had never experienced more joy than the voyagers so fortunately saved. To restore their spirits they hastily ate a little bread, and to obtain shelter they set up the tent on the *Céleste*'s deck. Cardounec moved away a short distance in order to look for some wood with which to light a fire, for their clothes were soaked, but he only brought back a few sparse handfuls of short and withered grass. In the end, they all wrapped themselves up in blankets and forgot, in the repose of sleep, their lassitude and violent emotion.

---

[29] In French argot, *schnick* is cheap alcohol; the word has only recently become a slang term for cocaine in parts of Ireland.

Before going to sleep, however, Valdy, Will Tooke and Ivan Kisseloff tried to figure out where they were.

"If we're on an island," said Valdy, "we've reached one of the Vigtens. If we're on the mainland, we ought to be somewhere near Drontheim."

"That's my opinion too," the Russian added.

"For myself, Messieurs," the American put in, "I think you're mistaken. The wind hasn't been blowing constantly from the west; it's sometimes veered to the south-west, and I'm authorized by that observation to affirm that we're on one of the Lofoten Islands."

"That's impossible!"

"We've crossed the Arctic Circle."

"At any rate, weather permitting, we'll calculate our position tomorrow."

The next day, the fourth of September, on looking around, the voyagers could see nothing but rocky and desolate land. Although the tempest had calmed, the sky remained veiled and the feeble light filtered through the gray clouds gave the day a wan and dubious tint. If the sun did not appear—as they anticipated—it would be impossible to read the apparent elevation of the star on the arm of the extant, and, in consequence, it would become very difficult to determine the longitude and latitude of their location.

"One means of getting out of difficulty remains to us," Valdy said. "We can rise up to a low altitude and head south, following the coast. We can stop to obtain information as soon as we see a town, a village or a hamlet."

Pickerreek remarked that the reserves of bicarbonate of soda and hydrochloric acid were running low, and that after an hour's flight there would be none at all left. Valdy was dejected. Norway had not been included in his itinerary, and if they were not lucky enough to find a sizeable town nearby in order to restock their supplies, the expedition would be over. Like all northern countries, Norway has large uninhabited areas and sparse human agglomerations in the midst of which one can only obtain the necessities of life.

It was, however, necessary to try everything to get out of the impasse in which they had ended up.

"We have an hour's fuel," said Valdy. "That's about a hundred kilometers we can cover, and perhaps..."

That 'perhaps,' pregnant with probabilities and disappointments, was interrupted by the arrival of a man, who stopped in alarm on perceiving the aeronef. Cardounet ran to him and reassured him by means of a thousand demonstrations of amity, offered him his most precious possessions—his pipe, a pouch full of tobacco and a few meager coins—and asked him by means of signs what the place where they were standing was called.

The man appeared to understand, accepted the graciously-proffered gifts, an repeated a single word several times: "Kjelwig."

Cardounet confessed in very good French that he had no idea what the word meant. Ivan Kisseloff came over; in his capacity as a Russian, he understood and could speak a little of the dialects in use in northern Europe, especially Finland, and which are derived from the Finnish language. He questioned the newcomer; the latter, delighted to be understood, gave the details request of him in a prolix fashion.

"We're neither in the vicinity of Drontheim nor in the Lofotens," Ivan Kisseloff said, turning to his companions. The tempest has driven us to the northernmost extremity of Europe. Messieurs, we're on Mageroe Island!"

"On Mageroe Island?" Valdy put in. "but that's impossible."

"It's at least seventy-one degrees of latitude and twenty-three degrees of longitude east of Paris," added Will Tooke.

"Messieurs, my informant is insistent. He claims that we're a short distance away from Kjelwig, the island's port, and that we'll see it if we go over the rocks in front of us."

Everyone climbed a rather steep slope, the culminating point of a depression in the ground, and they saw a few large huts set on a cliff violently carved by the action of the waters.

Cardounet grimaced in disdain. "That's Kjelwig!" he said. "Why, from the way the islander pronounced the word, I thought he meant a city as big as Le Havre or Brest. We won't find the ingredients necessary for the ascension of the *Céleste* in a place like that."

Indeed, the aeronef had landed on Mageroe Island, the European land closest to the pole, apart from Spitzbergen and Novaya Zemlya. With the aid of binoculars, they made out in the distance the three masses of granite that advance into the Arctic Ocean to form North Cape, and then the continent, with its promontories indented with profound fjords and its eternally snow-capped mountains.

If the reader studies a map of Europe, he will find the position of Mageroe Island to the north of Norway, a little above Finmark, the administrative district of which it is a part, and will see how well Pickerreek's perspicacity had served the voyagers. If the brave mariner had not realized that they were passing over land, the *Céleste*, driven by the impetuosity of the wind, would have been irredeemably lost in the abysms of the Arctic Ocean. The expedition was direly compromised, however, for steering toward the west of the Paris meridian and ending up eastwards of the same meridian is to move crabwise. From the fourteenth degree of west longitude they had been driven to the twenty-third degree of east longitude— a journey of thirty-seven degrees in the space of ten or twelve hours. That extraordinary velocity surpassed all their anticipations.

It is necessary to explain that those thirty-seven degrees crossed above the Arctic Circle only implied a distance of twenty-five leagues apiece, that being the relevant division of one degree, which represented 925 leagues. The parallels of the equator are reduced in circumference the further one moves away from it, and the distance between two meridians diminishes as one approaches the poles. Twenty-five leagues at the equator, it is only twenty-two at the thirtieth degree of latitude, sixteen leagues at the forty-ninth degree, twelve leagues at the sixty-first degree, eight leagues at the seventieth, four leagues at the eightieth and a quarter of a league at the eighty-ninth. It was therefore probable that the aeronef, borne by the wind and describing certain aerial sinuosities, had covered a distance of between four and five hundred leagues.

Valdy consulted a map of the region to which fatality had brought the *Céleste*, and recognized that it would be difficult to find the chemical elements required to produce carbonic acid, in the absence of unexpected circumstances. He did not despair completely, however.

"My friends," he said, "do you recall Crébillon's line: *Success is often a child of audacity?*"

Crébillon talked like an American," said Will Tooke.

"That's also my opinion," Valdy continued. "So we're going to go to the continent, to Hammerfest, Altengaard or Kaatfjord. If we don't succeed in finding hydrochloric acid and bicarbonate of soda, we'll manufacture them. Is that agreed?"

"Agreed," replied the voyagers.

Before embarking, Valdy examined the *Céleste* minutely, as he did every day. That inspection did not reveal any damage. Ivan Kisseloff was not entirely reassured, though.

"I know how much care you put into the construction of the *Céleste*," he said, "and I believe that her solidity is proof against anything, but don't you fear, after our long journey, a loss of hydrogen gas?"

"If gas is lacking, we'll have a vacuum inside the balloon, and its specific weight will diminish instead of increasing. In any case, I've thought of everything. Look."

Valdy lifted up two tiny trap-doors and showed the Russian tanned hides blacking two orifices fitted into the hull. "You know," he continued, "that the expansive force of gas increases as the external air pressure diminished, and that a balloon filled with hydrogen explodes as soon as it reaches a given height. The envelope of the balloon is a fabric whose variations in tension inform the experienced eye of an aeronaut of the danger of an imminent explosion; the latter prevents it by opening a valve that facilitates a loss of gas. But for an envelope like that of our aeronef, completely deprived of elastic materials, it became impossible to recognize the distention of the hydrogen. It was then that I thought of placing the tanned hides that I showed you in immediate contact with the gas. They're our safety-valves. When the external pressure is too low, the hydrogen reacts, the skins swell up and are projected outside like inflated blisters. Then I'm warned that it's necessary to descend. If circumstances force us to contrive a vacuum inside the hull, the hides act in the opposite sense and withdraw; from their concave tension I'll know the quantity of air that I'll be able to remove or return."

"But who not consult the manometric tubes that you've disposed in your apparatus?" said Ivan Kisseloff. "They'll inform you as well, if not better, than the skins."

"That's true, but although the manometers warn us, they can't protect us against explosion, while the skins split and prevent the hull from exploding. The wings, extending immediately as a parachute, slow the descent and we arrive on the ground without running excessively grave risks. Furthermore, we only have to fear those dangers if we go up to considerable heights, and I only expect to go up to three or four thousand meters on rare occasions. As for the hydrogen gas, I think our losses are very minimal, for our aerial vessel is absolutely impermeable. Giffard solved the problem before me, since the provision of gas that inflated his captive balloon did not have to be renewed for two months. 'A good balloon,' says Wilfrid de Fonvielle. 'ought not to lose its gas any more than a steamship loses its coal.'"

Chapter VII

These various explanations increased the confidence of the voyagers and made them forget the previous day's dangers. They made ready to take off immediately, and the *Céleste* rose up above Kjelwig. In less than a quarter of an hour they flew over Qvaaoe Island, or Whale Island, and landed near Hammerfest, the closest city to the pole anywhere in the world. The denomination of "city" is perhaps a trifle ambitious for a placed with a population of seven or eight hundred inhabitants, which has only a single street, but during the brief summer of the polar regions, Hammerfest exhibits a extraordinary animation. The harbor fills with ships, the warehouses open and exchanges are made; Norwegian and Russians traders arrive to barter cereals, flour, hemp and fabrics for dried fish, whale oil, reindeer hides, furs, eider-down and copper. Launches go back and forth across the bay in all directions, sailors come ashore, circulating in the street and mingling with the indigenes; it is a veritable fair, which lasts until the first frosts.

Toward the end of August and the beginning of September, the ships prepare for departure, chased away, not by the rigor of the temperature, which is still maintained above five degrees Centigrade, but by the anticipation of the equinoctial tempests, which are furious and terrible in that region. Winter is quite mild at Hammerfest; a branch of the Gulf Stream skirts and bathes the coasts of Finmark; the sea never freezes and the thermometer rarely descends to minus eight Centigrade.

On the fourth of September there were still two brigs and three schooners in the harbor. As soon as the *Céleste*'s arrival was known, the inhabitants of the town, the Laplanders camped on a nearby hill and the crews of the ships all came running to satisfy their curiosity. Valdy enquired as to the resources that could be made available to him, and quickly learned that there was neither hydrochloric acid nor bicarbonate of soda in Hammerfest. What should he do?

The safest and surest course was to embark to a brig departing for Bergen and go back to France—whereupon Harry Catlen, Esquire, would pocket a hundred thousand francs and laugh loudly at the temerity of the voyagers.

That idea exasperated Ivan Kisseloff, Pickerreek and Cardounet.

"We'll make up the lost time if we try," the last-named said. "Since the wind has been blowing from the west, it will soon turn to the east. That will be compensation for yesterday's tempest. We'll take advantage of the moment when the gusts are most violent, and set sail. We'll disembark in America in less than fifteen hours."

"The remedy's worse than the disease," Valdy said, smiling, "and I won't employ it."

Fortunately, there was a representative of an English foundry in Hammerfest, who had arrived from Kaatfjord. He chatted for some time with Will Tooke, and assured him that they could obtain a large quantity of sulfuric acid if the *Céleste* were transported to Kaatfjord. As for bicarbonate of soda, there was none. The American transmitted this information to Valdy, and the later ordered an immediate departure.

"I think we'll be able continue our journey without difficulty," he said, "when we have sulfuric acid at our disposal. That powerful reagent will assist us to replace the element we lack for the manufacture of carbonic acid."

The *Céleste* took off again, saluted by the cheers of the crowd, and disappeared in the direction of Kaatfjord. For the first time since their stopover at North Ronaldsay the voyagers saw trees: conifers, solitary and as if buried in the depths of valleys, but then gathered together on the mountain-slopes, forming immense forests that are the wealth of the circumpolar regions. The dark green hue of fir-trees, which has something sad and languid about it, cheered up the sight of our aerial explorers as if they were contemplating a meadow ornamented with dazzling flowers or one of those regions bathed with the light and warmth that creates the luxuriant vegetation of the tropics. It was a simple effect of contrast that Cardounet translated thus:

"In the country of the blind, the one-eyed are kings."

Finally, they distinguished Kaatfjord. The aeronef landed on a plateau situated about two hundred meters from the little town.

Kaatfjord owes its importance to a copper mine exploited since 1847 by an English company. As soon as the arrival of the *Céleste* was signaled, the director of the mine, his principal employees and several miners came toward the voyagers and offered them a gracious welcome. Valdy hastened to ask whether it was easy to obtain sulfuric acid; the reply was affirmative, and as much as he desired was put at his disposal, for sulfuric acid was is used in certain operations in the processing of copper ore, and Kaatfjord possessed abundant reserves of it. As for finding bicarbonate of soda, there was no possibility of finding it there; sodium chloride—marine salt—the primary material of soda, so widespread in nature, is imported into Sweden and Norway, the cold and humidity not permitting the establishment of salt-marshes and preventing all evaporation. Valdy was not greatly distressed by this latter inconvenience. He knew that bicarbonate of soda was not indispensable for the production of carbonic acid gas, since all carbonates release it in large quantities.

It was, therefore, necessary to find a carbonate—but that was not easy on the Scandinavian peninsula, a primitive terrain composed in the main of gneiss and micaceous schists. The formation of the ground has been so tormented, though, that one can encounter masses of the Secondary Era raised up and exposed. That was what happened; Valdy, accompanied by Pickerreek, Cardounet and Will Tooke, explored the environs of Kaatfjord and ended up discovering, on the slope of a large and deep crevasse, impure calcium carbonate, and eventually, a layer of chalk.

As chalk is very soft, it was easy to remove as much as they wished. Thanks to the help of the miners and the means of transport that the company director immediately organized, Valdy collected far more than he needed. The chalk was pulverized and introduced into the generator furnished with its tubular vessel full of sulfuric acid. Pickerreek activated it.

The experiment succeeded perfectly, except that it required more time than if they had been using bicarbonate of soda. The receptacles filled with liquefied carbonic acid gas. Valdy thanked all those who had lent him assistance warmly, and ordered the preparations for departure.

"My friends," he said to his companions, "our determination and energy will overcome all obstacles. Don't worry, Monsieur Kisseloff; Harry Catlen won't jeer at our endeavor and will lose his bet. This evening, we'll be in Drontheim, and there we'll find the resources that are lacking in Finmark. Then we'll head for the Shetland Isles, we'll take on the hydrochloric acid and bicarbonate of soda deposited there, which we left behind, and then we'll resume the normal conditions of our voyage—and, God willing, we'll make up the lost time."

That short speech was welcome joyously. A few minutes later, the *Céleste* took off and headed out to sea in order to avoid the rather elevated ramifications of the Kioelen Mountains.

The voyagers admired the Norwegian coast, strewn with gigantic rocks and numerous islands, indented by fjords and estuaries, like an immense lace. The aeronef did not rise above five hundred meters and always stayed close to the wind. The country they traversed was unremarkable. Somber forests intercut by ravines with foaming waterfalls, meadows in which sheep and reindeer were grazing, arid plains, occasional villages of wooden houses with kitchen gardens on the roofs, lakes surrounded by verdure—such was the aspect of the Nordland region between Kaatfjord and Drontheim.

It was almost dark when the *Céleste* arrived above the latter city. She landed on a promontory, near the railway station linking the stiftsamer—administrative districts—of Nordre-Drontheim and Sendre-Drontheim with the southern provinces of Norway and Sweden. In spite of the obscurity, the *Céleste* was seen executing her landing maneuvers. The news spread like a gunpowder-fuse. All of Drontheim headed for the aeronef, and the population saluted the French flag that Cardounet unfurled enthusiastically.

France—"beautiful France," as the Norwegians call it—finds a traditional sympathy in the cold northern lands, augmented by recent misfortunes. It is with love and respect that people out there talk about the brave and generous nation—and however lacking in chauvinism one might be, one is never insensible to those marks of affection, so Pickerreek and Cardounet distributed warm handshakes.

"Damn it!" said the latter. "How would we be greeted, then, if we'd thrashed *them* and taken Metz and Strasbourg back from them?"

"No, damn it—shut up!" replied the former. "Let's hope! *They* threatened Dunkerque; sooner or later, they'll pay me back for that!"

There is no need to describe every detail of the brilliant reception of the voyagers. That evening, one of the rooms of the Kongsgaard—the royal palace—was resplendent with light, and the whole of Drontsheim's social elite gathered there. The archbishop and the bailiff presented letters to Valdy and his companions that accorded them the title of citizens of Drontsheim. Thus had the municipality of Calais acted toward Blanchard when the intrepid aeronaut crossed the Pas-de-Calais in company with Dr. Jeffries. Madame Valdy became the object of the most delicate attentions, and the ladies graciously presented her with a fine jewel-case enclosing a forget-me-not wrought in gold and silver, ornamented with magnificent gems.

Drontheim, situated at the mouth of the Nid on a profound gulf called Trondheimsfjord, is not only an industrial and commercial city, but also a scholarly one. It has several notable scientific establishments, numerous schools, a museum, a public library, a mining directorate, etc. The kings of Sweden and Norway come to be crowned in the ancient cathedral of Saint Olaus, the most remarkable monument in the

Gothic style in the Northern countries. The streets are regular, but there are a great many wooden houses; fires are frequent and terrible; among those that have done the most damage we shall cite the fires of 1827, 1841, 1842 and 1846. Police regulations no longer permit any other material than stone in the construction of new buildings. The population is about seventeen thousand.

The environs of Drontheim are exceedingly romantic. It is a verdant oasis in the fog. The elegant villas are grouped picturesquely around three separate forts, the Moellenberg, the Christianteen and the Christianfield. On the isle of Munkholm stands the fortress of the same name—once a renowned and powerful abbey—like a protective giant.

Valdy asked whether it would be possible to obtain hydrochloric acid and bicarbonate of soda; he was told not to worry about anything, and that he would find aboard the *Céleste* everything that he might desire. The party continued, terminated by a splendid supper. Even Dernghuiz, at the insistence of his two "professors," Pickerreek and Cardounet, did full honor to the generous wines that were served, and went to bed "nodding his head," joyful and merry. The pupil was definitely coming along nicely.

The next day, at daybreak, all the healthy people in Drontheim and the surrounding area watched the preparations that always preceded the aeronef's departure. The houses and ships were decked with flags, as if they were celebrating a national holiday. The view of the port was splendid. After the final handshakes and adieux, the *Céleste* rose up majestically. Immediately, the cannons of the fortress of Munkholm thundered, the batteries of the warships released their volleys, and a mighty detonation brought the salute of a hospitable land to the voyagers' ears.

"Well!" said Valdy, setting a course southwards. "That's how one salutes kings!"

"Science is also a sovereign," said Ivan Kisseloff, "and they're rendering to your discovery the honors that are due to it."

Valdy searched for a current favorable to his direction, and found it at an altitude of eight hundred meters. The aeronef went along the Norwegian coast as far as the isle of Bremangerland and then set out across the sea. Nothing opposed the perilous crossing; in the evening, before it was completely dark, the *Céleste* came down on a plateau in the isle of Unst, which is the most northerly in the Shetland archipelago. Valdy inscribed the following in the ship's log:

5 September. We're behind schedule, but heading westwards again. We're on the isle of Unst, approximately 61°N latitude, 3° longitude W of Paris.

There was, in fact, a slight error in the position, but, as the advanced hour of the day did not permit taking and exact bearing, Valdy recorded an approximate one.

The islanders, frightened at first by the arrival of the *Céleste*, were rapidly reassured, and approached. Soon, a cordial intimacy was established on both sides. The bicarbonate of soda and hydrochloric acid, stored in the modest dwelling of a fisherman, were brought aboard the aeronef, and the brave man would not accept any payment.

The Shetlands, which number eighty-six islands of various sizes, are very similar to their nearest neighbors, the Orkneys; there is the same bare soil, with peat-bogs and pasturelands, the same damp and nebulous climate. The sea thereabouts is richer in fish, especially herring, so, when the fishing season arrives, veritable flotillas of English and Dutch boats cross paths in the region.

The sky seemed to support the courage and efforts of the voyagers, for the sixth of September advertised the most fortunate auspices: not a cloud on the horizon, not a breath of wind in the air; the most absolute calm—circumstances exceedingly rare in the Shetlands.

The *Céleste* departed and only went up to an altitude of three hundred meters. Valdy affirmed that they would arrive in

Iceland that evening. Iva Kisseloff seemed overjoyed to be leaving English territory.

"Monsieur de Kisseloff has a grudge against England," said Pickerreek.

"I know why," Cardounet replied.

"Bah! Why?"

"Because England is a land of fogs, because the sun resembles our moon there, because vines don't grow there and people have to drink beer instead of wine."

"Possibly!" Pickerreek concluded, seemingly content with that bizarre explanation.

After a few hours of travel, they recognized the Faroes.

"Aren't we going down," said Will Tooke, "to shake the hands of the good friends we left in those islands?"

"No," Valdy replied. "The slightest delay in these latitudes might be prejudicial to us, for variations of temperature hereabouts are abrupt and frequent. Let's take advantage of the calm while it persists."

Everyone endorsed this opinion.

"Do you see that little island in the distance?" said Valdy, pointing to a black dot standing out against the sea.

Binoculars were immediately aimed at the indicated spot and the voyagers made out a mountainous terrain covered with sheer rocks.

"What's remarkable about it?" asked the American.

"It's the isle of First Holm," Valdy replied, "and I'm bringing it to your attention because a remarkable event occurred there a few years ago, which victoriously contests the theories of those who claim that birds, when they fly, are as light as the air. An eagle carried away a young child and transported him to its aerie, set on the highest peak on the island, so steep that it had never been climbed by the reckless eider-hunters. The other, finding a superhuman courage in her grief, succeeded in reaching her child, but the poor boy had been killed by the raptor."

"The fact you're citing is conclusive," said Ivan Kisseloff, "And it's a pity that the story ended so tragically."

"Eagles," Valdy continued, "have tested their alary power many times in carrying off small children. Monsieur de la Blanchère cites several examples in his *Oiseaux utiles et nuisibles* that support my assertions.[30] This passage in his book made such an impact on me that I remembered them:

"'Some people,' the author says, do not believed that these animals are strong enough to carry off lambs and other quadrupeds of similar size in heir claws, but the fact is observed every day. Moreover, one even has examples of eagles taking children. We shall cite a few.

"'In Skye in Scotland a woman had left her child in a field momentarily; an eagle carried the child off in its claws and crossed the entire length of a lake in its flight. A few local people watching their flocks saw the bird deposit its burden on a rock and, hearing the child's cries, hastened to the spot, where they found the victim safe and sound.

"'In Sweden, the mother of another child was working in a field of ewes and had set her child on the ground a short distance away. Suddenly, an eagle swooped and carried the child away. For a long time the unfortunate woman heard the poor victim crying in the air, but here as no means of helping him. Soon, she could no longer see anything; shortly afterwards, she lost her reason.

"'In the spring of 1847 and eagle carried off a ten-year-old boy in the commune of Hery-sur-Alby in the canton of Geneva. The young scamp had just robbed a nest, from which he had taken the eaglets, and that act of aggression probably exasperated the father and mother. One of the two eagles immediately seized him and deposited him on a rock six hundred meters away. Fortunately, he was saved by shepherds who

---

[30] Henri de la Blanchère's *Les Oiseaux utiles et les oiseaux nuisibles aux champs, jardins, forêts, plantations, vignes, etc.* [Useful Birds and Birds harmful to fields, gardens, forests, plantations, vines etc.] (1870) was a very popular book, going through numerous editions, some of which were augmented. It remains notable for its engraved illustrations.

came running. The boy had sustained no other injury than a deep laceration caused by the bird's claws.

"'Moquin-Tandon[31] has communicated in inscriptions and belles-lettres from Toulouse to the Académie des Sciences, published in the *Mémoires* of 1839-41, a remarkable fact that attests the strength of a royal eagle. Two little girls in the vicinity of Alesse, in the canton of Vaud, one aged five and the other three, were playing together when an eagle of mediocre size swooped on the former and, in spite of her companion's screams and the arrival of several peasants, rose into the air. After an active search of the surrounding ricks, which had no other result than the discovery of a shoe, child's stocking and the eagle's aerie, in which there were only two chicks, surrounded by an enormous mass of bones of kids and labs, a shepherd finally found, the child's cadaver, nearly two months after the abduction, lying on a rock, half-naked, torn, bruised and desiccated. The rock was half a league from the place where the event had occurred.'"

"These examples," said Will Tooke, "are sufficient to prove the partisans of the heavier-than-air thesis correct."

"And if one harnessed a few eagles to a balloon," added Cardounet, "one would economize on the costs of aerial navigation."

"Unfortunately," Valdy said, "the education of eagles is very difficult, and falconers have given up on it. Even so, someone else has had Cardounet's idea—a German named Riesner. That blond son of Germany has even published a pamphlet on the subject. He has not only calculated the number of eagles that would be required by a balloon of a given size, but has described the harness of those new chargers."[32]

---

[31] The botanist Alfred Moquin-Tandon (1804-1863).

[32] I cannot trace the original of this pamphlet, but the assertion is widely cited in secondary sources from the late 1820s and 1830s, including a citation by Georges Cuvier, from which many of the others are presumably derived.

"That idea could only germinate in the head of a German," said Pickerreek. "Would he loosen the moorings as we do when the wind doesn't catch the sail sufficiently? If the ropes had tightened, crash! The eagles would have followed the plumb-line."

The brave mariner's reasoning as sound. His common sense rebelled against "the enormous naivety" of the German.

During this conversation the *Céleste* had left the Faroes behind and advanced rapidly toward Iceland. Nothing could be seen but the sea, weakly raised by the swell, and a few scattered ships, swaying gently and progressing under full sail. The crossing was truly being executed in ideal conditions— except hat, as they went further northwards, the thermometer dropped and it became cold.

Madame Valdy was the first to notice a flock of birds flying at a great height, fleeing at top speed toward Europe.

"A bad sign!" exclaimed Pickerreek. "It's rare that birds abandon the Arctic lands so soon. My friends, I'll only tell you this—that this year, it'll be cold enough at the North Pole to freeze all the whales and seals that live there."

"Indeed," added Ivan Kisseloff, "the extreme sensitivity of birds permits us o anticipate the rigors of the climate. The winter will be harsh—so let's act wisely and not linger long in the circumpolar countries."

"That's my opinion too," Valdy replied.

For a few more hours, the *Céleste* flew silently, but when the sun began to set its speed slowed. Mists rose up on the sea, sparse at first and as thin as puffs of smoke, and then more widespread and denser. Gradually, they invaded the air and spread a dangerous semi-obscurity. It seemed to be night when the voyagers recognized the coast of Iceland. They came ashore over the eastern region, a mountainous territory bristling with peaks, covered in glaciers and almost uninhabited. Valdy spotted a plateau situated on the side of a mountain and went down.

For the evening meal, Cardounet did not have to scavenge in order to prepare the dishes to his satisfaction; the site was rigged and devoid of wood. They took conserves from boxes. While our voyagers were refreshing themselves, the moon appeared, dull and veiled, above the mountains, gradually—to make use of the popular expression—"ate the mist" and expanded its gentle light over the surrounding objects.

Valdy and his companions were then able to admire the horrible beauty of the country that was serving as their refuge. Basaltic rocks formed an irregular circle; one might have thought that the hands of giants had set them up on their powerful foundations, so uniform and cleverly arranged were they. A few, carved like immense columns, seemed to be supporting the remains of a bizarre and gigantic fronton; at their feet, hump-backed layers of lava had taken the oddest forms as they descended, reminiscent, in the pale beams of the night-star, of a furious sea whose waves had been suddenly petrified. And in the midst of that chaos, there was no trace of vegetation, no indication of life. In the distance *joekuls*—glaciers—adhered forcefully to the flanks of mountains crowned with eternal snows, pressing with their jagged ridges upon the needles, spikes and peaks of schist that opposed an insurmountable barrier to them.

"But look what's happening above us," said Will Tooke, pointing at the summit of the mountain.

They all raised their heads, and they perceived a plume of smoke, sometimes thick enough to hide the moon.

"We're camping on a volcano, damn it!" exclaimed Cardounet.

"Yes," said Valdy, "but what volcano is it? It can't be Hecla, for its form and craters always render it recognizable; then again, it's deeper in the territory. Anyway, we'd be able to see the hamlet of Noefurholt, whose inhabitants serve as guides to the explorers of this desolate country—and here there's nothing, absolutely nothing."

"You're mistaken," Ivan Kisseloff put in. "There's someone—look at that narrow path along the mountain slope and you'll see an animal and a human being."

Indeed, a rather stout man mounted on one of the small, long-haired horses that render such useful service in Iceland was advancing, encouraging his mount with words and gestures. Sometimes, he writhed like a devil in a font, and a string of oaths escaped his lips, which the echoes repeated mockingly. It was obvious that the traveler felt a violent irritation at being late. The bag was walking slowly, with all sorts of precautions. One false movement, one false step, might have caused it to lose it footing and fall into the depths of some crevasse, and the intelligent animal, in spite of its rider's impatient cries, did not alter its tranquil gait. Finally, the man and the beast surged forth from behind a rock in the vicinity of the aeronef.

The rider stopped his mount and pronounced a few words that no one understood. Ivan Kisseloff tried to employ a half-Finnish and half-Norwegian patois to interrogate the newcomer.

The latter came forward and said, in the same language: "Be welcome, strangers." Immediately, he dismounted, shook Kisseloff's hand and bowed courteously to Madame Valdy. "What the devil are you doing here?" he asked.

"We've come from Europe."

"I know, I know—but since your arrival from Europe..."

"We arrived this evening."

"But where have you disembarked? The east coast is very bad and almost devoid of harbors."

"We haven't come by sea, we've come by air."

"What? I don't understand."

Ivan Kisseloff showed the *Céleste* to the Icelander and brief explained the mechanism and principle of aerial navigation.

"By all the saints in paradise," he said, "that's a curious and marvelous adventure. You're not making fun of me?"

"No."

Then, in spite of his small stature and corpulence, the islander ran to the *Céleste*, examined it and walked around it briskly several times. After he had satisfied his curiosity he

115

asked for something to eat. Cardounet served him, and the mariner was delighted with his guest, who ate and drank for four, repeating several times: "European foods are definitely more succulent than those of cold Iceland."

Ivan Kisseloff asked him who he was an where he had come from."

"I'm the Honorable Sturssen," he replied, "Sysselmand of the canton of Skalholt, a day's walk from Reykjavik."

"What's a Sysselmand?"

"The mayor, the judge, the preceptor, the notary—in sum, the head man—of the canton. You see that, in spite of my meager height, I've accumulated a goodly number of functions. My administrators are content with me, as I am with them."

"And what are doing, Monsieur Sturssen, traveling by night like this, alone and defenseless in a deserted land."

"Ha ha! How little you know of these lands of ice—and with all your civilization and all your comforts, you can't travel in Europe as safely as I can. Here, there are no gendarmes because there are no thieves or murderers. I've come from Diupavog, on the east coast, where I was settling some family business, and I'm going back to Skalholt. From Diupavog to here I've followed the coast so as not to lack nourishment, for the fishermen helped me. My intention was to go into the *Klofa-Jokull*—the snow-field—in order not to have the mountains in front of me, which are difficult to climb and would slow me down. I wanted to get around Oroefa tonight..."

"We're camping on Oroefa, then?"

"Yes—a volcano that only dates from 1724,[33] which doesn't prevent it, in spite of its youth, from getting angry at intervals and wailing and growling like its old colleague Hecla. And I ought to tell you that, if I was in such a hurry to get past Oroefa, it's because I noticed a few signs of an imminent eruption."

---

[33] Other sources represent Oroefa as an old volcano that had last erupted in 1362

"So there's danger in staying here?"

"Perhaps. Not because of the eruption itself but because of the *snoeflods*."

"I don't understand the last word."

"The *snoeflods* is an avalanche that often escapes from glaciers shaken by the volcano."

"When do you think the eruption will occur?"

"Who knows? Perhaps in a hour, perhaps tomorrow, or in a week. Our volcanoes are as capricious as pretty women."

And the Sysselmand, turning gallantly to Madame Valdy. Repeated a fine compliment of Fontenelle's by adding: "I don't say that about Madame."

Ivan Kisseloff smiled and translated the compliment for Madame Valdy.

Icelanders talk in a slightly affected way and often employ metaphor—a habit that doubtless comes from their repeated reading of the *Edda* and the Bible during the long winter nights. Generally, they are educated and their conversation is entertaining. There is no need to be astonished if Master Sturssen sometimes imported a refinement into his speech worthy of a good mind.

Oroefa was calmly emitting its plume of black smoke, and there was no sign of an imminent catastrophe. It was agreed that they would spend the night on the plateau. Pickerreek set up the tent and room was made within it for the Sysselmand. Soon, sleep weighed down all their eyelids and nothing could be heard but sonorous snores responding to the breath of the wind.

The Icelander did not sleep soundly; several times he woke up to look at the summit of the volcano and examine the sky. The atmosphere was calm, except that large white clouds were coming slowly from various points of the horizon and gathering above Oroefa's crater. Their mass thickened, extending and extinguishing the wan light shed by the moon and the stars. A few gleams, produced by the electric tension between the cloud and the volcano, lit up the air, and a dull

117

sound, as feeble as a whimper at first, but growing in a crescendo, was produced at unequal intervals.

"Wake up! Wake up!" cried the Icelander. "Wake up and let's get out of this accursed place; our lives are in danger!"

The voyagers were on their feet in an instant. Valdy immediately ordered all the accessories necessary for the *Céleste*'s departure to be prepared. At that moment, two oscillations shook the ground, and a frightful noise was heard.

"The *snoeflods*! The *snoeflods*!" cried the Icelander. "We're doomed! Save us, Lord!"

"Come on!"

And Will Tooke shoved the frightened Sysselmand on to the *Céleste*.

The aeronef rose up—just in time! The eruption was beginning to manifest itself in all its horror. An immense tongue of fire escaped from the crater; the volcano roared; its sides split and sulfurous matter vomited from large crevasses. The smoke whirled as if a furious wind were agitating it, and lightning bolts and crackling sounds like rumbles of thunder emerged from it. Finally, a terrible roar was heard, and immediately, enormous rocks, the broad surfaces of glaciers and entire peaks were detached from their bases and slid down the flanks of the mountain. The *snoeflods* was unleashed, with all its disastrous effects.

But the *Céleste* was already far away; it surpassed an altitude of three thousand meters and crossed the chain of mountains to which Oroefa as linked. Master Sturssen, slightly reassured and amazed, translated his astonishment into hyperbolic expressions and recovered his good humor. His presence was useful, for at night in an unknown country, it would have been very difficult to navigate and land; the worthy Sysselmand pointed out a terrain suitable for landing to Valdy. The aeronef came down.

They were about twenty-five kilometers from Oroefa, and in the black night they could make out the dazzling spray that it was launching, which ended up gradually dying down. The eruption was temporary. The upheaval of nature caused by the volcano's sudden activity was replaced by calm and tranquility. Pickerreek set the tent up again, and they all fell into a leaden sleep, some to wait for daylight, others to forget the violent emotion through which they had just passed.

The day of the seventh of September announced itself sadly, but not for Master Sturssen, who thought that Iceland was the most beautiful country in the world and that its dull and misty sky was better than that of Naples. Large gray clouds hid the sun; the cold became sharp enough to necessitate the wearing of furs. On Valdy's orders, the *Céleste* flapped its wings and flew off westwards in order to reach Reykjavik. During the journey, which was rapid and brief, they only saw the country superficially—a sad, desolate, arid land offering the sight of a disorderly series of basalts, lavas, masses of scoria, volcanic debris, conglomerates, glaciers, marshy plains and sterile mountains.

"To admire Iceland properly," said the Sysselmand to Ivan Kisseloff, "it's necessary to visit it in detail and not *grosso modo*, as we're doing marvelously at present. It's the most curious and most poetic country on Earth, 'set between the ice of the Pole and the fire of the abyss!'"

And Master Sturssen described volubly the principal curiosities of his island: the gigantic fissure of Almannagia, in the depths of which the river Oxeraa runs, and into which people condemned to death for adultery were once hurled; the volcanic wall of Ilrafnagia; the lake and plain of Thingvellir, in which is located the almost unapproachable enclosure in which the popular meetings known as the Althing are held in July every year; the cataracts of Stapafoss; the Great Geyser and the Strockur, with their jets of boiling water; the mountain of Husaell in the valley of Reykholt, whose summits are violet and the slopes blood-red; the crystalline mass of Spath Silfurdoekir—silver stream—transparent, pure and as iridescent as nacre; the basaltic crater of Dverghamrar; the little craters of Raudholar; the grotto of Surtschelliz; the cavern of Stapi; the hill of Kambell, overladen with colonnades that make it resemble an immense Gothic cathedral; and, finally, a

119

host of things whose marvels are indescribable, except in another book.

It was about eight o'clock in the morning when the *Céleste* arrived in Reykjavik, the capital of Iceland.

Reykjavik, which means smoky bay, is well-named. It is a sad, dark, languid place, only populated by seven or eight hundred inhabitants, who live in wooden huts. The dwellings of the bailiff and the bishop and two or three scientific establishments could lay claim to the title of "houses" but even they were paltry and very shabby. Thanks to Master Sturssen's loquacity, the principal inhabitants of Reykjavik were informed of the aeronef's arrival. When it became known that he was among the passengers, the most enthusiastic gave him a ovation and wanted to carry him in triumph, but the Sysselamd's modesty rebelled.

"What have I done to deserve it?" he asked. "The valiant explorers of the aerial regions have saved my life, for without them I'd be sleeping eternally beneath a thick layer of rock and ice. All the honor belongs to the stranger who has endowed the world with a discovery as prodigious, and to his courageous companions. I propose that the capital of Iceland should give them a quasi-royal reception; our country, which has always been a friend to science and progress, will show them that we are our fathers' sons and that we have not degenerated!"

This speech was loudly applauded and all Reykjavik came toward the voyagers. In the name of Iceland, the governor offered them princely hospitality, but Valdy refused to pause. He begged Kisseloff to translate his thanks, but they were behind schedule and had to make up the lost time. The bicarbonate of soda and hydrochloric acid deposited with the only pharmacist on the island were carried aboard the *Céleste* and Cardounet replenished the food supplies. Master Sturssen offered a veritable cargo of comestibles.

Finally, after three-quarters of an hour's rest, they exchanged adieux and the aeronef took flight in the direction of the sea. She crossed the huge bay of Faxa, passed almost directly above Mount Snaeffels, made famous by Jules Verne in his *Journey to the Center of the Earth*, and headed for Greenland, the coast of which was already in sight.

"Let's travel swiftly," said Valdy. "These regions are dangerous because of sudden changes of temperature."

The pressure was increased, the movement of the pistons accelerated, and the *Céleste* advanced with an extraordinary rapidity. Its speed was estimated at a hundred and fifty kilometers an hour.

Chapter VIII

As the reader can imagine, the passage of the *Céleste* over nations like France and England was noticed. No event had ever attracted so much public attention. The newspapers published more or less fantastic accounts, and the various *Céleste*/Valdy stories took precedence over all others for several days. The leading articles in Paris and London were full of discussions of aerial navigation, aerostatics, aeronefs, aeroplanes, atmospheric laws, air currents and so on. Politics, social and economic questions, and the deeds and speeches of statesmen were relegated to the background.

One German newspaper abandoned its habitual gravity and published the following article:

Hurrah for France! We knew that the French possessed levity, but according to what we have learned, the levity of their character has been entirely communicated to their actions. A Frenchman named Valdy has risen into the air without the air of a balloon. It is claimed that he made use of an apparatus of his own invention equipped with wings. Since his departure, nothing more has been heard of him. Really, all these flying men who surge from the ground from time to time have a seed of madness in their brains, and we would gladly laugh at them if their end were not always tragic, for from Icarus to Monsieur de Groof,[34] who killed himself recently, one can count nothing but falls and misadventures.

The French newspapers are enthusiastic; they are preoccupied with nothing but aviation and are heaping all kinds of praise on Monsieur Valdy. Le Constitutionnel *itself, he tranquil* Constitutionnel, *which owes its success to the invention of*

---

[34] The Belgian Vincent de Groof was killed in London in July 1874 while experimenting with an orihthopter launched from a balloon.

a few apocryphal animals and discovered the great sea ser-
pent, the complacent Constitutionnel, *has taken off its visor*
and aimed a telescope at the heavens. It has seen what it was
bound to see, the flying man describing his evolutions in the
aerial regions and disappearing into the photosphere of an
unknown sun.

We are informed that this famous experiment in aviation
has been attempted by an inhabitant of the banks of the Ga-
ronne. Until now, we have thought that hoaxes, in the sense
that the jargon of the press attaches to the word, came to us
directly from America, having received all the cares of Broth-
er Jonathan, but no one will be astonished to learn that they
have acclimatized perfectly in Gascony.

In France, when the contents of this insolent article became known, there was a general outcry. All the newspapers,
from the largest to the smallest, and from the most serious to
the most insignificant, responded in a forthright fashion and
fired off a volley of abuse at German literature. The
Constitutionnel had a fit of juvenile ardor and riposted with
the Attic wit and Gallic verve that the ponderous German
newspapers will never have. Its article concluded thus:

The Germans are not generous. They have defeated and
humiliated us; now they are insulting us. The day will come
when the roles will be reversed. Jena was the revenge of
Rosbach, Sedan that of Jena, but we believe in the system of
compensations. Alsace and Lorraine, or beloved sisters, your
vanquisher, in putting its heel on our throat, uttered the impi-
ous cry: 'Might is right!' Hope, Alsace and Lorraine, for we
reply: 'Science trumps force.'

The English newspapers debated and disputed. Some accepted without commentary or any hidden agenda the possibility of aviation, others brazenly denied it and formed a chorus
with their colleagues beyond the Rhine. Notable among the
former were the *Times,* the *Morning Advertiser*, the *Daily*

News, the *Morning Chronicle*, the Manchester *Guardian*, the Liverpool *Journal*, the Edinburgh *Witness*, the Glasgow *Courier*, the Limerick *Chronicle*, the *London Illustrated News*, the *News of the World*, *Lloyd's Newspaper*, *Punch*, etc., etc. Among the latter were the *Morning Post*, the *Morning Herald*, the *Standard*, the *Shipping Gazette*, the Manchester *Examiner*, the *Tablet, Freeman's Journal*, the *Weekly Times*, etc., etc.

The affirmations of eye-witnesses arrived from all parts of the United Kingdom, however, and letters cluttered the offices of the most widely-read papers. The editors' secretaries were working overtime to open the voluminous correspondence sent to them. As for the reporters and penny-a-liners, some were sufficiently daring to describe at length what they had seen and what they had not seen; they lied like toothpullers, but the benevolent public naively accepted the tall stories in the press.

Finally, a letter from Sir Walter Donderry put an end to the numerous contradictions that were surging from the brains of journalists. It was addressed to the Times and conceived thus:

Sir,

I beg you to insert in the columns of your newspaper the communication I am sending you with regard to the aerial voyage of the Céleste. *As incredulous as St. Thomas, I wanted to see in order to believe, and I witnessed the aeronef's departure. I think that my assertions will combat victoriously the negations of certain people who deny systematically, as Basile calumniates.*

In truth, I do not know how to describe to you my astonishment and my admiration. On the morning of the first of September, the Céleste, *manned by seven persons, left the ground near Parentis-en-Born in the Landes and rose gloriously into the air. It flapped its two immense wings forcefully and reached the upper layers of the atmosphere; we saw it like an imperceptible dot lost in the mists of the horizon; then it disappeared completely. I estimated its speed as that of a railway train traveling at full steam.*

I regret being unable to give you any technical details regarding this first apparatus of aviation, but I hope that its inventor, Monsieur Valdy, of whose general sentiments I am aware, will put his astonishing discovery in the public domain and furnish precise explanations to those interested in science and progress.

Aerial navigation has been discovered! I understand that the Germans are enraged, for it will change certain notions of the just and the unjust that Krupp's cannons have given them and will singularly compromise their triumphant warrior psychology.

The Céleste *has departed for a voyage of circumnavigation that will be effected in forty days. In my moments of incredulity I wagered two thousand pounds sterling against the voyagers; now I have seen and appreciated it, I will wager four thousand pounds that it will be in France within the appointed interval. That is how I translate my confidence in a discovery that will be the most extraordinary of the present century, so fecund in discoveries.*

Accept, Sir, etc.

Sir Walter Donderry

This letter caused a great stir and was reproduced by all the newspapers in Europe. The correspondents of the American press transmitted it to their editors by means of the various transatlantic cables and sacrificed large sums to amplify lies sensationally. The dispatch sent to the New York *Tribune* cost five hundred dollars.

The next day, the Times published the following item:

Lord W*** informs us that he will take Sir Walter Donderry's wager and that four thousand pounds will be deposited, to that effect, with Baring & Co.

We shall not mention the other wagers of various sizes that were laid, but *Punch* wrote maliciously that half the United Kingdom was betting against the other half.

In France, people debated and argued, and sometimes, unfortunately, lost their heads, but in the end, public opinion, so strong in our country, praised unreservedly the first serious attempt at aviation and pronounced in favor of Vardy and his companions. The caricaturists had some fun at the aerial voyagers' expense, but caricature is so witty here, so delicately mocking and simultaneously so good-humored, that no one thought of seeing any offence in the productions of Cham, Stop, Grevin, Daumier, Draner, Marcelin, Morland, Humbert, Morin, Hadol, Lafosse, Le Petit, Grafty, etc.

Once, fattened oxen were paraded every year in Paris. These placid ruminants were always pompously decorated and bear the name of an artistic success or the latest emergent celebrity; thus, Monselet,[35] the charming writer and disciple of Brillat-Savarin, was able to write: "No one is anyone in Paris until he has been a fattened ox." Today things have changed slightly. The fattened oxen have gone but Gallic wit remains, setting itself up as a sovereign and distributing fame. The *Éclipse*, that valiant little weekly periodical, seems to be one of its preferred refuges, thanks to the slightly Rabelaisian gaiety of its editors and the talent of its principal artist, Gill, the mordant, dazzling, extraordinary Gill.[36] Thus we can boldly

---

[35] The gastronome, journalist and novelist Charles Monselet (1825-1888).

[36] "André Gill", whose real name was Louis-Alexandre Gosset de Guines (his pseudonym was an homage to the English caricaturist James Gillray) pioneered the much-imitated device of enlarging the heads of the figures he drew relatively to tiny bodies. Although most of his contemporaries were avid to be caricatured by him, Napoléon III was outraged by a portrait in *La Lune* in 1867, which he promptly closed down—which is why Gill's career continued in the new publication *L'Éclipse*.

say: No one is anyone who has not been featured in the *Éclipse* collection.

That final glory was not refused Valdy. Gill represented him equipped with two immense wings, flying in the highest spheres of the Empyrean, among the suns and the stars, with Fouquet's pretentious motto as a caption: *Quo non ascendum?* The success of the burlesque was prodigious.

The Academies became excited too, but, in accordance with ancient and solemn tradition, their enthusiasm did not overflow. They informed one another that they would deliberate in public session, that they would accord their highest approval to the question of aviation, and that they would award the first aerial voyagers a worthy recompense.

Better late than never!

Gradually, the initial agitation calmed down, and news was awaited impatiently.

Chapter IX

Greenland! It really is the land of desolation, as Dr. Hayes called it. Nothing is as sad and harrowing as the sight of that country; from rocks of volcanic origin immense glaciers emerge, and the now, accumulating over centuries, has filled all the valleys. Milton's image of chaos is no more terrible or fearful. The *Céleste* advanced with a vertiginous rapidity, and Valdy rejoiced because he thought that he would reach Godhaven or Christianshaab, situated on the west coast, before nightfall, short as the days are in the Arctic lands in the month of September.

However, man proposes and God disposes. After a three-hour journey, one of the most rapid that the aeronef had furnished thus far, a fine but intense snow began to fall and the wind direction became to alternate variously. To complete the misfortune, the compass needle spun capriciously on its axis. The proximity of the magnetic pole and the electrical phenomena so frequent above the polar circle were disturbing it.

The situation became critical, because, the compass being useless and the sun being veiled by thick clouds, they could only steer by dead reckoning. Valdy attempted to pierce the layer of cloud that was hiding the blue sky and went up to more than three thousand meters, but he higher he climbed the more violent the tempest became. Moreover, the cold was so intense that carrying out maneuvers became difficult and it was necessary to descend again. The snow was swirling in all directions and the gusts sometimes blew horizontally.

"Let's descend to the ground," said Pickerreek, "and wait for the storm to end. The snow's building up on the deck and the wings; the excess weight will soon neutralize the *Céleste*'s movement."

"How do we know when this wretched tempest will end?" Valdy replied. "Sweep away the snow; it's necessary that we don't stop."

Dernghuiz, Pickerreek, Cardounet, Will Tooke and Ivan Kisseloff, armed with rods, sticks and anything that came to hand, gathered the snow into heaps and precipitated it into space, but their efforts remained fruitless; the snow immediately covered the places they had cleared once again, and the aeronef gradually lost height and slowed down.

Several times, Valdy was forced to land. As he knew that the slightest delay was prejudicial and risked causing his death and that of his companions, he fought, taking off again and skillfully taking advantage of winds that drove him, he assumed, toward the Baffin Sea. That maneuver was repeated several times during the five or six hours that they made difficult progress. In order to provide some relief for Madame Valdy, who was suffering in the bad weather, the tent was set up on deck, but a gust of wind carried it away after having torn it to shreds.

"All right!" said Cardounet, philosophically. "We'll sleep under the beautiful stars."

"Well," replied Pickerreek, "if you see a star, beautiful or ugly, you'll be damnably lucky."

"If you were better educated, Pick, you'd know that not all stars are in the sky, and that everyone has his own, no higher than a topsail."

"That's as may be," said Pickerreek, "and I understand..."

The brave mariner did not complete his sentence. A cry of fright escaped all their throats. The *Céleste* had just hit something. She suddenly stopped and tilted sideways. The impact knocked the voyagers down, but apart from a few bruises they were not seriously injured. A gust of wind had driven the aeronef into a spur of ice, a kind of monstrous iceberg almost isolated in a place where the snow, still falling in dense swirls, hid everything from sight.

After the first instant of surprise and stupor, Valdy examined the hull and perceived that it was ripped, and that no trace of hydrogen gas remained inside it. Pickerreek wanted to repair the damage and immediately set to work. Sheltered by a large blanket that was disposed as best he could over his head, the mariner took spare plates of cork, fitted them, and extended a layer of snow in the grooves that seemed to him to be suspect, which froze and blocked the passage of air. No cracks had ever been better filled, no mastic more impermeable. In order to depart again, it was only necessary to contrive a void within the balloon.

While Pickerreek carried out the necessary repairs, night fell. The exhausted and harassed voyagers did not know what dispositions to make to ward off the cold that was incessantly increasing in intensity.

"What if we imitate the Eskimos," said Will Tooke, "and build a snow-house? What do you think?"

"What's a snow house?" asked Madame Valdy.

"A very simple thing, Madame," the American replied, "which has already saved the lives of numerous voyagers lost on the ice-sheets or in these inhospitable lands. It's a hut made of snow. One of my friends, who accompanied Captain Hall in his exploration of the Polar Sea assured me that, if that improvised dwelling lacks comfort, it perfectly retains the animal heat that the human body gives off and permits temperatures that freeze mercury to be withstood. Tonight the temperature won't drop below minus fifteen Centigrade, and in our snow-house, wrapped in warm blankets, we won't notice the rigor of the climate."

"God idea, Will," said Valdy. "Let's get to work without wasting any time."

"Who'll guard the *Céleste*?" asked Cardounet.

"What do you fear for the *Céleste* in this desolate and un-inhabited region?"

"A visit from polar bears."

"Don't worry," said Ivan Kisseloff. "The season isn't far enough advanced and hasn't been rigorous enough to bring us those unwelcome visitors. Polar bears only become ferocious and troublesome after going hungry for long periods; they won't have suffered that yet, and we have nothing to fear."

A snow hut, conical in form and about twenty meters in surface area was promptly built. The low entrance opposed to the wind permitted penetration into the singular lodgings on hands and knees. Pickerreek and Cardounet took some of the food supplies provided by Master Sturssen into the snow-house, along with furs, blankets, weapons and ammunition.

A few moments later, the voyagers, illuminated by wine-spirit lamps, grouped in a picturesque fashion around the provisions deposited on the ground, were cheerfully having their evening meal, forgetting their fatigues and the tempest, henceforth impotent to reach them. Cardounet made tea, firstly in order to oblige Madame Valdy, and secondly for the dose of rum with which he intended to fortify his "warm water." That was what he called tea, and we firmly believe that all the mariners in the French fleet have the same scorn for the beverage, which is the delight of blonde misses and the Chinese. The red-brown perfumed liquid was poured into goblets, and, to kill the time, they began to chat.

"I've just had a thought, Messieurs," said Valdy. "If we hadn't undertaken to go around the world in forty days, we could attempt the exploration of the North Pole."

"Dangerous work," put in Will Tooke, "for we wouldn't find the depots of hydrochloric acid ad bicarbonate of soda essential for our return."

"Oh, I'd carry reserves for that purpose, and wouldn't embark without biscuit, as the vulgar saying has it."

"And you'd be acting wisely," said Ivan Kisseloff. "The bold navigators who have attempted the adventure had everything at their disposal that the most fecund resources of science have imagined, but still failed. They were fortunate when they didn't fall victim to their zeal and devotion."

"Is the Pole unreachable, then?" asked Madame Valdy.

"I don't claim that, Madame, but the geographical probabilities there are dead against human powers. Examine a polar map and you'll be astonished by the immense unexplored area, completely unknown and guarded by an insurmountable rampart of ice. What is there beyond it? Is there land or open sea?"

"Open sea," said Will Tooke.

"Yes, in all probability, the Polar Sea exists, but the affirmations of voyagers who claim to have seen it only rest on highly problematic hypotheses. Study the routes generally followed, and you'll convince yourselves, by the results obtained, that the unknown still retains all its mysteries.

"The Arctic Sea communicates in three directions with the Great Ocean and the Atlantic Ocean; there are three routes open: that of the Behring Strait; that of the Baffin Sea and that of the Atlantic Ocean. I'll pay particular attention to the last, which has been recommended by August Petermann, the illustrious geographer of Gotha, who has been followed by my compatriots, the Swedes and the Germans. It offers great advantages, for it's the closest to the European ports, and the Gulf Stream warms up the ice sheet, making a profound indentation.

"People have tried to advance by going along the coast of Greenland, traversing the sea that separates Spitzbergen from Novaya Zemlya, but success has been very limited in proportion to the effort, courage and energy of the explorers. In one direction, one runs into the land glimpsed by Cornelius Gilles in 1707, on the other, the unlimited ice-field. Only Captain Parry, aided with sleds and after unexpected fatigues, reached a latitude of 82° 45. No one has surpassed that; will anyone get any further?"

"You're counting without John Bull and Brother Jonathan," Will Tooke interjected. "England and America are stubborn nations; what they want, they want fervently, and their obstinacy often produced excellent results. If the Germans and the Swedes have seen nothing, it's because they went astray, and they ought to have taken the strait where Smith, Kane, Morton and Hayes glimpsed the Polar Sea—and no one dared raise doubts about the veracity of their accounts."

"You're mistaken, Monsieur Tooke; one of your compatriots has contradicted them—that's Captain Hall, who affirms in his journal that the Kane Sea is only a broad strait, and perhaps a bay, for in whichever direction he looked beyond the eighty-second degree of latitude, he saw land or indications thereof. Furthermore, some English and American geographers no longer have the same confidence as before, since they're advising navigators to take the Jones Strait, which is further to the west."

"What direction did Gustave Lambert want to take?" asked Madame Valdy.[37]

"That of the Behring Strait," Ivan Kisseloff replied. I confess, Madame, that in spite of the authority of Cook, who recommended that route and wanted to follow it, that it appears to me to be the worst of all."

"Gustave Lambert seemed to have full confidence in his plan, though."

"Captain Lambert had a noble heart and a valiant soul, and I'm convinced that if he had not been killed by a Prussian bullet he would have attempted extraordinary things, but I believe that he would have been thwarted by the climatic conditions that bar the Behring Strait route. Thus far, no one has been able to surpass $72° 40'$ of latitude. The encircling ice is immense and very thick; it advances as far as Cape Jakan in Siberia; to the north-west of the strait Wrangell Land has been identified, which appears even more insurmountable than the ice-sheet.

"So, according to you, the Pole will never be reached?"

"I don't know, Madame, but one really could believe that those regions are guarded by an Adamastor who, in his jealous

---

[37] Gustave Lambert (1824-1871) tried for twenty years to raise finance an expedition to the North Pole, and did contrive to carry our preliminary explorations of the Behring Strait in 1865, but as a staunch Republican he received only half-hearted support from the Second Empire and was eventually killed by Prussian artillery during the siege of Paris.

fury, breaks ships, sows death and terror in their crews, and says to audacious navigators: 'You shall go no further!'"

"Well," said Valdy, "where maritime navigation has failed, aerial navigation will triumph. By departing with an aeronef, we'd have nothing to fear from the hindrances encountered by voyagers such as Parry, Hayes and Payer when they ventured on to the ice-field, drawn by Eskimo dogs. The blocks of ice heaped on top of one another, the large crevasses, the hummocks and the gigantic icebergs stopped the continually, at the price of fatigues and exceptional dangers; it often took them a whole day to travel half a league. How many kilometers are there between our snow-house and the North Pole? Between fifteen hundred and two thousand. A bagatelle, as you see, since we could go there and back in four days. A member of the French society of aerial navigation, Monsieur Sivel, a former naval officer, has proposed exploring the pole by balloon.[38] And I confess to you that that original and bold means once seduced me."

"Has Monsieur Sivel discovered how to steer aerostats? Could he be certain of getting to the North Pole and coming back again?"

"No, of course not, but he had confidence in his boldness and his good luck. As for me, I declare frankly that I'd rather attempt the adventure in a balloon than in a ship. I believe that the dangerous would be less numerous and that the expedition would be terminated in less than a month."

"I don't believe it," Pickerreek put in.

"Perhaps you're right, for success would depend on certain atmospheric conditions that humans will never master completely—but if I were to perish, my sufferings would be less terrible and shorter than those endured in the cold of the

---

[38] Théodore Sivel, who put forward his plan for a polar expedition in 1872, was killed in 1875 before being able to attempt it, but an attempt to reach the Pole was eventually made by that means by S. A. Andrée in 1897; he and his two companions died.

Arctic winter. At any rate, we recognize now that it's impossible for a maritime expedition to surpass certain limits. There remains, in consequence, the aerial route, and that's the one I propose to take one day. With carefully-organized food supplies, a well-built aeronef and men of firm will, I'll succeed."

"Count on us—we won't abandon you," the travelers replied, unanimously.

Valdy thanked his companions for the confidence to which they were testifying, and the conversation soon lost all interest. Sleep made their eyelids heavy. Cardounet sealed the entrance of the snow-house with a sheepskin in order to prevent "that vagabond cold" from penetrating into the hut, and everyone, well wrapped-up in blankets, went to sleep, dreaming about distant excursions and voyages to the North Pole.

The following morning, at about four o'clock, Pickerreek was the first to wake up and emerge from the snow-house. At first, he could not make out the *Céleste*, buried under the snow; only the projecting rods and some of the rigging-ropes were protruding from the dazzling carpet. The storm had died away completely and the stars were shining rightly in a cloudless sky. On the other hand, the north wind was stubbornly keen and the cold more intense and more sensible than the previous day.

"Get up! Get up! All hands on deck!" shouted Pickerreek, in a stentorian voice.

"What's the matter?" demanded Valdy, suddenly appearing, with a loaded rifle in his hands.

"Nothing, Captain—but if we want to get under way, we need to dig the *Céleste* out of the snow and take advantage of the calm."

In less than five minutes the voyagers were on their feet and began clearing the aeronef. The operation presented a few difficulties, for the congealed snow was adhering strongly to the hull and the wings, and it was necessary to attack it with pick-axes. That violent exercise warmed up the explorers. Madame Valdy also set to work in order to combat the effects of the cold that she was feeling.

After two hours of hard work, the aeronef was completely freed. Taking turns, Pickerreek, Cardounet, Will Tooke and
Ivan Kisseloff moved the levers of the two pneumatic machines in order to evacuate the interior of the balloon. When
Valdy saw that the concavity of the tanned skins was sufficiently extended, and judged from the manometer that the rarefaction of the air was sufficient to obtain a specific lightness
equivalent to that given by the hydrogen gas, he ordered that
the apparatus be made ready for departure. The compass was
still crazed, but the sight of the Pole Star, which was fading in
the first light of dawn, determined the direction to be taken.

Day was breaking as the *Céleste* rose up into the atmosphere. As far as the eye could see, nothing was visible but
snow, taking on the most various hues in the first rays of the
morning sun. A few groups of ptarmigan and wild geese
passed over the aeronef, which maintained an altitude of three
hundred meters, troubling the absolute silence that reigned in
the desolate region with their discordant cries.

After traveling for about sixty kilometers, Dernghuiz
called his master's attention to something moving on the plain.
With the aid of binoculars they recognized a pack of dogs and
huts similar to snow-houses. It was an Eskimo village.

Hoping to obtain directions, Valdy landed a short distance from the village. Immediately, a frightful howling was
heard; the frightened Eskimos fled, shouting threats. In order
to reassure them, Pickerreek advanced on his own and invited
them to come back to meet him, but his demonstrations of
amity obtained no result. Then he went into a hut and found
himself in the presence of a tall fellow clad in sealskin, raising
a rifle and preparing to shoot. The mariner threw himself upon
the weapon, abruptly tearing it from his adversary's hands,
administering to his chin one of those famous uppercuts that
are the honor of noble English boxers and which always cause
those who receive them to "see stars."

"God damn it!" cried the man, falling backwards.

"Oh! You're not an Eskimo, then?" said Pickerreek, who
knew enough English to pronounce a few brief sentences.

"No, I'm English."

"You should have said so, imbecile! We're friends."

And Pickerreek, emerging from the hut, called to his companions, who hastened to join him.

On perceiving humans made of flesh and bone, like himself, and distinguishing a woman among them, the Englishman seemed cured of his great terror. He demanded explanations regarding the "enormous bird" that he had glimpsed in the sky. They satisfied his curiosity by taking him to the aeronef. Then, completely reassured, he told them his story. He was an unfortunate castaway. His ship, a whaler out of Aberdeen, had sunk in the Baffin Sea, and he was the sole survivor of the crew. After he had taken refuge on an ice-floe, the Eskimos had seen him, rescued him and taken him to Upernavik.

"I've been here almost a year," the Englishman continued, "waiting in vain for a ship to take me home. Wanting to make myself useful and no longer a burden on the inhabitants of Upernavik, I obtained employment as a hunter for a Danish company. We explore the country without straying too far and are sometimes fortunate enough to bring back rich provisions of fine furs to the factory. To be honest, this way of life is pleasant enough."

"So we're close to Upernavik, then?" Valdy asked.

"Yes—scarcely twenty-five miles away. When you set off again, head westwards and you'll get there."

"Well," said Valdy to his companions, "if the snowstorm has driven us off course, it's served to give us confidence in our apparatus. Yesterday we traveled more than fifteen hundred kilometers. If we travel at the same speed today, our deviation will soon be rectified."

The castaway called the Eskimos. The latter advanced circumspectly at first, but gradually grew bolder. Cardounet distributed some food to them; that small gift rendered them joyful and confident.

"You're not holding a grudge against me?" said Pickerreek, shaking the Englishman's hand.

"No," the other replied. "It's good to see European faces."

A few mouthfuls of whisky cemented that temporary friendship, and the *Céleste* resumed its flight, to the great amazement of the Eskimos.

After half an hour, they perceived the Baffin Sea, and then saw Upernavik, set at the foot of a hill, recognizable by its harbor striped by rocks, five or six houses built in stone and huts grouped around a little square. The aeronef landed on a hillock overlooking the coast. As usual, its arrival caused extreme fear in the first people who saw it.

Although Upernavik is the most northerly inhabited place in the world, since it is situated at 72° 40′ N, one encounters elements of civilization there that charm the traveler frightened by the surrounding country, the most arid, bare and desolate to be found anywhere.

The Danish Resident and pastor, altered by the public murmur, left their houses and came to meet the voyagers. Seeing that the strangers did not manifest any hostile intent, the Eskimos came closer. Pickerreek and Cardounet had to exercise the closest surveillance, for the indigenes of Greenland try to take hold of anything within arm's reach, no matter how dirty and greasy it might be. The pastor scolded his flock roundly, and the Resident, with the assistance of the four or five Danes who are always with him in his "town," drove away the unwelcome curiosity-seekers. A few blows with a switch delivered to the fingers of the latter had more effect than the eloquence of the pastor, although the latter was threatening them with eternal punishment.

"They're still children," said the latter, "With whom it's necessary to take a firm hand, but their inclination to theft is compensated by excellent. They're gentle, obliging, hospitable—all in all, the most honest thieves in the world."

"Your interpretation of honesty seems a trifle singular to me," put in Ivan Kisseloff, laughing.

"What do you expect?" replied the pastor. "Everything is relative, and these poor inhabitants of icy regions, deprived of everything, including food, succumbing to fatigue and hunger on a daily basis, are more worthy of pity than scorn. The climate is so harsh, the earth so cold, the privations so painful, that my heart finds a thousand reasons to excuse their peccadilloes. I'm here voluntarily to console and bring these disinherited individuals back to healthy notions of duty, and—dare I confess it?—my efforts are better rewarded than if I were exhorting the strays of that civilization of which people in Europe are so proud."

"You're here voluntarily, you say, Pastor?"

"Yes."

The Russian took off his hat and bowed respectfully. He had never seen such sublime and simple devotion.

The Resident offered them breakfast. The voyagers went into his house, followed by the Eskimos, who took them for quasi-supernatural being and never ceased to communicate the most bizarre impressions to one another. The wives of the resident and the pastor, assisted by two Eskimo maidservants, set up a copiously-served table. The paternal Danish government, anxious about the poor subjects of Greenland's western colony, and sometimes prevented from getting supplies to them, stored provisions in its coastal stations. Nothing was lacking: haunches of venison, vegetables conserved in ice, various game, good French wines, Spanish cooked meats, varied desserts, and coffee. Marveling at this extraordinary abundance, the voyagers did honor to the breakfast and thanked their host warmly.

Afterwards they thought about leaving, but they had counted without the caprices of the day star, which had warmed the inferior layers of the atmosphere sufficiently to melt the snow and thin ice. The luting contrived by Pickerreek turned to water; air penetrated the interior of the balloon. It was necessary to remedy that inconvenience. On the resident's orders, two Eskimos went to the stores, and soon returned with a mastic they had manufactured themselves. Pickerreek spread the coating skillfully in the fissures in the hull, in such a way as to render them completely impermeable, and they began evacuating it again.

When that operation as concluded, final handshakes were exchanged again, and the *Céleste*, rising up to a low altitude, took a southerly direction is order to head for Godhaven and Christianshaab, where they found deposited, thanks to Will Tooke, abundant provisions of bicarbonate of soda, hydrochloric acid and wine-spirit.

At Godhaven and Christianshaab, villages populated by a few hundred Eskimos, in the midst of whom lived some twenty Danes, the events that continually followed the arrival of the aeronef were reproduced: extreme fright at first, astonishment and admiration thereafter. The Europeans wanted to retain and fête the voyagers, but the latter refused to pause, wanting to take advantage of the good weather and make up the ground they had lost in the tempests that had taken them by surprise as quickly as possible. They hastily embarked the chemical raw materials and took off again, still heading southwards.

It was getting dark when they arrived at Cape Chudley, a little above the polar circle, opposite Cape Walsingham. The two promontories limited the Baffin Sea, forming the Davis Strait.

The night was not pitch dark, however. The innumerable stars and the reflections of the snow produced a twilight glow. On the other hand, the cold became more intense and the thermometer dropped to minus seven.

"Messieurs," said Valdy, "I think that it would be prudent to continue on our route. Let's take advantage of the good climatic conditions offered to us. The changes of temperature are so rapid in these regions that a new snowstorm might blow up at any moment. Furthermore, we don't have any long crossings to make. If fatigue overcomes us, we can rest when we please, for we'll remain constantly in sight of land."

After a brief deliberation, the plan was adopted. The voyagers donned their fur helmets, had a swift evening meal, and prepared to depart. The aeronef took off over the Davis

Strait and headed for Cumberland Island in the Baffin archipelago, unexplored as yet, but which presents all the characteristics of Arctic countries: no vegetation save for mosses, lichens, heather, sorrel, scurvy-grass and dwarf birch-trees; an abundant fauna of bears, foxes, reindeer, hares and other furry mammals, and numerous migratory birds.

The flight of the *Céleste* continued in the ever-solemn and majestic silence of the night. Nothing could be heard but the whistle of the air produced by the movement of the wings and the dull hum of the flywheels.

Suddenly, a pale and confused gleamed appeared below the Pole Star.

"Is daylight arriving early?" asked Cardounet.

"Wait," replied Will Tooke. "You're about to witness one of the most beautiful phenomena of the circumpolar regions. How is the compass needle behaving?"

"Like someone with St. Vitus' Dance."

"The aurora! The aurora!" exclaimed Ivan Kisseloff.

"Oh, how beautiful it is!" said Madame Valdy.

Luminous sprays, one in the east and the other in the west, slowly rose above the horizon. Tongues of fire streaked them in every direction, coloring them with the richest and most varied tints. Sometimes their glare hurt the eyes. The two fiery sprays incline toward one another and formed a dazzling vault. The segment of the gigantic arc was illuminated in its turn; flaming jets and sparkling rockets, passing from golden yellow to dark green, were launched toward the zenith, streaking the reddened atmosphere and forming a scintillating fringe for the immense aureole. Diffuse gleams snaked smoothly over the confines of the horizon, rotating in spirals, immersing themselves in the dark areas of the sky; elsewhere, they crackled like the flames of a conflagration, darting thousands of rays and sparks in every direction.

The *Céleste* was sailing—it can only be described in metaphorical terms—in a veritable sea of fire. The reflections of the aurora colored the faces of the voyagers; the masses of ice and snow took on pink or violet tones, according to their position, variously favorable to the refraction of the light, and resembled vast blocks of amethyst. The ridges and spurs of icebergs, diaphanously translucent, shone with an incomparable brilliance, deflecting the luminous rays and reproducing, in an indecisive half-light, the faint hues of the solar spectrum.

The phenomenon lasted for more than two hours; then the gleams faded and died away; the phosphorescence of the aurora diminished and the sky resumed its serene obscurity. Only the compass needle continued to agitate under the influence of the magnetic storm—but when the *Céleste* arrived on the western coast of Cumberland Island, it resumed its normal position.

It was five o'clock in the morning of the ninth of September when the aeronef landed on Salisbury Island, a deserted isle situated near the intersection of the Hudson Strait and the Foxe Channel.

"How shall we find the bicarbonate of soda?" asked Cardounet.

"Don't worry about a thing," replied Will Tooke. "One of my friends, Captain Knox, is cruising in these parts. He has everything aboard that we need—even a few strips of canvas to replace the tent we lost, and which would be useful to us now, for the cold is penetrating to the marrow of my bones. What do you think, Madame?"

"I agree with you," Madame Vardy relied.

"Good God!" said Ivan Kisseloff. "The thermometer has dropped to minus eighteen Centigrade."

Dernghuiz' teeth were chattering, and the poor fellow was shivering.

Pickerreek took pity on his pupil. He used his hatchet to cut down some dwarf birches, and a few branches from the emaciated fir trees that grew here and there, heaped them up and set them alight. Soon, the soothing heat of an ardent fire warmed the voyagers up and loosened their limbs. Madame Valdy, well wrapped-up in her furs and blankets, was able to go to sleep and recover the strength exhausted by her long night in the air. There was no shortage of fuel; Cardounet and

Pickerreek renewed it sever aims, and everyone waited philosophically, without experiencing too much suffering, for the return of daylight.

Finally, dawn appeared, crimson and tremulous. Will Tooke climbed a rise in the ground and inspected the points of the horizon with a naval telescope, but he could not see any ship.

Oh! he thought. *Can it be that my friend Captain Knox hasn't kept his word? This isn't a matter of haggling over the price of a consignment of cotton or rum—a commercial transaction that often transforms an honest man into an utter rogue. Here, science is at stake, and for that, a compatriot of Franklin, Fulton, Morse and Maury ought to keep his promises, even making sacrifices if need be. Knox, my friend, if you let me down, the New York* Tribune *will publish a letter from me in a few days' time that will publicize your conduct and reap you the opprobrium of the United States. And then, by all the devils in Hell, you'll have to reckon with me!*

Thee reflections calmed Will Tooke down slightly, but left him in a bad mood, which, but for the presence of Madame Valdy, would have burst out violently.

"Don't worry," Valdy said to him. "Your friend's doubtless waiting for us impatiently. We'll go look for him, and if he's cruising in these waters, we'll find him."

Immediately, the voyagers took their places aboard the *Céleste*, which rose up to an altitude between five and six hundred meters and moved through the air, following the contours of Salisbury Island. After a quarter of an hour, Pickerreek made out a schooner sheltered in the waters of a spacious haven, anchored some two cables from the shore. The starry flag of the Unites States was flying from the mizzen mast, flapping in the wind.

"It's the *Lincoln*! It's Captain Knox!" cried Will Tooke, joyfully.

The aeronef circled for a few moments and descended on to a bank bordered by small ice-floes. The American sailors who watched the aerial maneuver from their vessel uttered frenetic hurrahs, and saluted the valiant explorers with their repeated acclamations. A jolly-boat set off from the ship, came to shore and disembarked Captain Knox, a rather short, stout and sanguine man with the neck of a bull and a firm tread, martial in appearance.

"Good day, my friends, and may the Lord protect you!" shouted the captain of the Lincoln. "Where's my friend Will Tooke? Ah—there you are! Did you get lost in the atmospheric regions? As sure as my name's Sam Knox, I've been waiting for you for a week!"

Will Tooke briefly listed the misadventures that had delayed the voyage, and offered his apologies to the sailor.

"Forgive me," he said, shaking is hand cordially. "Not seeing you at first, I cursed you as a filibuster and a pirate, thinking that you'd failed to keep your promise. Pardon me for the momentary weakness, my friend."

"What? You doubted your old comrade Sam Knox? I forgive you, because of the frankness of your confession, but I'll get my own back. In your honor, there'll be a party today on board the *Lincoln*, and I'll keep you until tomorrow."

"We can't accept your offer."

"Why not?"

"We only have thirty days left to go around the world and we can't lose any more time."

"But damn it, you won't leave without having breakfast with me!"

"We accept," said Madame Valdy, who understood that a further refusal would annoy and disappoint the captain.

"Ah, you give me pleasure, Mistress; I like that sort of talk."

And Captain Knox, raising both hands to his mouth by way of a megaphone, hailed the ship. "Ahoy the *Lincoln!* Dickson, order the cook to get the freshest and most delicate food-supplies out of the hold. We're breakfasting on board. Order a double ration of whisky for the men. Today, we all rejoice!"

The jolly-boat transported the voyagers to the schooner. The sailors, using the leisure time created by the wait, had gone hunting, and there was no shortage of game. After a few minutes of culinary preparation, the cook, with the gravity of a maître-d'hôtel utterly devoted to his noble functions, announced that dinner as served. Naturally, the place of honor as reserved for Madame Valdy. Captain Knox preached by example, as they say; he ate with a hearty appetite, unceasingly encouraging his gusts, and drank like a Templar, but still remained polite; his tongue did not slip once; the libations had no hold over his rude nature.

While the voyagers breakfasted, the bicarbonate of soda, hydrochloric acid, wine-spirit and a spare sail were transported to the *Céleste*. Dickson, the first mate, took responsibility for organizing the transport, adding to it, on his own authority, a basket of fine wines and abundant food-supplies.

"You've read my thoughts, my lad," said Captain Knox. And he added, addressing Will Tooke: "Now you can go as you please. During the month of August, I followed the western coat of the Hudson Sea, and you'll find everything that was kept for you aboard the *Lincoln* at Forts Severn, York and Churchill. As for me, I won't stay here any longer, for the cold's beginning to make itself felt. One of these mornings we'll find ourselves trapped by the ice of we prolong our stay in these parts. I'll set sail for New York tomorrow."

"That's wise, my dear Knox."

The voyagers returned to shore and made their preparations for the departure.

Chapter X

Although the weather was splendid, and the sun was sending its warmest rays through the atmosphere, the temperature was still rather low, so the *Céleste* only rose up to a low altitude. Valdy headed westwards, in order to remain close to land. They soon lost sight of the *Lincoln*, flying all her flags; Salisbury Island gradually diminished and ended up confused with the waves.

"We're abundantly stocked with food," said Valdy. "It's necessary to travel swiftly. Load up the carbonic acid receptacles and generate all possible pressure."

The order was obeyed, and the aeronef's speed increased. She swiftly crossed the Foxe Channel, Southampton Island and the Roes Welcome Sound separating it from the mainland, and arrived in the territory of the Dominion of Canada, near the mouth of Chesterfield Bay, a profound inlet several hundred kilometers long, strewn with islets. Then the *Céleste* turned sharply southwards, following the step coasts of the Hudson Sea, traversed a rugged and deserted region that was wooded but covered with muddy marshes and bogs. They passed over a few lakes and a large number of fast-flowing streams and rivers, which were roaring as they poured their waters into the sea, but which winter would soon condemn to silence.

They eventually arrived at the mouth of the Missinippi and landed about five hundred meters from Fort Churchill.

During that journey night had fallen, and the arrival of the aeronef passed unnoticed. Our voyagers counted themselves fortunate to escape the curiosity that their passage had excited elsewhere.

"We haven't wasted any time," said Vardy. "Since our departure from Upernavik—which is to say, thirty-six hours ago—we've covered more than six hundred leagues."

"May the Devil take me," added Cardounet, "if a clipper or steamer exists that could do as much."

The travelers, exceedingly tired after staying up so late the previous night, felt in need of rest. They made a hasty evening meal and prepared for sleep. Pickerreek, aided by Cardounet and Dernghuiz, set up the sail provided by Captain Knox on the deck in the form of a tent, anchored it solidly, and exclaimed: "Now we have a shelter to ward off the cold.

In any case, as they headed southwards the rigor of the temperature had relaxed and become more tolerable. The thermometer was no longer below three degrees Centigrade.

"In truth," said Ivan Kisseloff, rolling himself up in his blankets, I'd far rather sleep here than accept the hospitality that we'd be offered at Fort Churchill."

"Why's that?" asked Will Tooke.

"Because the people at Fort Churchill are English."

"But what have the English done to you," asked Madame Valdy, "to make you hate them so much?"

"I'll tell you. A few years ago, I went to Constantinople with General Z***, undertaking a mission to the Sultan on behalf of my government. One evening, I was reading the newspapers in a café in the Pera district. On the next table some Englishmen were drinking tea and taking about our expeditions in Central Asia. I couldn't help overhearing the British islanders' conversation, and I never heard such gross boasting as that of a midshipman, who said with an imperturbable aplomb:

"'Russia, that barbaric nation, is trying to threaten our English possessions in Asia and frighten us, but we know how to put an end to its invasions and ambitions. Those Kalmuks and Cossacks, villainous bogey-men who swagger so boldly, melt in the sun like the lard they eat when the English stand firm against them. A single one of us can make ten of them retreat.'

"My patriotism rebelled. 'Monsieur,' I cried, 'I understand English and I have the honor of informing you in that

147

language that you're an insolent fellow and that one Russian, not ten, will reckon with your insults.'

"We exchanged cards. My adversary's name was George Simpson. The next day, we fought, and I received a formidable sword-thrust in the chest that put my life in danger and confined me to bed for six months."

"Damn," said Pickerreek. "That's enough to annoy anyone, Monsieur le Comte, and I understand now why you detest the English."

"When I was back on my feet," Ivan Kisseloff continued, "I enquired about my adversary, intending to challenge him again. I was told that he'd left for the China Seas. He'll doubtless come back some day, and the day when I hear of his arrival will be a fine one for me; the swords will flash in the sun again and I sense that hard and vengeance will guide my arm."

"We are bidden to forget insults and forgive offences," said Madame Valdy.

"Oh, Madame, I'm familiar with fine maxims on that subject, but I'm not perfect enough to put them into practice. Resentment and anger are poor counselors—so be it! Personally, I never turn the left cheek when I've been slapped on the right. Such principles make saints, but not men of action and courage.

"Bravo, Monsieur le Comte!" cried Pickerreek. "It's as if we were to say to the Prussians: 'You've taken Alsace and Lorraine off us; now take Lille and Dunkerque, if you please.' Our rancor will transform a generation of weaklings into resolute men."

Madame Valdy understood that the debate, led on to such terrain, would become thorny, and that the best of reasons would not convince her interlocutors. She held her tongue. Everyone went to sleep.

Early the following day, the tenth of September, the voyagers went to Fort Churchill to reclaim the deposit of bicarbonate of soda and hydrochloric acid left by Captain Knox.

Fort Churchill, one of the principal outposts of the Hudson Bay Company, is not, as its title of fort implies, a redoubt with bastions, towers, bunkers, drawbridges and so on; it is a commercial depot built of wood, surrounded by a pine fence; it is a caravanserai where provisions, weapons, pelts and all kinds of hunting apparatus are stored. The fort is situated at the mouth of the Missinippi or Churchill, a great river that flows into the Hudson Sea after a course of 1,450 kilometers.

The voyagers only encountered one principal factor, three secondary agents and twenty trappers, mostly French-Canadians, who still retained in the depths of their heart a reminiscence of the mother country, and only spoke French. These valiant hunters were astonished to receive such an un-expected visit, but their astonishment was redoubled when they discovered what kind of locomotion the strangers were employing. They transported the goods left by the *Lincoln* themselves, and examined the *Céleste* attentively.

A few Athaspaca and Knistinaux Indians also came to satisfy their curiosity. One of them, a chief, expressing himself in perfect English, asked for explanations that were hastily given to him. Then he became very pensive and exclaimed: "Nothing is impossible for the palefaces! The palefaces are masters of the earth; soon they will be masters of the heavens!"

Valdy ordered the departure. The aeronef took off, de-scribed a few coquettish circles as if to allow itself to be ad-mired, and headed southwards. Two hours later, it arrived at Fort York.

Once similar to Fort Churchill and all the outposts of the Hudson Bay Company disseminated over its vast territory, Fort York has acquired a capital importance in those icy re-gions, thanks to its location at the estuary formed by the mouths of the rivers Nelson and Hull. Today, it is a small town, the principal port of embarkation, depot and general warehouse of the hunting-grounds, the center in which the chief factors met. A director, delegated by the "proprietors"—more accurately, shareholders—resides there for most of the year. The town is built of wood and its appearance is dreary.

The travelers, as it is becoming tedious to repeat, were received with the greatest cordiality. The director invited them to breakfast. At table, they chatted for a long time. Valdy, Will Tooke and Kisseloff, eager to educate themselves, asked a host of questions about the organization of the powerful Hudson Bay Company.

"Its importance had declined considerably," the director told them, "for the number of furred animals has diminished, and it's now necessary to track then, at the cost of great fatigue, into the Barrens—the deserts of the North. Once, the company was sovereign, but in 1870 a parliamentary bill confiscated its immense territory to combine it with the Dominion of Canada, which has taken over its trading-posts with the surrounding land while leaving it a monopoly on the fur trade, with tax-exemptions."

"That's not too bad a share, all the same," Will Tooke interjected.

The director did not entirely agree with this opinion, but parliament had spoken and it was necessary to obey.

The Hudson Bay Company, like the East India Company, is evidence of the prodigies that can be accomplished by the spirit of well-organized association and perseverance. Businessmen, people hostile to adventure, have conquered and dominated two immense countries, have implanted civilization in the midst of barbarity, have undertaken gigantic construction projects, transformed peoples, cultivated land and imposed law. They have done better than that, certain English historians add: they have made a great deal of money!

All's well that ends well.

It was ten o'clock in the morning when the *Céleste* left Fort York. Valdy, sufficiently restocked, decided to head directly for the United States without calling at Fort Severn.

During the two to three days that followed, few incidents marked the progress of the aeronef, but in order not to lose track of it we shall temporarily consult the on-board log, filled in very evening with the most scrupulous exactitude by the captain.

10 September.

On leaving Fort York, we steered slightly westwards. As we went further south the temperature became milder and the country lost its grim aspect. To our right, the Nelson was visible, speckled with countless islets, appearing to us as a silver ribbon. The country over which we were passing was marshy and full of lakes. At midday, the progress of the aeronef was slowed by a southerly wind blowing rather violently. I sought a calmer layer of air and encountered one at an altitude of 1,400 meters. Then we advanced rapidly. At about two o'clock I was obliged to climb to two thousand meters. I opened the communication tap and let a little air into the interior of the balloon, which, without that precaution, was at risk of explosion, or at least ripping the tanned hides that are our safeguard. We discovered the great Lake Winnipeg. The wind dropped and we were able to fly at a height of eight hundred meters. Cardounet operated the levers of the pneumatic machine and extracted the air. We saw two steamboats on the lake. The country is becoming animated; we can make out flocks of sheep, farms and cultivated fields.

Joyful exclamations are escaping our lips. In addition to Lake Winnipeg we could see, with the aid of binoculars, a host of other lakes and lagoons, among which Will Tooke cited Lesser Winnipeg, Manitoba, the Lake of Woods, or Rain, etc. Now we're above the confluence of the Assiniboine and the Red River. The *Céleste* is landing two cables from Fort Garry.

11 September

‹At Fort Garry we have been the object of a sometimes-inconvenient but always-benevolent curiosity. Cardounet pointed me out to the colonists of the Red River as the inventor of the aeronef; his Gascon verve mingled exotic amplifications with the praise he lavished on me, and I could foresee a moment when the colonists would carry me in triumph. My modesty, put to a rude proof, as saved by the arrival of the factor-in-chief, who offered us amicable hospitality.

Fort Garry is already a small town; its location assures it a prosperous future; few places are better and more intelligently cultivated than its surroundings. Since 1869, the Red River colony has been part of the Confederation of Canada under the name of the province of Manitoba, and I am assured that the province has 60,000 inhabitants, including 40,000 semi-civilized Indians.

Before leaving Fort Garry we visited the Red River Academy, a school where the children of the Hudson Bay Company's agents are educated gratuitously. We were truly surprised by the marvelous organization of that educational establishment and the practical skills that are taught there. Whatever Monsieur Kisseloff thinks, the English have good in them, and they know that education is the base on which modern societies ought to rest.

We said adieu to our friends of 11 September and embarked. We were still heading southwards, following the contours of the Red River. Will Tooke showed me an assemblage of houses on the left bank of the river: Pembina, an outpost of the American Fur Company. Will Tooke saluted his fatherland with a formidable hurrah.

Our altitude was no more than five or six hundred meters; with our binoculars we could distinguish the country perfectly. To our right, the immense plains of Dakota unfolded; to our left, those of Minnesota. At about two o'clock in the afternoon we crossed the Sheyenne, a tributary of the Red River and arrived in Fort Abercrombie, where we renewed our provisions of bicarbonate of soda and hydrochloric acid.

After leaving Fort Abercrombie the *Céleste* veered south-eastwards and we began traversing a region of prairies. The savannah seemed infinite; it was a yellow sea, for summer had desiccated the grass. A fine and icy rain began to trouble our voyage but the clouds were quite low and we were easily able to rise above them. We then enjoyed a magnificent spectacle. While it was raining on the ground, the sun was shining its dazzling radiance on us; the azure of the sky contrasted with the white tint of the clouds; the latter where rolling over one another, colliding, becoming confused, taking on the most bizarre forms and sinking beneath the current of air created by the rapid progress of the aeronef. Sometimes, one might think that we were the nucleus of a comet drawing a gigantic tail of vapors in our wake.

While we were admiring the curious phenomenon to which we were the only witnesses, we heard a detonation and a sharp hissing sound. A tanned skin had burst and the balloon was filling with air.

"Great God!" cried Madame Valdy, "We're doomed!"

"Alert! Alert!" cried Kisseloff, hastening the movement of the piston—and we were saved.

"Don't be frightened," I said, in my turn. "Nothing is compromised."

In fact, I knew that the *Céleste*, losing its specific lightness, would not be as manageable, but the wings, flapping forcefully, maintained it, and the fall was accomplished in a slow glide. We passed through the cloud layer and I had time to select a place to land. Without exaggerating my assertions, I believed that we covered a distance of ten kilometers before touching down.

We found ourselves on the plateaus designated by geographers as the Missouri Hills. To one side us we saw a Redskin wigwam—Sioux, I think.

"A bad neighborhood," sad Will Tooke.

The Indians, frightened, abandoned their bison-hide huts, but we soon saw them again. They had put on their warrior dress—bizarre costumes if ever there were any. Some had deerskins over cotton shorts, and their heads were coifed with European hats; others wore trousers worn through in the seat; still others were dressed in old garments whose reek was detectable a league away; they all had necks, ears arms and hair overloaded with shells, bones and animal teeth; they all had tattooed faces, and the tattoos gave them a horrible appearance. The sachems lined up, brandishing their rifles and intoning a guttural chant. The warriors came next, then the squaws and the papooses. And they were all shouting, barking and hooting in the most discordant fashion. We have never heard such a frightful cacophony.

Pickerreek installed a spare skin, but it was impossible to leave before having evacuated the interior of the balloon—and operation that required quite a long time and thus favored the Indians' hostile disposition.

Will Tooke made a heroic resolution. He advanced on his own toward the Redskins, majestically unfolded a piece of crumpled paper and shouted three times: "A'hou!"—a term of greeting employed by the savage sons of the prairie. The latter ceased their singing and appeared to confer. Will Took, impassive, solemn and serious, continued moving forward and pronounced the following speech:

"I have come on behalf of the great Father who is in Washington, to renew the treaties of amity that have always linked the great nation of the Sioux to the white men. We are not here to dispute you hunting and your lands; we bring you peace…and gifts."

The last word had a magical effect on the three chiefs who spoke a little English. They persuaded the Indians to cease their shouting and threats, and advanced quite boldly. One of them shook Will Tooke's hand and said:

"The Sioux are poor, but their poverty does not make them jealous of the palefaces. The Great Spirit has created the Sioux to hunt the buffalo, not to herd cattle and work the earth. Let the white men respect our rights and our customs, and we shall be their friends and accept what it pleases them to offer us."

"I can give you powder and firewater," Will Tooke replied. "In small quantities, it's true, for I have distributed many provisions on my journey, but I will come back, and you will be satisfied with my liberality."

"The scalps will remain in our houses so long as you are among us."

Will Tooke knew his interlocutors and took advantage of their weakness. He gave them about a pound of gunpowder and two bottles of cognac.

The rest of us did not waste any time. Knowing, by hearsay, the extreme fickleness of Indians, faring that they might mistake the *Céleste* for an engine of destruction, we worked the levers of the vacuum pumps frantically. In less than half an hour the evacuation was complete.

The Redskins began to come nearer and examine the aeronef suspiciously. Some raised their voices in a bellicose tone that left no doubt as to their hostile intentions. We were ready to defend our lives fervently, but we would certainly have succumbed, for we could not repel and vanquish more than three hundred enemies. Finally, Will Tooke, still calm and impassive, took his place by our side. The *Céleste* flapped its wings and took flight...

Never has amazement been as emphatic as among those Indians. Their surprise was translated into shrill cries that reached our ears, and we saw them running away in all directions, showing signs of extreme terror.

Glad to have escaped the danger that threatened us, we felt an inexpressible mental wellbeing. The landscapes of the rich country that unfurled before our eyes appeared more cheerful and more beautiful to us. Finally, just as dusk was invading the limits of the horizon, we landed near Fort Pierre Chouteau on the Missouri. The commandant of the fort came to meet us and bid us welcome.

12 September.

After a night devoted to sleep, we left early in the morning, for I had resolved to arrive in Denver in the evening, and the distance was long. We rapidly crossed a country of plains very similar to the one we had crossed the previous day. The weather was fine, the breeze gentle, and we rarely exceeded an altitude of five hundred meters. Suddenly, between the Mankizitah and the Nebraska, two tributaries of the Missouri, we distinguished a moving black mass. They were bison. Their calls reached us. The herd was numerous and went by like an avalanche. Will Tooke wanted to stop for a while to hunt the great animals of the savannah, but as the hunt would

155

have brought us no profit and would have slowed us down I refused to land.

"It was after midday when we arrived at Fort Laramie. We were received by a captain and several soldiers, who seemed to us to be typical of the warrior-laborer imagined by Maréchal Bugeaud,[39] for since the Sioux, the Arikaras, the Mandans, the Cheyenne and other Indian populations have been driven back and confined, excursions have become less dangerous and travelers no longer need the same protection, so the soldiers have abandoned the rifle and the Bowie knife for the spade and the plough. Fort Laramie is a large village on the railway that is to extend into the state of Montana.

After having eaten a light meal and restocked our supplies, we resumed our aerial route. By rising up between one thousand and five thousand meters, we were able to make out the Rocky Mountains distinctly. Several of their peaks are covered in snow and their profiles stand out against the blue sky like motionless cumulus clouds.

Among the noises transmitted to us from the ground, our ears had only perceived thus far that of the breeze passing through the forests and those of waterfalls and rapids. Then we heard the whistle of a locomotive. That shrill note disturbed us and excited us. It is that of civilization appearing after having vanquished harsh nature and immense deserts; it is progress manifesting itself where barbarity once reigned!

We passed over Cheyenne City, the capital of Wyoming, and penetrated into Colorado, flying in a straight line as far as

---

[39] Thomas Robert Buegaud, Marquis de la Piconnerie, Duc d'Isly (1784-1849) distinguished himself in the Napoleonic Wars and resumed his military career after the July Revolution of 1830, undertaking a successful campaign in Algeria which led to the defeat and capture of Abd-el-Kader. A diehard opponent of democracy, he took a strong interest in the political organization of the colony, giving rise to the opinion cited above—a theory of colonial defence probably best represented by the South African Boers..

forty degrees north latitude. After a journey of three hours, we perceived a multitude uttering mighty hurrahs when the aeronef described a descending spiral and came to land on the plain.

We have reached Denver.

Chapter XI

The presence of the crowd was easily explicable. Fort Laramie is linked to the capital of Colorado by an railway line. After the departure of the aeronef, the commandant of the fort had hastened to send a dispatch the Denver. Will Tooke, who was originally, as we have said, from Kansas, one of the states bordering Colorado, had friends and acquaintances in the city. In America, in the Far west, people are neighbors when they live a hundred or two hundred kilometers apart. Furthermore, the railways have suppressed the desert between Kansas and Colorado. Will Tooke's relationships were quite natural, and we must confess that the greater part of the ovation that greeted the voyagers was reserved for him. The Americans were proud of having a compatriot in the first aerial vessel that was furrowing the atmosphere. However, after the initial moment of enthusiasm, they saluted Will Tooke's companions with their joyful cheers and prepared a triumphal reception for them.

Denver, "the city of the plains," whose present population is 15,500, is of recent foundation; in 1859 it did not exist. A few gold prospectors in quest of placers, having panned the sands of the Cherry Creek River, a small tributary of the South Platte River, found traces of the precious metal there. The news spread and squatters, backwoodsmen, colonists and adventurers hastened to the case. For several years, Denver was a true bandits' lair. Theft, murder, gambling, drunkenness and pillage were displayed there with impunity.

Gradually, mores improved, thanks to lynch law, often put into practice, to the influence of Governor William Gilpin, to the vigilance of Sheriff Robert Wilson and the presence of women who had followed their husbands into that Inferno and who organized meetings in which the slightest indecency was severely judged. Now Denver is one of the most elegant cities of the New World; it has a bank, a theater, schools, churches and department stores; it is the center of a very important market and linked to the Central Pacific Railway by two branches, one to Julesburg in Nebraska, the other to Cheyenne City in Wyoming.

The voyagers accepted the hospitality of one of Will Tooke's friends, named Charles Weston. Weston was entirely typical of the hardy pioneers who abound in the Far West. By turns a squatter, soldier, colonists and gold prospector, he had been poorer than Job, but today he was at the head of one of the largest banks in the country. His energetic personality, his indomitable courage and his adventurous character had triumphed in the incessant struggle that he had dared to sustain against dangers, fatigues, frustrations, disillusionments and harsh nature.

"I'm not the only one who has succeeded," he said, modestly. "At twenty, all Americans have the appetite of an ant, the strength of a mule and the courage of a lion. With those qualities, one makes one's way—provided that one doesn't lose one's hide in the process."

"The country is rich," Madame Valdy put in, "and I think that the strong and the valiant succeeded in easily vanquishing a nature that is not as ingrate as you seem to affirm."

"Ah, Mistress," replied Charles Weston, "the illusion is beautiful and the spectacle grandiose when one admires our vast plains from an altitude of several hundred meters, but their aspect changes when one travels them on foot. I know that Fenimore Cooper, one of the glories of young America, has embellished the immense solitudes with all the prestige of his imagination, but novelists distort the truth. The savannah is dismal; as soon as one goes into the ocean of verdure one 'loses sight of the land'—which is to say that one no longer perceives distant hills, trees, bushes and depressions in the ground; one is gripped by an ennui and an extreme discouragement. After several days' march, there's still the same silence and the same desolate uniformity. No trace of civilization. Life is only manifest in the presence of wolves, rattlesnakes, crows and prairie-dogs. Mirages are continually reproduced, and when the vision vanishes, the vast solitude resumes a more desolate aspect. And I won't mention the storms and the inconstancy of the temperature! Sometimes there's a change of thirty degrees. Just as you're admiring the mildness of the climate, the wind blows impetuously from the northwest, snow falls, the earth freezes. Woe betide the belated traveler then!"

"Will the savannahs never be colonized, then?" asked Madame Valdy.

"I don't say that at all, Mistress, but it will take time. Colonists still run into a host of inconveniences—mainly the ardor of the sun and the locusts—but when we've developed good irrigation systems and planted trees the climatic conditions will change and colonization will take possession of the steppes. We're only the advance guard of workers destined to transform this country radically. Our grandchildren will finish the work that we've begun."

Throughout the evening of the twelfth of September there was a festival in Denver. The houses were decked with flags, the shops closed. A splendid dinner was served at Charles Weston's house. Pickerreek, Cardounet and Dernghuiz soon abandoned the table. Arms linked, the three comrades roamed the streets of the city of the plains. It was noticeable, however, that they were slightly tipsy and that the mutual support they lent one another was necessary. What do you expect? No one in this world is perfect—and the wines of France have such an agreeable taste and perfume! When far away, it is the homeland in a glass.

"In foreign lands," said Pickerreek, "one ought to drink out of patriotism and devotion; that's all I know!"

The Tatar was singing and stamping his feet; one more mouthful and he would have been dancing.

"Dignity, damn it!" Cardounet said to him. "It's up to us to represent France and Russia!"

Dernghuiz did not understand, but he ceased fidgeting; his attention was caught by the presence of a compact crowd advancing in a disorderly manner. A few men were carrying banners bearing the most pompous and bizarre inscriptions:

Denver City is more glorious than St. Louis, Chicago, Cincinnati and New York; it welcomes the Christopher Columbus of aviation.

The king of the birds is here. Hurrah for Marcel Valdy! Flight is property.[40]

Etc., etc.

A few honorable businessmen profited from the opportunity to display colossal advertisements. T. Markett offered brown sugar at a cheaper price than all his competitors in the noble corporation of grocers. Hubson guaranteed the excellent quality of his whisky. One was practically giving away his merchandise. Another was boasting about a universal panacea that he claimed to have discovered—etc., etc.

Commerce, industry, fame, fine arts, politics and blackmail all march in step in America,

The crowd was going to Charles Weston's house to acclaim the voyagers of the *Céleste*. The street on which the banker lived was blocked and a band was playing, to the great joy of the spectators, what were supposed to be French national tunes: *Partant pour la Syrie, Clair de Lune*, the *Marseillaise, Marlborough s'en va-t-en guerre, Roi Dagobert, La Fille de Madame Angot*. Every piece had the honor of an encore. Valdy was obliged to show himself on the balcony several times. Will Tooke harangued the multitude, and was then followed by four or five orators who spoke at length about the merits of the astonishing new invention.

The final orator concluded his speech thus:

"France and America once fought for independence on the same battlefields. If we're now the foremost nation in the world, it's to the generous nation of Old Europe that we owe

---

[40] An untranslatable joke: the French *vol* [flight] also means "theft," so this unlikely slogan reverses Proudhon's famous dictum as well as celebrating the acquisition of a new prerogative.

161

it; so, I declare to you loudly that Valdy, the French Fulton, is a considerable man. He and his valiant companions are worthy of being Yankees..."

Nothing was more appropriate to flatter the crowd than that final sentence; there was an outburst of shouting, cheering and enthusiastic acclamations. Pickerreek, Cardounet and Dernghuiz, recognized in the midst of the crowd, were hoisted on to an artistically-decorated cart and paraded through the streets of Denver to the sound of the band. Numerous halts were made at drinking dens. Once, Pickerreek took off his hat to salute the spectators; one of them, misunderstanding the mariner's intentions, dropped a few dollars into it. His example was immediately followed by others.

"What!" said the worthy Pick, indignantly. "They're offering us money?"

"Take it," said Cardounet. "One never knows what might happen."

The parade continued for more than two hours, and the dollars were still falling!

When Pickerreek, Cardounet and Dernghuiz reappeared at Charles Weston's house, the general animation had calmed down and our three comrades' pockets were overflowing with money. Madame Valdy addressed a few severe reproaches to them regarding their escapade.

"Don't be annoyed, Madame," said Cardounet. "We haven't been wasting our time; we've brought back a nice nest-egg." And he displayed his dollars.

"You've been begging, then?" replied Madame Valdy. "That's unworthy of you."

"Oh, no. People gave it; we accepted it."

"Your exhibition has been well rewarded. I don't approve."

"That's as may be, Madame, but everything is paid for in this world. That's no reason to speak to us like an angry quartermaster. Our excursion was brief and fruitful, damn it! There must be many unfortunates in this land, even though it's filled with gold. I've heard it said that a certain Midas was never as unfortunate as when Jesus or Jupiter—I don't know which—gave him the power to turn everything he touched into gold."

"What does that prove?"

"It proves, Madame, that you should put away your reproaches, take our money and distribute it to the poor of Denver. What do you think of my idea, eh, Pick?"

"Of course! What would I do with so much money? You're educated, and you talk like a book."

Two tears gleamed in the corners of Madame Valdy's eyes. She was touched by that simple generosity, devoid of ostentation. The young woman took the callused hands of the two mariners and shook them effusively. "Forgive me, my good friends," she said to them.

"Forgive you?" said Pickerreek. "What for, Madame? We're the ones who are vagabonds who've drunk a little more than regulations specify—but we'll recover from it."

"It's still for Dernghuiz' education," added Cardounet. "That's our excuse."

"Well," Madame Valdy continued, smiling, "I congratulate your pupil on having such masters. Go on, you bad lots—the poor will bless you tomorrow. Drinking while doing good…I'll clink glasses with you."

Pickerreek, Cardounet and Dernghuiz emptied their pockets; they had 1,008 dollars—a little over five thousand francs. Madame Valdy took the money and gave it to the sheriff, asking him to use it for the relief of the poor.

"There's not much poverty here, properly speaking," the lawman replied, "and, with your permission, I'll give the money to a widow, the mother of three children, whose husband was killed recently by the Indians. She'll be able to set up a little business and thus provide for her needs."

"Act as you think best, Monsieur Sheriff—you have *carte blanche*."

The sheriff called a policeman and whispered in his ear. A few minutes later, a woman, still young and beautiful, but afflicted by grief and clad in mourning, came into Charles

Weston's sumptuous drawing room, escorted by the policeman.

"Victoria Lewis," the sheriff said, "thank the foreign voyagers; they heard about the misfortune you've suffered and wanted to help you. Here's 1,008 dollars; they're for you."

"Oh, Mistress!" said the young woman, falling at Madame Valdy's feet and kissing the hem of her dress. Then she burst into sobs.

"Here are your three benefactors," Madame Valdy replied, pointing to Pickerreek, Cardounet and Dernghuiz, who were standing as stiff and motionless as soldiers on parade.

"Oh, thank you, thank you for my children!" And Victoria Lewis took the hands of the three men in turn, raised hem to her lips and thanked them in tones of the most touching gratitude. Then she left.

"Well!" exclaimed Pickerreek. "Doing good does you good! But it stirs you up—I thought I was going to start crying, leaking like an old pontoon, and I nearly swallowed my plug. My heart's all confused."

"Madame Valdy will permit us to drink a glass of Bordeaux to put us right—isn't that so, Madame?" asked Cardounet.

"Go on, my brave incorrigibles," replied Madame Valdy, laughing. "You'll make me believe that wine makes men better."

Cardounet sang: "The wicked are drinkers of water/The deluge makes that clear."

The three friends headed for the servants' parlor. When they came back, their faces were colored by a hint of scarlet and their eyes were shining like carbuncles. In the New World, however, the laws of decorum never condemn a small gesture well judged and well supported, so the two mariners and the Tatar became the focus of attention. Men shook their hands and women addressed their most gracious smiles to them; in brief, they became the veritable social lions of the soirée for a while.

Meanwhile, Valdy wanted to fill the *Céleste*'s hull with hydrogen gas again. The director of the local gas plant placed himself at his disposal, but he could only furnish hydrogen bicarbonate or ordinary lighting-gas, and that gas, because of its weight—about 650 grams per cubic meter—reduced the ascensional force by more than half.

There was no possibility of manufacturing pure hydrogen by means of the chemical method used in laboratories—which is to say, by the action of sulfuric acid on water and iron or zinc—because the process requires considerable preparation and would take too long. Valdy remembered the method employed by Giffard when that clever engineer inflated his gigantic captive balloon at the Exposition Universelle of 1867. We shall borrow from Louis Figuier the scientific description of that preparation, which has the merit of being short and clear:

"The method employed by Monsieur Giffard for the preparation of hydrogen gas by means of the decomposition of water depends partly on known principles and partly on new equipment. It consists of facilitating out the decomposition of water vapor by coal, first driving a stream of water vapor over a fire of incandescent coke, which produces carbonated hydrogen and carbon oxide by reacting with the red-hot coal. To convert the carbonated hydrogen into pure hydrogen and the carbon oxide into carbonic acid, a further steam of water vapor is introduced at the other extremity of the furnace. That vapor produces pure hydrogen and carbonic acid when it reacts, by virtue of its oxygen, with the two gases filling the interior of the furnace.

"That mixture of carbonic acid and hydrogen is then directed through a depurator full of chalk, similar to the ones used in gas plants. The hydrogen in separated from the carbonic acid, with the result that pure hydrogen is obtained, which is directed into the interior of the balloon as it soon as it emerges from the chalk depurator."

By a fortunate hazard, the *Céleste* had landed a short distance away from the gas plant; it was only necessary to organize a metal conduit. Several men worked on that operation while the voyagers retired to the apartments provided for them.

Early the next morning, Valdy and Will Tooke proceeded with the manufacture of the hydrogen gas. By seven o'clock, the balloon was full.

It only remained to depart, but an obstacle that the voyagers had not taken into consideration barred the route to the west. The Rocky Mountains stood before them, their snowy summits reaching an altitude of between three and four thousand meters. It was certainly possible to pass over them, but it would be necessary to sacrifice some of the gas enclosed in the hull, because its tension risked causing an explosion.

Not far from Denver, the Rocky Mountains form a massif that radiates in transversal chains in all direction. That geological disposition has created profoundly sunken valleys knows as "parks," of which the principle ones are North Park, enclosing the sources of the Nebraska; Middle Park, in which the sources of the Colorado river and Grand River are situated; and South Park, in which the source of the Arkansas is found.

The gigantic mass of mountains contains a few passes, but they are only narrow paths solely accessible on foot, similar to the almost impracticable gorges in the Pyrenees known as "ports" and in the Alps as "cols." After an attentive study of the map and taking advice, Valdy decided to go a little way southwards in order to cross Middle Park at the southern extremity of North Park. He was sure of finding a depression there that would not oblige him to go up too high. If they encountered a peak of a certain height, they could go around it.

Charles Weston joined the crew. Business affairs, he claimed, were summoning him to Salt Lake City, and since the opportunity had presented itself, he would go to the Mormon capital by the aerial route instead of traveling on the railway. We think he wanted to try out the new means of locomotion. At any rate, we ought to applaud the banker's boldness. It was not in vain that Toussenel has made the vulture—a high-flying bird—the emblem of financiers!

Finally, the *Céleste* took off. All Denver had flocked to the place where the ascension was to take place. Cheers, hurrahs and enthusiastic acclamations escaped every throat. A thousand confused cries saluted the voyagers. In their delight, the American envied the fate of those first pioneers of the air, who were launching themselves so courageously into the unknown.

Chapter XII

The aeronef rose up to 2,500 meters. From that height, Valdy could easily study the topography of the country and take account of the difficulties presented by the elevation of the immense aggregation of mountains. The day of the thirteenth of September promised to be magnificent; the sun was shining in the blue sky; red-tinted bands of stratus cloud were skimming the prairies, stretching, thinning, separating, becoming transparent and, like the dew that had created them, evaporating as soon as the atmosphere warmed up. Charles Weston was wonderstruck; his American impassivity could not resist the beauty and magnificence of the spectacle.

They advanced for an hour in a southerly direction, and then Valdy set a course directly westwards and went up into the Rocky Mountains. All the crests were covered in snow and glaciers. The flanks of the chain were split in places by profound indentations, and the eye could no longer distinguish the depths of the abysses. Wild and desolate nature reclaimed its eternal rights at that altitude. Without the presence of the pines, larches and maples growing in the parks, the waterfalls roaring in the obscure gorges and the vultures flying in search of prey, they might have thought that they were contemplating a bleak lunar landscape.

The *Céleste* followed the mountainous sinuosities and fortunately reached the western depressions that inclined at a gentle slope, forming the eastern plateau of Utah and comprising the basins of the streams giving birth to the Colorado River. The aeronef descended to within five hundred meters of the ground, veered slightly northwards and made rapid headway, almost directly along the fortieth degree of north latitude, as far as the Wahsatch Mountains, and important ramification of the Rockies. The Wahsatch Mountains have an elevation varying between two and three thousand meters above sea level, but being situated on a plateau that is already elevated to between twelve hundred and fifteen hundred meters, their height, properly speaking, from base to summit is rather restricted, and the *Céleste* passed over them effortlessly. Soon afterwards they passed over the New Jerusalem, skirted the Great Salt Lake and arrived in Ogden.

Ogden is a principal station of the Pacific Railway. The voyagers were very surprised by the lack of enthusiasm of the inhabitants. Never in their long and painful peregrinations had they encountered such a glacial welcome. Save for a few old men and a few women, no one came to meet them.

"What's happening, then?" asked Charles Weston and Will Tooke. "Have the Indians devastated the country. Has an epidemic descended upon it?"

"No," replied an old woman. "Our people have gone to a revival held for several days by the venerable Mary Silver,[41] an eloquent preacher from the east, over there behind the hill you can see about a mile away."

Charles Weston explained what "revival" meant. "It is," he said, "a sequence of sermons made in the open air by ministers of different sects, to maintain the fervor of the faithful and convert to impious. These assemblies, veritable religious meetings, usually last several days, sometimes weeks."

"Well," said Cardounet, "I wouldn't be sorry to see that assembly close up and see whether the Reverend Mary Silver preaches as well as the curé of my village, Will you permit me to go as far as the revival, Captain?"

"As you wish," said Valdy.

"Are you coming, Pick?"

---

[41] There was a peripatetic evangelist named Reverend Mary E. Silver, or "Mother Silver," active in the mid-West in the late 19th century, but she would have been a teenager in 1875 and Brown's "Mary Silver" is a man. The selection of the name might be a coincidence—an odd one, if so—but if the real Mary Silver began her career as a child (not unknown for American tent preachers) Brown might have picked up the name from an oblique reference and misinterpreted it.

"Of course," replied the Dunkerquois, who never refused his comrade anything.

The two mariners headed toward the place indicated by the woman. From the top of the hill they witnessed one of the strangest and least edifying of spectacles. A vast encampment, swarming pell-mell with carts, horses, people, cattle and sheep was established in the valley. Large canvas tents were set up, with pennants covered in Biblical quotations floating above them. Fires, intended for cooking rather than sacrifices, spread clouds of acrid smoke lightly perfumed with the odor of fat. Women were busy with household duties; men were lying down on the withered grass, playing games, smoking or praying devotedly. The audience was very mixed; there were white men, black men, Redskins and half-breeds. In the middle of that veritable fairground, on an unhitched cart, the venerable Mary Silver could be seen. His precious person was protected from the sun's rays by one of those gigantic red parasols that charlatans exhibit in public squares. The preacher, a trifle stiff, bony, tall and angular, was waving his arms frantically, grimacing and howling a speech in which heavenly matters were bizarrely mingled with earthly ones.

Pickerreek and Cardounet drew closer in order to hear the orator's eloquent diatribes.

"I was filled with the spirit of the Lord," he cried, "and I heard a voice from on high saying to me: 'In the name of the God of Abraham, Isaac and Jacob, you shall take the word of truth into the West, into the West full of miscreants, over which Satan is extending his hooked claws. Another forty days, and Nineveh will be destroyed!' But how to come into the West without resources and without money? The Central Pacific Railway sells tickets at an exorbitant price. May the Lord confound the entrepreneurs of that infernal work, as once he confounded the arrogance of the Philistines…until the day when they lower their tariffs!

"Then the Almighty caused me to meet the venerable John MacDarney, a just man, living in the horror of sin and possessing two houses of commerce, one in St. Louis and the

170

other in Cincinnati. My faithful followers, you can buy tools and fabrics from him; I guarantee their quality. He sells at better prices than any other industrial company in the Union and sends his merchandise on payment, with a discount of ten per cent. Other merchants keep your money and the merchandise! I declare to you that John MacDarney is the Good Samaritan, and he said to me: 'Follow your vocation, Mary Silver; flee the delights of our impious cities, condemned to perish like Sodom and Gomorrah. Here's money, go into the Far West and offer the farmers and the gold prospectors excellent precepts and my merchandise...always on payment at a ten per cent discount! And now, Pharisees, buy and be converted!

"Another forty days, and Nineveh will be destroyed! The time is nigh; Azazel will choose the condemned. 'All the nations will assemble before him, and he will separate the some from the others as a shepherd separates the ewes from the rams; he will place the ewes to his right and the rams to his left.' That is what the voice of the apostle Matthew tells you by way of mine. And I..."

The preacher stopped suddenly. There was a great stir in the assembly, and no one was listening any longer. Someone had announced the arrival of the *Céleste*, and that news, spread by word of mouth, excite a murmur and a tumult that drowned out the voice of the orator. The latter wanted to know the cause of the unexpected disturbance, and a revivalist told him what was happening. Then his indignation overflowed.

"What!" he cried. "Instruments of the black demon, you're deserting the Lord's field to satisfy the curiosity that doomed Lot's wife, Dinah and David, and was the cause of Actaeon's transformation into a deer—the curiosity that, on the part of Pandora and our mother Eve, unleashed all the evils that are harassing humankind! I warn you, the Lord will know his own and will abandon you!"

But no one was listening to Mary Silver's tirade; everyone was preparing to decamp, laughing and cheating. That indifference wounded the preacher, and it was angrily that he continued:

"In truth, you're not worth the trouble of a man inspired by the Holy Spirit coming to redeem you. In truth, I tell you this: you're nothing but peasants;[42] in truth..."

He was not given time to finish the threatening speech. A storm of boos greeted the final phrases and a veritable rain of fruit, vegetable stalks and crusts, the debris of the most recent meal, fell upon the orator. The infinite number of projectiles obliged him to flee; then the cart was invaded and tipped over in the blink of an eye, and the faithful fought fiercely over a few rags.

Cardounet and Pickerreek, wanting to protect the poor preacher, threw themselves into the melee and distributed a few rude slaps. Soon they rendered themselves masters of the terrain; the members of the audience, admiring their strength and skill, applauded them warmly. In America, physical strength is always appreciated. Then Cardounet grabbed the big red parasol, closed it and brandished it like a sledgehammer. A negro attempted to steal the glorious trophy from him, but a terrible blow from the handle applied to his head sent him flying.

"Hurrah! Hurrah!" cried the crowd.

"Here, brave man," said Cardounet, addressing Mary Silver—who, seeing that he had support, was reassured and was calmly readjusting his clothing. "Here's your brolly."

"Keep it, valiant defender of holy causes," the preacher replied. "Keep it in memory of me. May it protect you from the iniquities of this world, as it has protected me from the sun and the rain. Everywhere that hazard takes you, display it as a specimen of the merchandise of John MacDarney, a saint in this vale of tears, who owns two stores, one in St, Louis and the other in Cincinnati, and sends goods on receipt of payment, at a ten per cent discount."

"Understood!" replied Cardounet, and set the umbrella on his shoulder in order to carry it way.

---

[42] *Croquants* [peasants] has a double meaning, also implying a crunchy sweetmeat.

The "Lord's field" was gradually emptying, and the multitude was heading for Ogden. When Pickerreek and Cardounet arrived at the landing-place they saw Valdy, Kisseloff, Will Tooke, Dernghuiz and Charles Weston, armed with carbines and revolvers, standing guard sternly around the aeronef.

"What's wrong?" asked the two mariners. "Are we under threat?"

"No, but the curiosity of these people is intolerable," Valdy replied. "They're overwhelming us, and if we let them do as they liked, they'd devastate the *Céleste* in a matter of minutes."

Indeed, everyone, wanting to see at close range, was pushing and pressing upon his neighbors; there was jostling, shoving and trampling, which often degenerated into brawls. Will Tooke harangued the crowd and obtained a certain reserve on the part of the most eager. A few men of good will put themselves at the disposal of the voyager, planting pickets, extending ropes, and exercising an attentive surveillance. The tide of curiosity-seekers was increasing by the minute; all the old Mormon townships grouped around the New Jerusalem were almost completely abandoned by their inhabitants. In less than three hours, Ogden became the location of an immense assembly. The sheriff distributed arms to several militiamen, established a guard post, and ordered them to make certain of the safety of the voyagers and the aeronef.

"You have nothing to fear from the crowd," the lawman said to Valdy, "but you need to watch out for the Mormons."

"I don't see why they'd be our enemies. Having arrived today, we'll be gone tomorrow without leaving any trace of our passing."

"I'll explain it to you," said the sheriff. You doubtless know the history of the Mormons as well as I do. You know that, having been chased out of Nauvoo, Illinois, where their great prophet Joseph Smith was killed, they emigrated eastwards en masse, led by Brigham Young, the lion of the Lord, president of the twelve apostles, and came to settle on the banks of the Salt Lake. They colonized the region admirably and transformed the desert, but they set up immoral institutions that a social state that wants to persist ought to reject firmly.

"Americans are very tolerant, but they never suffer the violation of the fundamental laws of the nation. Persecution is of no account when it's a matter of combating fanatical sects, so they were attacked morally and physically—morally by sending books, newspapers and schoolteachers, physically by constructing roads and railroads, putting them in daily contact with the civilization they rejected and from which they'd voluntarily separated themselves.

"When the Central Pacific Railway was built, the Mormons knew full well that they were threatened by an invasion of *gentiles*, as they call us disdainfully; they fulminated against the work of progress, and if they'd been strong enough, the whistle of a locomotive would never have been heard in the territory of Utah. But railways can't climb mountains and drive, without a goal, into deserts, and the Latter Day Saints thought they'd found a remote corner of the earth where nothing could reach them. The sight of your marvelous apparatus will dispel their last illusions. Aerial navigation suppresses distance and effaces difficult configurations of the ground. Do you understand, now, why the Mormons will be hostile to you?"

Valdy thanked the sheriff and promised to be vigilant.

Between Ogden and the New Jerusalem, extra trains were organized. For the Central Pacific Railway Company, it was an excellent opportunity to make money by satisfying the general curiosity. The engineers, mechanics and stokers—in sum, all the railway personnel—came to visit the aeronef and compliment Valdy. One chief engineer, William Reading, examined the *Céleste* at length, praising its skillful construction, but seemed astonished when its extraordinary speed was mentioned.

"I doubt," he said, "that you can travel faster than an express train traveling at thirty miles an hour."

174

"We can go much faster than an express train," replied Will Tooke.

"That's almost impossible."

"Well, follow us tomorrow."

"Where are you going?"

"To Unionville, in the state of Nevada."

"I'll make you a proposition. I'll send a train to Unionville; I'll travel with the mechanic and the stoker. If you overtake me, I'll admit your superiority."

"Agreed," said Valdy.

The voyagers renewed their provisions of bicarbonate of soda and hydrochloric acid, and made sure that the hull of the aeronef was still in good condition.

"A locomotive and the *Céleste*!" said Pickerreek. "It's as if a whiting wanted to race a whale!"

In spite of the sheriff's less-than-reassuring apprehensions, the night passed peacefully. By way of precaution, the voyagers slept on board. The preparations for defense and the sight of the militiamen must have calmed the ardor of the most bellicose Mormons. The next day, a colossal poster was displayed on the walls of Ogden station, thus conceived:

Today, 14 September
FANTASTIC STEEPLECHASE
All out contest
between
Terrestial Locomotion and Aerial Locomotion.
Hurrah! Hurrah!
Long live PROGRESS
Long live the UNION
A train of six wagons guided
by
Chief Engineer William Reading
will depart from Ogden at seven a.m. for Unionville
The aerial vessel the CÉLESTE will accompany it!
The stake: 100 dollars.

175

"The aerial vessel the CÉLESTE will accompany it!" was a masterstroke, but in America, advertising has been raised to the level of a principle. Needless to say, the engineer took all kinds of precautions to clear the track, in order to advance without encumbrance, and that there was fierce competition for seats, in spite of the high price. Many people were turned away.

The Pacific Railway extends without long detours and without ramps. Utah and the state of Nevada form what geographers call the "Great North American Basin," a plateau extending between the Rocky Mountains and the Sierra Nevada, watered by rivers that pour their waters into inland lakes. The appearance of the country is generally arid, almost a desert. Only the Humboldt River Mountains break up the uniformity of the vast sterile plains. The Central Pacific Railway, which changes its name at Ogden to become the Union Pacific, cuts through those mountains by means of insignificant ramps sheltered by "snow-sheds" that permit the trains to circulated feely throughout the winter.

At the designated hour, the *Monroe*, A Crampton-type locomotive with slender wheels, draped with flags and pennants, covered with bunting and richly decorated, sounded its shrill whistle and launched forward. At the same time, the *Céleste* flapped its wings and rose into the air, saluted by the enthusiastic acclamations of the crowd. Charles Weston, who wanted to share the glory of his new friends, asked to deploy the flag of the United States alongside the French flag floating at the prow of the aeronef.

"Do it," said Valdy. "The two standards flew together when we fought for your independence; they ought to be side by side for the victories of peace and progress."

The train was traveling at an extraordinary speed. William Reading, placed on the footplate, was encouraging the mechanic and the stoker. The passengers arranged on the external benches followed the maneuver and promised a gratification of a thousand dollars if they beat the aerial vessel. The stoker stuffed—the word is appropriate—the furnace with coal. The piston was beating at fifteen thrusts a second and the train was traveling at a speed of a hundred kilometers an hour.

In order to go up to an altitude of seven or eight hundred meters to find a favorable air current, the *Céleste* slowed down and allowed the train draw ahead, but when she found favorable conditions, she headed directly westwards and advanced at a prodigious velocity. All the crew members were at their posts: Pickerreek, Cardounet and Dernghuiz were manufacturing carbonic acid to replace the fuel consumed; Will Tooke and Ivan Kisseloff were supervising the transmission, the straps and the wings; Charles Weston and Madame Valdy were serving as lookouts; Marcel Valdy, as usual, was fulfilling the function of an experienced pilot. After an hour, the aeronef caught up with the train; a few minutes later it had overtaken it.

The frantic race continued in that fashion all the way to the Humboldt Mountains. There, the *Céleste* suffered a considerable delay. Either because the configuration of the ground changed the atmospheric conditions or because the air current varied in its direction, a violent contrary wind suddenly got up and impeded her maneuvers. During that time, the *Monroe*, traveling at full steam, took the lead again, crossing the mountain ramps and running into the plain.

William Reading thought that he had won.

"Faster! Faster, lads!"he cried. "The honor of the Central Pacific Railway is at stake. "Faster! Faster!"

And the train pulled further and further ahead.

Valdy experienced a violent resentment, akin to a fit of rage. He glimpsed defeat and humiliation. His companions were uttering curses.

"A thousand thunders!" said Pickerreek. "Let's climb! The wind won't be as bad beyond the mountains. At sea, the slightest cape obliges us to put on more sail."

"That's a good idea," Valdy replied. "Let's climb. Watch the tanned skins, and when the gas pressure's about to burst them, warn me!"

The *Céleste* rose up to more than four thousand meters. At that height they no longer felt the effects of the contrary wind, but the temperature dropped to a few degrees above zero.

To increase the expansion of the carbonic acid gas, they turned up the flame of the spirit lamps; then the aeronef plunged earthwards and its speed increased dramatically. Pickerreek's anticipations were justified; beyond the mountains, the *Céleste* rediscovered the atmospheric current that had favored it on departure, caught up with the train, and gained a considerable lead on it.

William Reading understood that he was beaten, but he did not want to let his disappointment show. "Faster! Faster!" he cried, incessantly.

And the passengers joined in with him in chorus, promising to double the tip.

The stoker was black, and steaming with sweat. "Impossible to go any faster," he said. "If I heat up the combustion, the boiler will blow up."

"Let it blow up, as long as we get there!" replied a Californian.

The *Monroe* was traveling at a truly fantastic speed, if it is permissible to express it thus, and the train was gliding rather than running on its rails—but that frantic course could not be continued for long without danger. The locomotive resumed its original speed. When it pulled into Unionville station, the *Céleste* had arrived three-quarters of an hour before.

The population of Unionville, alerted by telegraphic dispatches, was feverishly awaiting the result of the great contest. It acclaimed the aerial voyagers when they landed in a meadow on the bank of the Humboldt, then flocked to the vicinity of the railways station and vigorously applauded the arrival of the Monroe. The victors and the vanquished were entitled to the same manifestations, as everyone had done their best.

William Reading flung his arms around Valdy and embraced him.

Honor to you, my fortunate adversary," he said, emotionally. "Your discovery is marvelous, and like Goethe after the battle of Valmy, you may say: "Here, a New Era begins!"

Chapter XIII

The rest of the day was devoted to public rejoicing. Unionville fêted the bold voyagers worthily and joyfully. Charles Weston, still marveling, bade them farewell and began the return journey to Denver that evening.

The following morning, the fifteenth of September, the *Céleste* quit Unionville and departed in a northward direction. Initially it traversed a country of lakes and lagoons, fed by small watercourses, reminiscent of Switzerland, and arrived in the territory of Oregon not far from the Blue Mountains, which are an immediate prolongation of the Sierra Nevada. Those mountains, of limited height, the culminating point of an immense plateau of steppes and forests, presented no obstacle to the progress of the aeronef. Valdy set a northwestward course in order to reach Salem, the capital of Oregon, and drew nearer to the ground. Until the Cascade or President Mountains, there was nothing to be seen but sparse Indian huts, herds of moose, bison and antelopes, and packs of wolves, which, along with a few other mammals, composed the fauna of the region.

The Cascade Mountains owe their name to the rapids of the Columbia, a great river that has carved out a route through the granite mass and often runs between two sheer banks, gigantic walls three or four hundred feet high. The mountains in question form an alpine region; their summits are snow-capped, their flanks dotted with pasturelands and magnificent forests. The principal peaks are Mount McLaughlin, Mount Jefferson, Mount Washington or Hood, the volcanoes Mount St. Helens and Mount Harrison, Mount Baker, etc.

Between Mount Jefferson and Mount Hood, on the forty-fifth degree of latitude, the chain is subject to a depression. In order to go through it the *Céleste* only had to go up to an altitude of fifteen hundred meters, and then glide toward Salem, which it reached at about four o'clock in the afternoon. Salem

180

is a city with a quarter of a million inhabitants, situated on the Willamette, a tributary of the Columbia, which waters one of the most fertile valleys in northern America.

Nothing surprised our voyagers as much as the luxurious vegetation of that region. They noticed trees of colossal dimensions, giants compared with which our oaks and elms would seem pygmies. The west coast of the United States, between the thirty-fifth and forty-fifth degrees of north latitude, is admirably favored by the climatic conditions; excessive heat and rigorous cold are completely unknown there. The strip of land bordered on one side by the Pacific Ocean and on the other by the Cascade Mountains and the Sacramento and St. Joachim, rivers flowing into San Francisco Bay, enjoys a perpetual spring, interrupted—or, at least, diminished—by the rainy season that begins in November and lasts until the end of April—but the rains do not present the continuity of those of the tropics; after a deluge of a few days the sky resumes its serenity and the temperature its habitual mildness.

That exceptional climate explains the vigor of the vegetation; in some places, one finds the giant cypresses that the American call "mammoth trees."[43] The most remarkable are those in the Yosemite Valley of California. Some are more than a hundred meters tall and ten meters in diameter; their lowest branches are seventy meters from the ground. The number of concentric layers in the trunk prove that they are more than four thousand years old. Four generations of Methuselahs could not have seen them born or see them die.

In Oregon, one sees little vegetation as extraordinary, but it is not rare to encounter trees there between sixty and eighty meters high. Our tallest plane trees and oaks do not surpass thirty meters.

---

[43] *Sequoia gigantea*, the giant redwood, only grows in California; its Oregonian relatives are more modest. The allegation that some are more than four thousand years old is an exaggeration; the oldest known specimen is only 3,500 years old.

The voyagers did not stay long in Salem; they hastily renewed their bicarbonate of soda and hydrochloric acid and resolved to take advantage of the rest of the day by going to Olympia, the capital of Washington State, about fifty leagues away. The *Céleste* departed, rose up to a low altitude and followed the rich valley of the Willamette. To the east, the limitless sea was visible, reddening in the rays of the setting sun, and to the west, the dazzling snow eternally crowning the peaks of the Cascades was perceptible. They passed over Oregon City, Portland, Columbia and St. Helens, cities of considerable size destined for a brilliant future. The Columbia River was crossed at Monticello, a large town not far from its mouth, and they arrived in Olympia at dusk.

Like most of the new cities of young America, Olympia, an excellent harbor on Puget Sound, an inlet of the Strait of Georgia, presents a bizarre and picturesque appearance. Wooden cabins sit side by side with well-constructed edifices, streets that are scarcely traced out end in irregular public squares, hotels and splendid cafes are next door to abject hotels and gambling-dens. All contrasts are displayed there, and rub shoulders—but all that will not last; American activity will realize prodigies there, as elsewhere, and transform the nascent capital of Washington, which, in the meantime, is growing rich on the export of cereals, flour and timber for construction.

The inhabitants of Olympia gave the crew of the *Céleste* the most sympathetic welcome. The governor of the territory offered hospitality. Valdy accepted, on condition that the reception would be very intimate, for the late nights and tumultuous celebrations are exhausting and tedious. The governor did his best to satisfy his guest's desire, and only invited a few friends. They dined simply—without any fuss, as Cardounet put it—took tea and then at about ten o'clock, everyone went to bed.

On the sixteenth of September, at about six o'clock in the morning, the *Céleste*, abundantly resupplied, resumed its aerial journey. A thick fog covered the ground and the crew could not make out the jagged contours of the Strait of Georgia, Victoria, the principal settlement on Quadra's and Vancouver's Island, Fort Bellingham, or New Westminster, the capital of British Columbia, the nearest towns.

The aeronef was about to venture once again into regions where barbarity, save for rare exceptions, rules as absolute sovereign. At about ten o'clock the sun's rays dissipated the layer of fog, and the voyagers were able to see the country over which they were passing. At that moment, they were following the course of the Frazer River, which descends from the Rocky Mountains, to which the recent discovery of gold deposits has given a universal reputation. The Frazer, the most important watercourse in the English possessions of the northwest, runs through a landscape covered in forests, whose exploitation it facilitates. For some years, steamboats have been traveling along it; unfortunately, the rapids at them mouth prohibit navigation.

Suddenly, Cardounet uttered a strident cry.

"What is it?" asked Valdy.

"Look over there," the mariner replied. "Look at that cloud, growing and advancing toward us."

All eyes looked in the direction indicated.

"I know what it is," said Will Tooke. "They're passenger pigeons."

Scarcely had the American pronounced these words that the *Céleste* was invaded by birds. They passed everywhere, above and below, their number increasing with every moment. It was an indescribable host. The sun could not penetrate the compact mass, and the pigeons' excreta fell upon the aeronef, soiling the voyagers.

"Up! Up!" cried Valdy.

A tug on the tiller inclined the *Céleste*, which succeeded, after some effort, in rising above the migrating flock. As far as the eye could see, the winged flocks were perceptible, tightly-packed and numerous. They were carrying out the most capricious evolutions, which produced sudden changes of color as the metallically-colored feather reflected the sun's rays. Never had any king's or fairy's mantle given an idea of richer or more sparkling colors; gold, green, scarlet, silver and red shone by turns, scintillating in the atmosphere like a splendid jewel-box.

Pickerreek tried to count the flocks but gave up; they passed by for more than an hour, heading south. Finally, the last ones disappeared, and Will Tooke provided a few details of the habits of the birds.

"The migrant dove or passenger pigeon—Linnaeus' *Columba migratoria*," he said, "is one of the most remarkable species of North America. It migrates from the Dominion of Canada to the Gulf of Mexico, but its migrations bear no resemblance to those of birds like the quail and the swallow, which flee the rigor of the seasons; they're regulated by the means of subsistence offered by the countries. Audubon, our great naturalist, gave us our first information about the habits of the animals. Nothing is more interesting than the story his observations tell. In 1813, while traveling in Kentucky, he saw a hundred and sixty-three flocks pass overhead in twenty minutes; the flocks overlapped, the sky was darkened, bird droppings feel like thick snow and the repeated flapping of the wings produced a monotonous noise like that of a distant rumble of thunder.

"To estimate their number he made the following calculation: 'Let us suppose a column a mile wide; let us suppose that it takes three hours to pass overhead; as its speed is a mile a minute, its length will be 180 miles, each comprising 1,760 yards; if each square yard in occupied by two pigeons, one finds that the number of the birds is one billion, one hundred and fifteen million, one hundred and thirty-six thousand: 1,115,136,000. Now, each individual consuming half a pint of fruit peer day, the nourishment of a flock requires eight million, seven hundred and twelve thousand—8,712,000—bushels of grain per day.'"

"What an appetite!" exclaimed Cardounet. "Well, I wouldn't like to feed such a well-stocked aviary."

"When the pigeons discover the fruits and grains necessary to their alimentation," Will Tooke continued, "they settle *en masse*, stripping maples, mulberries, elms, oaks, beeches, fields of rice or wheat, and when they've fed they retrace their route to their point of origin. Their roosts are often situated more than a hundred leagues from their refectories. During their feeing trips they're subjected to the attacks of falcons, but birds of prey aren't their most terrible enemies; humans subject them to far more murderous slaughter.

"To sleep, the pigeons take refuge in the high forests; it's there that the hunters wait for them. When evening comes and their countless legions are circling in the air, coming to settle in the trees, the massacre and carnage immediately commences; rifle shots ring out; the high branches give way beneath the weight of birds; they break, and as they fall, they crush birds perched on the lower branches. There's an indescribable confusion and tumult. While they are killed, and killed incessantly, and the victims pile up in enormous heaps, the pigeons arrive in their millions. Sometimes it's after midnight and the last flock is still flying over the forest, but the carnage continues until dawn. Then the birds resume their flight without their number seeming sensibly diminished.

"After the hunters come the wolves, the foxes, the bears and the lynxes, which come to claim their share of the kill; then the carnivores are replaced by the vultures, the eagles, the buzzards and the crows, and all the scavengers attracted by the odor of blood and the racket of the night."

"Is there no means of getting rid of these inconvenient guests?" asked Monsieur Valdy.

"Only clearance. As the plow conquers the forest, the number of pigeons diminishes. Audubon did not encounter them again in the same locations as in 1813. Civilization has driven them westwards; soon their flocks will be thinned out and humans will no longer have to fear their depredations."[44]

---

[44] An accurate prediction; after a catastrophic decline between 1870 and 1890 the species was extinct by 1914.

While Will Tooke was talking, the *Céleste* was advancing rapidly. It reached Fort Chilcotin, a hunting outpost situated on a tributary of the Frazer, also intended to keep watch on the still-savage Indians inhabiting British Columbia. That immense country, which formerly formed the fourth department of the Hudson Bay Company, extends from the great Ocean to the Rocky Mountains, and from the United States to Alaska. After the Simpson River at 54° 40′ north latitude, it takes the name of Stekeen Territory. In 1857 it formed a colony and in 1870 was combined with the Dominion of Canada. On the coast, thanks to currents from the south, the climate is quite mild, but in the interior it is harsh and rude. The vegetation is, however, richer than that of the lands east of the Rockies in the same latitudes. The gold deposits of Frazer, Stekeen, the mines of Caribou and Omineca, discovered in 1857, attract a large number of immigrants, and the population, almost as mixed as that of California, is beginning to undertake serious agricultural endeavors. The south of the Columbia will become one of the commercial centers of the Pacific one day.

The commandant and all the agents at Fort Chilcotin received the visitors deferentially.

"When I was sent the deposit of bicarbonate of soda and hydrochloric acid," the Commandant said, "and the employment destined for the chemical agents was explained to me, I tell you frankly that I was incredulous. It mortifies me to admit it, but I believed that it was a hoax."

"Of course," muttered Ivan Kisseloff, between his teeth. "That doesn't astonish me on the part of an Englishman."

"Receive my apologies," the Commandant continued. "Your enterprise is bold and your work admirable. I'm proud to welcome you and I hope that you'll accept the hospitality I offer you. At Fort Chilcotin, I step aside before you; gentleman, you are now the absolute masters; command, and you will be obeyed."

"Well, Monsieur Kisseloff," said Madame Valdy, softly, "for a Englishman, he speaks well, it seems to me."

"Bah!" the Russian replied. "He's seeking to repair his blunder."

As not everyone had Ivan Kisseloff's prejudices, however, Valdy thanked the Commandant warmly and Pickerreek called him a "brave man." It was agreed that they would have lunch at the fort and would then leave immediately for Fort Simpson. The Commandant treated the voyagers in a princely fashion.

Ivan Kisseloff agreed that some Englishmen had some good in them, but perhaps he was only talking about their food.

After the meal, they got ready to depart.

"Permit me to give you some advice," the Commandant said to Valdy. "Don't land before you get to Fort Simpson. Savage, cruel and bellicose Indians inhabit the forests and steppes over which you'll pass; if they see you, they'll look for a fight. The authority we exercise over them is very limited, and they detest palefaces. The most redoubtable tribes are the Nagaïls, the Manscouds, the Sloud-Couss and the Carriers.[45] They never give any quarter and you'll inevitably be killed if you fall into their hands.

"Don't worry about us, Commandant," said Pickerreek. "We're able avoid being eaten."

The aeronef rose up above Fort Chilcotin and headed north-west. Nothing impeded their progress. At five o'clock in the evening, they landed on a small cape in the Strait of Vancouver, a short distance from Fort Simpson. There, Will Tooke found compatriots again, for Fort Simpson, situated at the southern extremity of New Cornwall, belongs to the region known as the territory of Alaska, ceded by Russia to the United States in 1867 for the sum of 7,200,000 dollars.

---

[45] These tribal appellations appear to have been obsolete even in 1875; they seem to have been taken from Conrad Malte-Brun's *Géographie mathématque* (1803-1812) or, more probably, one of the subsequent texts that merely recycled information therefrom.

As always, the reception given to the visitors was very enthusiastic and amicable. Valdy, Madame Valdy, Will Tooke and Kisseloff slept in the fort. Pickerreek, Cardounet and Dernghuiz wanted to stay on board the aeronef. The two mariners loved the *Céleste* as they had loved their ships, and they could not bring themselves to abandon it.

During the night the sky clouded over and a cold dense rain fell violently. Pickerreek, Cardounet and Dernghuiz made what arrangements they could to combat the bad weather, while savoring two bottles of a generous wine that "happened" to be within arm's reach. When the sun's light appeared, the rain was still falling and the west wind was blowing forcefully.

"Lousy weather!" said Cardounet. "The Captain won't be pleased."

Valdy was, indeed, annoyed. He feared the consequences that a long exposure to cold and rain might have for his wife, delicate by nature and accustomed to comfort.

The latter divined her husband's apprehensions. She wrapped herself up in a fur cloak, covered her head with a moose-fur cap, put sealskin boots on her feet and appeared in that bizarre accoutrement. "Now I'm impermeable," she said, gaily. "When are we leaving?"

"As soon as we've take the same precautions as you, Madame," relied Will Tooke, laughing.

Thanks to the generosity of the fort's inhabitants, the voyagers acquired complete costumes of the kind customary in that damp region.

The *Céleste* departed. At first it skimmed the ground in order to be better sheltered from the wind, but that maneuver was difficult to execute and hindered the flight. Then they climbed high enough to overlook a few islands in the Prince of Wales Archipelago. The wind was still pushing them toward the land.

"How high are the clouds?" Valdy asked.

"About two thousand meters," Pickerreek replied.

"Let's get above them."

The aeronef rose up and penetrated the clouds. No ray of sunlight appeared to brighten them. They went up further, but still in vain. The cloud layer, however improbably it seemed, was several kilometers thick.

"The wisest thing is to tack," said Pickerreek. "We won't go fast, but we'll make headway."

This advice was put into practice. The *Céleste* maintained an altitude of about five hundred meters, and presented its prow obliquely to the wind direction. In moments of calm it made progress, and struggled advantageously against the gusts. Without the rain, which never ceased falling, the delay would have been insignificant. Finally, after a long day of effort and fatigue, the aeronef landed on a rock close to New Archangel.

"Since our departure from Europe," Valdy said, "we've never sailed as long and advanced as little as today, the seventeenth of September. We've only covered about three hundred kilometers."

In spite of the bad weather, the inhabitants of New Archangel left their dwellings ad came to examine the *Céleste*. The governor of Alaska, the factors and the principal agents of the Russo-American Company, a rival of the Hudson Bay Company, offered their services to the voyagers. The latter accepted gladly and went into the town, desirous above all of warming their cold-numbed limbs.

New Archangel is a wretched town. It is situated on the western coast of the island of Sitka in the King George Archipelago. The fortifications, the habitations, the barracks and the warehouses are made of wood. The population is about fifteen hundred.

Soon, Valdy and his companions were sitting around a stove stuffed with pine-logs and red with heat.

"You don't appear to have a good impression of our region?" said the governor.

"I confess, Governor," Valdy replied, "that I've judged it rather unfavorably."

"That's your fault, to some extent. You've arrived at the moment of the equinox, at the beginning of the rainy season, climatic conditions that send us long tempests and spread a humidity that gets in everywhere and makes all our trees spongy, but the rest of the year our abode is quite tolerable. Although the Alaska territory experiences harsher temperatures in the lands bathed by the Behring Sea and the Arctic Ocean, it's not the same for those bordering the great Ocean. It's not as cold here as in other regions situated on the latitude of Sitka Island, but that's counterbalanced by more rain and more fog."

"The compensation isn't in your favor."

"Yes it is, for the humidity develops a vegetation that's typical of more southern regions."

"In fact, your forests are beautiful."

"They only constitute the least part of our riches. Our principal products are those of hunting and fishing. Sometimes, our warehouses are full to bursting with salted or smoked fish, the oil of whales seals and walruses, furs of all sorts, especially sables, foxes, ermines, beavers, squirrels, otters and marmots. When the fine season arrives, the sad Sitka became the center of major commerce and cheers up.

The governor pleaded *pro domo sua*[46] and his interlocutors approved deferentially.

A solid meal restored the voyagers' strength; then, as they could not go out, for the rain was still falling, they went into a lounge where there was a numerous gathering, gave the mot minute details of their aerial exploration and went to bed at about ten o'clock in the evening.

The next day, the eighteenth of September, the rain had stopped, but the westerly wind was still blowing. Valdy gave the order to depart.

All the inhabitants of New Archangel gathered on the promontory where the *Céleste* had landed; they saluted the bold voyagers and the aeronef rose up, taking a northerly di-

---

[46] For his own house.

rection. She traversed Sitka Island and the Cross Strait, and went along the territory of New Norfolk, indented by inlets and small gulfs reminiscent of Scandinavian fjords. In the distance, Mount Fairweather was visible, a volcano 4,550 meters high; then, beyond the Behring Sea, Mount St. Elias, 5,400 meters high. The summits of the two mountains were lost in the clouds.

At about two o'clock in the afternoon, they crossed the sixtieth degree of north latitude and ventured over a country beginning to present the character of Siberian regions. The vegetation became stunted and bare rock appeared here and there, completely deprived of vegetal soil. When the *Céleste* was several leagues beyond the river Ahtna, whose estuary forms Controller Bay, Valdy noticed that one wing was going up and down irregularly. The principal armature was doubtless in need of urgent repair. He descended into a small valley, wild and picturesque.

Pickerreek discovered that an iron bar was twisted. While he was straightening it, Cardounet perceived a group of bizarrely-dressed men on a nearby hill. They were Chugaches, indigenes of Alaska, as savage and cruel as all the Indians inhabiting the peninsula. They drew nearer, at first with circumspection, and seemed to be examining the crouching aeronef with surprise. Seeing that only seven persons were guarding the mass, they did not hide their hostile disposition.

"Hurry up, Pick!" said Valdy. "Everyone else, grab your weapons."

Everyone picked up a rifle, a revolver and ammunition.

The Chugaches uttered shrill cries; they were immediately joined by sixty warriors of their tribe. Those reinforcements increased their audacity, and the advanced, brandishing spears, tomahawks and hatchets.

"Damn it!" exclaimed Pickerreek. "I'll miss the party."

"Madame Valdy will stay with you," said Ivan Kisseloff. "We don't want her to take any risks,"

Madame Valdy smiled. "I'm not afraid," she replied, simply.

The savages were still getting closer, confident in the few poor firearms they possessed. A chief fired the first rifle-shot.

"Ah, my dears, you're starting the dance," said Cardounet. "Well, we'll supply the sugared almonds."[47]

A second bullet passed over the *Céleste*.

"Fire!" commanded Valdy.

The carbines burst forth like thunder. Three Chugaches bit the dust.

"Charge!" said Ivan Kisseloff. "Our attitude will frighten that rabble!"

The five men launched themselves toward the Indians, discharging the first two shots from their revolvers almost at point-blank range. Four more enemies fell. The wounded howled like men possessed. That first movement intimidated the Chugaches, who imagined that the palefaces were unleashing lightning from their hands, for they were unfamiliar with the use of revolvers. Valdy commanded a general discharge.

Immediately, the Indians disappeared behind the hill, proffering threats and uttering cries for help.

"Let's run to the *Céleste* and get out," said Will Tooke. "I know what savages are like. They'll come back with reinforcements. An entire host will fall upon us, and we'll succumb to the weight of numbers."

"That's the most prudent course," Valdy replied.

As they ran to the aeronef, Dernghuiz perceived a head striped with tattoos behind a clump of dwarf willows. Had he been left behind? Was he a scout, a sentinel or a spy? The Tatar ran toward the Indian; the latter, realizing that he had been seen, brandished his tomahawk and threw it. Dernghuiz avoided the blow; then, as rapid as thought, he ran behind the Chugach and smashed the butt of his carbine into his head. The savage fell to the ground, stunned. Ivan Kisseloff came to help his courageous servant. The two of them disarmed the prison-

---

[47] *Dragées* [sugared almonds] has a double meaning, also referring to buckshot or grapeshot.

er, bound his hands and shoved him in front of them to the *Céleste*.

"What shall we do with our captive?" asked Ivan Kisseloff.

"We'll have to give him the delights of an aerial voyage," said Cardounet. "That will show him what we can do."

The Indian was hoisted on to the deck of the Céleste, but his eyes suddenly glittered and he made a violent effort to break the bonds restraining him. In the distance, he could see all the warriors of his nation approaching. There were two or three hundred. What could the palefaces do against that number? Resistance would become impossible. He was about to be rescued!

"All ready, Captain," shouted Pickerreek.

The voyagers embarked immediately and he aeronef flapped her wings.

The Chugaches opened fire, but the old weapons they were using only had a limited range; the bullets did not reach the *Céleste*, which was already heading westwards.

The prisoner's amazement was indescribable. A convulsive trembling took possession of his limbs and he tried to hurl himself into space. Pickerreek grabbed him by the arm and held him back, saying: "Don't be afraid—we're not going to eat you."

Cardounet added, sententiously: "We want the conversion of the sinner, not his death."

Frightened by these speeches, which he did not understand, the Indian darted anxious glances around and manifested an extreme terror. The voyagers took pity on him. After a trajectory of twenty kilometers, they deposited him on the ground. No gesture of friendship could reassure the Chugach, who fled rapidly and disappeared.

The aeronef continued on its course, traversed the inlets of Prince William Sound and arrived at Fort St. Nicholas at the end of the day.

,At Fort St. Nicholas, designated on some maps as Fort St. George, the voyagers were warmly welcomed, and the trappers who lived there, under the authority of a factor, were amused by the adventure that had overtaken the Chugach prisoner when it was elated to them.

"Now," the factor said to them, "you have no more to fear from attack by the local populations. On your route you'll encounter the Kenais, the Koniags and the Aleutians, tranquil semi-civilized peoples converted to Christianity, but who have a pronounced taste for whisky and all spirits."

On the nineteenth of September, the sun's rays did not reach the ground. A thick fog—a fog one could "cut with a knife"—extended through the atmosphere and presented objects from being distinguished ten paces away. Valdy was determined to leave, though.

"We'll go slowly," he said.

"The *Céleste* took off and rose up high enough not to run into the mountain chain that follows the coast and forms the principle artery of the Alaskan peninsula. Enveloped on all sides by thick fog, the aeronef advanced slowly and prudently. Finally, at about three o'clock in the afternoon, they reached Fort Alexander, situated on the watercourse that connects Lake Iliamna to Bristol Bay and landed on a small hill overlooking a marshy region.

The people confined in Fort Alexander only saw, at long intervals, the rare Russian and American vessels that came during the summer to take on cargoes of pelts, so their surprise and admiration overflowed enthusiastically when they discovered the form of locomotion that the voyagers had employed in order to visit them. There was a celebration during the evening of the nineteenth of September at Fort Alexander, and the factor lavished cares and attention on his guests of a day.

"I have only one regret," he told them, "and that's knowing that you're traveling through our region at the approach of the autumn equinox. The tempests are terrible hereabouts, and I fear a catastrophe. Our prayers go with you and we wish you all the success that your efforts deserve, but they can't master the storms."

"Bah!" Cardounet replied. "The *Céleste*'s seen many others."

"Well, you're valiant; Providence will aid you."

"We're counting on it," said Madame Valdy.

The twentieth of September contrasted with the three previous days. The sun, without being bright, cleared the air, dissipating the mists, and the breeze blew gently from the south-east. In these latitudes, one could not ask for better weather conditions. The aeronef launched into the atmosphere. It followed the Alaskan peninsula, a rocky and mostly sterile terrain inhabited by populations living by fishing. We ought to say that the region is surrounded by seas exceedingly rich in fish, and that life is relatively easy there.

They traversed the Isdnotski Strait, which separates the first of the Aleutians from the American continent, passed over several islands, of which the principal ones were Unimak and Akun, and came down to land on the western tip of Unalaska.

The Aleutians have been compared to the piles of an immense bridge linking America to Asia. The comparison is just. To the south, they border the Behring Sea, and form three principal groups. A few geographers admit five, which are the Behring islands, the Shumagin islands, the Rat islands, the Andreanof islands and the Fox islands. They are volcanic in origin and manifest the traces of violent geological commotions. Several volcanoes there are still active and warm springs are very numerous. Save for stunted bushes, grasses and lichens, they are almost devoid of vegetation. The inhabitants, of Kamchatkan origin, obtain their principal resources from fishing and hunting; they are mild and peaceful. The number of Aleutians has been estimated at a hundred and fifty, occupying an area of about 450 square myriameters.

At Unalaska, the voyagers renewed their bicarbonate of soda and hydrochloric acid and departed immediately. They passed over the islands and islets of Unimak, Tskugidi, Tanginak, Ullaga, Yunaska, Seguam, Atka, Tagalak, Gareloi and Adak, and finally arrived at Tanaga shortly after nightfall.

The *Céleste* had covered the entire distance between the 160th ad 180th degrees of longitude west of Paris. We know that between the fiftieth and sixtieth parallels the distance of a degree is about thirteen leagues; they had, therefore, covered 260 leagues, which is 1,040 kilometers—a perfectly ordinary trajectory for the aeronef if nothing hindered its progress.

Apart from the Aleutians living on Tanaga Island, Ivan Kisseloff encountered three of his compatriots, former agents of the Russo-American Company who had been acclimated by a long sojourn in that hash environment and were, moreover retained by family ties, for they had married indigenous women. The latter were introduced to the voyagers, but we have to confess that they did bore no resemblance to the Medici Venus. Cardounet could not help saying that "it would be necessary to have killed the father and mother to espouse such she-apes." Like everything else, beauty is often a matter of convention; the Aleutians had charmed and inflamed the hearts of the Russians, who appeared to be excellent husbands.

The good and peaceful inhabitants of Tanaga offered their services to Valdy, who thanked the effusively and distributed a few bottles of tafia rum, the most agreeable gift one could offer them, and then made preparations to spend the night.

So they had reached the 180° meridian!

In spite of the accidents, the detours, the retreats, the delays, the tempests and the contrary winds, the *Céleste* had traveled half way around the world in twenty days!

Aerial navigation was henceforth a reality. The air was conquered!

Chapter XIV

The next day, the Céleste left Tanaga. Valdy wrote in his log:

In crossing the 180° meridian I add a day to my calendar, without which, on our return to Europe, we would find ourselves a day behind schedule, for in heading westwards we gain four minutes per degree, which is twenty-four hours for the globe's 360°. Our friends in France will see the sun pass the meridian forty times while we shall only see it pass thirty-nine until the tenth of October. That is why I need not arrive in Bordeaux until the eleventh of October, after forty actual days of travel, and why I am writing 22 September at the head of my log entry, although it is only the twenty-first for us.

The weather was almost fine and the wind quite favorable. Valdy told his companions that they would land on the Asiatic continent in the evening if no inconvenient circumstances cropped up. The aeronef passed rapidly over the islands of Ilak, Amchitka, Rat, Kiska, Buldir and Agattu and landed at midday on Attu, where they were to find the last deposit of bicarbonate of soda and hydrochloric acid arranged by Will Toke.

As soon as the refueling was complete, the *Céleste* took off again and advanced over the sea. Now it was necessary to increase speed, for there were no longer any points of relief. For reasons of prudence, Valdy did not want to fly directly toward Petropavlovsk; he veered slightly northwards again, skirted Bering Island and Medny Island, and reached Asia at Cape Kronotsky. He followed the Kamachatkan coast, passing close to the volcano Avacha, and arrived at Petropavlovsk at about eight o'clock in the evening.

In spite of the darkness and a cold north wind, the inhabitants of the capital of Kamchatka came to meet the voyagers as soon as they heard of their arrival. Moreover, Ivan Kisseloff was, as he put it in jest "at home," and when he had listed his titles and qualifications, and shown the letters of recommendation that he was carrying, the Russian functionaries put themselves entirely at his disposal. Several of them spoke French fluently, and that pleased Cardounet and Pickerreek.

"They must be worthy folk," said the former.

"And scholars too, since they speak French as if they'd invented it," added the second.

Petropavlovsk—the port of St. Peter and St. Paul—in the depths of Avacha Bay, is a small city of five thousand souls. Its harbor is spacious and safe. The houses are made of wood, the fortifications of earth supported by tightly-bound fascines. It has a terrible neighbor in the volcano Avacha, which constantly threatens to bury or destroy it. On 8 August 1827 the volcano emitted such a large quantity of ash that it was feared that the town might suffer the fate of Pompeii and Herculaneum. On 6 May 1841 the entire country suffered a violent earthquake and several houses collapsed.

The governor, the principal commissar of the Russo-American Commercial Society and the officers of the garrison lavished cares upon the voyagers and were delighted to find one of their compatriots among the first aerial navigators. It will be remembered that Will Tooke had encountered the same sentiments among the Americans. Vanity is universal, in all times, all nations and all latitudes.

On the twenty-third of September, before the healthy population of Petropavlovsk, the *Céleste* rose up into the atmosphere. Its progress was awkward and uncertain to begin with, hindered by a rather strong north-easterly wind, but after several evolutions at fifteen hundred meters she found an air current favorable to her new direction. Valdy wanted to traverse Kamchatka, go back up the western coast as far as the fifty-seventh parallel and then head for Okhotsk, across the arm of the sea that forms the two guls of Pinjinsk and Ijiginsk.

The region of Kamchatka between Petropavlovska and Bolsheretsk to the west was rapidly traversed.

Pickerreek noticed that the Sea of Okhotsk was changing its appearance and taking on a milky tint. In addition, the waves were becoming "fleecy" and colliding with one another. "Captain," he said, "the people who warned us to beware of the equinoctial tempests weren't lying. There must be a general upheaval below us."

"You think so, Pick?"

"Do I think so? As surely as I'm going to die one day and my mother's a good woman! The swell's breaking angrily on the shore and the wind's hissing like all the snakes in Hell."

"Will it reach us?"

"That, Captain, I don't know yet."

The sky, which until then had been streaked by white cirro-cumulus clouds, was covered over by clouds with leaden and coppery tints. They were running from the south-west, a point opposite to the direction from which the wind was blowing.

"That's bizarre," said Ivan Kisseloff, watching the clouds race.

"The explanation's quite simple though," Valdy replied. "On the days that precede and follow the equinoxes, nature undergoes a universal upheaval. The sun, having reigned for six months over one hemisphere, warming the atmosphere, breaks the equilibrium of the temperature when it passes to the other side of the equator. The exceedingly cold air of the poles descends toward the torrid zone, while that of the latter zone flows back toward the poles. There are, in consequence, two air currents, which produce the phenomenon that we're witnessing, but which often intersect and give birth to those reversals of the wind that are so terrible in the Channel and the Atlantic Ocean, to the mistral of the Provençal coasts, the typhoons of the China Seas, the tornadoes of the African coasts, the *pomperos* of Brazil and the *nortes* of the Gulf of Mexico."

During his brief explanation, the aeronef was advancing over the sea, and the voyagers lost sight of the cliffs of Kamchatka. They continued for an hour without feeling the effects of the tempest that had been unleashed in the lowers atmospheric layers. In any case, Valdy was not afraid of squalls, because he knew that land was not far away.

Suddenly, the aeronef was subjected to several oscillatory movements. At the same time three detonations were heard.

"Damn!" cried Valdy. "The hull's breached!"

The detonations multiplied.

"No, no," replied Pickerreek, "It's the alarm cannon of a ship. Look—down there…she's struggling in the tempest. She's breaking up."

With the aid of binoculars they made out an English corvette tossed by the waves, deprived of part of its rigging.

"Captain!" said Pickerreek. "Are we going to let the crew of that ship perish without trying to rescue them?"

"No, damn it!" Valdy replied. "Everyone to his post!"

The *Céleste* descended toward the vessel, describing a long spiral. When it arrived two hundred meters above the surface, however, it was gripped by a crosswind that spun her around several times. To complete the misfortune, torrential rain began falling at that moment, blinding the courageous rescuers.

Twenty times Valdy tried to reach the corvette, which was gradually sinking; twenty times he was driven back by gusts of wind or overshot the vessel. Pickerreek, Cardounet, Dernghuiz, Will Tooke and Ivan Kisseloff redoubled their efforts, giving no thought to the dangers that threatened them. They only saw the unfortunates terrified by the storm and the saddened appearance of the aeronef. The latter appeared to be reassured when they heard voices coming from the sky shouting: "Hold on! Hold on!"

The English sailors succeeded in putting a launch into the sea. The vessel's commander, standing on the bridge, gave orders with an intrepid composure, and made sure that the embarkation took place in an orderly manner.

"He's got guts!" said Cardounet, in amazement.

The launch, sufficient laden with men and food supplies, drew away. The commander followed it with his eyes momentarily, and then ordered the other lifeboats to be made ready. No other means of salvation remained.

The launch, tossed by the waves and caught by the wind, which changed direction by the minute, was driven back against the corvette and smashed into its flank. Desperate cries were heard over the tempest. The commander made a gesture that signified: *No more hope!* Then he summoned the rest of the crew, who silently gathered round him on the bridge.

There, beneath the rain that was precipitated in large dense drops and he gusts of wind that caused the masts to creak and bend, he picked up a Bible and began to read the sixth psalm of penitence, the psalm imprinted with such a sad melancholy, which the English have adopted as the prayer for the dead under the title *De profundis*.[48] As the reading continued, the corvette disappeared into the abyss, to the accompaniment of the passage that depicts the patience of repentance: "My soul waiteth for the Lord more than they that watch for the morning..."

The corvette sank.

And the waves and the wind continued their fierce roaring.

The *Céleste* passed over. It was so low that its wingtips were touching the crests of the waves.

"Our good will is futile, then?" cried Will Tooke.

"May the Lord's will be done!" replied Madame Valdy, wiping away her tears.

"Captain!" Cardounet interjected. "I can see one of the victims, swimming and fighting the swell. Let's go back—we can save him!"

While the aeronef described a parabola that would bring her back to the location of the sinking, Cardounet took a long rope, attached crosswise thereto the famous red umbrella that he had obtained from the eloquent Mary Silver and threw it into the sea. The swimming man grabbed hold of it. The

---

[48] Psalm 130.

Céleste was now running into the wind, and its speed was insignificant.

"Hold hard! Hold hard!" cried the aerial rescuers. And they hauled on the rope with all their might, hoisting the umbrella and the shipwreck-victim up on to the deck of the aeronef.

The man saved so miraculously hid his face in his hands and sobbed, murmuring: "My beautiful corvette! My friends! All dead!"

As he raised his eyes, he perceived Ivan Kisseloff. The two men looked at one another with an indescribable expression.

"Ivan Kisseloff!" cried one.

"George Simpson!"cried the other, simultaneously.

And George Simpson, overcome by so many diverse emotions, lost consciousness.

The *Céleste* regained the upper regions. At an altitude of two thousand meters it found the current favorable to its course again, orientated itself, and eventually reached the Siberian shore near the Gulf of Tauisk. Two hours later she landed close to Okhotsk.

During the journey, George Simpson, surrounded by care and concern, recovered slightly. He thanked his rescuers; then, overcome by fatigue, exhausted by his long battle against the elements, racked by the fever that took possession of him, he went to sleep believing that he was dreaming. At Okhotsk, he woke up again. Sleep had replenished his strength and given his thought all the clarity of intelligence. When the fashion in which he had been snatched from certain death and transported to land was explained to him, he remained mute with astonishment and admiration.

"You didn't see us, then?" Will Took asked him.

"Yes, but vaguely. Through the rain driven horizontally by the wind I made out a black mass that passed over the masts several times, and I thought I was seeing a cloud driven by the wind. A few sailors assured me that they heard voices coming from the sky, but I thought that fear had led them astray and that they were troubled by a hallucination. Then again, I was too busy commanding the maneuvers to pay any attention to an unusual object."

"It was you in command of the corvette, Monsieur Simpson?" said Cardounet.

"Alas, yes. A big wave had just carried the captain away."

"It was you on the bridge?"

"Yes."

"Well, you're a brave man, and I'm delighted to have helped to rescue you."

That compliment brought a slight grimace to Ivan Kisseloff's face, but as the Russian was a man of honor, he suppressed any impulse of hatred, talked to the commandant of the port of Okhotsk and commended George Simpson to his benevolence.

Okhotsk is merely a maritime station, which has lost its importance since Russia has withdrawn its Siberian frontier to the River Amur. The city, with a population of between a thousand and twelve hundred, built in wood, is wretched in appearance. The winters there are extremely rigorous.

The voyagers were cordially welcomed by the Russian functionaries relegated to that corner of the Earth. After dinner, they repaired to a vast dilapidated hall: no ceiling, no tapestries, no curtains, no luxurious furniture, but, by way of compensation, wooden benches on which were piled soft furs, carpets made of luxurious and precious skins, and a cast-iron stove, which hummed gently and spread a gentle warmth through the room.

Everyone, according to his taste or temperament, took coffee or tea, skillfully prepared by a Cossack cook. Then they chatted about the marvels of aerial locomotion.

Simpson, completely recovered and restored, remained sad and silent, thinking about the incidents of his rescue, his sunken corvette, his friends and comrades swallowed up by the waves. He was no longer the hot-headed midshipman of Constantinople. Distant voyages, accompanied by their inseparable dangers, had matured his reason and calmed he effer-vescence of his youth; today, he was a lieutenant in the service of Her Britannic Majesty, and his superiors reckoned him one of the most experienced and capable officers in the English navy.

During quiet hours on watch, either in the calm of serene tropical nights or wintering in the polar seas, he had often re-membered the man he had killed—he had thought that Ivan Kisseloff was dead—and reproached himself for his insolent provocation. His victim pursued him everywhere and some-times appeared to him, as fearful as Banquo's ghost. That was why he had fainted on seeing Count Ivan Kisseloff.

Madame Valdy, with the tact characteristic of women, sensed the immense grief that was overwhelming Simpson, and tried to console him.

"Monsieur Simpson," she said to him, "Tell us about those the tempest stole from you. Memory is a second life, and you will be with them again."

"Alas, Madame," the lieutenant replied, "the wound from which my heart is suffering will never heal. My superiors, my equals, my brave mariners—I loved them all! For two years we've been sailing together, two years during which we shared the same discomforts and the same hopes. They were my family."

"Monsieur Simpson, God takes pity on the unfortunate and disinherited of this world; He will not abandon you."

"I've never doubted God, for his designs are impenetra-ble."

"How did you come to find yourself in these distant seas when the tempest came to assail you?"

"I'll tell you that."

Everyone who understood English drew closer to the shipwreck-victim.

"For several months," Simpson went on, "we were sta-tioned in the China Seas, and our principal base was Honk Kong. Captain James Reynolds, the commander of out cor-vette, received orders to return to Europe. The Admiralty, confident in his skill, his experience and his knowledge, instructed him to explore the Asiatic shore, the Aleutian islands and the American coast from the Alaskan peninsula all the way to Cape Horn. It was a veritable scientific expedition. Our principal aim was to study the meteorology of the climates contained between the sixtieth degrees of north and south latitude.

"After having passed through the Tatar Strait and taken on provisions at Nicolayevsk, we headed for Okhotsk. We'd just passed St. Jonas' Island when the tempest hit us. Captain Reynolds tried to reach Port Ayan or some haven on the Siberian coast, but the gusts of wind falling on the corvette drove her out to sea. Then, furling the sails and putting on steam, we were out in the open when we began taking on water in the coal-hold. Had we touched a reef? Was the hull breached? I don't know. Just as the commander as ordering all hands to the pumps and enormous wave swept over the bridge of the ship and carried him away. As the senor lieutenant on board I took his place.

"Soon, I realized that the pumps had become blocked and could no longer take up water. The fire, reached by the water, went out and the corvette began to sink. Then we fired the cannon and I made my preparations to abandon ship, ordering the lifeboats to be made ready. You, my friends, who have snatched me from the jaws of death, saw me at work; you know that I tried everything to save my unfortunate comrades!"

"Lieutenant," said Pickerreek, "you're as brave as the bravest captains of the Dunkerque whalers. I know what I'm talking about!"

"Alas," George Simpson continued, "my efforts were in vain. God had condemned us to death." And the poor lieutenant hid his face and wept. Everyone shared his emotion and respected his grief.

Simpson, a zealous puritan, as religious as seamen are, thought that the Almighty had unleashed his wrath upon the crew of the corvette because he was a hardened sinner; internally, he blamed himself, and was mortified. "My God! My

God!" he murmured, sobbing. "If you required a victim to appease your wrath, why didn't you choose me? The voice of fate designated Jonah, and calm succeeded the tempest. Lord, I have sinned and I alone was guilty!"

To create a diversion from that painful scene, Madame Valdy asked the lieutenant what his plans were.

"I shall stay here," he replied, "until I find a means to return home."

"Why not come with us?"

"Oh, Madame, you're answering my most secret prayers. I feared embarrassing you on your aerial vessel."

"You need new friends—be ours."

"Madame, you have my eternal gratitude. I'll come with you as far as India. There, I'll put myself at the disposal of my country's authorities."

It was agreed that George Simpson would augment the crew of the *Céleste*. Only Ivan Kisseloff had a few mental reservations, in which hatred spoke more loudly than generosity, but he did not let his ill-humor show.

The party continued for a little longer, and then everyone made arrangements for the night's rest.

The tempest was still blowing on the twenty-fourth of September and the wind, lees variable, was blowing from the north-east. The sharp cold obliged the voyagers to don their furs. The *Céleste* rose up to a low altitude, followed the Siberian coast, passed over Port Ayan and arrived at Oudskoi.

At Oudskoi, a Russian outpost surrounded by Tungus tribes, the principal inhabitants of the region, the voyagers ate a hasty breakfast, took on the bicarbonate of soda and hydrochloric acid deposited in the fort at the mouth of the river Uda and continued their aerial journey.

In spite of his bitter thoughts and black melancholy, George Simpson allowed himself to be gained by enthusiasm. He admired the marvelous apparatus that was carrying him through the air with vertiginous rapidity without restriction, and warmly praised the genius that had conceived it.

"Your work is beautiful and extraordinary," he said to Valdy. "Thanks to your endeavor, the day will come when we are able to brave tempests with impunity; mothers and wives will bless you then."

After leaving Oudskoi the aeronef crossed the ramifications of the Stanovoi and Khinghan Mountains and penetrated into a region that was not as harsh and wild as the one they had been traveling through.

"Behold the land of Amur!" exclaimed Ivan Kisseloff. "It's a Russian conquest; we've been its definitive masters since 1858, and we've already transformed it completely. The immense country was once only traveled by nomadic populations: the Tungus, called after the animals that accompany them in their migrations, Tungus dogs, Tungus reindeer and Tungus horses. Now towns are being constructed, the steppes colonized, steamboats go up the rivers and industry is making progress!"

They laughed at Kisseloff's chauvinism—especially Cardounet, who said: "I prefer my Landes, Monsieur le Comte."

However, when they reached the Bureya, a tributary of the Amur, they discovered cultivated fields, verdant meadows, semi-European and semi-Asiatic villages, herds of animals, hamlets in which nomad tents were sheltered by colonists' farms, and they agreed that the Russian had no exaggerated unduly in his pompous description.

To reach her destination the *Céleste* had only to follow the course of the Bureya, which snaked through a fertile valley. She passed over Irkutsk,[49] a large town and agricultural center with several forts of various sizes, and landed at about five o'clock in the afternoon at Blagoveshchensk.

---

[49] Brown's geography goes seriously awry here; Irkutsk is more than a thousand kilometres west of the Bureya, which has no large towns; he might have confused the name of the river with that of Buryat, a region which lies directly to the east of Irkutsk.

That small town, situated at the confluence of the Bureya and the Amur, is recently-founded. Emperor Nicholas had it constructed almost at the same time as Nicolayevsk, the capital of the province of the eastern Siberian shore. It is the hub of a circle administrated by officers, for the Russians colonize their immense possessions militarily.

The Amur, the beautiful river named Sahaliyan by the Manchus and Heilong-Jiang by the Chinese, separates Siberia from Manchuria. Cossacks and Tungus on the left bank, Manchus on the right, perceived the aeronef carrying out its final aerial maneuvers. At first they experienced an extreme fright, but were reassured when they saw the Russian authorities marching resolutely toward the gigantic bird and shaking the hands of Ivan Kisseloff and his companions amicably.

The commandant of the Blagoveshchensk region, fearing that the curiosity of those under his administration might lead them to commit thefts and depredations, had the *Céleste* guarded by a platoon of soldiers, took the voyagers to his house, and treated them in a princely fashion.

The following day, before more than ten thousand people who had come from all directions, the *Céleste* rose into the atmosphere and continued her journey. The wind was still blowing from the north-east, but it was less violent. The aeronef crossed the northern part of Manchuria, an almost independent Chinese province governed by three viceroys or Fu-Yu, inhabited by Manchu nomads and sedentary Chinese.

"One thing I've noticed," said Cardounet, "is that we're in a land of veritable ugliness. Dernghuiz isn't handsome, but he's twenty times better than the indigenes we can see."

"Damn! That's no way to talk about your pupil!" said Ivan Kisseloff, smiling.

"I'm not criticizing him; he's a charming individual…morally speaking. He's useful, drinks wine now without pulling faces, and clinks glasses like a true matelot."

"What does that prove?"

"It proves, Monsieur le Comte, that Dernghuiz, thanks to our cares, has acquired a false European appearance that brings him closer to us, and takes him further away from the villainous types of these lands."

"You're a trifle mistaken, my brave Cardounet. Dernghuiz doesn't belong to the same variety as the peoples in the midst of whom we find ourselves. Like the Kirghiz, The Bashkirs, the Turkomans and the Baluchis—in sum, all the peoples living west and south of the Pamir Plateau, he belongs to the Indo-Germanic race, while the majority of those to the north and east belong to the yellow or Mongolian race, characterized by the broadness of the face, prominent cheekbones, small and widely-separated eyes, cleaved obliquely, large ears, a broad nose, a pointed chin, thick lips, an ill-furnished bard and a yellow-tinted skin."

"I'm not as knowledgeable as you, Monsieur le Comte," Cardounet continued, "although I studied…once…but it seems to me that you're painting a portrait of Dernghuiz."

"I don't say that there isn't a certain relationship between the two human species with which we're concerned, for in central Asia there's a commonalty of language and mores that proves that the ere once confused, but you'll agree that in Dernguiz the type is less accentuated than among the Mongols we saw in Blagoveshchensk."

"Which is to say that he's the Apollo of the Bel Air—that, I think, is what that citizen of the pagan paradise is called…"

"No, of the Belvedere."

"All right, the Belvedere! Well, he's that Apollo compared with all the apes that we visited at Blago…your Russian names are a kilometer long and one can never pronounce them entirely without drawing breath and taking a drink."

"Some of them are quite short," said Ivan Kisseloff, laughing, "and don't require similar precautions.

"Those," replied Cardounet, in the same tone, "we can pronounce twice over right away."

After having crossed a series of steppes and the Khinghan mountains, the *Céleste* passed over an uneven country, fairly well cultivated, irrigated by numerous watercourses and sufficiently wooded. They passed over the Argun, and two hundred kilometers further on they reached the Shilka—the two rivers that join up to form the Amur. A few minutes later they came down at Nerchinsk, the objective of the journey of the twenty-fifth of September.

Chapter XV

Nerchinsk is a town of eight hundred souls in the province of Transbaikalia, formed in 1851 from the southern part of the government of Irkutsk and Daourie. It is famous for the lead, silver and gold mines found in the region; it is almost a European city, coquettishly located at the mouth of the Nercha, a pretty river that flows into the Shilka.

Ivan Kisseloff introduced his companions, including George Simpson, to the civil and military authorities, the administrators and mining engineers, and gave the latter a tour of the aeronef, giving them all the explanations they requested. Some of the Russian functionaries spoke French and they offered their compliments to Valdy in that language. Madame Valdy became the object of their most delicate and polite attentions, and during the splendid diner and brilliant soirée that the Administrator General gave the voyagers, the places of honor were reserved for her. A deputation of miners came to beg her to accept three small ingots, one of lead, one of silver and one of gold. The most literate worker made a small speech in Russian, which was immediately translated and was not too badly phrased.

Madame Valdy thanked the poor miners warmly. The Administrator General said to her, laughing: "Literacy is taking root everywhere, Madame; it's a sore by which it's necessary not to let oneself by infected. So, to punish the workers, I'll give them a day's paid leave."

"You couldn't be more agreeable to me, Monsieur," Madame Valdy replied.

"It seems to me," Will Tooke interjected, "that not all the miners are of Russian origin."

"That's true, the Administrator replied. "There are a few Buryats among them, who, subject to our civilizing influence, have abandoned their nomadic habits and shaken off their traditional idleness in order to demand from labor a well-being

211

and ease that they never knew on the steppes, especially when the winters raged in all their rigor."

"Are the Buryats numerous in this province?"

"About a hundred thousand of them have been counted between Lake Baikal and the Argun, and they can put twenty thousand warriors on campaign, for their adolescents and old men bear arms. They've been Russian subjects since 1644, and choose their own chiefs, save for governmental confirmation, which gives them a dagger, the symbol of their dignity. In summer they live in huts that resemble Bedouin *gourbis*; in winter they shelter in fur tents. Their religion is a mixture of Buddhism and idolatry. In their eyes, women are impure and inferior beings who cannot approach their idols and domestic gods. If a Buryat wants to sit down where a woman has sat down before him, he purifies the place with perfumes, ablutions and prayers, but those who get close to us gradually forsake their customs and prejudices."

The party went on long into the night, and the voyagers did not surrender to the delights of sleep until after midnight.

On the twenty-sixth of September the sun rose bright and radiant. Not a breath of air stirred the atmosphere. Good weather had finally replaced the equinoctial torment that had raged for three days. The *Céleste* departed, acclaimed by the entire population of Nerchinsk, and headed westwards. The mining administrator immediately sent a dispatch to Kyakhta to announce the arrival of the aeronef. During a journey of about a hundred myriameters, no incident troubled the voyage. The country over which they passed resembled the already-familiar terrain of Transbaikalia: pastureland on the banks of the rivers, sterile steppes at the feet of the mountains.

In Kyakhta, more than twenty thousand people greeted the *Céleste* with their cheers when she came in view.

If one consults a geographical text for information about Kyakhta, one generally finds very little: "Kyakhta, a small town on the southern frontier of Siberia, in a poor and desolate country. There is considerable trade between the Chinese and Russians. Population 1,200."

Had curiosity, then, attracted twenty thousand people to a small town? No—the majority of geographical guides are mistaken in what they say about Kyakhta.

Kyakhta is famous throughout Central Asia for its great fair in the month of December; it is the center of trade between the Russians, the Siberians, the Mongols and the Chinese. Every year more than a 100,000,000 francs changes hands there. Kyakhta is, so to speak, merely a suburb of Troitskosavsk,[50] the official Russian city with a population of 12,000, and is only separated from the Chinese city of Maimaichin by wooden palisades. At that location, therefore, three towns come together, and we are no longer astonished to encounter a numerous population there.

The Céleste landed on a kind of rocky tumulus. Al the Russian authorities, with the governor of Troitskosavsk at the head, came to wish the voyagers welcome. It was only four o'clock in the afternoon, and Ivan Kisseloff tried to take advantage of the time by proposing to his companions that they visit the here towns. The governor offered to be their guide. Two carriages were hitched up and they began with Maimaichin.

"Although we're in China," the governor said, "you can see how great our influence is here. The people of Maimaichin almost recognize us as their suzerains and live in the certainty of soon being incorporated into Transbaikalia. Except for the soldiers sent by the court at Peking, all the inhabitants treat us as friends. They know that they owe the development of their commerce and industry to us, and they are grateful to us. What sentiments would you expect China to have for a government of which it hardly ever has word and which seems to have forgotten it? Here, we are doing more than safeguarding our interests and extending our commercial relations we're fulfilling a civilizing mission that will inevitably attract toward

---

[50] Troitskoavsk was a collective name temporarily given by the Russians to Kyatkha and Maimaichin (now Altanbulag), although it has since reverted to Kyatkha.

213

us brutalized and disinherited people whom the Celestial Empire allows to huddle in their ignorance and poverty without ever helping them."

They arrived in Kyakhta.

"Kyakhta, the governor continued, only owes its importance to its location. Initially, it was merely a fortress protecting the route followed by the caravans coming from the land of the Khalkas and the Gobi desert, but when Russia created markets and a fair here, it became the center of all the commerce of the Asiatic and Siberian regions. The fair is held in December.

"You'll doubtless be astonished that the most rigorous time of winter was chosen to effect commercial transactions, but one doesn't have European comforts here; the roads are often full of potholes and the rivers have no bridges. In winter, snow and ice level the terrain and establish direct communications. All the watercourses freeze, and facilitate the passage of convoys that would otherwise only arrive after long detours and great expense.

"Our fair in exceedingly curious; Russians, Mongols, Buryats, Manchus, Chinese, Tatars and Jews all come to it— some people travel more than two thousand *versts* to reach it. Some camp, others build huts, and everybody mingles and trades. Nothing is more bizarre than the disparate picturesque costumes that clash with our somber and severe garments. Our traders exchange leather, felt, furs, wool, animals and metals for tea, rhubarb, porcelain, raw silk and cotton. Kyakhta being 658 myriameters from St. Petersburg, it used to require two years to complete a commercial operation engaged between the two cities; now we have the telegraph and a few good roads protected by forts, which abridge the distance. However, we're waiting impatiently for the decree for a railway that will put Siberia in communication with Europe."[51]

---

[51] The Trans-Siberian Railway was, of course, built, its Far East section being inaugurated in 1890, but it by-passed

214

"That's good thinking, Governor," said Will Tooke. "The Central Pacific Railroad has done more for the prosperity of America than a hundred years of colonization."

Next they visited Troitskosavsk.

"Messieurs," the governor continued, "here we're almost in Europe. The city is built in an orderly manner and possesses all the elements that constitute civilization: churches, a printing works, a library, a museum, hotels, cafés—or, rather, tea-shops. A great deal of tea is consumed here; the excellent caravan tea renowned throughout the entire world, but which is only savored here, for it only arrives in distant lands after adulteration and mixing that remove its delicious aroma."

We shall not describe the celebrations that followed the voyagers' reception. That evening there was a dinner, a ball, illuminations, and European comfort rubbing shoulders with Asiatic luxury everywhere. Ivan Kisseloff asked whether the supplies of bicarbonate of soda and hydrochloric acid that he had ordered to be sent from China had arrived.

"I received a veritable cargo," said the governor, "which went by the river route from Nicolaevsk to Chita, and overland from Chita to here. I've conformed to the instructions that were given to me and passed on your supplies to caravan chiefs, instructing them to leave them at the designated places. I've taken the names of the depositories and I hope that you'll find everything in order. The bicarbonate of soda and hydrochloric acid are no use, and even unknown, to the people who are holding them; as they're exceedingly avaricious and I've promised them, in addition to the agreed price, a rich reward if they fulfill the prescribed conditions faithfully, I think that you'll be able to continue your exploration without delay. The great caravan that goes to Tibet every year to visit the holy city of Buddhism, should have left a considerable deposit in Lhasa. Anyway, here are the indications that you'll need."

Kyatkha and the town's importance as a trade link diminished in consequence.

The governor handed a portfolio to Ivan Kisseloff, who immediately passed it on to Valdy.

"I have one piece of advice to give you," the functionary continued. "Be prudent in your dealings with the people of Central Asia; they're crafty and suspicious. By day, don't stop near towns; wait for nightfall before going to look for the bicarbonate and acid. Your aerial vessel will sow fear wherever it passes. As you can imagine, the barbaric populations, thoughtless and cruel, will not forgive you for their terror if they get hold of you. Until you reach the Gobi desert announce loudly that you're Russian, and you'll be respected, for Russia is feared and the countries neighboring Siberia are subject to our influence, but beyond it, be watchful and circumspect."

Valdy promised to follow the governor's recommendations. Before going to bed, he took cognizance of the information he had been given, and studied his itinerary.

At daybreak on the twenty-seventh of September the voyagers shook hands with their hosts, responded with salutes to the acclamations of the crowd that pressed around them, and departed in a southward direction. A few minutes later they were in China, in the land of the Khalkha Mongols, a mountainous country irrigated by the tributary rivers of Lake Baikal. At nine o'clock in the morning they arrived at Ourga. There, no equivocation was possible; the chemical raw materials had been confided to the Russian consul.

Ourga is a city of eighty thousand inhabitants. It is a holy city and possesses the Guison Tamba, an incarnation of the Buddha, who is nevertheless obedient to the supremacy of the Dalai Lama in Lhasa. A city does not become holy without consequence, so Ourga contains a multitude of temples served by more than thirty thousand lamas. It has three very distinct districts: the Russian, the Chinese and the one consecrated to the divinity, into which the profane never penetrate.

The stir produced by the arrival of the *Céleste* in Ourga is easily imaginable, but before visitors became too numerous the visitors had restocked their supplies. Ivan Kisseloff presented his respects, on behalf of his comrades, to the Russian delegation, and the aeronef took off again. It veered slightly westwards and passed over a region of steppes announcing the imminence of the desert. The voyagers observed a few badly-maintained caravanserais, close to which poor Mongols lived, organized into improvised tribes and whose only wealth comprised sickly flocks. They also made out caravans traveling over the arid ground, which stopped in the grip of alarm when they saw the *Céleste*.

Eventually, in the distance, they saw a thin thread of water snaking through the middle of stunted plants. That was the Orkhon, a tributary of the Selenge—the Orkhon, so celebrated in Mongol pomp, whose limpid waters bathe Karakorum, once the capital of Genghis Khan's empire, today a dilapidated town.

"Everything passes and everything dies," said Will Tooke, philosophically. "Behold what remains of the great Asiatic conqueror!"

"Conquerors are condemned by God," Valdy replied, "For they ordinarily rule over nothing but ruins, slaves and cadavers. The day will come when their sanguinary exploits will be compared to the humble labors of artisans, the discoveries of scientists, the masterpieces of geniuses known and unknown, and the martyrs of ideas, and impartial posterity will judge the former severely, while blessing the latter."

"All the same, I don't think it will happen soon," said Cardounet.

"Unfortunately for humankind," added Valdy.

"The *Céleste* touched down on the bank of the Orkhon, a short distance away from Karakorum. The bicarbonate of soda and hydrochloric acid were in the home of a lama relegated to the sad village. He delivered all that he had to the voyagers, and they gave him a few gold coins.

While the aeronef was being refueled, Madame Valdy, Will Tooke, Ivan Kisseloff and George Simpson paid a rapid visit to the ruins to the ancient capital of the Mongol Empire. The latter two found themselves alone momentarily.

"Monsieur Simpson," said Ivan Kisseloff, abruptly, "I haven't forgotten the past. While we were on Russian territory, the simplest notions of propriety commanded me to be reserved in your regard; now, I no longer have conventions to maintain, and I hope that matters between us are not concluded."

"I am at your disposal," replied George Simpson, simply.

Madame Valdy understood by the faces of the Russian and the Englishman that something had happened between them. She made a resolution to watch them closely, to prevent any duel and perhaps to bring about a reconciliation between them.

The *Céleste* took off again and flew into the Gobi desert. Nothing can describe the bleak desolation of the solitudes they were traversing. The arid plain and the powdery soil extended as far as the eye could see. The heat soon became unbearable and the air currents, warmed by contact with the ground, produced numerous mirage effects.

"Funny country," said Cardounet. "One can't see a cat or the slightest bush."

"And yet, we're traveling over the most frequented and least extensive part of the desert," replied Ivan Kisseloff. "What would it be like if we were flying over its broadest extent? Dernghuiz, who has undertaken the voyage, claims that there aren't five trees between Ourga and the Khinghan Mountains, over a distance of between a thousand ad twelve hundred kilometers."

"Damn! What will become of us if we don't have enough carbonic acid gas to cross this vile country?"

"Don't worry," Valdy put in. "Our provisions from Kyakhta, Ourga and Karakorum are sufficient to get us across the whole of China. We have abundant reserves of hydrochloric acid, and if we were to run out of bicarbonate of soda we could replace it with the natron I can see beneath us."

"What's natron?"

"Know first, my brave Cardounet, that we're traversing the bed of an ancient inland sea; it needn't astonish you, then, if there are abundant quantities of salt. Under various influences, nature produces on a large scale what we perform on a small scale in our laboratories—which is to say that it transforms that salt into carbonate of soda, or, to put it another way, natron."

The *Céleste* continued on its way, almost skimming the ground. Knowing that they would not find any hills or obstacles in front of them, the voyagers were profiting from that rare topographical circumstance to examine the little-known country over which they were passing attentively.

The Gobi desert or Sha-Mo—sea of sand—is the center of the Great Asian Plateau. It extends from Chinese Turkestan in the west to Manchuria in the east, and from the land of the Khalkhas and the Dzungars in the north to the Khoukhounoor and Chara-Mongolia in the south. Its edges have an elevation of about twelve hundred meters, but going toward the center it is subject to a depression varying between six and eight hundred meters. Alexander von Bunge has recognized that it is a kind of dried-up Caspian, having conserved a few essentially aquatic vestiges: salt lakes, and, in certain places, a marine vegetation of reeds and seaweeds. The fauna is as poor as the flora; one only finds hamsters, rare herds of antelopes, argali sheep and wild donkeys. I summer, the climate resembles that of the tropics; in winter the cold is intense and the wind it. At all times tempests blow up there: whirlwinds of sand that swallow everything in their path.

In the Gobi, there are no oases like those in the Sahara. Palm trees do not grow there. The streams that emerge from the highest massifs wind slowly through marshy terrain and always die away, either into the sands of lakes presenting the various characteristics of African *chotts*. However Mongol hordes live in the desert; in the mild season, their herds browse the short, fine grass that grows in damp places, and during the bad season they retire to the mountains or camp around the caravanserai that China has established along the caravan route.

The aeronef, continuing its exploration, passed over a few almost-dry lakes, of which the largest are Olok, on the forty-fifth parallel, and Sogoh-Noor 250 kilometers further south, which receives the Tho-Sa, a trickle of water passing through Sou-Tcheou. It was almost dark when the voyagers glimpsed Sou-Tcheou, a town situated in the confines of the desert, famous in China because it is a short distance from the western extremity of the Wen-li-Tchang-Tching—which is to say-, endless fortress—known simply to Europeans as the Great Wall.[52] In conformity with the instructions of the governor of Kyakhta, Valdy chose a solitary location for is descent, half a league from Sou-Tcheou. The information said that the chemical products had been transported by a camel-driver answering to the name of Si-Ye-Ki, whose house stood on the left bank of the Tho-Sa to the north of the town.

With the aid of directions provided by Ivan Kisseloff, Dernghuiz promised to find and ring the man.

After an hour's wait, they saw Dernghuiz arriving with Si-Ye-Ki. The Chinaman as driving mules carrying the bales and bottles entrusted to his care. Ivan Kisseloff rewarded the faithful Si-Ye-Ki handsomely, and sent him away.

"We're too close to the town," Valdy said, "and since we've been recommended to show ourselves as little as possible, let's go back some distance; that way, we'll guarantee our safety and perhaps our lives."

They took advantage of the twilight to load the *Céleste*. Twenty minutes later, they were fifty kilometers north of Sou-Tcheou and landed on a plain that showed no vestige of human presence.

---

[52] The term Wen-li-tchang-tching seems to have been borrowed from Charles de Chassiron's *Notes sur le Japon, la Chine et l'Inde* (1861), from which the other exotic names—unorthodox even in 1875—in this paragraph are probably derived. Sou-Tcheou would now be rendered Suzhou, but the reference is obviously not to the city of that name in Eastern China.

Pickerreek and Cardounet prepared the evening meal; they deposited a few provisions and several bottles of a wine recommended by its age and vintage on the stony oil. Soon, nothing could be heard but the sound of jaws fulfilling their function, and the glug of wine poured into goblets.

"Before we go to sleep," said Cardounet, "I'll make you some of that caravan tea I was given at Kyakhta, that tea..."

Suddenly, a savage clamor resounded. The voyagers looked at one another in amazement, but before they could make a move—before they could even assume a defensive attitude—they were surrounded, seized and tied up by men who surged forth like wild beasts.

Dernghuiz was in the midst of them. He was encouraging them with voice and gesture. Ivan Kisseloff heard him say several times: "I was the prisoner of these foreigners. When they took my liberty they took everything from me: my horses, my mules, my camels. I want to avenge myself; these people are mine!"

"The villain," murmured Ivan Kisseloff—and he informed his companions of what was happening.

Pickerreek and Cardounet swore like men possessed and cursed Dernghuiz, employing the least polite expressions in their marine vocabulary. Alas, that was all they could do.

The crew had been surprised by a detachment of Tatars from Turkestan, veritable pirates of the desert, living by rapine, pursuing caravans to pillage them or exact a tribute.

The Tatars lit a fire, tied up their horses and camels, and gathered in a circle around the man who seemed to be in command. Madame Valdy was taken into the hideous circle. All eyes were shining with a savage and lascivious ardor.

"That woman belongs to me," said Dernghuiz. "She's my slave. Woe betide anyone who touches a hair on her head!"

"You who speak with so much assurance," said the chief, "who are you?"

"Why are you interrogating me?"

"You're disguising your person and your thought; you're a dog, and the son of a dog; you're not one of us."

"What does it take to be one of you?"

"Not to belong to the Buddhists and to venerate the Quran."

"I'm a *hadji* and I'm coming back from Mecca."

Did they believe him? That response changed the sentiments of the Tatars and caused them to respect Dernghuiz as if he were a saint. Fanaticism renders ignorant and force natures supple."

"You've seen the *Hajr al Aswad*?"[53] demanded the chief.

"I've touched it and purified myself by its contact," Dernghuiz replied. "It has borne the imprint of my lips. I have drunk the water of the Well of Zamzam. I have made the tour of the tower of Masjid al-Haram, the holy mosque as many times as the Prophet prescribed, and the remission of my sins has been granted to me.

It was impossible to conserve any doubts; Dernghuiz belonged to the Muslim religion.

In religious matters however, Dernghuiz had always shown the greatest indifference. Instead of putting into practice the precepts of the Quran, he defied them on a daily basis by remaining in the service of a Christian and drinking wine like a disciple of Bacchus. As for his prayers, he always forgot them. He was definitely cut from the cloth of a dyed-in-the-wool hypocrite. Knowing the various Tatar dialects in use in the regions of Central Asia he could, according to circumstances, be a zealous Muslim or as Buddhist sectarian.

"Tel us how you became the prisoner of the infidels?" demanded a Tatar.

"Favored by the holy Prophet, I had traversed Turan and Thian-Chan-Nan-Lou[54] in the east of Turkestan with impunity,

---

[53] The author inserts a footnote to clarify that the reference is to the sacred "Black Stone" contained within the Kaaba, the object of veneration of the Haj pilgrims.

and I was walking in small stages to return home, though the country of the Khalkas, when I was attacked by the miscreants."

"He lies! He lies!" shouted Ivan Kisseloff, loudly.

"If you budge again, of if you pronounce a single word," Dernghuiz continued, tranquilly, addressing his former master, "I'll blow your brains out, for you're a son of a dog."

"Well said, Brother," said the chief. "Take back your slave—the woman belongs to you. The holy book commands us to soothe the unfortunate and protect pilgrims."

Dernghuiz took Madame Valdy away, put a camel-hair rope around her neck, and attached her solidly to a stake driven into the ground. The poor woman did not pronounce a single word of complaint.

"The wretch!" said Valdy, trying to break his bonds.

"Let's resign ourselves and pray," said Simpson.

"What's that?" asked the chief, pointing at the black mass of the *Céleste*.

"Eh? How do I know?" replied Dernghuiz. "Perhaps it's the infidels' abode."

The Tatars drew nearer to examine the aeronef, but its eccentric form and strange disposition held the back superstitiously for a few moments.

"There's some rich booty or you," continued Ivan Kisseloff's emancipated servant. "You can share it out tomorrow. Come on, come with me."

He climbed into the *Céleste*, followed by the most courageous. Some of the thieves threw a few bales of bicarbonate of soda down on the ground and two bottles of hydrochloric acid. As it spread out the hydrochloric acid sizzled, burning everything it touched. A burnoose was reduced to tatters and its owner burned his fingers. Surprised and terrified, he uttered a terrible scream.

"What's wrong?" demanded the chief.

---

[54] Malte-Brun's appellation for the region English sources usually called Bukharia

The Tatar held up his injured hand.

"Why did you touch that without my permission?" Dernghuiz demanded, angrily. "After Allah, I'm the master here! A descendant of the Prophet gave me that water, which comes from the Well of Ishmael,[55] and in order that it would not be stolen from me, he gave it the virtue of burning until I have arrived in my tent."

Suddenly, the Tatars thought that they had among them not merely a hadji, a saint but a sorcerer, a djinni.

"I told you," said Dernghuiz, "that tomorrow the infidels' spoils will belong to you, but it's necessary that I take back what was stolen from me."

"You're right," the chief replied.

Another looter discovered five or six bottles of wine, but he broke them with scorn and indignation, for the law of the Prophet forbids the use of wine. However, having perceived the food-supplies, he took them.

"Eat," said Dernghuiz, "but let's leave the infidels' dwelling. I invite you to be my guests, and I offer you the food that has been stolen from me."

The Tatars, living meanly, like all nomadic populations, and having a substantial meal in prospect, did not need the invitation they had been given to be repeated twice. They squatted down on their heels and waited for the promised distribution.

There are at least forty starvelings, Dernghuiz thought. *How am I going to give them all a feast?*

The sobriety of the guests got him out of the difficulty though. Everyone ate, and drank...wine, cognac and rum.

To begin with, Ivan Kisseloff's servant brought a few bottles of champagne. He pretended that it was a marvelous

---

[55] The well of Zamzam, near the Kaaba, is also known as the Well of Ishmael, supposedly having sprung forth at God's command when Hagar, expelled by Abraham, was in dire straits, at which time an angel told Hagar that her son, Ishmael, would become the founder of a great nation (the Arabs).

water, the gift of a venerated dervish, assuring those who drank it all the felicities of paradise and God's forgiveness. To give more weight to his assertions, he recited verses from the Quran, prostrated himself toward the east, pronounced cabalistic formulae and poured it all around. The Tatars licked their lips and their eyes shone with pleasure.

"Pilgrim, pilgrim," said the chief, "praise God and glory to you! It's the beverage of the houris that you're serving to us."

"Drink!" Dernghuiz continued, still pouring out the sparkling liquid. "Drink the celestial dew! Allah only gives it to the elect!"

When the champagne had run out, Dernghuiz offered the cognac and the rum. Again he claimed that it as a product of the Well of Ishmael. The Muslims hold Ishmael, the patriarch glorified by the descent of Mohammed, in too great a veneration to refuse anything recalling his memory, and the Tatars drank the spirits. Some grimaced, others did not wince, and almost all of them, after a few moments, asked for more. Used to drinking the brackish water of the desert, they were already feeling the commencement of the drunkenness that cheers without making the head heavy or producing stomach cramps.

They were, in fact, in such a good mood that they proposed to massacre the prisoners and sing victory songs. Killing is mere child's play for barbarians.

Dernghuiz opposed the massacre, and appealed to their cupidity. "Today," he said, "is a blessed day for you and for me; we should not stain our hands with blood. There will be time tomorrow. The infidels have dug up treasures; they will want to buy their freedom. We'll collect their ransom and then kill them. Besides which, if we kill them immediately, who will return my camels, my horses, my tents, my servants and all the sacred objects that I was bringing back from Mecca? The infidels deposited all that near Sou-Tcheou, in a place they will show us."

"Pilgrim," said the chief, "the wisdom of God is with you. Your advice is that of a pious and experienced man. Your words shall guide us."

Night fell, and its darkness was increased by vapors that rose slowly from the ground into the atmosphere, gradually becoming impenetrable even for the most clear-sighted eyes. The Tatars set up their yurts between the Céleste and their prisoners and got ready to go to sleep. To avoid any escape, the chief appointed four of his men to mount guard on Valdy and his companions. Dernghuiz volunteered to watch with them, and his offer was accepted.

Two or three hours went by. Dernghuiz chatted with his new friends about trivial matters. Suddenly, he offered them a goblet of the houris' beverage. "By chance," he had found two intact bottles. The guards did not have to be persuaded, and savored long draughts of the delicious champagne, delighted by not having to share the windfall with their comrades. Egotism is universal.

Dernghuiz went to lie down at the feet of Madame Valdy, who was still attached by the neck and weeping silently. The young woman made a gesture of repulsion, but Dernghuiz took her hands and raised them to his lips respectfully. Then he waited and watched.

The sentinels soon felt the effects of the champagne; their eyelids grew heavy and their thoughts became vague; their heads slumped on to their breasts and they eventually feel into a profound sleep.

The night was still black and the fog denser and colder. Dernghuiz untied Madame Valdy, put a pistol in her hand, bid her to keep quiet and not to move, and left her.

The prisoners were shivering. Understanding that they had no hope with regard to the bandits, and, believing that they had been betrayed by Ivan Kisseloff's servant, they were resigned and thoughtful, Valdy most of all.

So his discovery was to be futile! The fruit of his study and his labor would serve as a plaything for barbarians—and he, who had dreamed of the glory and applause of nations, would die leaving nothing behind, taking the secret of aerial navigation with him!

Suddenly, Ivan Kisseloff felt warm breath caressing his face and a hand pressing on his shoulder.

"Silence, Master, it's me," said a voice.

"Dernghuiz?"

"Yes. Don't talk. Our salvation depends on your silence. Give me your arm so that I can cut the cords binding the. Good! Now take this knife, free your legs and follow me."

The two men made their way to the *Céleste*, crawling, and stopping every time they heard a noise. After a detour, they finally arrived behind the aeronef. There they were able to talk in whispers without fear of being overheard.

"What about our friends?" asked Ivan Kisseloff.

"Master, begin getting the machine ready, so that we can leave without delay. I'll take charge of saving you all."

Ivan Kisseloff carried out an inspection by touch, for the night was too dark for him to distinguish anything, and he made sure that nothing had been removed or broken in the mechanism responsible for the transmission of movement. In addition, he established that a receptacle was sufficiently full of carbonic acid to facilitate a journey of about sixty kilometers.

Dernghuiz came back with Valdy and Madame Valdy. Twice more he made the difficult and perilous journey, and brought back George Simpson, Will Tooke and Cardounet. He had not been able to find Pickerreek.

Dernghuiz went back again, but after an absence of ten minutes, which seemed like ten hours, he came back alone.

"Master," he said to Ivan Kisseloff, "our friend was not with you. I'll swear to that on my life."

What should they do? Ought they to wait for daylight? Should they attack the Tatars while they were asleep? But if Pickerreek was no longer there, what good would it do to risk themselves needlessly?

The *Céleste* could not be raised on its support rods without making a slight sound. That sufficed to wake the guards, who, perceiving the disappearance of the prisoners, uttered cries for help. A savage howling replied to them. The Tatars emerged from their yurts and rushed at the aeronef in disorder.

But the *Céleste* flapped its wings, wounded the closest marauders or knocked them down, and disappeared into the fog.

Chapter XVI

After a journey of about thirty kilometers, the *Céleste*, hampered in its flight by the mist and the darkness, landed on the crest of a small hill, one of the last foothills of the Nan Shan Mountains, which separate the Khoukhounoor from the Gobi desert.

"Let's not go any further," said Valdy. "At daybreak we'll retrace our steps and go back to recue Pick."

"What if the Tatars have killed him?" asked Simpson.

"Then woe betide them!" cried Cardounet, angrily.

"Do you think," asked Ivan Kisseloff of his servant, "that the bandits will respect the life of your friend Pick if he succeeded in getting away?"

"I'm certain of it," Dernghuiz replied. "For them, everything that happened last night—the distribution of water from the Well of Ishmael, your liberation and our flight through the air—are incomprehensible and supernatural things, and they'll take our friend for a djinni. A Muslim would never raise a hand against a djinni."

"Let's hope that you're right."

After that, everyone wanted to know about the subterfuges Dernghuiz had employed to bring his work of liberation to a successful conclusion. The brave servant recounted his deceptions, his ruses and his speeches. Ivan Kisseloff translated his story as he went along.

"Master," Dernghuiz added, "why did you doubt your slave? Have I not always been faithful and devoted?"

"Forgive me, Dernghuiz. You're no longer my servant—you're my friend. Anything it pleases you to ask of me—money or land—I will give you."

"Keep your land and your money. My needs are insignificant and I want to remain with you forever. Your friendship is sufficient for me."

"Your heart is valiant and generous, Dernghuiz; I shall be more than a friend; I shall be your brother."

"Master, ask the lady if she forgives me for having handled her roughly and tethered her. By acting thus, I probably saved her honor and her life."

The Russian transmitted his servant's question to Madame Valdy. She immediately came to squeeze his hands effusively. Valdy, Simpson, Will Took and Cardounet did likewise.

To avoid any new surprise, the voyagers armed themselves and stood watch until morning. Only Madame Valdy slept for a while—a repose very necessary after so much emotion.

Finally, daylight appeared; the sun dissipated the fog; the immense plain extended like a sea. Only a few streams and partly dried-up lakes broke the monotony of the vast solitude. The *Céleste* took off and Valdy steered it toward the Tatar camp. The latter had disappeared. Broken bottles, the debris of the meal, the bicarbonate of soda trodden underfoot and the droppings of the camels and horses indicated the location of the halt.

Dernghuiz examined the terrain carefully, looked attentively at the imprints left here and there by the animals—in brief, following the track—and announced with certainty that the caravan had headed north. The aeronef rose up a thousand meters, and the voyagers aimed their binoculars at the horizon.

Between two indentations in the terrain Will Tooke made out a party of men and beasts of burden marching raggedly, but he could not be certain that they were the previous evening's enemies.

Dernghuiz, however, was in no doubt. "Them! Them!" he cried, several times.

The *Céleste* set out in pursuit of the troop and reached it in less than five minutes. The Tatars stopped, surprised and terrified.

Ivan Kisseloff and Will Tooke were strongly tempted to take their revenge and fire a few bullets, but Dernghuiz dissuaded them from doing so.

"Let's stop," he said. "I'll bring Pick back without our having to shed blood. You keep watch—that's all I ask of you."

The aeronef landed two hundred meters from the caravan. Gripped by terror, the Tatars prostrated themselves and begged for divine mercy.

"Bunch of Bedouins!" shouted a voice, with scorn mixed with a certain measure of mockery. It was Pickerreek's voice.

All the voyagers shivered with joy. Dernghuiz headed toward the bandits and demanded in an imperious tone to talk to the chief.

"What do you want?" said the latter, trembling with fear.

"Your prisoner."

"There he is. We haven't done him any harm. We've respected him..."

"You've acted wisely, for my vengeance would have been terrible."

"Who are you, then, you who drink the water of paradise and command the earth and the air?"

"I'm a servant of the Holy Prophet; he sent me to you to tell you to quit the life of murder and pillage. Repent and be humble; if not, a terrible punishment awaits you all."

The Tatars prostrated themselves, giving signs of the utmost desolation, and murmuring prayers. In the meantime, Dernghuiz and Pickerreek went to the *Céleste* and embarked.

We shall not describe the transports of joy that welcomed the worthy Pick. The aeronef took of immediately and veered away. Now she could continue her journey freely.

"What time is it?" Valdy asked.

"Eight o'clock."

"We haven't lost much time. If nothing goes wrong, we'll still arrive in Lhasa today, the twenty-eighth of September, and take on abundant food supplies, bicarbonate of soda and hydrochloric acid."

The voyagers rapidly traversed the final plains of the Gobi, crossed the Nan Shan mountains and the northern part of Khoukhounoor—a Chinese province that owes its name to a great lake, the Blue Sea—and rose above the Baian-Kara-ula mountains, several of whose peaks are covered in eternal snows. From that point on they were obliged to maintain an altitude varying between three and four thousand meters, for the Tibetan plateau on to which they were penetrating presents a succession of chains that rise up one after another like the steps of a gigantic circus, all the way to the Himalaya.

That immense terrace doe not, however, have the elevation that certain geographers attribute to it of between four and five-and-a-half thousand meters. The plateaus and the peaks have doubtless been confused. Alexander von Humboldt's calculations only estimate it at 3,500 meters, and, according to the most recent information, the sacred lakes on the banks of which a numerous population lives are only 3,700 meters above sea level.

In response to Madame Valdy's request, Pickerreek related what had happened to him.

"It's quite simple," he said. "When we were captured and tied up by the Blackamoors I said to myself, *Pick, it's not these apes who'll have your hide*—and I resolved to set us free. First, it would be necessary for me to break my bonds, then I'd break yours, and then—forward into battle! I thought that each of us was worth four or five Tatars-that as the proportion I established in my intellect. And I said to myself again: *Pick, my friend, you're going to play a trick on them of which they'll only see the smoke!*

"When I saw that they were asleep, I dragged myself behind the horses and camels, quietly, to the place where they'd piled up the saddles and the rest of their trinkets. I was mad at Dernghuiz and I swore to kill him as sure as my name's Pick and I'm from Dunkerque! *Brigand, you've betrayed us*, I said to myself. *You'll pay me back for that, or I'll perish, strangled by all the Flying Dutchman's bowlines*. Then I found the pommel of a saddle decorated with brass wire and edged with a strip of metal that was quite sharp.

"I rubbed the rope tying my hands against that blade. I rubbed for a long time, for I was holding my breath like a porpoise and I did it softly so as not to raise the alarm. I rubbed so hard and so long that I wore away the accursed rope. Good— my arms were free. As for the legs, that was no longer difficult, and I said to myself again: *Ah, my lads, I'll prepare a trick for you that'll make you sicker than if you had perpetual seasickness!*

"As I was getting ready to come for the rest of you, I heard a frightful racket, and howling that would have made all the devils in Hell quiver—then I saw you taking off. You were saved! That was the essential thing, damn it! And I was more content than if I'd been appointed a naval captain or an admiral! Five or six Blackamoors found me and fell on me, but one knows how to box, and kick-box...and *bang! bang!*—fists in the face and kicks in their crotch; a body-check there and a trip there...al that fell on them like misery on the poor, and I got rid of all that vermin!

"Then the chief arrives; he gives me a speech in his gibberish, which I don't understand; naturally, I reply to him in French, and I say to him: *My worthy fellow, don't bother with so much eloquence; I warn you that if you touch a single hair on my head, I have friends who'll find you and take away your appetite for biscuit, and likewise for your comrades.*

"Well, would you believe it? That little speech had its effect. The Tatars approached me respectfully; some of them knelt down and came to kiss my feet and the hem of my jacket. That didn't do me any harm, so I let them do it. I understood that they took me for some kind of god. Not wanting to be outdone in politeness, I offered the chief a plug of tobacco. He took it, but instead of putting it in his mouth, he put it in a bag hung around his neck like a scapular and tucked it under his shirt, over his breast."

"Oh, of course!" exclaimed Ivan Kisseloff, laughing. "The chief mistook your stick of tobacco for an amulet."

"Much good may it do him," Pickerreek continued. "Then, at daybreak, we left. The Blackamoors were still looking up in the air and seemed anxious. Me, I was hoisted on to a camel, which shook up my guts in a rude fashion, but I consoled myself, because I hoped to see you soon. Finally, I spotted the *Céleste*, like a black dot in the sky. *Ha ha!* I said to myself, again. *Everyone has his turn, comrades, and we're going to see you dance to the violin!*

"I was expecting a battle, and then I saw Dernghuiz arrive. I realized then that something had happened that I didn't understand, and I followed him to come and find you. Oh, if you'd seen the Tatars when you arrived! They were trembling in every limb and opening their eyes like a carp's. Truly, they were falling apart with fear."

"But you, my brave Pick—you weren't afraid?" asked Valdy.

"No—I knew you'd come to recue me, and that you'd get me back, even if I were a hundred feet underground."

"That confidence does us as much honor as you," said Will Tooke. "To save you, we'd have made any sacrifice."

"Of course," said Pickerreek, and made a gesture that signified: *I always counted on you; count on me!*

Meanwhile, the *Céleste* was passing over mountains, profound valleys, lakes and rivers at an extraordinary velocity. Sometimes it skimmed the terrain of high plateaus. Then it frightened the inhabitants of the desolate regions, the ruminants of the depths and the birds of the glacial summits; little troops of goats and sheep ran over the abrupt slopes; yaks fled and ibexes launched themselves with prodigious bounds from one escarpment to another; eagles and bearded vultures abandoned the inaccessible crags and flew away, uttering raucous and discordant cries.

Finally, at about four o'clock in the afternoon, the aeronef rose up to more than six thousand meters above sea level to cross the last mountains forming the plain of Lhasa, through which flow the rapids and cataracts of the Tsang-

Tsiou,[56] a tributary of the Tsang-Po or Brahmaputra. At that height, the air was not too rarefied because of the incessant evaporation of the watercourses and great lakes, such as the Buka Noor and the Tengri Noor. Even so, the voyagers felt some oppression; their vision became blurred and their throats dried out.

"Our malaise won't last," said Valdy, encouraging his comrades. "We're going down—I can see Lhasa, the objective of today's journey."

At that moment, there was an atmospheric disturbance that caused the *Céleste* to pirouette and lean to port in a terrifying fashion.

A cry escaped every throat...

Cardounet had just been tipped overboard!

His fingernails traced a groove over the cork sheets; his hands sought convulsively for something to hold on to, but only encountered the red umbrella given to him by Mary Silver—and the umbrella, not being retained by anything, followed poor Cardounet in his fall.

"Damn it!" cried Valdy.

"Cardounet! Cardounet!" shouted Pickerreek, several times. And the mariner wiped away the tears that were running down his tanned face.

"If the Tatars had killed me," he went on, in a voice punctuated by sobs, "I wouldn't have witnessed my friend's death! That would have been better for me, for I won't survive this!"

"Perhaps Cardounet isn't dead," said Will Tooke. "He could have fallen into a river or a lake, or tall trees that would have deadened his fall."

"Ah!" Madame Valdy put in. "You're giving us hope, Mr. Tooke—and I have confidence in it."

"God has protected you thus far, Madame," Simpson added, "and in his infinite bounty, He'll protect you still."

---

[56] Presumably the Kyi Chu

The aeronef was almost flying over Lhasa already, but she turned back and Valdy headed for the point where Cardounet had fallen. He landed there.

For more than an hour the voyagers searched, calling out and shouting, but only echoes replied. There was no trace of Cardounet—not even a cadaver.

"He's dead, well and truly!" said Pickerreek, dejectedly.

"And yet, we haven't found his body," said Ivan Kisseloff.

"Before reaching the ground he fell at least three thousand meters, and in his fall he'd have been flattened, or even buried in some loose ground—unless rocky spurs tore him apart."

They feared that Pickerreek was right. Unfortunately, all the probabilities favored his assertions. Madame Valdy tried to console him, but the young woman had as much need of consolation as the mariner. Dernghuiz appeared to be gravely afflicted; he loved his joyful "professors" so much!

"Our search is futile," said Valdy, sadly. "We can't stay here any longer. Let's say a prayer for the first victim of aerial navigation and then let's go."

The voyagers knelt down on the ground and invoked the mercy and generosity of God on behalf of their lost friend. The Almighty must certainly have been listening to their humble supplications, because no more fervent prayer ever escaped mortal lips.

Then the *Céleste* resumed its flight and went to perch on a steep mountain ridge about a league from Lhasa, the culminating point overlooking the valley of the Tsang-Tsiou, which did not permit any surprise. Valdy consulted the information furnished by the governor of Kyakhta and read the following:

The bicarbonate of soda and hydrochloric acid are in the safe-keeping of the leader of the caravan formed in the south of the Gobi Desert at Ngan-si Chau; he is to hand the chemical elements over to a Chinese functionary, the supervisor of

236

the tardjoums[57]—way-stations—who resides in Lhasa. According to the indications I have received, the house of this functionary is easily recognizable by its elevation, its architecture, more Chinese than Tibetan, and the detachment of Chinese soldiers guarding it. It is situated to the north of Lhasa, on the road leading to the fortress of Potala, the residence of the Dalai Lama.

In order to introduce yourselves to the supervisor of the tardjoums, act prudently; put on local costume and show him the sheet of paper covered in Chinese characters that you will find in a pocket of the portfolio. It is a letter from the mandarin at Maimaichin; his dignity gives you the right to speak in the name of the Emperor of China, and his recommendation is all-powerful.

"Provided that the caravan has arrived safely," said Will Tooke, "we'll find the bicarbonate and the acid easily. The Russian governor's information is remarkable in its clarity and precision."

"That's true," Valdy replied, "but there's no point going I search of them this evening, for it's getting dark and Lhasa seems to me to be a city large enough to get lost in."

"Waiting would be wiser," agreed Ivan Kisseloff.

The voyagers found a few provisions that had escaped the voracity of the Tatars and ate, but their meal was sad. They could not help thinking about Cardounet, whom they would never see again. Pickerreek, his eyes moist with tears, set up the tent, wrapped himself in his blankets and lay down. Everyone else did likewise.

In those high regions, one hears nothing but the harsh cold wind passing through the fissures in the rocks and moan-

---

[57] This word does not appear to be found anywhere outside the present text except for the 1868 issue of a periodical called *L'Année Géographiqe*, edited by Vivien de Saint-Martin, where it is used to signify a measure of distance.

ing. One might think that the sounds were sighs mingled with lugubrious plaints.

Poor Cardounet!

The next day, the twenty-ninth of September, as soon as dawn broke, Dernghuiz, furnished with the letter from the mandarin of Maimaichin and in possession of the directions necessary to find the supervisor of the tardjoums, descended into the plain and headed toward Lhasa. His Tatar costume, which he had never forsaken for European clothing, was little different from that of the Tibetans, and nothing drew attention to him.

When he went into Lhasa he was astonished to see an immense crowd. He even recognized individuals belonging to distant countries bordering the Pamir plateau. He hesitated to enquire as to the cause of the assembly, however, fearing that he might be taken for an intruder. Finally, he approached a man whose placid face inspired some confidence in him.

"Praise God!" he said,

"Glory to Buddha!" the man replied.

"May the Dalai Lama be blessed!"

"It's today that the Dalai Lama is reborn, but his spirit has been watching over his servants since he has deprived himself of his mortal envelope."

Dernghuiz knew enough. If anyone interrogated him he could reply. He continued on his way and eventually arrived at the house of the supervisor of the tardjoums. When he tried to go inside the soldiers pushed him back; then he showed the mandarin's letter. The commander kissed it respectfully and rapped twice with his staff on a gong, which resonated with prolonged vibrations. Three richly-dressed officers immediately appeared.

"What is it?" they asked, in Chinese—a language that Dernghuiz did not understand.

"Orders from Tsien-Tse, Hoang-ti"—the Son of Heaven and Sublime Master—said the chief guard.

The officers disappeared and soon reappeared with a fat man clad in a floral-patterned satin robe and a blue crepe surcoat. It was the supervisor of the tardjoums, a military mandarin of the second class and one of the most important individuals in Lhasa. He took the letter that Dernghuiz held out to him and read it, making gestures of the most profound respect.

The bicarbonate of soda and hydrochloric acid had been in his house for more than a month.

The mandarin spoke one of the dialects in use in both Tibet and Turkestan, and was able to converse briefly with Dernghuiz.

"What are you going to do with these substances?" he asked.

"I don't know their purpose. I'm carrying out the orders I was given."

"Who commanded you?"

"Powerful and rich servants of the Son of Heaven."

"Did they not tell you that they would reward my zeal?"

"Yes." Dernghuiz took twenty gold coins out of his pocket and handed them to the Chinaman. Four hundred francs! That is a fortune in Tibet.

The mandarin's face blossomed like a flower caressed by the first rays of the rising sun, and he gave orders to have the bales and bottles confided to his care loaded up. Dernghuiz, followed by mules, horses and two Chinese servants, left the house of the supervisor of the tardjoums, but in spite of his best efforts he could not move forward. An innumerable multitude of men and women was blocking the road, uttering shrill cries. Lamas were singing the praises of Buddha and burning incense. It was a Buddhist procession. Everyone prostrated themselves, including curiosity-seekers. In order not to stand out, Dernghuiz bowed in devotion—but curiosity over-rode fervor, and he raised his head.

Then his heart started beating as if to burst out of his breast. He had seen...no, it was impossible! He was the victim of a hallucination or a dream. His eyes were deceiving him.

When he looked up again, he saw nothing but the immense crowd disappearing around a bend in the rod, and could no longer make out the object that had impressed him so powerfully.

He gave the order to depart, and while his voice encouraged the animals that he drove in front of him, he smiled in a strange fashion.

Before leaving Lhasa he bought food-supplies—rice and oatmeal pancakes, dried fruits, poultry, etc.—and an assortment of old Tibetan and Chinese clothes that he spotted in a shop.

Dernghuiz was definitely planning something.

Having arrived close to the place where the *Céleste* was resting, and not wanting to show it to the Chinese domestics, he had them unload everything the mules and horses were carrying on to the side of a narrow path, gave the servants a few coins and sent them away. Valdy, Kisseloff, Simpson, Will Tooke and Pickerreek transported the chemical products, foodstuffs and old clothes to the aeronef by hand.

"Now let's go," said Valdy.

"Master," said Dernghuiz to Ivan Kisseloff, "tell the Captain that we can't go. I've seen Cardounet."

"What! You've seen Cardounet?"

"Yes, Master."

"But that's impossible."

"Like you, I doubted it—but certainty has entered my mind now. I saw our friend among the lamas celebrating the glory of Buddha."

"Where was that?"

"In Lhasa."

"Dernghuiz, Dernghuiz. You're driving me mad. Think hard. Haven't you been misled by some resemblance?"

"Master, I assure you that it was Cardounet."

"Messieurs, Messieurs!" cried Ivan Kisseloff, breathlessly. "Cardounet's alive!"

The voyagers' surprise was indescribable.

"Ah! By all that's holy!" said Pickerreek. The mariner extended his arms, went frightfully pale, and fell over.

"What's the matter, Pick?" asked Madame Valdy.

"Pay no attention, Madame…Cardounet's not dead! That news gave me so much pleasure that…this time…I swallowed my plug!"

A few pinches of an emetic taken from the pharmacy box rid Pickerreek of his involuntary ingurgitation. It was agreed that Simpson, Ivan Kisseloff and Dernghuiz would go back to Lhasa to make sure of Cardounet's identity and to liberate him.

The Englishman and the Russian put on the old clothes, wrapped their faces in pieces of cloth similar to those worn by nomadic populations to protect them from the sun's ardor—an indispensable precaution to hide their European features—picked up weapons and gold, and followed Dernghuiz.

Chapter XVII

Dernghuiz' eyes had not deceived him; Cardounet was not dead!

You will recall that in trying to cling on to the aeronef, Cardounet had not encountered any point of support except for the famous red umbrella given to him by Mary Silver, the preacher at the Ogden revival. While the *Céleste* flew on toward Lhasa, the mariner, precipitated into space and obedient to the law of gravity, had descended toward the earth at a velocity that, according to the equation specifying that the distance traveled is proportionate to the square of the time elapsed, was accelerating with every passing second.

Either by chance or the effect of a voluntary movement—Cardounet was never able to give precise information on that subject—the umbrella opened and was transformed into a parachute. The mariner clung convulsively to the handle with his clenched fists, and let himself drift in the atmosphere. The descent slowed down; initially vertical, it became somewhat oblique. Cardounet finally touched down without experiencing any shock.

Suddenly, he was surrounded by men who showed him the greatest marks of respect and hastened to take him to Lhasa. The aerial castaway was reassured, and meekly allowed himself to be guided.

The men leading him were lamas who had retired to the location to mortify themselves, fast and pray. They had seen a gigantic bird flying across the sky, and then a mass detach itself therefrom and fall from a prodigious height into their midst. Buddha was manifesting his power; he was sending one of his celestial messengers! It was a miracle—a miracle without parallel—that would make pious souls rejoice and would confound the impious. No doubt was possible; they had seen it with their own eyes.

The lamas certainly had no thought of taking advantage of that marvelous event to influence the people, for the events seemed as supernatural to them as to the most ignorant of Tibetans.

In Tibet, Buddha is worshiped as a supreme god, and his earthly representative in the Dalai Lama, the leader of spiritual power. Surrounded by Asiatic pomp and magnificence, he resides in a palace called Buddha-Lha—the happiness of wisdom[58]—built in the fortress of Potala, a kilometer to the north of Lhasa. No woman may pass the night in his abode. He receives the adoration of the faithful seated on a richly-decorated throne—or rather, an altar. When he dies, the spirit of Buddha is assumed to determine how and when he will resume his mortal envelope, completely rejuvenated—but the Chinese government, which knows how much political and religious influence these resurrections exercise on the Tibetan population, ordinarily takes charge of substituting for the spirit of Buddha.

In order to replace the dead Dalai Lama, prayers and fasts are ordered. In Lhasa, all hands agitate prayer-beads; incense is spread in profusion, and pilgrimages to Buddha-Lha are incessant. Families that believe they possess the infant called to succeed the Dalai Lama notify the Chinese authorities and the yan-wang—temporal regent—in order that it can be determined whether he has the necessary attributes.

As soon as three infants bearing the signs of the resurrection of the divinity have been found, they are taken to Lhasa and the principal lamas of the States were Buddhism is prevalent are alerted; they convene an electoral assembly, spend six days in Buddha-Lha praying, fasting and mortifying themselves, and on the seventh day pieces of paper on which the

---

[58] There appears to be a confusion here of two versions of Potala; the supposed derivation is false (*lha* actually means "divine"); most authorities think the name is actually derived from Mount Potalaka [something akin to "Brilliance"], the mythical dwelling of a Buddhist bodhisattva.

names of the infants are written are placed in a golden box; it is shaken, and the oldest lama takes out one of the pieces of paper.

The infant whose name is drawn is proclaimed Dalai Lama. He is surrounded by riches and solemnly paraded through all the streets; the faithful prostrate themselves before him. The other two competitors are returned to their parents.

The twenty-eighth of September, the day of the *Céleste*'s arrival in Lhasa and Cardounet's fall, was the sixth day of prayers for the election of a new Dalai Lama. The principal priests, informed of what had happened, firmly believed that Buddha had sent them a being from his paradise, and resolved to take advantage of this fortunate circumstance.

Cardounet was dressed in a silk robe embroidered with gold and silver, coiffed with a colossal bonnet and introduced to the people, who acclaimed him with enthusiasm. The following day, he was hoisted on to a palanquin ornamented with precious fabrics and stones, and paraded through the streets of Lhasa—and everyone prostrated themselves as he passed. It was during that parade that Dernghuiz, emerging from the house of the supervisor of the tardjoums, thought he had recognized his friend.

Cardounet was anxious, though.

How will all this end up, and when will I be liberated? he thought. *I can see that they've mistaken me for the good Lord, since they're getting down on their knees in front of me, but that scarcely makes me into these folks' good Lord. And what about my friends? They think I'm dead! That's understandable—I took a jolly plunge, and without the American preacher's umbrella, I'd have been flattened like a cod or a herring dried for seven years! Which proves that a good deed is never wasted! I protected that joker of a preacher from the people who were knocking him about, and he gave me his umbrella. Thanks, brolly! I'll keep you until the end of my days, and if you get broken, I'll have your repaired, as good as new.*

What's become of the Céleste? *While I was being taken away and was still confused by what had happened to me, I*

244

saw her pass overhead. I'm sure the Captain wanted to give me an honest burial, and that Madame Valdy recited a Pater *and an* Ave *for me—good people! And Pick? There's one who must be missing me! I certainly missed him when that filthy rabble of Tatars took him prisoner, and if they hadn't given him back, I'd have been heartbroken. But we were hoping that Pick was alive, but I'm dead for him...for all of them! And since this morning they've been parading me around like a fattened ox back home. This is at least my twentieth stop. They burn incense to me, they venerate me, and may the Devil carry me away if they aren't worshiping me a little, but all that isn't worth one of our rapid journeys through the air...*

My friends, my good friends, if you knew that I still existed, you'd look out for me and come to my rescue! My friends, shan't I ever see you again?

Cardounet felt his eyes welling with tears, and his head sank down to his breast.

Suddenly, cries of delight were heard and the frantic stamping of feet. The Dalai Lama had been named, and his sumptuous cortege was emerging from the fortress of Potala. The new incarnation of Buddha was a rather amiable child aged between five and six. The poor mite, raised on a golden palanquin, seemed utterly bewildered, but the old lamas were radiant.

Cardounet raised his head again to see what was happening. Immediately he quit his palanquin, shoved his way through the priests who opposed his passage, shook his umbrella menacingly and embraced two men who came to a halt beside him.

"Dernghuiz! Monsieur le Comte!" he cried. "Oh, it does me good to see you again."

"Cardounet, you're dooming us and dooming yourself," said Ivan Kisseloff, indicating the circle that was forming around them.

"What? What? Aren't I the good Lord of these filthy Moors? If they so much as look at you sideways, they'll have me to deal with!"

245

But the lamas were shouting about profanation and perjury. Dernghuiz and his master were seized and bound. Cardounet tried to defend them, but people moved respectfully aside before him and left him to act in a void. He foamed at the mouth and ripped his beautiful clothes.

"Load of donkeys!" he said. "You think you can get away with his? Ah, a thousand million hawsers! I'll have to disembowel a dozen of you if you don't respect me friends."

Ivan Kisseloff shouted to him: "Carry on playing your role, Cardounet. George Simpson's with us, but I can't see him anymore. He'll warn our companions, and they'll save us."

"So much the better—for the moment, I can't help you; my worshipers are so uncivilized that they don't understand a word of French."

"Keep an eye on us—that's all I ask of you."

Dernghuiz was dragged away with his master.

As if nothing had happened, Cardounet returned to his palanquin and took his throne, with a majesty of which no one would have thought him capable.

The festival and parade continued.

George Simpson, fully understanding the dangers of Cardounet's imprudence, hid his face in order not to be recognized and drew away. He ran back to the *Céleste* as fast as he could, and recounted the new misadventure that had occurred.

"Dernghuiz and Kisseloff are doomed," said Valdy, "for Chinese justice is swift."

"On the day of the proclamation of a new Dalai Lama," the lieutenant said, "it's forbidden to shed blood. We can save them."

"Tell us what to do—we'll obey without question."

"We're going to get two horses. Will Tooke will come with me..."

"What about me?" asked Pickerreek.

"You stay here. Help Monsieur Valdy fly the aeronef; Madame Valdy will lend a hand. It's necessary that the

Céleste lands on the plain in an hour's time. You'll need three people to operate it."

"All right," said Valdy.

"With the binoculars, can you make out the road from Lhasa to the fortress of Potala?"

"Yes."

"Be on the side of that road in exactly one hour, near the clump of trees that we can see. Don't get out—remain constantly ready to depart."

"I'll carry out your orders."

Will Tooke and Simpson put on some of the old clothes brought by Dernghuiz and drew away.

Before arriving in Lhasa, George Simpson spotted a camp of Mongols attracted by the solemnities of their religion, possessing a certain number of beasts of burden. By means of sign language he made them understand that he wanted two horses. The tribal chief refused at first, but a few gold coins deftly slipped into his hand made him more obliging. The well-known cupidity of such individuals speeds up the bargaining process. Simpson was able to acquire two wiry, bright-eyed and fast horses. Admittedly, he paid four times their true value for them.

The two men headed for the fork in the road they had designated.

"Are you a good horseman, Mr. Tooke?" asked Simpson.

"Yes, I was one renowned on the prairies of Kansas and Colorado."

"So much the better, for I have an important role planned for you."

"What are we going to do?"

"Kidnap the Dalai Lama."

"What!"

"There's no other means to save our companions."

"Then let's kidnap the Dalai Lama."

"You'll be on your horse and you'll hold mine by the bridle. I'll hand the child to you. Then run away as fast as you can, to where the *Céleste* will be waiting for you. Top speed!"

"What about you?"

"Make your escape without worrying about me. After all, what does it matter if I'm captured? Possession of the Dalai Lama will render us masters of the situation, and the Tibetans won't dare to do us the slightest harm for fear of reprisals."

"Good, good—I understand the plan. You can count on me, Mr. Simpson."

"Understood."

The Englishman and the American waited another quarter of an hour. The former looked at his watch and said: "In five minutes, the *Céleste* will be at the designated spot. The Dalai Lama's procession is coming toward us. Mount up, Mr. Tooke and let's get ready."

The strokes of the gong resounded at regular intervals; a large crowd drew nearer. When the Incarnation of the Buddha appeared, everyone knelt down and prostrated themselves. Momentarily, Simpson was the only one standing, save for the principal lamas. The latter advanced to order him to bow down, but the lieutenant, moving as swiftly as thought, snatched the child in his muscular arms and handed him to Will Tooke.

The confusion that followed that bold act was indescribable. The lamas launched themselves toward Will Tooke, but the American, digging his heels into the flanks of his horse, galloped away at top speed. Almost forgotten, Simpson had time to mount up and disappear in his turn.

An immense clamor rose up toward the heavens. The lamas prostrated themselves in the dust. Desolation took possession of every soul. The Chinese horsemen forming part of the cortege launched themselves in pursuit of the kidnappers—but Will Tooke and Simpson were traveling at an extraordinary speed. The horses, vocally encouraged and kicked in the flanks, were galloping frantically.

The *Céleste* landed.

"Quickly! Quickly!" cried Simpson. "They're after us!"

Will Tooke dismounted, climbed into the aeronef by means of the rope-ladder that Pickerreek threw down to him and handed the Dalai Lama to Madame Valdy. George Simpson hoisted himself up on to the deck by the strength of his wrists.

The horsemen arrived—but the *Céleste*, taking off again, rose up majestically, described a few spirals, passing over the fortress of Potala and the palace of Buddha-Lha several times, and disappeared.

The frightened horseman turned round and rode back toward the city. The amazement and cries of terror were succeed by a mad rage. The lamas tore their garments, raked their faces with their fingernails and turned all their wrath upon the prisoners they held. Cardounet was wrenched violently from the palanquin on which he was still posing and, god or not, became a captive in the company of Ivan Kisseloff and Dernghuiz.

"Oh, damn it—I prefer this!" said the mariner.

The crowd was murmuring and proffering threats, however, calling for the death of the prisoners and demanding the honor of tearing them into pieces or stoning them.

Dernghuiz, Ivan Kisseloff and Cardounet were taken into the fortress of Potala.

"What are they going to do to us?" asked Cardounet.

"Uhu!" the Russian replied, in a significant tone.

"But you have weapons?"

"Yes—four revolvers and two daggers."

"Well then, my worshippers are in trouble."

Dernghuiz reflected. Suddenly, he perceived the supervisor of the tardjoums emerging from the Buddha-Lha, escorted by his officers. He asked one of the soldiers guarding them to summon the mandarin. The soldier refused brutally.

"If you do what I ask," Dernghuiz said, "I'll give you two gold pieces. Here's one—you'll get the other when the supervisor of the tardjoums is informed."

"Agreed," the soldier replied, heading toward the Buddha-Lha.

"Do you have much gold on you, Master?" Dernghuiz asked.

"Some. Why do you ask?"

"Because my people have a proverb, which says that a golden key opens all doors."

"All peoples have that proverb, my friend."

"I've always suspected as much."

The supervisor of the tardjoums appears. He recognized Dernghuiz immediately and addressed reproaches to him.

"This is no time to argue," said Dernghuiz. "My masters scolded me because I wasn't generous enough in rewarding you for your fidelity and your care in looking after you-know-what. Here's another twenty gold pieces."

"They're very rich, then, your masters?"

"Rich and powerful, as I told you this morning. When they learned that we were prisoners they stole the Dalai Lama."

"The men who fly in the sky like eagles are your masters?"

"Yes. If we're respected, they won't harm the Dalai Lama, but if we're killed, they'll kill him. Tell that to the administrators and the lamas."

The mandarin turned to his retinue and repeated what he had just heard.

"Now," Dernghuiz continued, "this is the proposition we offer: we'll be put under your guard; you'll accompany us with ten of your men and take us out of the fortress, to the place where the Dalai Lama was taken. There, I'll call my masters..."

"What if your masters don't come?"

"They'll come. The Dalai Lama, who's doubtless floating above the clouds, must be impatient; he'll be returned to you as soon as we're free. As for you, your good offices will be recognized and we'll reward them. In the name of my masters, I promise you a hundred gold pieces."

"Will your masters keep your promise?"

"Yes."

"I need to inform the governor, the yan-wang, the Teshu-Lama[59] and the principal lamas. Be patient; I expect to bring you good news."

"I forgot to tell you," Dernghuiz continued, "that if we die, a frightful vengeance will follow close behind our murder. In the air, our friends are invincible and they'll spread terror through the city and the surrounding country. The lamas and the important people will be their first victims. Now go."

The last threat produced its effect. No matter how brave one is, who can fight against beings ungraspable on the ground?"

The supervisor of the tardjoums disappeared and spread the news of the prisoners' proposition along his way. The crowd calmed down and no longer uttered cries and imprecations. Buddha's representative would be returned to them.

After an hour's absence, the mandarin reappeared. He was free to act as he saw fit, provided that he brought the Dalai Lama back to his desolate faithful. He took ten soldiers, had the prisoners come with him, and went with them to the site of the abduction.

Cardounet and Ivan Kisseloff looked up into the blue sky, but could not see anything. The supervisor of the tardjoums was already trembling for his hundred piece of gold.

"I'll make them come," said Cardounet. "Have someone bring me a long pole and three large pieces of cloth, one blue, one white and one red.

Dernghuiz transmitted Cardounet's request to the mandarin. The latter took off his blue surcoat; Ivan Kisseloff offered his handkerchief; and, eventually, a soldier handed over a red

---

[59] The author inserts a footnote: "The Teshu-Lama, also known as Panchen Erdeni, comes after the Dalai Lama in the religious hierarchy of Buddhism." The cited name, routinely used by Europeans, derived from the Panchen Lama's traditional residence, the Tashilhunpo or Teshu-lumbo monastery.

251

scarf. With a piece of thread, Cardounet stitched the three objects together, attached them to the pole and set it upright.

"There," he said. "It's the French colors. Pick will make them out from the utmost depths of the atmosphere; for him, it's the fatherland, friends, hope."

"I can see the *Céleste*!" cried Ivan Kisseloff.

"Is it coming toward us?"

"Yes."

"Well, what did I tell you?"

Indeed, the aeronef was approaching with an astonishing rapidity. It changed direction slightly and passed above the pole.

"Come down to earth!" shouted Cardounet, making a megaphone of his hands. "Come down—there's no danger; we're safe!"

The *Céleste* landed fifty paces from the group formed by the prisoners, the soldiers and the supervisor of the tardjoums.

"Where's the Dalai Lama?" demanded the last-named.

"Come with us," Dernghuiz replied. "You'll be given the reward I promised you."

The mandarin hesitated, and did not seem confident. Finally, cupidity triumphed over fear and he followed Dernghuiz, Ivan Kisseloff and Cardounet.

Madame Valdy brought the child, still frightened by his aerial voyage. To console him, she had put a gold chain around his neck, along with her watch. Although he was a representative of God, the child seemed to be delighted with the gift, and was amusing himself with the *tick-tock* he could hear. The supervisor of the tardjoums received the Dalai Lama with marks of the greatest veneration. The crowd maintained at a distance by the soldiers, burst out into fanatical cheering.

"Now," said Dernghuiz, "here are your hundred gold pieces. You've been helpful to us; Buddha will bless you. My masters will also give you the two horses they used to steal the Dalai Lama. They've been bought and paid for, and no one will reclaim them."

"Where are the horses?"

"Over there, grazing at liberty."

"Your masters are generous and powerful; may Buddha come to their aid."

Having pronounced that wish and pocketed his gold, the supervisor of the tardjoums left. The soldiers were carrying the Dalai Lama in order that his precious person did not touch the impure earth trodden by other mortals.

"Hurry up!" shouted Valdy. "The multitude might fall upon us to punish us for our temerity. Let's go!"

Everyone embarked and the *Céleste* rose up above Lhasa. Then it headed southwards.

As one can imagine, Cardounet received warm congratulations. Pickerreek embraced his friend, said the most extravagant things, and nearly swallowed another plug of tobacco. Joy transformed and rejuvenated him.

The aeronef crossed the Dsang-Po and Lake Palte, remarkable for its altitude—4,115 meters—and the island it encloses: an island fifty kilometers long and fertile, populated mainly by monks and nuns. Then it arrived at the first buttresses f the Himalaya.

The chain of the Himalayas—"land of snows" in Sanskrit—describes a great arc of a circle 230 myriameters long between the Indus and the Brahmaputra. On the Tibetan side, from which our friends reached it, the mountain forms a relatively gentle slope, dominated by peaks whose height attains gigantic proportions: Gaurisankar, 8,840 meters; Kanchenjunga, 8,590 meters; Dhawalagiri, 8,200 meters, etc. Valdy examined the places where the crest was subject to some depression, and rose up to an altitude that the aeronef had never reached before. The mercury column in the barometer vacillated between thirty-two and thirty-three centimeters. They were, in consequence, about seven thousand meters above sea-level.

The voyagers felt the effects of the rarefaction of the air, the glacial cold and he phenomena so often observed and described by aeronauts, which provoke a lassitude, an inertia leading infallibly to death if one does not react against it.

"Courage! Courage!" shouted Valdy, his voice slightly enfeebled. "I can see the southern slope. A few more minutes and we'll be flying over the most beautiful country on Earth!

Beneath the aeronef the landscape was horrible and grandiose. Eternal snows and tormented glaciers reflected the rays of sunlight, taking on all the colors of the rainbow. Spurs of ice surged forth here and there with the most eccentric contours, like the giant sentinels of the giant mountains. There was desolation and silence everywhere. If they had not been able to glimpse in the distance the final plateaus of Tibet and the profound valleys of Bhutan, they might have thought that they were in the bleak circumpolar regions.

Finally, they crossed the cliff of the Himalaya and the *Céleste* descended three thousand meters. Valdy set a course westwards to reach Katmandu, the capital of Nepal, which was still more than a hundred leagues away. They traversed Bhutan, an independent, mountainous and infertile state inhabited by undisciplined, violent and barbaric bandits, whom the English have been obliged to chastise several times. Moreover, the Bhutanese exact a tribute from the English in commercial terms; every year their government sends caravans to Bengal, which take on supplies of European merchandise. Sooner or later soldiers and cannon follow merchandise; the time can already be foreseen when England will add Bhutan to its Indian possessions.

The aeronef traversed Sikkim, the state that separates Bhutan from Nepal and was combined several years ago with Bengal. Then it entered Nepal.

From that point on the voyagers could hardly make out the country over which they were passing. The shadows of the mountains extended over the plains. They only had an imperfect view of Nepal, which seemed to them to be physically similar to Bhutan. It had the same alpine aspect, the same sterility, and the same climate.

Finally, after a rapid fight that continued for a further two hours, Katmandu came into view, recognizable in the obscurity by a few tremulous gleams shining in the darkness like the reflection of stars. Valdy shone an electric light to the ground and searched in every direction for a location sufficiently steep to be safe from any surprise; he came down a few leagues from the city, on an isolated summit of the mountain chain forming the first southern ledge of the Himalaya.

The provisions bought by Dernghuiz in Lhasa were distributed. Pickerreek and Cardounet regretted not having any wine, for the Tatars had broken or drunk all the bottles, but, glad to find themselves together after a separation filed with perils, they forgot the "juice of the trellis" while telling one another about their adventures and drinking fresh water.

"We've both been gods," said Cardounet. "It's our specialty—but if I'm ever given the choice, I want to be Bacchus."

Chapter XVIII

On the thirtieth of September the sun appeared above the snowy peaks of the Himalaya and promptly dissipated the thick vapors covering the valleys. In the distance, they could see Katmandu.

"Let's get closer to the city," said Valdy, "and pick up the provisions of bicarbonate of soda and hydrochloric acid deposited there."

The *Céleste* took off, and, in a few minutes, was very close to the capital of Nepal—but far enough away not to be noticed.

George Simpson and Will Tooke went into the city.

Katmandu is one of the most picturesque cities in Asia. The streets are quite well paved—an unfamiliar luxury in those regions—and the houses have a particular architecture reminiscent of that of Swiss chalets, or, more accurately, the edifices with ornamental gables, sculpted balconies and over-hanging roofs that characterize the constructions of the Middle Ages. Its population is approximately 30,000.

Will Tooke and Simpson searched in vain for the depository designated by Ivan Kisseloff. They only encountered three or four English traders, who were unable to give them any information because they had only recently arrived in Katmandu, and were preparing to go on to India, not having permission to stay in the country for long. Nepal is not yet directly governed by the English, but is "protected" by them. It is under the dependence of a rajah who exercises great authority, while being obedient to English politics, which he fears. Generally, he respects the Europeans attracted into his possessions by curiosity or business, but he often imposes more or less vexatious conditions on them.

Will Tooke and Simpson went back to the *Céleste*.

"How much bicarbonate and acid do we have?" asked Valdy.

"If we make good progress," Pickerreek replied, "we can make our next thousand kilometers."

"Good. That's reassuring. Let's hope that we'll be luckier at our next stop. We're only three hundred kilometers from Oude—we'll soon be there."

"If we don't find anything in Oude," Simpson interjected, "we can push on as far as Lucknow—it's an important center, and I can count on the English authorities to furnish everything we need."

The aeronef rose up to hundred meters above the mountains surrounding Katmandu and headed westwards. The traversed part of Nepal and the Terai diagonally.

On the Hindustan side, the Himalaya rises abruptly in an interrupted fashion, thus forming three principal chains, three immense steps of a gigantic ladder, each having a distinct climate and vegetation. From the base of the mountain, a strip of insalubrious marshes extends, covered with reeds, brushwood and impenetrable jungles, inundated during the rainy season and favorable to the growth of tropical plants. That is the Terai.

The *Céleste* then penetrated into the Presidency of Allahabad, and nothing troubled its rapid journey until it reached Oude, at about ten o'clock in the morning. Oude, Aoude or Audh, on the Gogra, a tributary of the Ganges, is an old city, whose importance and splendor has greatly declined. However, it still encloses beautiful monuments—principally, the mosque of Aurangzeb.

Here, the visitors were not longer forced to exercise the restraint that had hindered them so much in Central Asia. They took the aeronef to the very gates of the city.

The authorities, officers, soldiers, English businessmen, sepoys and Hindus of all ranks and castes clustered around the *Céleste*. What had marked the passage of Will Tooke in America and Ivan Kisseloff in Siberia was renewed for George Simpson. The lieutenant was warmly acclaimed by his compatriots.

"Good, good," said Pickerreek. Our turn will come when we traverse Algeria and when we arrive in Bordeaux."

In accordance with the satisfaction given to national pride, the English functionaries welcomed the voyagers benevolently. The bicarbonate of soda and hydrochloric acid were deposited in the establishment of a merchant. The commandant of the detachment of sepoys sent some of his men in search of the chemical products and offered them a morning meal.

"We'll drink a toast to your admirable invention," he said to Valdy.

"Thank you, Commandant," Valdy replied, "but our time is limited. We only have a few more days to get back to France and we can't lose any time."

"That's annoying for me, for I would have been honored to accommodate you."

"Well, Commandant," said Madame Valdy, "we're going to look for food supplies, because we've run short, and you can share our breakfast."

"You have no food-supplies?" cried several officers. "Don't worry about a thing—we'll take care of it." And they disappeared, taking several soldiers with them.

Five minutes later, a cart pulled by an elephant poured a veritable avalanche of provender on the ground nearby. Cardounet started arranging it carefully in his storage-lockers, and his eyes lit up with pleasure when he found numerous bottles in the heap.

"Pick! Pick!" he said. "Come and see! Look at these labels. It's wine, and I wish that a royal might fall on the back of my neck if an admiral ever drank better. There are all regions and vintages."

"That's lucky! When the opportunity arises, we'll have a few."

"And Dernghuiz. It'll complete his education."

"And quite some education."

"Well, if these bottles don't reconcile Monsieur Kisseloff with the English, I don't know what will."

258

"Bah! I think that's already done."

They ate informally. The crew replied to the Englishmen's toasts by drinking to the prosperity of India and the health of Queen Victoria; then hands were shaken, farewells were exchanged and Valdy made ready to depart.

The aeronef continued on its route. She passed over Lucknow, a city of 300,000 souls, famous for its industry and for the uprising of 1857; she crossed the Ganges, the railway line between Calcutta and Lahore; the Kuwana, a tributary of the Ganges; and traversed the country situated between Agra, with it 125,000 inhabitants, the ancient and splendid residence of the Great Mogul Akbar, and Gwalior, with 60,000 inhabitants, one of the strongest places in Hindustan.

The voyagers noticed the dazzling, varied and magnificent vegetation of that rich country. Méry[60] alone has been able to describe that exuberant, vivacious, radiant nature. The landscapes are grandiose, and the forests, with their precious essences, have the majesty of those of the New World. Around the cities and in the plains, large-scale agriculture make progress by the day, presenting enormous terrains where cereals, indigo, cotton, poppies, castor-oil, mustard, betel, turmeric, safflower, bananas, etc., are cultivated.

Then the *Céleste* traversed a region of plateau, a sort of moorland intermingled with jungle, crossed the Aravalli Mountains and arrived in Ajmer.

It was only five o'clock in the evening when the aeronef landed beside that city. The first inhabitants who perceived her uttered cries of fright and rushed in great haste to warn the English garrison, announcing that a gigantic monster was about to bring death and desolation to the city.

---

[60] The Romantic novelist whose full names was Joseph Méry made a major contribution to the French literary mythology of "the Orient" in various novels set in India and the East Indies. Some of the descriptions to which Brown is referring, albeit not among the more luxurious ones, can be found in the title story of the Black Coat Press collection *The Tower of Destiny*.

The officers and the governor, disturbed by this news, ordered a detachment of soldiers to take up arms and advance toward the place where the *Céleste* was resting—but when they saw George Simpson coming to meet them with a entirely British placidity and phlegm, they laughed at their mistake and welcomed the aerial visitors deferentially.

"I'll admit to you frankly," said the governor of Ajmer to Simpson, "that you gave us a fright. I didn't really believe the rumors assuring me that we had a fabulous creature to combat, but I thought it might be an attack by one of the tribes we administrate, the Rajputs."

"I thought that the Rajputs were entirely submissive," said Valdy.

"Hmm!" said the governor. "They're submissive as long as we keep a close eye on them, but if they thought for a single instant that our vigilance was lacking, a formidable insurrection would break out. At any rate, gentlemen, I hope that you'll accept the cordial hospitality I can offer you, and I don't think I'll have any need to go out on campaign for so long as you care to stay here."

"We owe you some compensation, Milord," said Madame Valdy. "We're at your disposal."

The governor set a platoon of soldiers to guard the aeronef, offered his arm gallantly to Madame Valdy and went into the city, followed by the voyagers and a numerous crowd attracted by curiosity.

Ajmer, the capital of the state of the same name, has about 30,000 inhabitants. It once belonged to the Mahrathas, who ceded it to the English in 1818 after a long and bloody struggle. There is nothing remarkable about it, save for the tomb of a Muslim saint, visited by a multitude of pilgrims. Situated on the northern slope of the Aravalli Mountains, it is at a high enough altitude to experience harsh winters. Its position permits it to overlook the plateaus that extend from Merwara to Sind.

The governor of Ajmer did everything possible to be agreeable to his guests. He treated them with the luxury that has made the reputation of the nabobs of India, and hosted a soirée in their honor to which he invited the principal Rajput chiefs dependent on his government. The reception hall had a magical aspect. Garlands of flowers and clumps of greenery from which enormous bouquets of Kashmir roses protruded decked the walls and perfumed the atmosphere; the light of chandeliers sparkled, and richly-framed mirrors reflected it in all direction. Here and there, under the branches of orange-trees and lemon-trees laden with their gilded fruit, soft cushions and rugs ornamented with fantastic designs permitted the guests to relax. The Rajput chiefs, with their brilliant indigenous costumes, their turbans surmounted with scintillating crests, their waistcoat embroidered with gold, their dazzling and delicate shawls, their silken belt and their daggers enriched with gems, seemed to be the animated flowers of that miniature Eden.

Dernghuiz, Pickerreek and Cardounet were veritably wonderstruck.

The party went on long into the night and the voyagers went to bed a little late, but the following day they were up early, thanked the governor for his splendid hospitality and embarked in the midst of an enormous crowd of curiosity-seekers.

The *Céleste* followed the course of the Luni, a river that emerges from the Aravalli Mountains and fades away in the marshes formed by the Rann of Kutch, passed close to Jodhpur, a large city of 150,000 souls, and set out over the southern tip of the saline desert that Sind extends toward Punjab and bears the various Indian names for desert—Thar, Marusthali, etc. They could then travel within three hundred meters of the ground without encumbrance.

"Today is the first of October," said Valdy. "We have eleven days left to arrive in France."

"This is my final stage of my aerial journey," Simpson put in.

"You don't want to accompany us to Europe?"

"No. I've been waiting to arrive in a seaport in order to put myself at the disposition of the Admiralty. This evening we'll be in Karachi, and I can't go any further without being derelict in my duty. I thank you for your help and your friendship, and I shall be eternally grateful for all that you've done for me. I owe you my life, and..."

"Don't mention it, Monsieur Simpson—you've repaid that debt generously. Without your admirable devotion in Lhasa, Cardounet, Dernghuiz and Kisseloff would have fallen victim to the Tibetans."

"I can't claim any merit for my action, for you and your companions would have devoted yourselves to their salvation."

"That's true, but would we have come up with the idea of kidnapping the Dalai Lama?"

Simpson smiled. Then he resumed a serious tone. "Tell me frankly and without procrastination, Monsieur Valdy—do you think that Monsieur Kisseloff is still my enemy?"

"I've noticed one thing: since we left Lhasa, Kisseloff no longer speaks ill of the English."

"Out of politeness, perhaps..."

"No, out of gratitude.

"He avoids me, though, and affects a wounding coldness in my regard."

"There's a final conflict taking place within him, but his natural generosity will hold sway over hatred. He's the youngest of us all, and you know how difficult it is for youth to be reasonable when self-esteem and vanity are at stake. In compensation, youth keeps awake the noble sentiments of the heart that command the forgiveness of insults and gratitude. Now, Kisseloff is a man of honor, and I believe that he'll offer you his hand before you leave us."

"My God hear you!"

The *Céleste* continued its rapid flight; the voyagers could distinguish the country over which they were passing perfectly. They encountered a few wretched villages inhabits by djats—agricultural laborers—and a few camps of Baluchis, the feeble debris of the race dominant in Sind prior to its conquest by the English. At about two o'clock in the afternoon they perceived pools of water bordered by aquatic plants and tall grasses that were sometimes dense enough to form jungles similar to those of the Terai.

"We're approaching the Indus!" Valdy shouted.

"How do you know, Captain?" asked Cardounet.

"By the pools that are under our feet. Like the Nile and the Ganges, the Indus has periodic floods that inundate the neighboring land. The floods commence with the melting of the snows of the Himalaya in the months of April and May, reach their highest point in July, and conclude in the September current. It's only a fortnight since the river returned to its bed. However, it's not the principal branch of the Indus that we're about to encounter—that's still a hundred kilometers away—but a secondary arm, a sort of large ditch that irrigates the heart of Sind over a distance of fifty myriameters and joins up with the river in the delta near the Sea of Oman.

Scarcely had Valdy concluded his explanation than rifle shots and sharp cries were heard.

"Are we under attack?" asked Pickerreek.

George Simpson picked up his binoculars and examined the ground.

"No one's threatening us," he said. "They're hunting tigers of Gujarat lions, the two most terrible felines of the country we're traversing."

"Since we have time in hand, for we'll be in Karachi is less than two hours we can take a closer look at the hunt."

The *Céleste* veered sideways and landed in the plain, a short distance away from a group of men who were watching the maneuver in alarm.

"Don't worry," George Simpson shouted, in English. "We're friends."

Several hunters approached. They were mostly Baluchis and Hindus, but there were three Englishmen among them who looked at the aeronef in surprise and engaged the voyagers in conversation.

"What animal are you hunting, Gentlemen?" asked Will Tooke.

"Tiger," one of them replied. "Or rather, two tigers. We were in Hyderabad when we heard that a pair of the animals was ravaging the region. We resolved to hunt them down. Until now, though, our efforts have been fruitless, and the terrified indigenes dare not emerge from their houses. Our tigers aren't content to steal oxen, horses and sheep; they've killed half a dozen people and devoured them. Today, djats have seen them close to here, and we hope that the carnivores will make the acquaintance of our buckshot."

"Will you permit us to join you, Gentlemen?" asked Will Tooke.

"With pleasure. One can never be too many in hunting that game."

It was agreed that Pickerreek, Cardounet and Dernghuiz would stay on the *Céleste* with Madame Valdy. Will Tooke, Ivan Kisseloff, Simpson and Baldy armed themselves and joined the hunters.

The Englishman who had spoken to the voyagers, whose name was John Berley, was in charge of the general direction of the hunt. Berley was a distinguished Nimrod. He had killed more than twenty felines—tigers, panthers or lions—and often risked his life in the perilous encounters that he sought with passion. His experience was not to be disdained.

The tigers had taken refuge in dense brushwood that was visible about fifteen hundred meters away, which the Indus flood had temporarily transformed into a marsh covered in tall grass and reeds. The Baluchis spread out behind the hunters and the latter headed for the brushwood. It was necessary that no one penetrate the thicket in isolation, for it was sufficiently dense to permit the animals to surge forth unexpectedly. In addition, the mud would impede progress. Berley examined the tiger-tracks attentively, and indicated the direction to follow. Will Tooke, Simpson, Valdy and Kisseloff were beside him, and two Hindus were behind them with spare guns, already loaded. The other two Englishmen formed the rear-guard, along with several indigenes.

To flush out the tigers, the Baluchis howled like maniacs and threw stones into the jungle, but these provocations seemed to have little effect on the animals, for neither of them showed itself. Suddenly, a roar was heard and an agonized scream. A tiger had just pounced on a Hindu, whom it had carried a few paces away, and whose body it was raking with its powerful claws.

"Fire! Fire!" shouted Berley.

Everyone discharged his weapon. As soon as the smoke had dissipated, Berley advanced alone, holding his rifle at the ready in order to fire his second shot. In front of him, however, he could see nothing but the torn and disfigured cadaver of the Hindu. The tiger had disappeared. It must have been wounded, however, for its howls resounded three times, becoming fainter.

The hunters went in pursuit; they penetrated further forward into the thicket and stopped in a little clearing. Suddenly, a furious roar was heard. The tiger was fifteen paces away, crouched on its legs with its body tensed, ready to pounce.

More impatient than prudent, Ivan Kisseloff fired. The feline launched itself upon him and knocked him over. Before it had time to sink its claws into the Russian's body, however, George Simpson advanced and discharged both barrels of his rifle at point-blank range. The animal collapsed on top of its victim; it was dead. Ivan Kisseloff was freed; he only had minor bruises. After an initial moment of stupor, perfectly comprehensible in the circumstances, he asked who the bold hunter was who had so fortunately saved him.

"It was George Simpson," Valdy replied.

The Russian went to the lieutenant. "Mr. Simpson," he said, "will you forget the reasons for my rancor and the insolent words I pronounced in Karakorum, and count yourself among my friends?"

George Simpson threw himself into Ivan Kisseloff's arms. "Oh, Count," he exclaimed, "you make me the happiest

of men! I've long deplored the causes that led to our duel—
that barbaric custom unworthy of mean of heart, which choos-
es its victims indifferently among the offenders and the of-
fended. The intoxication of anger is not courage, and there is
more merit for you in being one of the first pioneers of the air
than in legally killing or wounding the people who might
doubt your bravery."

"Mr. Simpson," Ivan Kisseloff replied, "be assured that I
shall never forget the services that you have rendered me, and
that I shall conduct myself in accordance with the noble precepts that you have been so well able to put into practice."

That reconciliation took place in the thicket, in front of
the indigenous and foreign hunters, a few paces away from the
tiger that was lying on the ground.

"Gentlemen," said Berley, "I understand that there has
been a violent dissent between you, but I declare to you that
I'm delighted to see you friends, for in you"—he indicated
Ivan Kisseloff—"there is a nobility of character and a chival-
ric frankness, and in you"—he indicated George Simpson—
"moral qualities and a reflective boldness that denote superior
intelligence. Gentlemen, I believe that you were made to understand one another and love one another. Now, if you
please, let's return to the hunt."

The dead tiger was a superb animal; it belonged to the
species known as royal tigers; its length, from the muzzle to
the tip of its tail, was two meters twenty-five. It had received
four wounds, but the pelt was not too badly damaged, so the
Baluchis hastened to skin it.

"There's no point in pursuing the other one," Berley said.
"We won't catch up with it—our gunshots have frightened it.
A tiger never attacks an organized troop of men advancing
noisily. It will come back at nightfall, but then all the chances
will be in its favor."

"Will it flee very far?" asked Valdy.

"No, not if we don't pursue it."

"Well, then, we'll hunt it with the aeronef."

"That's an excellent idea, Monsieur, and if you'll permit me to embark with you, I can guarantee that the tiger won't escape us."

"I intended to make that proposal to you."

The Hindus carried away their compatriots cadaver and everyone emerged from the brushwood. Valdy, Ivan Kisseloff and Berley headed for the *Céleste*. Simpson, Will Tooke and the two Englishmen remained with the indigenes to keep watch on the thicket.

On the way, and at the request of his traveling companions, Berley provided a few details regarding tigers.

"They're redoubtable animals," he said, "and dangerous neighbors for humans. They don't always live in jungles and marshy ground; one also encounters them in the vast Indian forests. The tiger is the largest and most robust of all the cats; it mostly prowls in the evening, before and after sunset; its lies in ambush, concealing itself in bushes on the banks of rivers, beside roads and paths, and near isolated springs; when it had discovered its prey, it creeps closer and leaps upon it with a prodigious bound. When driven by hunger it has an extraordinary audacity, and has been seen in broad daylight penetrating into villages in search of human prey. Sometimes it has attacked detachments of travelers and troops. Laggards often fall victim to it. Francis Hamilton Buchanan affirms that in less than two years, these carnivores killed eighty people in a single village. James Forbes adds that in a single night they devoured three well-armed sentinels and that couriers charged with caring dispatches are often taken, although they always travel in groups of five or six. In Gujarat, at a crossing on the river Gumeah, traders disappeared every night for a fortnight. In the gorge of Kutkum-Sandhi, a single tigress killed several people every day, of all kinds, for more than three months."

"Damn!" said Valdy. "India isn't a land of Cockayne, as certain travelers claim."

"Oh," John Berley continued, smiling modestly, "English hunters, less timorous than the Hindus, have put a stop to the misdeeds of tigers. The government gives ten rupees for every head, and in some years the sums distributed run into thousands of pounds. The Indian chiefs hunt the tiger mounted on elephants; rich Englishmen do likewise, but their hunts aren't as fruitful as those that amateurs like me undertake on foot. In four years, Lieutenant William Rice killed sixty-eight tigers, three panthers and twenty-five bears. During his lifetime, Judge Henry Ramus killed three hundred and sixty tigers. You see, Messieurs, that Hindustan can oppose worthy rivals to Bombonnel the panther-killer and Jules Gerard."

While chatting, the three men arrived at the aeronef. Berley equipped himself with some stones the size of an egg, and everyone embarked. In the blink of an eye, the *Céleste* was over the thicket. There, it descended to within fifty meters of the ground and advanced slowly; it seemed to be floating. It only beat its wings once every five seconds. Enthused, John Berley completely forgot the hunt, and Ivan Kisseloff had to remind him that there as a tiger in the brush.

Finally, they saw the animal. It was crouched down, staring at the unfamiliar object that was passing overhead. It seemed to be terrified. They saw it slip away through the bushes, keeping low, stopping occasionally to look about anxiously, seeking some refuge where it might hide.

"The tiger's definitely frightened," said Berley. "There'd be little honor for us in killing it in its shelter; we need to flush it out." And he threw a few stones.

The wild beast roared, but its roar had something plaintive about it; one might have thought that it was conscious of a danger impossible to brave. Berley resumed his attack, hurling stone after stone forcefully.

The tiger bounded, and ran off at lightning speed. The *Céleste* immediately accelerated and pursued it. Berley fired; twice he hit the carnivore, but each bullet that hit it seemed to revivify it. It howled more loudly and fled more rapidly. It was a magnificent race, a steeplechase every bit as fantastic as the one sustained by William Reading on the Central Pacific Railway.

Finally, after ten minutes of frantic pursuit, Berley shot the animal in the head and killed it. The aeronef landed in the jungle. The Hindus, preceded by the two Englishmen, Will Tooke and Simpson, arrived at a run and showed their delight at being rid of their dangerous guests.

"If I had a apparatus like this one you steer so well at my disposal," Berley said to Valdy, "I'd take responsibility for freeing all the English possessions of all the malevolent animals they contain."

"Hope," replied Valdy. "England, which is the industrial nation *par excellence*, will not lag behind when it's a matter of creating an aerial fleet."

The hunters bade farewell to the voyagers, and the latter departed again immediately. The *Céleste* rapidly crossed the distance separating it from the Indus, passed over Hyderabad, the capital of Sind, without penetrating into the delta, followed the railway line linking Bombay to Karachi, and arrived in the latter city at about five o'clock in the afternoon.

Chapter XIX

Scarcely had the aeronef touched down than it was surrounded by a curious multitude. Indigenes, Europeans and mariners jostled one another to examine the marvel at close range. Suddenly, a fat man, as red in the face as a lobster, emerged from the bosom of the crowd, panting and sweating, out of breath.

"Oh, my friends, my good friends!" he cried. "What a great day for me! I've finally found you again!" And he distributed rude punches right and left.

"What!" said Valdy, utterly astonished. "Is that you, Sir Walter Donderry?"

"Eh? Yes, of course it's me. Am I not recognizable to the naked eye? Has my corpulence diminished and my belly caved in since you last saw me?"

"Certainly not, but I'm surprised..."

"To see me here, no? Me too—but you're a matter of discussion."

"What do you mean?"

"I'll explain later. At my request, a detachment of soldiers will guard the *Céleste*. The captain of the port, one of my friends, is waiting for us at his home. Let's go."

Sir Walter gallantly offered his arm to Madame Valdy, and penetrated into Karachi with the aplomb of a triumphant victor of ten battles. The port captain welcomed the voyagers with the urbanity that distinguishes naval officers and placed himself, his house and his servants at their disposal.

An hour later, the aerial crew and a few guests sat down around a splendidly furnished table. During dinner they chatted.

"Oh, my friends," said Sir Walter, "they're talking about you in Europe. No Affair of State has ever been discussed as much as your voyage. People are forgetting everything, even politics, in order to occupy themselves specifically with aerial navigation. It's a veritable frenzy. The newspapers, the literary magazines, the scientific journals, pamphlets and publications of every sort are examining the past, present and future of aviation. Some were laughing, others denying it, and it was necessary for me to write to the *Times* to affirm your departure. In spite of my letter, I think there are still people who aren't yet convinced. They're the true Ratapoils[61] of progress!"

"A lot of paper must have been blackened in America too," Will Took interjected.

"That's quite possible."

"And what about Harry Catlen?" asked Cardounet, nudging Ivan Kisseloff's elbow.

"He's incredulity incarnate," Sir Water replied. "Every time I've shown him in the English newspapers—the only ones he'll read—the dispatches from various telegraphic agencies announcing your passage through some country or some city, he never ceases to laugh in my face and treat Monsieur Valdy as a 'Bedlamite,' certifying that our machine will break down within a week, convinced that he'll win his bet."

"He's got some nerve, that Mossieu Catlen!" said Cardounet. "He'd better take it back, or I'll dip him in some exceedingly peppery soup!"

"Out of friendship for me, I hope you'll leave him in peace. He'll be punished enough when he has to shell out the four thousand pounds that you're well on the way to winning from him."

"One will keep quiet—because of you, Sir Walter—but one will think it nevertheless."

---

[61] The illustrator Honoré Daumier published "Proclamation du Colonel Ratapoil" in the satirical periodical *Le Charivari* in 1850, and its protagonist became a widely-cited type-specimen of a militaristic individual nostalgic for the glorious days of Napoléon I's conquests. Daumier's subsequent depictions of the character often bore a strong resemblance to Louis Napoléon, then President of the nascent Republic—which ceased to seem amusing after the coup-d'état of 1851.

"Think what you please on the quiet, my brave Cardounet. In every hundred people you'll always find one imbecile who'll criticize the endeavor in which you're taking part, and ninety-nine who approve. So much the worse for the imbecile."

"You're right. It's necessary to treat them with scorn and not to punch them on the nose."

"Do tell us how and why you come to be in Karachi," said Valdy.

"When I wrote to the *Times*," Sir Walter replied, "my letter caused such a sensation, affirming so clearly what I had seen, that I immediately became an individual of note, a celebrity. You'll remember that there were only two witnesses to your departure—Monsieur Dambielle and me. Monsieur Dambielle has said nothing and written nothing; he has allowed the discussion to go on, listening to the blunders of some and the enthusiasm of others without deigning to respond. It was a wise decision—he's avoided a host of annoyances."

"How so?"

"Listen to me and judge for yourself. So there I was, one of those overnight celebrities—celebrities who fade away as rapidly as they surge forth, and whom the wise always mistrust. To begin with, I received letter after letter asking me for information, details, and so on, and begging me to reply. Ten speedy secretaries wouldn't have been enough for that job! Then I received visits from a multitude of people coming to submit projects, plans and ideas. Finally, I couldn't take any more and closed my door—but they lay in wait for me. Whenever I went out I was followed, accosted and surrounded. The curious, the bothersome and the importunate harassed me, no longer giving me a single moment's peace. Then I resolved to flee. I knew your itinerary, and I knew that you were due to stop at Karachi to take on supplies. I embarked at Marseilles on a steamer laving for Bombay, and from Bombay I came here by rail. Now I'll go back to France with you, if you'll accept me as a traveling companion."

"Gladly," Valdy replied. "You can replace George Simpson, whom we're losing."

The conversation continued and the voyagers were obliged to relate the principal adventures they had undergone. Sir Walter Donderry, his friend the port captain and the guests marveled at what they heard and raised the roof with their applause when Pickerreek recounted, with his picturesque expressions, his naïve modesty and his abrupt and frank gestures, the fortunate rescue of Lieutenant Simpson. The later shed affectionate tears.

At eleven o'clock, the voyagers, weary after their late night in the home of the governor of Ajmer, asked for permission to retire.

"Sleep well," said Sir Walter, shaking their hands. "Your fatigue demands reparative rest. Personally, I shall wait impatiently for daybreak, dreaming that I'm transformed into a sylph, that my Silenian paunch has disappeared and that I'm flying in the ethereal realms, as light as a dragonfly."

The next day, the second of October, Valdy and his companions, followed by the port captain and a curious crowd, prepared to depart, George Simpson said his adieux in emotional terms.

"You've become my dearest friends," he said, "and God placed you in my path to replace those I have lost. You consoled me in my affliction and put hope in my heart." Then he turned to Madame Valdy and added: "And you, Madame, be blessed for the kind words and encouragements that you have never ceased to lavish upon me. When my courage faltered, you have sustained me. Bless you, for you have been my Providence."

Ivan Kisseloff threw his arms around the lieutenant. "Mr. Simpson," he said, "you've done better than reconcile me with the English; you've taught me to love my fellows. I thank you for that sincerely. My vanity and my pride are humbled before you, who have saved my life when I was your enemy. Your noble example will henceforth trace my duty."

"Those are good and generous words," proclaimed Sir Walter, extending his hand to Ivan Kisseloff, "and I'll permit you to mock the English as much as you wish."

"What if I abuse that permission?" Kisseloff asked, smiling.

"I won't withdraw it."

"No, no—it's good to be able to hold one's tongue: a word often does more harm than a sword-thrust."

"You're right—and as Sancho Panza said: 'Taking too much harms, and scratching too much spoils,'"

George Simpson embraced the voyagers and the latter embarked. The *Céleste* took off and headed westwards. A few minutes later it left Hindustan and flew over Baluchistan. Sir Water Donderry looked alternately at the sky and the earth, and remained mute with surprise and admiration. Eventually, his enthusiasm overflowed and was translated into exclamations and hyperbolic expressions.

"Away with steam!" he cried. "Away with steamships and lumbering locomotives. With those powerful machines one crawls, dragging oneself along; but here, distance belongs to us, our horizon is limitless and the immensity is overcome. We have wings: 'Wings to fly over the sea/in the redness of the morning!'"

"After having crossed the lower ramifications of the mountains of Hali and Onachati, the aeronef flew at a height varying between two and three hundred meters, following the bare, arid and scantly-indented coast of Baluchistan. Nothing remarkable struck the voyagers' gaze; they only perceived small tribes of nomads, three or four watercourses, and wretchedly ill-constructed and poorly-populated villages. The entire sea-coast of Baluchistan is a bleak country; it is the Mekran of the Persians, the Gedrosia of the ancients, the antique land of the Ichthyophages where Alexander and his army suffered from hunger on their return from the Indus.

In spite of his good nature, Sir Walter Donderry was amused by the fear generated in the region's poor inhabitants by the *Céleste*'s passage. He saw boats at sea capsize as their occupants tried to see better, or flee with all sails aloft to escape an imaginary danger.

"What do you expect?" he said. "It's the rule for progress to inspire fear; it frightens the foolish and the ignorant, and then reassures them. The first hydrogen gas balloon that came down in the countryside, at Gonesse, was mistaken for a monster and torn apart by frightened peasants. In England, peasants attacked an aeronaut after setting fire to his aerostat. It was, if my memory serves me right, a man named Young. He was surrounded in the forest of Lancaster, where he landed, struck, wounded, knocked down and finally left for dead at a crossroads."

Before noon, the Céleste landed at Gwadar, sixty degrees of longitude east of Paris. Gwadar is the place where the submarine telegraph departing from Basra—an important section of the direct link between London and Bombay—ends. A certain number of English functionaries are based there, who exercise a great influence. The voyagers received a perfect welcome, but they only stayed long enough to take a light meal and pick up the chemical products deposited in the city.

"We've made rapid progress," said Sir Walter, "and I'm curious to know how many kilometers we've covered since this morning."

"Five hundred," Valdy replied.

"Five hundred! That's astonishing!"

"It's our moderate speed. When we're in haste, we can double that distance in the same lapse of time."

"But that's marvelous. The Indian mail-coach, Mercury, the envoy of the gods, and Iris, the light-footed messenger, are mere tortoises compared with us!"

The aeronef resumed her journey, continuing along the coast. She crossed the Mashkel, the only important watercourse in Baluchistan, which is scarcely navigable, but irrigates a fertile valley. She passed over a few scarce villages, meager settlements in a country as dismal and deserted as the one they had traversed in the morning, and arrived on the shore of the Strait of Hormuz. She penetrated into Persian territory and came down at dusk about two thousand meters from Bandar Abbas.

Bandar Abbas is located on a small island near the coast of Moghistan. It has a good harbor and does considerable trade with Basra, Arabia, India and Oman. Its population is estimated at twelve thousand. Unfortunately, the climate there is exceedingly unhealthy, and the heat intense. The English, who are gradually becoming the masters of the entire Persian Gulf, have a consul in the city; it was with the agent in question that the bicarbonate of soda and hydrochloric acid had been deposited. Will Tooke, Ivan Kisseloff and Sir Walter set off for Bandar Abbas, traversing the narrow arm of the sea separating it from the mainland by boat, and went straight to the consul.

The latter was exceedingly surprised.

"It's real, then!" he cried. "Aerial navigation exists!"

"Yes," Sir Walter replied, "it exists, my dear compatriot, and you have before you three passengers of the first aerial vessel that has flow through the atmosphere."

"Receive my congratulations, Gentlemen. I'll have the chemical products I my possession transported immediately, and if you'll permit, I'll accompany you to the place where your marvelous apparatus is stationed."

"With pleasure."

The consul gave orders to his servants and embarked with the voyagers. When he arrived, he examined the aeronef attentively, and let the most enthusiastic expressions of admiration escape his lips.

"Sir," he said to Valdy, "you have surpassed Watt, Stephenson and all the ingenious minds with which England is honored. Your discovery will render immense services to humankind, so it's necessary to keep it safe."

"Do we have some danger to fear?"

"Perhaps. The populations of this coast are ignorant and fanatical. If they perceive your arrival, they'll tear your apparatus to pieces, firstly because you're Christians, and secondly because the old dervishes and inflexible imams—the entire religious caste, in fact—are resolute enemies of progress."

"Where should we go?"

"Leave the Ghermasir—that's the name of this coast, meaning 'hot ground'—and take refuge on one of the numerous islets cluttering the entrance to the Persian Gulf. That way you'll avoid your enemies, and perhaps a bout of fever, for the Ghermasir is extremely unhealthy."

"I've always heard it said that the islands in these parts are the lair of pirates."

"Oh, don't worry; pirates rarely travel by night. In this part of the sea, navigation is exceedingly perilous and difficult, and there are always two or three English frigates anchored in the straits, keeping a lookout for pirates and holding them at bay."

The bicarbonate of soda and hydrochloric acid arrived. Pickerreek, Cardounet and Dernghuiz hastened to load them on board. Valdy thanked the English consul for the information he had furnished and ordered the departure.

The aeronef set out over the sea. She traversed Kish Island , the principal base of the English cruiser, and after a few evolutions, landed on a bare, arid and deserted islet surrounded by coral reefs.

"I think we'll be safe on this rock," said Will Tooke.

"To avoid any surprise," Valdy put in, "We'll each take a turn on watch during the night. It's a useful precaution, which would have saved us a great deal of trouble if we'd taken it when we camped in the vicinity of Sou-Tcheou."

"We'll take sentry-duty and keep our eyes open," said Cardounet, "but we'll need our keep our strength up for that. Let's break a crust."

The voyagers squatted on their heels and made a considerable breach in their provisions. The wines provided by the officers at Oude stimulated the gaiety of Pickerreek and Cardounet, and Sir Walter Donderry, put in a good mood by the two mariner's witticisms, opined that he had never had such a fine meal.

It was one of those beautiful Oriental evenings so often celebrated by Saadi, the bard of the roses of Shiraz, an in-

277

spired poet, the Persian Virgil and Anacreon. The blue tints of the sky fused with the extreme rim of the horizon in the evening twilight, and the stars, those flowers of the night, radiant and nuanced by transparent vapors floating in the atmosphere, sparkled and twinkled in the infinite. The calm and limpid sea sang its eternal song softly, its waves breaking nonchalantly on the rocks covered with brightly-colored mollusks and red algae. One might have thought it the sigh of a bride, the stifled sound of a kiss or the whimper of a baby awakening to smile at its mother.

Sir Walter Donderry, touched by the magnificence of the simple and grandiose spectacle, offered his impressions in monologue. "O holy poetry, daughter of Apollo," he said, "celestial inspirer who puts the sentiments of truth, beauty and the sublime in all of us, you raise the soul above those miseries against which paltry humankind struggles. Your leaps are irresistible, your conceptions divine. You console us and fortify us when we are bent down beneath the burdens of misfortunate; you ennoble everything that binds us to the earth, that vale of tears, and you enable us to glimpse..."

Sir Walter was interrupted by a detonation.

"Eh? What's that?" he demanded.

"To arms! To arms!" cried Pickerreek. "A thousand curses! We're under attack!"

"Well," murmured Sir Walter, picking up a rifle, "here's something designed to bring you back to reality." And he fired at a black mass agitating at the foot of the rock. The shot must have struck home, for a howl was heard, and furious clamors.

"They're pirates!" cried Valdy. "Come on, all together! Fire!"

The voyagers discharged their weapons.

"Now the revolvers!"

Detonations rang out and bullets whistled. The pirates hesitated; they dared not cross the slope of the cliff, for they would be exposed to the gunfire of those they were attacking.

"Lie face downwards," said Pickerreek, "and when the sea-raiders rush us, we'll greet them and avoid their fire, for they won't be able to make us out in the darkness."

Everyone lay down on the rock. Cardounet crept forward to observe the pirates' maneuvers.

There were about fifty of them. Three boats, tartans of the kind commonly used in the archipelagoes of the Persian Gulf, had brought them to the islet. They were hiding beneath a ridge wound around by a path, preparing to launch an assault. The black mass quivered.

Suddenly, a voice rang out, shouting in English: "Don't worry—we're friends!" And a formidable volley of shots rang out.

The pirates ran down—or, rather, tumbled down—to the sea, uttering exclamations of fear, embarking tumultuously in the midst of an indescribable disorder and confusion. The boats drew away, but, rapid as their flight was, they received another volley of grapeshot, which must have damaged them and killed a number of men.

The voyagers watched what was happening in astonishment. By a providential hazard, no one was wounded. Madame Valdy had bravely discharged six revolver shots at the assailants.

"Well," said Sir Walter, having recovered somewhat from his surprise, "there's help that arrived at the right time."

"You think so?" asked a man who appeared, escorted by a dozen English sailors. "I'm very glad for you and for me, Sir Walter Donderry."

"You know me?"

"Who doesn't know Sir Walter Donderry, since he wrote that famous letter to the *Times*, advertising aerial navigation?"

"Has that letter gone around the world, then?"

"Don't complain—today it contributed to your salvation."

"So much the better, I'm owed some compensation for all the annoyances it's caused me. May I know to whom I have the honor of speaking?"

"To the Commodore in command of the English cruiser in the Persian Gulf."

At that moment two launches arrived at the spot where the pirates had landed. The Commodore approached them to give orders.

"We'll spend the night here," he said. "Half of the crew of each launch come ashore, with arms and ammunition. Every hour, a launch will explore the environs of the island, under the surveillance of an officer. If anything new happens, warn me."

Eight cadavers were lying on the ground, and four or five wounded pirates were moaning.

"Take the wounded aboard," the Commodore went on. "We'll hand them over to the Persian authorities tomorrow, and their account will soon be settled. As for the dead, throw them in the sea; the bellies of the sharks will serve as their tomb."

On the part of the voyagers, the Commodore received all the marks of a profound gratitude, and hastened to satisfy their curiosity.

"As soon as you'd left the vicinity of Bandar Abbas," he said "the news of your passage spread and produced an extraordinary sensation. Europeans, Persians, Arabs and Guebres were talking about nothing else but the bird with gigantic wings they'd glimpsed in the sky. Some were frightened, predicting the greatest calamities, others thought it as an optical illusion. There was an overall anxiety, though, a vague apprehension, as if some unprecedented catastrophe were imminent.

"My frigate was anchored in Bandar Abbas harbor. The consul came to find me and told me what he knew. I shared his admiration and scolded him for not having alerted me. 'But where have these valiant voyagers gone?' I asked.

"'If they've followed my advice,' the consul replied, 'they've landed on one of the numerous islets situated between the isles of Kish and Hormuz. Among them is Sir Walter Donderry, the gentleman who wrote that famous letter to the *Times*...'

"'That's impossible; Sir Walter Donderry wrote his letter in Europe, after the departure of the aeronef.'

"'Yes, but he went to meet it in Karachi and embarked in that city.'

"The news spread that the gigantic bird was nothing supernatural, and that it was a machine of recent invention. All foreheads cleared. However, I noticed something unusual in some familiar faces, and I acquired the certainty that an expedition was being prepared to rob and kill you. My duty was clear; I had a compatriot to protect, human lives to save and a marvel of science to preserve from the impious and savage depredations of barbarians, and I resolved to come to your aid personally. Another motive also guided me; I wanted to shake your hands, compliment you on your boldness and examine your apparatus at close range."

"Monsieur le Commodore," said Valdy, "we are too obliged to you to refuse anything it pleases you to ask of us."

"During the night it was impossible to think of cruising these waters in my frigate," the brave officer continued, "for the reefs are numerous and the straits dangerous. I immediately fitted out two launches equipped with four light artillery pieces, crewed by intrepid men, and set out, making a detour, for the islet on which it was presumed that you had landed. Two miles from here I ordered all the lights to be extinguished, in order that nothing would betray our presence, and we waited. I disembarked on the point opposite the one from which the pirates attacked, in order to reassure you and avoid a surprise—and you know the rest as well as I do."

"Thank you, Commodore," said Sir Walter, shaking his compatriot's hand. "As soon as I reach Europe, the Admiralty will know of your noble and courageous conduct."

"Now reassured, the voyagers chatted with the Commodore for some time, recounting the incidents of their aerial explorations, furnishing the technical information that was requested of them, and then asked for permission to retire.

"Sleep," said the Commodore. "I'll keep watch."

All night long, the launches circled the island. Sentinels placed on the culminating points of the rock kept watch; patrols commanded by midshipmen supervised the hastily-organized safety measures.

When the first light of dawn reddened the horizon, Valdy, followed by the Commodore, inspected the aeronef minutely. No bullet had reached the hull; the leathery skins were still taut, the loss of hydrogen reduced to negligible proportions. If no accident occurred, they could hope to reach France without recourse to the vacuum pumps and without renewing the gas.

The commander of the English cruiser shook the hands of the people he had saved and protected, one last time, and Valdy gave the signal to depart. The *Céleste*, saluted by the artillery aboard the launches, rose up to a feeble height and steered southwards. In a few minutes, it reached the Musandam flats on the Strait of Hormuz and penetrated into Oman, a vast country of the Arab peninsula.

The voyagers perceived Sharjah, a city of 25,000 inhabitants with a large slave market, the port of the Dhorra Coast, once known as the Pirate Coast. Then here were a few cultivated fields, a few clumps of palm trees, and finally the desert, with its frightful nudity. As far as the eye could see, there was nothing but sandy hillocks grouped in stages like heath-land dunes. The aeronef crossed the Tropic of Cancer. The sun's rays, reflected by the white-colored sands, produced a stifling heat. Cardounet opined that they were "breathing fire."

In order to find a slightly fresher air, Valdy was obliged to rise up to fifteen hundred meters and continue his route while maintaining that altitude. With the aid of binoculars, they saw three or four caravans, probably heading for Mascate.

"Damn!" said Pickerreek, wiping his forehead, which was streaming with sweat. "I believe that it's better to travel by air than on land in this satanic place."

"Indeed," replied Sir Walter Donderry. "And I speak from experience."

"You know Arabia?" said Ivan Kisseloff.

"A little—mainly the south. After the Palgrave expedition of 1862, which crossed peninsula from the north-west to the south-east, several Englishmen, including me, resolved to visit the regions unexplored by the celebrated voyager. We left Aden with the intention of reaching Mascate by crossing the unknown regions forming the deserts of Rubr-al-Khali and El-Akkaf, but we didn't succeed in our enterprise. After marching for several days beyond Wadi Doan in the Hadhramaut, and penetrating into the Dahna—the fiery desert—driven back by hostile populations, robbed by our men, sick with fever and deprived of all assistance, we reached the coast and arrived at the port of Keshin, exhausted and at the end of our tether. However, I've seen enough, suffered enough and studied enough to inform anyone who might want to attempt the adventure after me."

"When we have time," Valdy said, "we'll attempt it by air."

"I advise you to do that, for by land, it presents serious difficulties, especially for Europeans."

"It's a villainous region, then?" Cardounet put in.

"Villainous isn't the right word, but in certain places, it's one of the least pleasant in which to travel."

"Tell us what struck you most," said Will Tooke. "Since its accursed heat prevents us from getting closer to the ground, your story will substitute for what we might have seen."

"It's precisely that heat, Mr. Tooke, that spoiled Arabia and my expedition for me. This country forms a rectangular peninsula extending from 12° 30′ to 34° north latitude and from 30° 15′ to 57° 30′ east longitude. Much of it is, therefore, in the torrid zone, and there's no need to be astonished that the heat is so intense. At Mocha, which is on the sea shore, the thermometer often rises to fifty-five degrees. When the simoom blows, it's fire that one breathes, to make use of our friend Cardounet's expression; it burns everything in its passage and contributes all too often to the spread of cholera and the plague. In the deserts, it whips up grains of sand of an extreme fineness and swallows caravans.

"The Dahna is the most frightful and most horrible desert on Earth. By comparison, the Sahara and the Thar are veritable gardens. Everywhere, the eye discovers nothing but immense sand expanses, with gigantic crevices, gulfs as profound as those of the sea. There is no trace of humidity anywhere, nor of animal or vegetable life. It's chaos in its frightful desolation. The dryness is a consequence of the heat, and water is lacking almost everywhere. There are no rivers; merely meager stream close to the coast.

"When rain falls, it is immediately absorbed by the friable soil, and that absorption creates a curious phenomenon. The water accumulates underground and forms veritable subterranean rivers. Thus, the existence has been determined of the Oued Roumen, which traverses almost all of Arabia from north to south along an extent of 1,300 kilometers. The Arabs reach those waters by digging wells at distant intervals."

Sir Walter Donderry was interrupted in is explanation by a faint noise—a sort of crackle coming from the inferior layers of the atmosphere.

"Damn!" said Pickerreek. "There's something going on beneath our feet."

The *Céleste* descended, and they distinctly perceived seven or eight hundred men charging one another. It was a battle—a veritable barbarian battle. Only a few of the warriors were equipped with firearms; the others were fighting with spears, sabers and clubs. War cries could be heard, along with the howls of the wounded, the moans of the dying, the imprecations of the defeated and the insults of the victors. The bloody melee continued with such fervor that no one noticed the aeronef.

"I have a yen to calm these savages down," Cardounet said, "by sending them few bullets."

"Why would you do that?" replied Sir Walter. "Do you know which side is in the right and which in the wrong? Are you entitled by legitimate self-defense? Why usurp a role that belongs to Providence alone?"

"Perhaps the parties are both wrong."

"Well, in truth, that's quite possible. In Europe, that's always agreed once the war is over and thousands of families are in mourning."

"Let's frighten the combatants, then, to oblige them to cease their horrible butchery."

Cardounet discharged two shots from his carbine into the air.

At that detonation, which seemed to come from the depths of the heavens, the warriors raised their heads, perceived the *Céleste* flying overhead, uttered cries of terror, and ran away in all directions, abandoning the dead and the wounded.

"Good," said Cardounet. "At least I've interrupted the battle for the moment."

"I don't think it'll start again," added Valdy.

"So much the better, then! I had a good idea."

The *Céleste* continued on her way and arrived within sight of Hasik at about four o'clock in the afternoon. Hasik is a small city situated in the Gharah, the name borne by the southern coast of Arabia west of Oman. The country, streaked by small mountains of volcanic origin, contrasted in its relative fertility with the desert they had just crossed.

Dernghuiz and Pickerreek easily found the sheikh who was holding the bicarbonate of soda and hydrochloric acid, and had the chemicals transported to the aeronef, which had landed three kilometers from the city. The sheikh received a rich gratification and offered hospitality. Sir Walter Donderry thanked him but declined; he knew from experience that the Arabs are far from having all the generous qualities attributed to them. The *Céleste* drew away for ten leagues and landed again in a wild, uncultivated area with no trace of human presence.

Chapter XX

On the fourth of October, after a tranquil night, our voyagers guided the *Céleste* toward the coast. The temperature, refreshed by sea breezes, was bearable. Although recalling the nature of Africa soil, the Arabic coast, Hadramaut, presented several fertile and cultivated areas. Clumps of palm trees, figs, olives, bananas and aloes stood out against the charred ground and heir verdure, slightly gray-tinted, cheered up the view. In the distance the Kuria and Muria islands, English since 1857, which furnished a great deal of guano, were visible; then there were several small ports: Morebat, Djaffar, Kechin, Raida, Sihout, Mukalla, and Haura at the mouth of the Khabb, the principal river of Yemen.

Several times, the tribes disseminated over that vast territory seem to the gripped by fear on seeing the aeronef traveling swiftly toward their douars; the most intrepid Arabs "let the powder talk" by firing into the air, but the bullets fired by wretched flintlock rifles rarely passed a height of a hundred and fifty meters.

Finally, they distinguished ships and oats bobbing on the blue waves of the sea, going in various directions, but announcing, by their number the neighborhood of a important port. Indeed, they soon saw Steamer Point Bay and Aden.

It was four o'clock in the afternoon. Since that morning, the *Céleste* had traveled twelve hundred kilometers.

The aeronef landed on the sea shore two cables from the city's fortifications. It was immediately surrounded by a compact and exceedingly heterogeneous crowd. There were Arabs, Jews, Parsees, Egyptians, Somalis and Europeans. The governor of Aden came to meet the voyagers, confided the guard of the *Céleste* to a platoon of soldiers, and everyone went into the ineradicable city, the Gibraltar of Arabia.

Aden, situated at 12° 43′ north latitude and 42° 52′ east longitude, has belonged to the English since 11 January 1839.

They have made it one of the strongest military bases in the world. It is surrounded by arid hills bristling with rocks of volcanic origin. Its port, or rather, the harbor of Steamer Point, which neighbors it, is a rendezvous for steamers bound for India, China and the Mascarene Islands, which call in there to renew their coal supplies. Apart from the commercial warehouses, which are expanding by the day, the population is almost exclusively occupied in the trade in gum and coffee. It has thirty thousand inhabitants.

Sir Walter Donderry had spent time in Aden before. He hastened to take his companions to see the immense cisterns constructed long ago by the Queen of Sheba and cleared and augmented by modern engineers. They are gigantic impermeable stone vats, which can contain potable water for more than a year. One might think that they were the work of giants,

The Governor, officers of the garrison, civil functionaries and Arab sheikhs crowded around the voyagers, complimenting them and giving them a splendid reception. Madame Valdy appeared to be a phenomenon for the indigenous chiefs, for the Mohammedan religion disparages and humiliates women, reducing them to the condition of slaves and brutalizing them; they could not conceive that a woman might be bold enough to launch into the atmosphere to attempt to fly around the world in forty days.

The next day, the fifth of October, Sir Walter Donderry and Valdy thanked the governor of Aden, the officers, the functionaries and all the people whose acquaintance they had made the day before, on behalf of the crew, and the *Céleste* departed, saluted by the frenetic cries of negroes and Arabs and the enthusiastic cheers of the English. She followed the coast as far as the strait of Bab-el Mandeb, which it crossed, passing over the English-controlled isle of Perim, and went into Africa near the Bay of Asab; then she veered northwestwards along the shore of the Red Sea, although she was hampered by a moderately strong contrary wind blowing from the north.

"We won't advance as rapidly as yesterday," said Valdy. "This wind is untimely."

Sir Water, who had traveled a great deal in Africa and knew a great deal about its climatological conditions, passed on a few instructive details.

"In all the gulfs," he said, "the air and the waves are almost constantly agitated. The causes of that agitation are explained by the contraction to which the ground is subjected. In the Red Sea, other causes combine with that—firstly, its relatively shallow depth; secondly, the rarity of watercourses flowing into it; and thirdly its evaporation. Extending between 30° and 12° 40′ north latitude, it's exposed to blazing sunlight, which warms its waters to thirty-five degrees centigrade. The evaporation is so strong that the Gulf of Arabia would dry out in sixty years if Bab-el Mandeb were sealed, but a strong current from the Indian Sea makes up the deficit created by the evaporation, incessantly filling the vast basin. Under the combined action of that current and the heat, the air warms up, expands, rises up to higher regions, is replaced by denser air coming from the northern lands, and produces this northerly wind that is causing you so much inconvenience—and almost permanent wind, which renders navigation perilous and difficult. Thus, only steamboats can easily travel the Red Sea."

"Tell me, Sir Walter," asked Cardounet, "why is this gulf called the Red Sea? The water is the same color as other seas. It's certainly not because the lobsters in it are cooked by the heat."

"The Red Sea owes its name to its numerous coral reefs, its red-tinted sands, and, principally, to the presence of a red alga called *Trichodesmium*, with simple filaments bound together by a mucilaginous substance, which floats on the surface of the water and produces stains like pools of blood.

"Thank you, Sir Walter; there's more knowledge in your little finger than my whole body; I'll interrogate you whenever I want to know something."

"As you please, my friend."

288

The *Céleste* was flying awkwardly. Valdy tried to find a tranquil layer of air, but he always encountered a contrary wind.

"If this continues," he said, "we'll be obliged to descend."

"Avoid that if you can," said Sir Walter. The coast of Samara, which we're following, is extremely inhospitable. It's the land of the Dankali, made up of fanatically independent tribes, populated by coarse, ignorant, deceptive, suspicious negroes, avoid and cruel thieves."

"Let's continue on our route."

The aeronef went around, as best it could, the mountainous sinuosities the formed the coast of Samara, sometimes succeeding in avoiding the wind, and finally arrived at the Bay of Zoulla in the evening.

Zoulla! Pickerreek and Cardounet opened their eyes as if they had perceived something strange. They rubbed their eyes four or five times to render their vision clearer. Was it possible? Was not a deceptive mirage playing tricks on them? They could see the French flag flying on a signal-post, flapping its pleats in the wind. They saw several men clad in dark blue uniforms, coiffed in the coquettish little waxed hats that pose so daintily on the heads of our mariners.

"Oh, yes!" shouted Valdy, enjoying his two companions' astonishment. "Yes, it's France, the fatherland! Zoulla has been one of our possessions since 1867."

"Well, by all that's holy!" exclaimed Cardounet. "That makes me feel ten years younger."

"Oh, Captain," said Pickereek, "this emotion is stupid, but it disturbs the temperament. Look—I nearly swallowed my tobacco plug again!"

And the two mariners could not tear their eyes away from the tricolor standing out against the azure sky. We even suspect that their eyelids dampened slightly.

The *Céleste* landed on a sandy beach on the coast of Zoulla.

At Zoulla the voyagers were greeted by a young naval ensign. The officer had the city and the shore of the bay under his command. The superior authorities were resident in the Île Dessi, also acquired in 1867, and the principal center of our naval base in the Red Sea.

The mariners charged with the service of the port made a fuss of Pickerreek and Cardounet—and Dernghuiz, who never quit his two friends. They talked for a long time about the absent fatherland, and drank to their beloved France. They drank for such a long time, and so often, that their tongues thickened and their eyes misted over slightly, but no one got drunk; they were merely slightly tipsy. Even Dernghuiz was merely fidgeting agitatedly, as if mercury were running in his veins; his yellow-tinted face was radiant with satisfaction and pleasure. In the company of Pickerreek and Cardounet he had learned a few French words, and he cried joyfully: "French, all friends, all professors!"

Cardounet explained the significance of the final term in the Tatar's mouth, and then the old frank Gallic gaiety that is our privilege convulsed every spleen and Homeric laughter elevated every rib-cage.

The good and worthy mariners! They were delighted to welcome comrades.

We know full well that the manner in which we have presented them belies the romantic tradition that has created a sentimental, disheveled, somber and fatalistic mariner with a heart filled with feverish passions, of which Eugène Sue has described several specimens, but we think that the truth is better than the fiction. Yes, our mariners are jesters and heavy drinkers, but what men they are! Abnegation, devotion and bravery are the order of the day in them, and a hundred qualities compensate for their sight faults.

For his part, the ensign did his very best to welcome Valdy, Will Tooke, Ivan Kisseloff, Sir Walter Donderry and Madame Valdy.

"We owe thanks to the wind that was blowing today," Valdy said to the ensign, "For without it, we would have taken on supplies in order to leave immediately and perhaps wouldn't have made your acquaintance."

"Why is that?"

"The wind has slowed our progress and we've been constrained to stop to Zoulla, when we wanted to reach Souakim."

"I thank the wind in my turn, but for tomorrow's journey, I'll tell you a means of avoiding its effect. On leaving Zoulla, go some way inland, behind the mountains that border the coast; I'm convinced that, a few leagues from the sea, you'll find a tranquil atmosphere."

"Of course, that's true," said Sir Walter, "but none of us thought of such a simple thing. It's even probably that we'll encounter a current that will come to our aid."

The soirée terminated with a punch, of which the station's mariners had a good share, and then the ensign offered his apartments to the travelers to shield them from the chill of the night. In those latitudes the days are very hot but the nights are sometimes quite cold.

Early on the sixth of October, every healthy man in Zoulla and the surrounding area was up and about. The wind was still blowing strongly from the north-north-west. Compliments, embraces, handshakes and good wishes were exchanged many times over, and the *Céleste* took off.

Valdy steered inland, and after half an hour he set a northward course. The ensign's predictions were realized; the air was almost calm. The voyagers passed over a landscape presenting the features of Saharan regions, strewn with numerous oases inhabited by the Ghazi, the Bedouin, the Bejas, the Beni-Amer, etc.—negroes with European faces and close relatives in their mores, their religion and their customs to the Dankali. At about ten o'clock in the morning they arrived in Souakim.

Since the piercing of the isthmus of Suez, Souakim has taken on a certain importance. Its harbor, facing numerous sandy islets, is frequented by small boats and its commerce is becoming more extensive. It is the ancient capital of Turkish Habech, the Nubian coast, ceded a short time ago to the Viceroy of Egypt. One encounters black and white Arabs, Egyptians and a few Europeans there. One of the latter, Maltese by birth and an innkeeper by profession, had custody of the deposit of bicarbonate of soda and hydrochloric acid. In exchange for payment, he hastened to transport the chemical agents aboard the aeronef. The *Céleste* departed immediately and headed westwards, following the nineteenth degree of north latitude, heading toward Dongola, the heart of Nubia.

The country over which they were passing was nothing but an immense desert of desolate aspect; bushes, mimosas and tufts of agoul or pilgrim grass, *Poaceae*, paniceas, *Capparaceae* with prickly branches and rugged calices formed the meager ornamentation of that vast solitude. Three caravans were however, visible making their way toward the coast beneath a sky the color of lead. They were heading for some port to trade ivory, gum, wax, myrrh, ostrich plumes, gold dust and musk for the products of European industry. Sir Walter Donderry assured them that the caravans dealt in slaves, and that they had no scruple about raiding the weak tribes they encountered along their route. It is true that the favor was often returned, with interest.

The aeronef passed over the rather elevated ramifications of Djebel Barkal and subsequently discovered the mountainous masses of Robatat, Monassir, Chaighieh, etc. There they crossed the Nile. A hundred kilometers further on they crossed it for a second time above the fourth cataract. In that place, the great river describes a curve and only resumes its northward course after having turned back on itself between 19° 30′ and 18° north latitude.

Before sunset, they perceived Marakah or New Dongola, the capital of the province of Dongola. The Céleste landed some distance from the city. The voyagers feared, not without reason, the bellicose and piratical humor of the men of that country. Sir Walter Donderry, who had once taken part in a scientific expedition charged with traveling up the Nile as far as Khartoum in upper Nubia, was familiar with Marakah. Accompanied by Ivan Kisseloff and Will Tooke, he headed boldly for the city, went into it, found a host of indigenes there attracted by curiosity, and asked in Arabic—a language that he spoke fluently—to present his respects to the Pacha of Dongola.

By a fortunate chance, the Pacha of Dongola was the same man that Sir Walter had visited during his expedition. "Fortunate chance" is not an exaggeration, for in most Muslim sovereignties, if not all, functionaries submissive to the arbitrariness of despotism are moved and disappear continually.

Sir Walter explained to the Pacha the motives that had brought him into his presence. "A caravan led by an Egyptian from Aswan ought to have confided bales to a man in Marakh named Si-Djilali-ben-Hussein to be given to *roumis*.

"Si-Djillali-ben-Hussein is one of my *chaouchs*,"[62] the Pacha replied. "He will give you what belongs to you. Now, tell me how you came to Marakah. You and your Companions have surely not traversed the Korosko and arrived here without being accompanied, and yet I see neither your camels nor your convoy of servants."

"We haven't come by land."

"So you came up the Nile?"

"No."

"Have I failed in the duties of hospitality or lacked respect for you that you mock me thus?"

"I'm not mocking you at all."

"By Allah, what are you saying? If you have not come either by land or water, what means have you employed?"

"Eagles and vultures come to Marakah, and they do not walk on the ground or sail on the water."

---

[62] The author inserts a footnote: "Agents of Muslim police, and sometimes executioners. It is well-known that in Africa there is nothing degrading about the latter profession, which is even honored." Later in the paragraph the author adds a parenthetical definition of Korosko as "desert."

"Do you take me for a simpleton? Do you think that you can make be believe that you have a bid's wings at your disposal?"

"Give orders to your *chaouch* to bring us what belongs to us, come with us, and judge for yourself."

The Pacha, who was one of those old Egyptians for whom routine has all kinds of attractions, and was, moreover, imbued by his education, his religion and his mores with the most absurd prejudices, decided to verify his interlocutor's assertions."

"If you are making fun of me," he said, "so much the worse for your head."

"I am English," Sir Walter replied, firmly, "And never lie. If your threats are put into execution, I warn you that my nation will demand justice from your master the Viceroy, and you will perish in your turn. Now come!"

This firm and arrogant language impressed the Pacha, who softened to the point of becoming gracious. While the bicarbonate of soda and hydrochloric acid were being loaded and horses were being saddled, Ivan Kisseloff, Will Tooke and Sir Walter paid a rapid visit to Marakah.

The city only has five thousand inhabitants. It is of recent foundation and located on the left bank of the Nile. The houses, build of sun-baked bricks and unshaped stone, are small and uncomfortable. It is defended by a castle-fort built according to the plans of the celebrated microscopist Christian Ehrenberg, who traveled in Nubia in 1820 on a scientific mission for the Prussian government.

The Pacha, followed by a number of Shaigiya horsemen mounted on the famous thoroughbred horses of Dongola, told the voyagers that he was ready to accompany them. They mounted the horses that had been provided for them and the cavalcade moved off, raising clouds of dust.

Sir Walter and the Pacha marched at the head; after half a hour's ride the Englishman pointed to a black mass that was easy to distinguish in the sandy plain.

"There are our wings," he said.

The Pasha looked at him askance.

Eventually, they arrived at the aeronef. Si-Djillali-ben-Hussein had the chemical products unloaded, received a rich reward and returned to take his place beside his master. All the horsemen looked at the *Céleste* with curiosity mingled with dread; its strange and unknown form inspired assort of respect in them.

"Well, Sidi, are you convinced?" asked Sir Walter.

"I understand," replied the Pacha, having reflected for some time, "that this machine has come here guided by a superhuman force, but I doubt that it has the lightness of a bird. Listen, I will give you some good advice. Either you are telling the truth, or you are an impostor. In either case, I warn you that if this machine remains in proximity to Marakah, the population will come running to destroy and pillage it, because you are *roumis*. Take my advice. If you do not rise up into the air your imposture will be recognized and punished; if you can fly like our eagles, imitate them and fly away."

"Thank you. Watch, and be convinced."

Valdy gave orders to take off immediately. The *Céleste* rose up on its supportive struts, its wings beat the air violently, and it rose into the air. Sir Walter, his eyes glued to his binoculars, wanted to enjoy the skeptical Pacha's surprise. He saw him raise his arms to the heavens and remain in a sort of ecstasy. The horsemen seemed anxious and afraid.

After having traveled fifty or sixty kilometers, the voyagers landed in the desert. Night fell almost immediately. As a precautionary measure, it was agreed that everyone except Madame Valdy would take turns on watch until morning. Pickerreek set up the tent and began the sentry duty while his companions slept. Until daylight the sentinels relieved one another regularly, but nothing troubled the calm of the immense solitude.

Finally, the radiant sun emerged behind the mountains that close the valley of the Nile in almost all of Nubia, and its dazzling light suddenly invaded all the points of the horizon.

"Get up! Get up!" cried Sir Walter, joyfully. "Today, the seventh of October, we're going to travel across one of the most celebrated countries in the world."

"We won't have much time to admire it," said Valdy, "for we'll be traveling flat out. This evening we'll be in Medinet el-Fayoum, more than twelve hundred kilometers from here."

"The Bible assures us that the Israelites led by Moses took forty years to cross the desert. If they'd had aeronefs at their disposal, their journey would have taken less than forty hours!"

After this reflection by Sir Walter, the *Céleste* rose into the atmosphere, returned toward the Nile and followed the great river, maintaining a height of two hundred meters. She passed over the isle of Argo near Marakah, where colossal statues and Ethiopian ruins have been found, and continued on its way above a country covered in rocky massifs, called by the Arabs in their expressive language Batn-el-Hajar, which means belly of stone.

It would be fastidious to name the numerous villages scattered on the two banks of the river, so we shall only identify the people that inhabited them. After the Dongola one encounters the Mahas, the Sokkots, the Hadjas and the Barahas, a mixture of negro and white hybrids, most descended from Turks and Mamelukes.

Toward midday, the aeronef landed near Aswan, and was immediately surrounded by a curious crowd. Valdy took on the supplies of bicarbonate of soda and hydrochloric acid deposited with A Copt—a Christian descendant of the ancient Egyptians—and gave the order to depart.

"It's a pity that we can't stop here for a few hours," said Sir Walter.

"Why's that?" asked Cardounet.

"Because there are important ruins to be seen in Aswan. It's the ancient Syene from which were transported the beautiful granites and syenites extracted from neighboring quarries in colossal blocks, which served for the edification of a great many Egyptian monuments. Then, opposite is the island of Elephantine, the Djeziret-el-zahir, or flowery island, of the Arabs, which European visitors call the Garden of the Tropic. Elephantine is covered in rich antiquities; one, once could see a nilometer there described by Strabo, and two temples constructed by Amenhotep II 1,700 years before our era. But modern civilization has replaced those magnificent edifices with two large barracks. Where the priests of the Pharaohs celebrated the glory of Kneph, the good genius, and Osiris, the resplendent sun, Muslim mercenaries smoke their chibouks and live in filth and indolence."

The *Céleste* then followed the beautiful plain fertilized every year by the Nile floods, famous for the historic memories it recalls. On the banks of the river stood, imposing and majestic, palaces, ruins, colonnades, obelisks, temples and grandiose monuments, confused with recent towns, and still surrounded by a verdant corset of palm trees, sugar canes, orange groves, sycamores and banana-trees.

They perceived Edfou, the *Apollinopolis Magna* renowned for its temple of Horus; Esneh, the Latopolis of the Greeks, where two zodiacs were discovered and the hypogeas of Eileythyia; Luxor, from which the rose granite monolith decorating the Place de la Concords in Paris comes; Karnak and Medinet Habu, on the site of Thebes of the Hundred Gates; Denderah, ridiculed in the satires of Juvenal for its pretentious disputes with the inhabitants of Ombos, a few leagues north of Syene, its magnificent temple still standing: Keneh, formerly Coenopolis, with ten thousand inhabitants; Madfouneh, the ancient Abydos; Girga, on the canal of Joseph; South, near the debris of Lycopolis; Achmoumeyn, almost opposite the great Hermopolis, a miserable village constructed on the ruins of the superb Antinoe; Minieh, where bardaques—porous vases—are manufactured; and Beni Suef, a center of commerce and cotton manufacture.

All the crew admired the vast panorama.

"Oh," exclaimed Sir Walter Donderry, "what you could see if you remained for a entire year in this ravishing country!

During the months of July and August the valley of the Nile resembles a vast sea strewn with islands, with causeways that lead from ne village to another; the trees, gathered in clumps, show their crowns above the waves; the muddy waters roll their silt over the arid sands that they will fecundate. The spectacle is magical! The inundation is not torrential like those produced in our European rivers; it invades gently and gradually, pianissimo, the banks dried by the ardor of the sun and the burning wind of the Khamsin; it extends in an undulating sheet to the limits of the desert.

"During the months of December, January and February, when the frosts are rigorous and nature dies in almost all the climates of the temperate zone, Egypt wakes up. It's the verdant season! The atmosphere is embalmed by the orange-tees, the lemon-trees, the laurier-roses, the tamarinds and other odorant bushes. The fertilized soil is covered with crops and flowers. The insects, in the revivified grass, and the birds in the refreshed and perfumed air, sing the song of spring."

Near Beni Suef the *Céleste* turned westwards, passed over a country criss-crossed by canals, and arrived shortly at Medinet, the capital of Fayoum.

Chapter XXI

The aeronef was soon surrounded by a numerous crowd composed of Muslims and Copts. The news of its arrival spread through Medinet like wildfire. The governor of Fayoum came to verify for himself that there was to exaggeration in what he had been told. He was a modern Egyptian—which is to say, one of the sons of great families sent by the Khedive to complete their education in European schools, enlightened men who do not reject any improvement and render useful service to their country on a daily basis. He spoke English and French fluently. Sir Walter Donderry had met him before in the social circles of London and Paris, so he was delighted to renew his acquaintance.

The governor, who was about forty years of age, was named Mourad-ben-Ghazalli-Bey, or Ghazalli-Bey for short. "Messieurs," he said, in French, "welcome to Egyptian soil. Henceforth I shall count the day of your gracious visit as one of the happiest of my life." Then he turned to Madame Valdy and added: "Madame, our mores have not yet emancipated women, but if they had your boldness they would soon bring about the regeneration that Egypt awaits in order to recover its ancient splendor and power."

"Educate them," Madame Valdy replied, "And I'm sure that they would understand their civilizing and social mission."

Ghazalli-Bey made no reply. Egypt is a nation in which it is not yet permissible to discuss such issues.

The governor confided the *Céleste* to the guard of a platoon of soldiers and took the voyagers to his house. He received them with the customary pomp and courtesy of rich Orientals, and the delicacies that ennoble hospitality.

"I am glad," he said, "that it is a Frenchman who has discovered aerial navigation."

"It could not be otherwise," Cardounet put in, laughing. "All the peoples of the world agree in repeating that the French are the 'lightest' human beings in existence."

"No, no," replied Ghazalli-Bey, "their lightness is often merely apparent, behind which serious and commendable qualities are concealed. Our country owes a great deal to France; it has retained the traces of her glorious army and the numerous scholars that accompanied it. Then, the great nation was our enemy, but she pursued a civilizing mission whose effects we still feel. For our vanquished fathers, France became a sort of revelation, and when they aspired to progress, it was from France that they requested instruments and men to spread the first seeds of education among them. Without the tenacious perseverance of Monsieur de Lesseps, would the piercing of the Suez canal, that marvelous and gigantic project that had defeated the pharaohs, have been achieved? I doubt it. So, every time that I can render justice to the French, I do so promptly and gratefully."

Valdy thanked Ghazalli-Bey; Pickerreek and Cardounet shook his hand, with such ardor that one might have thought that they were trying to dislocate his arm.

In the evening, the voyagers toured Medinet, favored by splendid moonlight and guided by the governor and a number of his subalterns. Medinet-el-Fayoum, constructed on the site of the ancient Arsinoë, resembles the majority of Muslim cities: narrow streets; low houses without openings in their facades; mosques with gracious minarets; heavy and oppressive public edifices—all that was on view. The factories making white shawls, linen cloth and rose essence are renowned. Its population is in excess of twelve thousand.

"You will find it different from your European cities, so animated and luxurious," said Ghazalli-Bey. "In Egypt, therefore, it is not our cities that it is necessary to visit but our magnificent countryside. The province of Fayoum is an immense garden. Nature deploys all her riches there. And yet, it was once nothing but a wild and uncultivated desert. The deviation of the waters of the Nile carried out three thousand years before the Hegira by a Pharaoh of the dynasty of Manetho transformed the land completely. The Bahr Yussef—the canal of Joseph—formed Lake Moeris, permitting the creation of an ingenious irrigation system, and fertilized the arid sands."

The voyagers thanked the governor for all his kindness and asked to rest, for their long journey and the heat had wearied them.

The next day, the eighth of October, in the presence of almost all the inhabitants of Medinet-el-Fayoum, the Céleste prepared for departure. Ghazalli-Bey gave Valdy a letter of recommendation for the sheikh of the oasis of Siwa and offered Madame Valdy a valuable ornament, a veritable artistic masterpiece, fashioned by the most skillful Egyptian workmen.

At eight o'clock in the morning, the aeronef quit Medinet, passed over Lake Keroum, the ancient Lake Moeris and continued on its westward course. Nothing remarkable struck the voyagers' gaze. The desert extended into the distance; only a few encampments and caravans broke the lugubrious monotony.

After a journey of three hundred kilometers, the soil seemed to cast off its sandy envelope to some extent and became subject to undulations step enough not to be attributable to the action of the wind. In the distance, they distinguished veritable rocky hillocks, and eventually hills and mountains. At about one o'clock in the afternoon, they spotted the oasis of Siwa. The *Céleste* drew nearer to the ground, but soon became the object of hostile demonstrations.

"Be prudent," said Sir Walter. "The people down below don't seem to want to welcome us as friends."

"That's because they're afraid," said Ivan Kisseloff.

"All the more reason to be circumspect."

The Arabs came out of their houses and uttered cries; horsemen raced into the plain at the gallop. The alarm seemed to be general. Several rifle shots were fired at the aeronef and

Valdy had to climb out of range of the bullets. Then he circled over Siwa, looking for a favorable opportunity to descend.

"I've got an idea," said Cardounet.

"What?"

"Give me the letter from the Bey of Medinet and steer the *Céleste* over that group of people I can see over there to one side of the town. There must be a chief among them."

Cardounet took the letter and wrapped it round a silver five-franc piece, thus forming a little packet on which the air had no purchase, and threw it overboard. They followed the letter with the aid of binoculars. As soon as it hit the ground a child picked it up and took it to the man in command. The latter read it and dispatched four or five horsemen in the various directions where "powder was still talking." As if by magic, the detonations ceased, and silence replaced the tumult and the din.

Ghazalli-Bey, who knew the suspicious and bellicose character of the desert Arabs, had employed both persuasion and command in what he wrote.

Sheikh of Ouah-el-Siwa, he said in his letter, *you will share bread and salt with the men who will arrive among you flying like the birds. They do not mean you any harm. Do not be afraid of their machine, which you will see in the sky. These individuals have been inspired by the Holy Prophet; they are my friends and are under the protection of the Khedive. You will give them what they request and offer them hospitality. I shall take account of your generosity; you will be richly rewarded when you come to Fayoum with your caravans. If you greet them as enemies and combat them, I shall inform the Khedive of your treachery and I will personally bring war and desolation to Siwa. May Allah protect you and render you kind to strangers.*

The sheikh, understandably, made the greatest efforts to reassure the voyagers and persuade them to descend. Sir Walter, who spoke Arabic fluently, heard the word *aroua*, which means "come." Then the aeronef settled gently on a hillock, sufficiently far away from the group surrounding the sheik.

The latter understood the foreigners' hesitation, and launched his horse forward at a gallop, approaching on his own, while invoking Mohammed and Allah.

Sir Walter came forward. "Who are you?" he asked.

"I am the Sheikh of Siwa."

"Are you a friend or a enemy?"

"I am a friend of Lord Ghazalli-Bey. He tells me to receive you as friends because you bring me peace. Be welcome; you are my guests; you are the envoys of God."

"Come on," Sir Walter called o is companions. "We're the sheikh's guests; we no longer have anything to fear. No Arab has ever betrayed the duties of hospitality."

The *Céleste* was entrusted to the guard of a few horsemen, and everyone headed toward Siwa.

Siwa, the principal town of the oasis, is built on a small hill, conical in form and quite steep; it has three thousand inhabitants, who are mostly crop-growers, camel-drivers and caravan guides. The bicarbonate of soda and hydrochloric acid had been brought from Alexandria[63] and handed over to a Jew who stayed in the town for a few months every year, occupied in the date trade. The Jew seemed delighted to get rid of his deposit and did not want any payment for having taken care of it. Nevertheless, Valdy got him to accept a thermometer, and Sir Walter explained the various uses of the instrument to him.

The oasis of Siwa forms a valley surrounded by mountains, well irrigated, enclosing small lakes and producing an abundance of dates, water-melons, pomegranates, grapes, olives, broad beans, barley, wheat and rice. It owes its fame not to its extraordinary fertility but to the numerous ruins with which it is covered. Once it was the oasis of Zeus-Amon; it was there that the pagans of antiquity went to consult the most famous of their oracles; it was there that Alexander the Great received the pompous title of the Son of Zeus; it was in the

---

[63] The author inserts a footnote saying that caravans make the journey from Alexandria to Siwa in fourteen days.

surrounding desert that the army of Cambyses perished when that cruel king tried to sack the divine temple.

Our voyagers made a rapid visit to the ruins nowadays known to the Arabs as Omm-Beyda and took part in the *diffa*, the meal offered in their honor by the sheikh. Sir Walter rewarded the chief of the oasis generously by giving him a few banknotes.

"Do you often go to Alexandria?" he asked him.

"I go every year to deliver the tribute that we pay the Khedive."

"Present these papers at a banking house or a commercial establishment, and you'll be given gold."

"May Allah bless you!" And the sheikh pocketed the banknotes. Rich or poor, all Arabs are avaricious, and Sir Walter Donderry knew them well enough to know that nothing would be more agreeable to his interlocutor than the hope of realizing a tidy sum.

The Céleste took off again, but no approval or acclamation accompanied her. The Arabs were more dazed than amazed, and they saw the aeronef's ascent as something supernatural, which they could not imagine. Some contended that the magic of the djinn and the peris was no stranger to that marvelous event.

The voyagers followed their course into a country less bleak than the desert, but thinly populated and rather arid. They soon left Egypt and passed over the Barca plateau in the Regency of Tripoli, formerly Cyrenaica or Pentapolis. They traversed the desert of Barca, which separates the oasis of Awjila from the coast, and distinguished the Djebel Akhdar, a mountain chain extending from the Gulf of Sidre to the Egyptian frontier. Finally they arrived at Benghazi jut as the sun was launching its last rays into the atmosphere and seemed to be swallowed up in the iridescent waves of the Mediterranean.

Benghazi, the ancient Berenice, is on the sea shore. The Garden of the Hesperides was placed in its vicinity. Its harbor, protected by a line of reefs, is very mediocre. Its population is about 6,000, and trades with the island of Malta and Oudai in the Sudan.

Night spread its shadows over the earth; Valdy did not judge it wise to go into Benghazi as yet in search of the chemical products deposited with an Italian established in the city for some years. The *Céleste* landed on a small hill in the Djebel-Akhdar, in an isolated spot, sheltered from any surprise. The voyagers ate supper cheerfully, chatted for a while and slept like logs. At dawn the following day, the ninth of October, Pickerreek, Cardounet. Sir Walter and Will Tooke went into Benghazi and came back an hour later with a convoy of mules carrying the bicarbonate of soda and hydrochloric acid. No one in the city had any inkling of the proximity of the aeronef.

The *Céleste* launched forth like an arrow over the sea. Instead of following the coast, which curves to form the Great Syrte—the Gulf of Sidre—Valdy preferred to undertake a crossing; it shortened his journey by three hundred kilometers. Indeed, the distance from Benghazi to Tripoli in a straight line is only about sixty myriameters, while it is more than ninety along the shore, which is sterile and almost uninhabited. Then again, our voyagers were weary of passing over immense and tedious terrestrial solitudes. Always the same appearances, the same uniformity of the sandy plain; nothing but thorny mimosas or meager bushes to cheer up the landscape! The oases, sometimes seen from a rather elevated altitude, had appeared to be so may tufts of grass scattered in a devastated field.

But the sea! The sea, with its vaporous horizons, its terns, its petrels and its gulls describing their gracious curves above the foamy crests; the sea, with its constant agitation and its eternal murmur, is joy and life! *Thalassa! Thalassa!* The sea! The sea! cried the ten thousand men led by Xenophon, delightedly, when, worn out by fatigue and exhausted by their long march, decimated by war and privation, they perceived the waves of the Pont-Euxin. The sight of the sea awakens mysterious sentiments of grandeur and admiration, which, in the words of Captain Matthew Maury "reveals new marvels at

305

every step; and one does not take long to see in that liquid mass, which seems inanimate at first glance, a veritable world, alive and moving, obedient to determined laws. The further one advances the more gripping the impression of that majestic spectacle becomes."

The *Céleste*, "sailing in the redness of the morning," traversed the Great Syrte, famous for its depths, its shifting sands, its tidal waves and its numerous shipwrecks, and reached land again at Cape Mesurata. From there on she followed the coast as far as Tripoli, where she arrived at about one o'clock in the afternoon and landed near the harbor.

Tripoli is a city of thirty thousand souls, the residence of the Dey and the administrative center of the entire Regency. Thus, when the aeronef was perceived, all the functionaries and all the European consuls and their personnel hastened toward the spot where it had landed. The Dey came in person, accompanied by a numerous escort, to visit the aerial marvel, and had his felicitations presented to Valdy by a French interpreter, a dragoman. The consuls wanted to welcome the voyagers appropriately and begged them to remain until the following day, but Valdy refused their offers, on the pretext that he had no time to lose in returning to France. As soon as he had taken on supplies he made ready to depart.

Suddenly, the attention of the crowd was diverted from the *Céleste* by a black dot that appeared in the sky. Will Tooke and Ivan Kisseloff recognized it as a balloon. There were two aeronauts in the nacelle. The balloon rose, descended, rose again and drifted over the sea, in a direction almost parallel to the coast.

"I know that maneuver," said Pickerreek. "That balloon's in distress."

Indeed, the aerostat as seen to skim the waves several times, then rise up in prodigious bounds, only to fall again further on. No help was possible. The two aeronauts seemed condemned to certain death. Cardounet estimated their distance at about six kilometers; no boat, no matter how fine a sailor it was, could arrive soon enough to pick them up. The balloon was still traveling rapidly, continuing to bound eastwards—which is to say, out to sea.

"Quickly, quickly!" shouted Valdy. "All aboard! We'll save those two unfortunates."

The anxiety was general, even among the Arabs, Moors and negroes, who constantly maintain a chilly impassivity. The *Céleste* flapped its wings and launched forth over the waves. In a few minutes, she reached the balloon, the name of which as legible in large letters: *L'Algérien.*

"A thousand thunders, they're French!" exclaimed Pickerreek. "We'll save them or I'll lose my name!"

But how was the rescue to be effected? The half-deflated aerostat sometimes dipped its nacelle in the water and hid the two aeronauts in its folds. There was no possibility of lifting it up, for its weight might have raged the *Céleste* down into the abyss. They could not advise the aeronauts to cut the rigging in order to free the balloon, because it was supporting the nacelle.

What could they do?

Pickerreek had an inspiration. "Captain," he said to Valdy, "get us close enough for them to be able to hear me."

The aeronef skimmed the surface of the sea and turned in a tight circle.

"Try to climb!" shouted Pickerreek. "Your salvation lies in a new ascent."

"We have no more ballast!" replied one of the aeronauts.

"Get rid of everything heavy you have on you. Take off your clothes and throw them in the sea."

The two men undressed almost completely and followed Pickerreek's order. Immediately, the balloon, relived of a certain weight, straightened up, cleaved the air like an arrow and climbed to a height of about fifteen hundred meters.

"I understand," said Valdy—and he steered toward the aerostat.

"Let's position ourselves underneath it," said Pickerreek, "and wait."

Having obeyed the ascensional impulse, the balloon began to descend again, but slowly and obliquely. The *Céleste* waited for it, presenting her prow.

Cardounet, Pickerreek and Will Tooke grabbed the nacelle and held it in place. The two aeronauts, in their underwear, somewhat chilly, stepped on to the deck of the aeronef. The balloon, completely disengaged, rose up into the blue sky and disappeared.

The *Céleste* veered away and returned to land near Tripoli. Applause, acclamations and frantic hurrahs greeted her return.

The two voyagers, so miraculously rescued and utterly astonished by their adventure, looked around in alarm, initially unable to find words to express their surprise.

"But it's not a dream!" one of them finally cried. "We're alive, we're saved!"

"Well, yes, old chap," Pickerreek replied, "and you ought to light a fine candle to the chance that led us here today. You owe another to Captain Marcel Valdy, who has invented a machine to fly in the air, a machine compared to which locomotives, steamboats and balloons are just rubbish."

And the brave mariner explained succinctly, in his own fashion, all the facts related to aerial navigation.

"And what about you?" he added. "Tell us a little about how and why you cast off your moorings and almost took the big plunge."

"I'm an aeronaut by profession," replied the man who had spoken previously, "and my traveling companion is an amateur. I went to Constantine to effect an ascension with my balloon, *L'Algérien*, and this morning, when its inflation with bicarbonated hydrogen gas was concluded, my comrade and I took off. The wind was blowing from the north; I thought we were going to come down in the vicinity of Batna, but at an altitude of two thousand meters, and aerial current seized us and drove us eastwards with extreme violence. I wasn't worried about it, because no danger threatened us. In order to descend I waited until we were close to a sizeable town, because

I had everything to fear from the inexperience and ignorance of the Arabs living in douars. I didn't discover any. Suddenly, my comrade cried; 'The sea!' I opened the valve to let gas escape and descend, but the current increased its velocity and carried the balloon like a wisp of straw out over the Mediterranean. We left the coast, perceived the Kerkenni islands, and then the open sea. What can I add? The loss of gas continued, and we had no more ballast hen you snatched us from the jaws of a frightful death."

The two aeronauts thanked the crew of the *Céleste* warmly, and Sir Walter offered them his pecuniary services, for they had abandoned and lost everything in their shipwreck. The French consul hastened to lend them first aid, and begged them to accept his hospitality, until a favorable opportunity presented itself for their repatriation.

Escaping from the numerous marks of sympathy and admiration that were lavished on them, the voyagers re-embarked as quickly as possible and the aeronef rose up majestically above Tripoli. They flew along the African coast as far as Gabes, a large city in Tunisia, which gives its name to the gulf formerly known as the Little Syrte, then steered westwards and passed over the region of *chotts* that extends from the sea to the foothills of the Aures Mountains in the province of Constantine, which Captain Élie Roudaire proposed to transform into an inland sea. The *chotts,* or *Seb Khas*, are depressions devoid of any issue for the watercourses that come together there. In winter, one would consider them to be lakes of a considerable surface area and depth, but in summer the waters evaporate in the heat and disappear almost completely.

"They are then covered in magnesium salts," says Roudaire in "Une Mer interieure en Algérie,"[64] "and resemble, to the extent that they might be mistaken for, immense plains

---

[64] The article cited appeared in the *Revue des Deux Mondes* (15 mai 1874). Roudaire's subsequently expanded into a book *Le mer intérieure africaine* (1883).

covered in white frost. When one ventures into the interior of the chotts, one experiences a heavy and crushing heat. The eyes are dazzled by the reflection of the sunlight from the tiny crystals of magnesia that carpet the ground. Objects placed on the edges are reflected there with as much fidelity as in the most transparent water. The illusion is complete; one might think one were on an islet in the middle of a veritable lake."

Monsieur Roudaire has recognized in the *chotts* the great bay of Triton, a narrow gulf of the Mediterranean enclosed by land, like a sort of Red Sea, but busy and possessing large town towns on its shore actively engaged in trade. He proposes restoring the sea's ancient limits and fertilizing the south of Algeria. Let us hope that he can realize this grandiose conception.

As long as the daylight lasted, the *Céleste* continued westwards. At about six o'clock in the evening it landed in Algeria, a short distance from the Tunisian frontier, near the western point of the Sebkha-el-Gharnis. Our voyagers had nothing to fear for their security, for the environs of the *chotts* are sparsely inhabited and there are many quicksands; it is imprudent to risk oneself there by night and without a guide. Quicksands, muddy holes that even experienced eyes do not always perceive, swallow anyone who attempts to cross their dry bed. Entire caravans, camel-trains and detachments of soldiers are said to have been buried without leaving the slightest trace of their passage.

The night was tranquil. Nothing could be heard but the cried of hyenas and jackals attracted by the odor of the culinary debris that Cardounet had strewn on the ground. About midnight, that strange concert ceased, and everyone slept soundly until morning.

"Today, the tenth of October," said Pickerreek, "is the penultimate day of our voyage."

"Tomorrow we shall be in Bordeaux, laughing at Harry Catlen's long face," Cardounet added, to Ivan Kisseloff.

"Be careful," Madame Valdy interjected. "Croesus was afflicted by the instability of human things. Who knows what might happen to us?"

"Oh, Madame," said Sir Walter Donderry, with a slight tone of reproach, "you, so valiant and so courageous, no longer have the confidence, then, that has sustained you thus far?"

"I still share your hopes, but how can you be sure that the rudest proofs are not reserved for us during the last two days of our excursion?"

"Well, we shall fight. The combat of humans against nature is a condition of progress."

"Let's embark, then," shouted Valdy.

The *Céleste* departed in a westward direction, only rising up to a low altitude. They traversed the Melrhir *chott*, encountered vast plains, some deserted, other irrigated and fertile, and the numerous oases of Belud-el-Djerid—the land of dates—Larbaa and Ksour, followed by Oued Djeddi—Goat-kid River—and arrived at El-Aghouat shortly before midday.

At El-Aghouat, Pickerreek's patriotic anticipations were realized; from the senior commandant of the circle to the humblest soldier, and from the richest colonist to the poorest, everyone welcomed the voyagers with transports of delight. The houses were decked with flags and the streets strewn with odorant greenery. Thanks to the efforts of the officers of the garrison, the cooks in the mess improvised a delicious and copious lunch. The place of honor at the table as reserved for Madame Valdy, who became the object of the gracious attentions that our military men are able to lavish so elaborately and so gallantly. Pickerreek and Cardounet were confused by the thousand courtesies that were extended to them. Will Tooke, Ivan Kisseloff, Sir Walter Dondery and Valdy were delighted by their hosts' tact. Dernghuiz stayed sober and ate with a hearty appetite. There was a long conversation about aerial navigation and its future consequences.

"Your discovery is admirable," said the commandant of the circle to Valdy, "and I hope that it will help us in Africa. You'll render the desert—the immense Sahara, the tomb of so many travelers, the insatiable gulf of victims—irrelevant; you'll push the limits of Algeria back to the Equator. What a conquest! And without shedding a single drop of blood, without risking a single human life. Science is more powerful than the strongest armies, and conquerors, so acclaimed and so vaunted, are mere pygmies when compared to the energetic and devoted men who have sometimes used up their lives in order endow humankind with an invention!"

"I'm planning an expedition to the North Pole," Valdy replied. "If I succeed, I'll come back to Africa and explore its heart. I'll do everything I can to be a worthy rival of René Caillé, John Speke, James Grant, Stanley and Livingstone!"

It was necessary to part. The officers wanted to retain the voyagers, but the latter told them about the engagements by they were bound, and resolved to leave immediately in order to reach Nemours that evening.

The *Céleste* took off and rose to an altitude of twelve hundred meters. She flew along the upper reaches of the Oued Djeddi, crossed the small mountains where northern ramifications of the Djebel Amour meet the Djebel Lazereug and the Djebel Senebla, and penetrated into the desert of the province of Oran. There, a feeble southerly wind began to rise.

"Good!" said Cardounet. "There's a zephyr that won't oppose us—just as long as it lasts during our return to France."

"Don't worry, my friend," said Sir Walter. "When a southerly wind rises in Africa, it does so crescendo, and is maintained for several days. It'll be stronger this evening; tomorrow, it'll be almost violent."

"So much the better! We'll cross Spain more rapidly."

They passed over the Chelif, the largest river in Algeria, the Oued Masser, and the El-Chergui *chott*, the most remarkable of the Algerian *chotts*; it is a hundred and thirty kilometers long and twenty broad. Its banks and cliffs, as high as thirty meters in places, are rocky and sheer. They bear the traces of the sojourn of the waters.

After that, the aeronef arrived in a region of high plateaus, host to Arab nomads in summer, and penetrated into the Tell near Daya. From then on, they maintained an altitude of about two thousand meters above sea level, for the mountainous massif of the Tell, which extends from the thirty-third and thirty-fourth degrees of north latitude to the Mediterranean, is strewn with spurs and peaks. Here and there, in the narrow valleys and the lower mountain slopes, they perceived Arab villages, farms inhabited by European colonists, *bordjis*—forts—and caravanserais surrounded by fig-trees, orange-trees, jujube-trees, pomegranates, carobs, tamarinds, olive groves and large pastures of alfalfa and Artemisia. Then the *Céleste* passed over Tlemcen, the ancient capital of the kingdom of the same name, traversed the Tafna, a river famous for the treaty concluded on its banks on 30 May 1837 between Abd El-Kader and General Bugeaud, and arrived at Nemours or Djamaa-Ghazouah a few minutes before sunset.

"Damn!" said Cardounet. "You were right, Sir Walter; the wind's stronger now than when it began to push us. In truth, I think you're as knowledgeable as Mathieu de la Drôme!"[65]

Sir Walter Donderry smiled.

---

[65] Mathieu de la Drôme (1808-1865) was the author of a book promoting a method of predicting the weather by means of lunar phases, *De la prédiction du temps* (1862). He subsequently published an almanac based on his predictions, which employed tremendous success in spite of the unreliability of the method.

Chapter XXII

At Nemours the reception was as enthusiastic and as cordial as that at El-Aghouat. The voyagers dined with a numerous company in the house of the superior commandant of the circle and stayed up until midnight. Before thinking about sleep, however, they loaded aboard the considerable supplies of bicarbonate of soda and hydrochloric acid deposited with a French colonist.

"Finally," said Cardounet, "that's the last load."

"Yes," Valdy replied. "Tomorrow, barring accidents, we'll be in France—we'll be in Bordeaux."

"I've got an idea, Captain."

"What?"

"The wind's good, he sky's completely clear of clouds, and there's enough moonlight to make out an inn sign aft fifty meters. Let's profit from all those advantages and leave immediately. We'll arrive in Bordeaux in the morning of the eleventh of October instead of the evening. That way, no one can quibble over matters of timing. In addition, if, for some unknown reason we're obliged to abandon the *Céleste*, there are railways in Spain, and I think we could get to Bordeaux soon enough for Harry Catlen not to be able to jeer at us."

"What do you think of Cardounet's proposition, Messieurs?" Valdy asked.

"It's quite practicable," said Will Tooke.

"Cardounet's right," said Iva Kisseloff.

"Let's go!" replied Sir Walter, Pickerreek and Madame Valdy.

The superior commandant, the officers of the garrison and the colonists raised a few objections regarding the dangers of a nocturnal flight and tried to deter the voyagers, but the latter reassured them and embarked immediately.

The *Céleste* set out over the Mediterranean, which, under the influence of the wind, was agitating it waves and growling

314

dully. They rapidly traversed the arm of the sea between the African and Spanish coasts, whose average width is a hundred and sixty kilometers, and arrived over the point of Eténa near the city of Almeria. Henceforth, there were no great dangers to fear.

"It's comfortable traveling like this," said Cardounet. "One has only to let oneself go."

The wind was still blowing strongly, and the aeronef progressed with an extraordinary speed. The moon spread its pale light over the earth, and in the distance the silhouettes of mountains stood out jaggedly against the sky. By virtue of a sort of repercussion that the night produce, the shrill whistle of locomotives could be heard, along with the rustle of trees and forests, the roar of rivers and streams when they formed cascades. They perceived sleeping towns and villages, recognizable by street-lighting or he lanterns carried by night-watchmen on patrol.

All the sierras that steak Spain from east to west, for the Sierra Nevada to the Bay of Biscay, were crossed without inconvenience. The *Céleste* traveled on and on with a rapidity that it had rarely attained before. At the approach of dawn, shortly before six o'clock, the voyagers perceived the Atlantic Ocean. Not wanting to make the last leg of the journey without sufficient guarantees, Valdy steered the aeronef to a little promontory and landed there. He examine the *Céleste*'s hull, making sure that it still contained an adequate quantity of hydrogen, and that all the mechanisms of the apparatus were functioning properly.

"Do we still have enough bicarbonate of soda and hydrochloric acid?" he asked.

"Don't worry about that, Captain," Pickerreek replied. "There's enough to go all the way to England, if you want to."

"Good. Now I want to know whereabouts on the Spanish coast we are."

"I'll find out for you," said Cardounet, "for I can see a citizen riding a mule over there, and I'll ask him."

Like many children of the Landes, Cardounet could speak Spanish passably. He advanced toward the individual he had just spotted—a peasant almost as thin as his illustrious compatriot Don Quixote, who was singing a *montagnard* song as he trotted along on his mount. After a few minutes of conversation he came back and said to Valdy: "Captain, we're in the province of Santander, between Santillana and San Vicente de la Burquera."

The position was immediately located on the map.

"Aha!" said Sir Walter Donderry. "We've drifted westwards. From the fourth meridian, we've almost reached the seventh."

"The wind pushed us off course," said Ivan Kisseloff.

"Or perhaps," Will Tooke put in, "it's our skillful pilot who, in order to get over the mountains and avoid sinuosities, has abandoned a straight line and edged slightly to the left."

"That's possible," Valdy replied. "Come on, Messieurs, let's go. In less than three hours we'll be having breakfast in Bordeaux."

The *Céleste* rose up over the ocean and Valdy set a north-easterly course. In spite of the resistance offered by the southerly wind he advanced quite rapidly, with the prow angled. In the middle of the trajectory, however, when they had lost sight of the Spanish coast and had not yet sighted the French cost, there was a hitch. The gusts suddenly increased in violence, and vertical atmospheric currents, launched like jets of an irresistible force by the turbulence in the Gulf of Gascony, collided with the horizontal currents; then the wind turned to the south-east and redoubled its fury. The aeronef was carried away like a feather. It was a veritable avalanche of air that as driving it out to sea.

"Damn it!" cried Pickerreek. "We're adrift, and we're going to be lost in the Atlantic!"

Valdy tried to escape the danger threatening them. He went up to an altitude above four thousand meters in order to search for a favorable current, but encountered the accursed south-easterly wind everywhere that was driving them away from land.

Then he struggle against the gusts. The generators were charged with bicarbonate of soda and hydrochloric acid, the receptacles filled with liquefied carbonic acid, and the manometers marked an extraordinary pressure. The piston obedient to that pressure went back and forth in its cylinder four or five times a second, and the wings fluttered with a feverish and jerky movement.

Like a mountain deer, exhausted by a long, fast chase, which resolves to stand up to the furious pack, the aeronef presented its prow to the tempest, and every time there was a brief calm it advanced slightly—but the violence of the wind soon drove it back.

That formidable struggle lasted for four long hours.

"Are we condemned to perish just as we were about to reach port?" said Ivan Kisseloff.

"Oh, Madame," said Sir Walter to Madame Valdy, "you warned us. God has kept his most cruel proof in reserve."

"May His will be done!" replied Madame Valdy.

"Madame!" cried Will Tooke. "Those are words of discouragement. Remember your admirable conduct during the tempest at the beginning of our voyage, which drove us all the way to Norway."

"I'm not in despair; I'm resigned!"

"Come on, come on!" Cardounet interjected. "There's a proverb which says that God helps them who help themselves. Let's put it into practice."

"Look who's talking," said Pickerreek.

"Look! Look!" cried Valdy, pointing straight ahead.

Everyone turned in the direction indicated by Valdy, and distinguished an almost-imperceptible black line—a line that appeared and disappeared by turns, according to the undulations to which the *Céleste* was subject.

"It's the coast," said Pickerreek.

It was, indeed, the cost, but almost invisible and very distant, scarcely distinguishable from an altitude estimated at two

317

thousand meters. Hope returned to the voyagers' hearts, however, and they competed in self-composure.

"Charge the receptacles!" Valdy commanded. "Charge!"

And the Céleste, like a swallow pursued by a bird of prey, made several detours, describing zigzags in flight, seemingly bounding in repeated somersaults, and made headway.

Suddenly, a formidable detonation rang out.

Two receptacles had just exploded, and their far-flung shards had caused irreparable damage. The ropes and metallic rods supporting the wings were broken; the tubes conducting carbonic acid were cracked and severed; the cylinder of the piston was staved in; all the rigging was damaged to some extent—but the hull remained intact. Fortunately, no one had been hit by the debris of the receptacles.

The *Céleste* spiraled downwards. Pushed by the wind, still obedient to the final impulse of the wings, it landed obliquely on the sea, without sinking. The terrified voyagers clung to anything that came to hand. Not a word or a scream had been uttered during that frightful fall. Supported by the hull, still filled with hydrogen, the aeronef floated, its two wings held it in equilibrium and formed a sort of gently-sloping embankment over which the angry waves broke and spread in seething sheets.

Cardounet, ever the jester—or, rather, wanting to shake his comrades out of their torpor—responded to that terrible blow of fate with a joke.

"Good," he said, "after strenuous exercise, a bath always does you good."

No one replied.

"Well," he continued, "why despair? All's not yet lost. A ship might spot us and pick us up."

"Alas," replied Sir Walter, "with this wind blowing, no ship will venture into the redoubtable region of the Gulf of Gascony."

"To die," cried Valdy, desperately, "so close to success!"

"The adventure of Icarus is no fiction," added Sir Walter, bitterly.

And all those men, so valiant and so strong, whom nothing had held back in their perilous voyage, had an instant of weakness that made sobs break out in their breasts. Whichever way they looked they saw nothing but the infinite sea, confused at the horizon with the sky: the swelling sea, groaning in a sinister manner, rolling its menacing waves over its unfathomable abyss.

Madame Valdy, who had seemed so resigned initially, was the first to recover the strength of her soul and envisage the peril without trembling.

"Let's not get discouraged," she said. "We still have two resources."

"What are they?" demanded Ivan Kisseloff.

"The tide and signals. The wind has almost lost its grip on us now, and the tide might perhaps push us toward the shore."

"I can scarcely anticipate our salvation by that means," said Sir Walter.

"Then let's organize distress signals immediately."

"Good, Madame!" cried Will Tooke. "That's the way I was waiting to hear you talk. It seems to me that you have been, and still are, our guardian angel. Your boldness revives my courage, and puts some sentiment of hope into my heart, which tells me that we'll be saved."

"Madame," added Sir Walter Donderry, "you give us the faith that, in the words of Scripture, moves mountains. Bless you—and let's get to work."

Cardounet, Pickerreek and Dernghuiz tied fragments of rope and metal rods together as best they could, and succeeded in setting up a kind of flexible mast, at the end of which they hung strips of cloth and brightly-colored pennants.

That critical situation was prolonged for the greater part of the day. At about three o'clock in the afternoon, however, the wind dropped slightly and the swell diminished. The aeronef, half-submerged, stayed afloat and was in fairly good condition. In spite of the fragile envelope of the hull, no leak was manifest.

"Our salvation depends on the resistance of the balloon, converted into a launch," said Pickereek.

All points of the horizon were scanned and scrutinized with naval telescopes, but absolutely nothing was discovered. Finally, however, about forty minutes before sunset, they perceived the mast of a vessel.

"Which way is it headed?" demanded Valdy.

"It appears to be coming straight toward us," replied Will Tooke.

Then all eyes lit up with hope. The shipwreck-victims no longer took their eyes off the masts, which grew as they approached. First they made out the royals and the topgallants, then the maintops and finally the shrouds, the funnel and the entire mass of the ship.

To attract attention to them, the voyagers discharged all their firearms simultaneously and waved pieces of cloth. The maneuver was successful. The vessel, vomiting clouds of smoke as she put on steam, arrived in a hurry and stopped a few cables from the *Céleste*. She was a steamer from Bordeaux, the *Fonfrède*, coming from Lisbon and heading for Pauillac to unload her cargo. Two lifeboats put to sea and collected the aerial castaways. Valdy was able to saved his log, a few instruments and some precious objects. The commander of one of the boats, an old quartermaster, who had "seen all the colors" in the course of his active existence, was astonished by the bizarre form of the aeronef.

"Holy paper bags!" he said. "I never saw the carcass of a ship like that one floating there. I won't offer my compliments to the master of the shipyard who launched that vessel, and may I go to the bottom of the sea if..."

"That carcass wasn't constructed to sail on the water, but to navigate in the air," Cardounet put in.

"Tell that to the marines, Matelot. I might be an imbecile but I'm not an idiot."

"Even so..."

There were shouts from the *Fonfrède,* and the appeals interrupted the discussion begun between Cardounet and the quartermaster. The mariners plied the oars vigorously, the boats glided over the crests of the waves, and hooked on to the sides of the steamer. The *Fonfrède*'s captain welcomed the shipwreck-victims aboard immediately, and lavished all the cares upon them required by their condition.

Valdy went on to the afterdeck, and for as long as he could see the *Céleste* he gazed at it with dolorous affection—but soon, he could no longer make out anything but a black patch on the agitated sea…and then nothing…

Then two large tears rolled down his cheeks.

That surge of regret and affliction on his part was certainly excusable. The fruits of all his patient research, his painful efforts, his long study and his hopeful dreams were all about to be swallowed up by the Ocean.

He was, of course, conscious of his talent and his worth, and he was already planning to construct a new aeronef—but he had wanted to arrive in France with his apparatus, to fly over Bordeaux with his companions.

What a triumph, and what glory, for the courageous inventor, had his dream been realized! The detractors, the jealous and the envious would have been confounded forever, and France, so unfortunate, so direly tested a few years before, so ridiculed by her enemies, would have recovered all her former prestige at a stroke, and become once again the sanctuary and hearth of progress that had once accorded her first place among the nations!

The captain of the *Fonfrède* had heard talk of the aerial expedition, and was not astonished by the facts that the people he had just saved recounted to him.

"Although you've completed your voyage around the world in forty days," he said, "you'll lose your bet if you don't arrive in Bordeaux his evening?"

"Yes."

"Well, you'll arrive there—I give you my word of honor. According to my estimate, we're on the forty-fifth degree of north latitude and four degrees west—which is to say that we're less than a hundred kilometers from the Pointe de

Grave. The sea's calmer now, and the wind's becoming favorable. We'll be in the Gironde in three hours."

The captain took the helm himself and ordered full steam ahead. The steamer cleaved through the waves with extraordinary speed, and soon, in the darkness, they saw the Cordouan lighthouse. Pickerreek and Cardounet assisted with the maneuvers; it seemed to them, so great was their impatience, that they would never arrive. They wanted a dazzling success for their friend Marcel Valdy.

Finally, they distinguished the beacons of the Pointes de la Coubre and Royan. They were no more than a few kilometers from the coast. In the darkness, and the wind that was blowing, it was becoming difficult and dangerous to penetrate into the Gironde, but Cardounet, who "knew his river, his Garonne," like no other mariner in Gascony, fulfilled the functions of harbor-pilot and boldly plowed through the surf of the mouth. The *Fonfrède* dropped anchor a short distance from Verdon.

"I can't go any further," said the captain, "but I'll have you taken ashore. With the railway, you'll be in Bordeaux before midnight. Now, good luck!"

The voyagers thanked the captain warmly and embarked in the launches. Eight o'clock in the evening was chiming as they went into Verdon station. They requested a special train, which was immediately granted to them, for night trains are rare on the Medoc line, and they arrived in Bordeaux shortly after eleven o'clock. Two cabs transported them from the station to the Place de la Comédie, and they went into the Café de Bordeaux.

At that exact moment, Harry Catlen, Esquire, who was sitting at a table with several of his partners in the wager and Dambielle, looked at his watch and said, joyfully: "Quarter to midnight, Gentlemen. The forty days requested by Monsieur Valdy have run out. In a quarter of an hour I'll be four thousand pounds in credit."

"Don't be in so much of a hurry!" shouted Ivan Kisseloff, who was the first to appear. "And transfer the four thousand pounds to your debit. We've won our bet."

Dambielle embraced Valdy. "What!" he said. "It's you...it's you...I'd despaired of ever seeing you again. God be praised! You're here, safe and sound."

Then he shook hands vigorously with Pickerreek, Cardounet, Will Tooke and Ivan Kisseloff, and presented his respects to Madame Valdy. On perceiving Sir Walter Donderry, however, he could not hold back an exclamation of surprise.

"You too, Sir Walter?"

"Why not?" replied Sir Walter. "I was getting bored on the ground, so, in spite of my corpulence, I went into the sky to meet your friend." Then he turned to Harry Catlen and added: "My dear compatriot, I've lost two thousand pounds with you; I can assure you that these Messieurs have not stolen them, and that all the conditions have been met exactly."

"Oh well!" exclaimed Harry Catlen, gripped by the general enthusiasm, "I don't regret my money. I deem myself fortunate to have contributed to stimulating one of the noblest and most glorious enterprises of our era."

"No hard feelings, then!" said Ivan Kisseloff.

And the Russian offered his hand to the Englishman.

The next day, the accounts were added up. The construction of the *Céleste*, the expenses of the voyage and unforeseen expenses rose to approximately three hundred thousand francs. The voyagers did not make any profit—but we know how small a place financial considerations played when they had decided to undertake their aerial exploration, so they considered themselves very fortunate to have gone around the world in forty days. "Gratis," Pickerreek added.

Then, while Dernghuiz, in the company of his two "professors"—or, to put it better, his two intimate friends—drank a stirrup-cup, because the Tatar would soon be leaving them, Valdy, Madame Valdy, Dambielle, Will Tooke, Ivan Kisseloff and Sir Walter Donderry chatted about their hopes for a further excursion.

"We were pressed for time," said Valdy, "and weren't able to devote ourselves to scientific studies, but before long we'll follow in the tracks of Gay-Lussac, Biot, Robertson, Glaisher, Coxwel, Bixio, Flammarion, Wilfrid de Fonvielle, Tissandier, Crocé-Spineli and Sivel, and I hope that science will find us to be useful and devoted champions."

"I've lost fifty thousand francs betting against you," Sir Walter Donderry put in, "but I've won a hundred thousand from Lord W . I'll put that sum at your disposal when you construct a new aeronef.

"Thank you, Sir Walter," Valdy replied, "but now that I've demonstrated all the advantages of aerial navigation, I want to address myself to France; I want to request the initial capital for my future enterprises from its people. I hope that there won't be any lack of subscribers, and that my fatherland, that sentinel of progress, will hear me and respond to my voice!"

SF & FANTASY

Henri Allorge. *The Great Cataclysm*
Guy d'Armen. *Doc Ardan: The City of Gold and Lepers*
G.-J. Arnaud. *The Ice Company*
Charles Asselineau. *The Double Life*
Cyprien Bérard. *The Vampire Lord Ruthwen*
Aloysius Bertrand. *Gaspard de la Nuit*
Richard Bessière. *The Gardens of the Apocalypse*
Albert Bleunard. *Ever Smaller*
Félix Bodin. *The Novel of the Future*
Alphonse Brown. *City of Glass; The Conquest of the Air*
André Caroff. *The Terror of Madame Atomos; Miss Atomos; The Return of Madame Atomos; The Mistake of Madame Atomos; The Monsters of Madame Atomos; The Revenge of Madame Atomos*
Félicien Champsaur. *The Human Arrow; Ouha*
Didier de Chousy. *Ignis*
Captain Danrit. *Undersea Odyssey*
C. I. Defontenay. *Star (Psi Cassiopeia)*
Charles Derennes. *The People of the Pole*
Georges Dodds (anthologist). *The Missing Link*
Harry Dickson. *The Heir of Dracula*
Jules Dornay. *Lord Ruthven Begins*
Alfred Driou. *The Adventures of a Parisian Aeronaut*
Sâr Dubnotal *vs. Jack the Ripper*
Alexandre Dumas. *The Return of Lord Ruthven*
Renée Dunan. *Baal*
J.-C. Dunyach. *The Night Orchid; The Thieves of Silence*
Henri Duvernois. *The Man Who Found Himself*
Achille Eyraud. *Voyage to Venus*
Henri Falk. *The Age of Lead*
Paul Féval. *Anne of the Isles; Knightshade; Revenants; Vampire City; The Vampire Countess; The Wandering Jew's Daughter*
Paul Féval, *fils. Felifax, the Tiger-Man*
Charles de Fieux. *Lamékis*
Arnould Galopin. *Doctor Omega; Doctor Omega & The Shadowmen*
Judith Gautier. *Isoline and the Serpent-Flower*
Léon Gozlan. *The Vampire of the Val-de-Grâce*
G.L. Gick. *Harry Dickson and the Werewolf of Rutherford Grange*

Edmond Haraucourt. *Illusions of Immortality*
Nathalie Henneberg. *The Green Gods*
V. Hugo, P. Foucher & P. Meurice. *The Hunchback of Notre-Dame*
Michel Jeury. *Chronolysis*
Gustave Kahn. *The Tale of Gold and Silence*
Gérard Klein. *The Mote in Time's Eye*
Louis-Guillaume de La Follie. *The Unpretentious Philosopher*
Jean de La Hire. *Enter the Nyctalope; The Nyctalope on Mars; The Nyctalope vs. Lucifer; The Nyctalope Steps In; Night of the Nyctalope*
Etienne-Léon de Lamothe-Langon. *The Virgin Vampire*
André Laurie. *Spiridon*
Gabriel de Lautrec. *The Vengeance of the Oval Portrait*
Alain le Drimeur. *The Future City*
Georges Le Faure & Henri de Graffigny. *The Extraordinary Adventures of a Russian Scientist Across the Solar System* (2 vols.)
Gustave Le Rouge. *The Vampires of Mars The Dominion of the World* (w/Gustave Guitton) (4 vols.)
Jules Lermina. *Mysteryville; Panic in Paris; To-Ho and the Gold Destroyers; The Secret of Zippelius*
Jean-Marc & Randy Lofficier. *Edgar Allan Poe on Mars; The Katrina Protocol; Pacifica; Robonocchio; Tales of the Shadowmen 1-9*
Xavier Mauméjean. *The League of Heroes*
Joseph Méry. *The Tower of Destiny*
Hippolyte Mettais. *The Year 5865*
Louise Michel. *The Human Microbes; The New World*
José Moselli. *Illa's End*
John-Antoine Nau. *Enemy Force*
Marie Nizet. *Captain Vampire*
C. Nodier, A. Beraud & Toussaint-Merle. *Frankenstein*
Henri de Parville. *An Inhabitant of the Planet Mars*
Gaston de Pawlowski. *Journey to the Land of the 4th Dimension*
Georges Pellerin. *The World in 2000 Years*
Ernest Pérochon. *The Frenetic People*
Pierre Pelot. *The Child Who Walked on the Sky*
J. Polidori, C. Nodier, E. Scribe. *Lord Ruthven the Vampire*
P.-A. Ponson du Terrail. *The Vampire and the Devil's Son*
Henri de Régnier. *A Surfeit of Mirrors*
Maurice Renard. *The Blue Peril; Doctor Lerne; The Doctored Man; A Man Among the Microbes; The Master of Light*
Jean Richepin. *The Wing; The Crazy Corner*

Albert Robida. *The Adventures of Saturnin Farandoul; The Clock of the Centuries; Chalet in the Sky*
J.-H. Rosny Aîné. *Helgvor of the Blue River; The Givreuse Enigma; The Mysterious Force; The Navigators of Space; Vamireh; The World of the Variants; The Young Vampire*
Marcel Rouff. *Journey to the Inverted World*
Han Ryner. *The Superhumans*
Brian Stableford. *The New Faust at the Tragicomique; The Empire of the Necromancers (The Shadow of Frankenstein; Frankenstein and the Vampire Countess; Frankenstein in London); Sherlock Holmes & The Vampires of Eternity; The Stones of Camelot; The Wayward Muse.* (anthologist) *The Germans on Venus; News from the Moon; The Supreme Progress; The World Above the World; Nemoville; Investigations of the Future*
Jacques Spitz. *The Eye of Purgatory*
Kurt Steiner. *Ortog*
Eugène Thébault. *Radio-Terror*
C.-F. Tiphaigne de La Roche. *Amilec*
Théo Varlet. *The Golden Rock. The Xenobiotic Invasion; Timeslip Troopers* (w/André Blandin); *The Martian Epic* (w/Octave Joncquel)
Paul Vibert. *The Mysterious Fluid*
Villiers de l'Isle-Adam. *The Scaffold; The Vampire Soul*
Philippe Ward. *Artahe*
Philippe Ward & Sylvie Miller. *The Song of Montségur*

MYSTERIES & THRILLERS

M. Allain & P. Souvestre. *The Daughter of Fantômas*
A. Anicet-Bourgeois, Lucien Dabril. *Rocambole*
A. Bernède. *Belphegor*; *Judex* (w/Louis Feuillade)
A. Bisson & G. Livet. *Nick Carter vs. Fantômas*
V. Darlay & H. de Gorsse. *Lupin vs. Holmes: The Stage Play*
Séamas Duffy. *Sherlock Holmes in Paris*
Paul Féval. *Gentlemen of the Night; John Devil; The Black Coats ('Salem Street; The Invisible Weapon; The Parisian Jungle; The Companions of the Treasure; Heart of Steel; The Cadet Gang; The Sword-Swallower)*
Emile Gaboriau. *Monsieur Lecoq*
Goron & Emile Gautier. *Spawn of the Penitentiary*
Steve Leadley. *Sherlock Holmes: The Circle of Blood*

Maurice Leblanc. *Arsène Lupin vs. Countess Cagliostro; Lupin vs. Holmes (The Blonde Phantom; The Hollow Needle); The Many Faces of Arsène Lupin*
Gaston Leroux. *Chéri-Bibi; The Phantom of the Opera; Rouletabille & the Mystery of the Yellow Room Rouletabille at Krupp's*
Richard Marsh. *The Complete Adventures of Judith Lee*
William Patrick Maynard. *The Terror of Fu Manchu; The Destiny of Fu Manchu*
Frank J. Morlock. *Sherlock Holmes: The Grand Horizontals; Sherlock Holmes vs Jack the Ripper*
Antonin Reschal. *The Adventures of Miss Boston*
P. de Wattyne & Y. Walter. *Sherlock Holmes vs. Fantômas*
David White. *Fantômas in America*

SCREENPLAYS

Mike Baron. *The Iron Triangle*
Emma Bull & Will Shetterly. *Nightspeeder; War for the Oaks*
Gerry Conway & Roy Thomas. *Doc Dynamo*
Steve Englehart. *Majorca*
James Hudnall. *The Devastator*
Jean-Marc & Randy Lofficier. *Royal Flush*
J.-M. & R. Lofficier & Marc Agapit. *Despair*
J.-M. & R. Lofficier & Joël Houssin. *City*
Andrew Paquette. *Peripheral Vision*
Robert L. Robinson, Jr. *Judex*
R. Thomas, J. Hendler & L. Sprague de Camp. *Rivers of Time*

NON-FICTION

Stephen R. Bissette. *Blur 1-5. Green Mountain Cinema 1; Teen Angels*
Win Scott Eckert. *Crossovers* (2 vols.)
Jean-Marc & Randy Lofficier. *Shadowmen* (2 vols.)
Randy Lofficier. *Over Here*

HEXAGON COMICS

Franco Frescura & Luciano Bernasconi. *Wampus*

Franco Frescura & Giorgio Trevisan. *CLASH*
L. Bernasconi, J.-M. Lofficier & Juan Roncagliolo Berger. *Phenix*
Claude Legrand, J.-M. Lofficier & L. Bernasconi. *Kabur*
Franco Oneta. *Zembla*
L. Buffolente, Lofficier & J.-J. Dzialowski. *Strangers: Homicron*
Danilo Grossi. *Strangers: Jaydee*
Claude Legrand & Luciano Bernasconi. *Strangers: Starlock*

ART BOOKS

Jean-Pierre Normand. *Science Fiction Illustrations*
Raven Okeefe. *Raven's L'il Critters; Rave's Faves*
Randy Lofficier & Raven Okeefe. *If Your Possum Go Daylight...*
Daniele Serra. *Illusions*